Mumbo Jumbo

Short Stories

Ben Gilbert

GARUDA
BOOKS

GARUDA BOOKS

Published by Garuda Books

Cover by Russell Pond
Formatting by Paul Salvette

First edition: October 2015
Second edition: November 2019

CONTENTS

*"Black Magic is everywhere
Especially in your head"*

——Black Magic Poem by Ben Gilbert

NON-FICTION

High Altitude and Chocolate

Published in Scarlet Lead Review (January 2021)

Tall Boy was huge, six feet six inches or more, with the backpack to match.

Chekhov, not as tall, was a respectable 5 feet eleven inches. His backpack had a girth that matched his sizable shoulders.

Two men: one fit, experienced and seasoned; the other, young, strong and totally full of himself. They stood together, eyeing the contents of their backpacks, which they had both neatly laid out on top of a blue painted wooden dining table.

The entire expedition crew of eighteen were crammed into a small mountain lodge, the last before the team left the main trail to head up into a little visited and remote Himalayan enclave in Nepal. Outside, warm rain fell.

The crew milled around, drinking tea, checking supplies, making sure any last forgotten details were remembered. Stuff was everywhere, yet there was a sense of order in the chaos, as things were checked, packed, unpacked and checked again. But no one else had laid things out neatly as these two. It was as if they were presenting or selling something at a bazaar. They were showing off.

Sticky was leading a fourteen day expedition in search of elusive snow leopards and didn't want a foolhardy competition between these two men.

Their copious amount of paraphernalia, although impressive, was complete overkill – so many unnecessary things. Chekhov was carrying 23 kilos at least; and Tall Boy, with an added camera bag containing enough kit for a professional shoot, had more than thirty five kilos. For an expedition in the Himalayas, on steep rocky ground above five thousand metres, this was madness. But before Sticky could voice her concerns, she had to stare hard at a sizable pile of what looked like silver bullion wrapped in brown designer paper wrappers.

Could this be…Swiss Chocolate?

Not just a few bars but a horde. How many kilos worth? She would never know, but ten would seem an underestimation.

After her initial bafflement, she laughed. The chocolate was for the crew she quickly learned, a gesture of good will. Then let's share it out, she suggested, the crew was large and there was enough for… she didn't know, a few bars each, at least! But Tall Boy wasn't parting with his bullion, and started packing it all away.

If he wouldn't part with his chocolate, then at least he could lighten the load by allowing one of the crew to carry the camera equipment; after all, that's part of their job, to carry gear – they get paid handsomely, and besides, are used to it.

He wasn't budging on that either and, to make the point, put the full pack on his back with the extra camera bag fastened to the top. He had not long returned from an expedition in the Altai Mountains, Russia, and should have known better. Sticky tried to reason with his stubbornness.

Chekhov did the same, put on his full backpack, unaware of the high altitude reality awaiting with open jaws and gnashing teeth. She tried to reason with naivety.

She lost on both occasions, and now they stood tall, grinning, and ready to take on the world and leave her standing in their dust.

Later, when everyone was eating, Sticky snuck outside to where the packs and baskets for the trip were all neatly lined up against the side of the lodge wall. She tried on the two demon packs. Although the packs were ridiculously too large for her back, she felt their full weight, the heavy pull to earth, knowing she wouldn't have a hope in hauling them over a mountain range. Whose knees would crumble first: Tall Boy or Chekhov?

The following morning, in vain, she had one last try at convincing them to share their loads. She gave up. The team had snow leopards to track over a lot of high and challenging ground. Sticky had a scientist, clients and a crew to look after; high altitude weight lifting would have to wait.

Up and up they went for two days, twisting through pines, into clouded bamboo forest, then giant rhododendron trees before the vegetation thinned until they were finally hiking through juniper. They passed a man chopping the juniper with an axe and saw a filthy pit where it was being distilled to extract the oil. No doubt to be later sold in Paris and New York as a rare eco friendly sustainable Himalayan oil using secret and ancient methods – hack the forest down, without any thought of tomorrow. He was the last person they saw. Base camp was made where the juniper no longer grew, next to a fast flowing glacial stream.

Food is always central to any expedition. It gathers people at the end of the day, warms and soothes the weariness of altitude. But, it's never that simple. The porters had been pilfering the dried yak meat, pulling it from their baskets as they hiked, scoffing it out of sight. So they thought, until Sticky caught them red-handed. The cook should have been on top of this one but he wasn't, and she had to do a sergeant major shouting act to get things straight. All the menus had been carefully worked out – why weren't they eating chocolate instead of Yak?

For Europeans, *Swiss Chocolate* is a treat. It is a kind of treasure. Nepalese, especially hard working porters, see *rice* as something special. They happily eat two large cereal bowls full of steaming rice with a sprinkling of watery lentil gravy full of salt and chilli. And, their tea is sugar with some hot tea added to make it into a drink. So, chocolate just isn't their thing. However, someone was eating it: the trash was full of silver and brown paper.

Chekhov was a personal trainer and paranoid of losing his well earned muscles. To ensure he kept perfect physique, he turned to food.

Not only did he eat two huge portions of client food (that meant a really large meal, twice), he also joined the crew to eat rice and lentils, with yak meat. Again, he ate two enormous portions. He did this every mealtime. No one could quite believe it. It was like a circus act, but instead of sustaining weight, he lost it, like everyone does at altitude. His unwanted weight and muscle loss, combined with the oncoming onslaughts of altitude sickness, was never going to be pretty. He would soon be in meltdown.

Sticky took a trip with two crew members to the top of a non-snowy peak. It was high with splendid views of the Himalayas. This isolated enclave is hidden by three six thousand metre peaks. She could view one glacier, an impressive gorge with a raging torrent, a huge imposing rock face below a massive snow covered mountain, and a six thousand metre monolithic rock spire overlooking a vast forest. The forest held red panda and black bear; the rocky high ground, snow leopards and blue sheep. She surveyed for routes and good places for research.

On her return, Sticky noticed the messy brown lips of chocolate scoffing. The team had tucked in. That would ease Tall Boy's burden.

The following day, Chekhov wanted to go up the non-snowy peak. He went with two young porters who rushed him up. They all wanted to be the fastest. The problem being, the porters had lived here all their lives and the altitude was irrelevant to them. Sticky had warned Chekhov about altitude sickness – take it slow, she said. That had fallen on deaf ears. The others ambled way behind, taking time. Sticky had stayed at base camp, and now, looking up to the top, everyone appeared like tiny specks to her.

And this was when the trouble all began. The following morning, she found Chekhov's sunglasses by the stream. He was uninterested in their return, shrugged, sat looking into space and irritable when expected to answer back. Altitude sickness is a strange thing: it has Stubborn as a best friend. Take a rest, go down for a day, take a porter with you and come back up tomorrow or the next day. All advice was duly ignored. Strangely, his appetite was not affected. Muscles before health, before all else! But some days later, he did go down, forced down by feeling very rough indeed. He descended at least a thousand metres to a lodge. Sticky gave him an English speaking porter to carry his heavy pack and look after him. He never did come back, consuming the lodge's food supplies until the team returned to find him some weeks later. He refused to speak about what had happened.

The chocolate was being distributed. Sticky must have had three or four bars in total. It tasted good.

Tall Boy was still refusing to let anyone help him with his load. With the kerosene and food supplies going down, some of the porters had little to carry, so there really was no excuse. Sticky didn't pay too much attention to him as she was distracted by snow leopard tracks in the snow – a mother and a small cub. So there was excitement all round. The tracking took the group to a pristine high altitude lake where they spotted twelve blue sheep, one with huge curled horns. Getting down from this high spot was very tricky. Sticky didn't want to go back the way they had come, that was the wrong way on their circular route. The only other option was to follow the lake overflow. It quickly formed a stream. The stream seemed to cut a route through the rocks. On either side of the stream were boulders one could hop along. Sticky said she would do a reconnaissance, but the further she got, the steeper it became until she was dropping down from one boulder to the next, as the stream became a waterfall. Going back was going to be gruelling. She noticed the others watching her from above and edging along the top of the cliff she was descending. They indicated that they would try and go another way. All her focus had to be on her own descent. It was long and very physical and she broke out into a sweat thinking this might have been a mistake.

That morning, at the last night's campsite, they had left the crew to make their own way to a designated spot and could now see them below in a small alpine valley. They had taken over an old herding hut. The welcome sight and smell of wood smoke meant food and tea. It drove her on.

On arrival, she looked back to the cascading stream dropping down and through the rocks. The lake was a very long way up. High above to the right, the rest of the team were toing and froing along the rocks trying to find a way down. They seemed to be having difficulties in finding a route and it wasn't until some hours later that they arrived, utterly exhausted. Tall Boy collapsed, his legs giving way. His feet had problems, his shoulders hurt and he was unable to speak. The others told Sticky he had still refused to share his load. She didn't mention the weight of his pack again.

Sick of chocolate, Sticky refused any more. Surely it all must have been eaten by now? The whole team had been enjoying it. The porters had even shared some amongst themselves, except they ate it in small cubes rather than whole bars.

Sticky didn't know what to do with Tall Boy. There was a steep downhill descent that would take all day, non-stop, morning until dusk. He wouldn't make it in his condition with a load. Time for a sergeant major episode, not exactly as he was a client; however, it took some convincing but Sticky did manage to get him to hand over his camera gear to a trusted porter. It weighed about the same as her own back-pack. He then refused to hand over his backpack. Oh well, she had tried.

The descent was relentless and hard on the knees. The team couldn't afford to be stuck in the forest after dark as there was no water and no flat ground for tents.

It was a silent event with a lot of slipping, muffled curses and a few hard landings. But everyone made it, unscathed.

Tall Boy staggered in last, bow-legged and half slipped, half fell to a resting position where the team and crew all sat. Nearby, no more than twenty minutes walk was a lodge, and that meant food and drink for all, even alcohol, always an important end of trek moment.

Tall Boy's backpack had come open. More bars of chocolate than Sticky could count, lay strewn around. No, he even had some in his pockets! It was like contraband. He was off-loading it, leaving it all behind, now desperate to ease the load. There must have been at least another ten kilos. This chocolate had nearly finished him off.

Some kids sauntered by, eagerly eyeing the treasure, silver wrappers shining in the twilight. They were immediately rewarded but didn't hang around too long, taking off in case he changed his mind.

Everybody laughed, at the kids but more likely at Tall Boy. Everyone was just baffled and perplexed.

Sticky looked across the inky sky. A few hours away, somewhere in the darkness, was Chekhov's lodge. She wondered what the restaurant bill would be. That's tomorrow's problem. Now, the bar.

CRYSTAL NIGHT

Published in: Twisted Vine journal, Western New Mexico University (Dec 2019); Bookends Review (April 2020); pacificREVIEW, a west coast arts review annual sdsu (2020, Synchronous Theme); Fear of Monkeys (December 2020)

Cold crystals beautifully shaped and delicately formed into soft snow or the harsh ice on an inaccessible mountain. This is what the word crystal conjures up for me.

For others, it may be the cure of crystal healing or the devil calling in piece of crystal meth, an expensive cut-glass thing or just a pretty stone. I had even known a girl called Crystal, whose beauty had the magic of a piece of crystal rock.

Berlin. November 9th 2014.

The bar was dimly lit. In fact, from the outside it barely looked open. There were no customers, not even a barman was visible. The only clue that it may be open was the flickering of candles burning on top of empty wine bottles, thick with teardrop wax. There was a candle on every empty table.

Just like this one, most semi rundown areas of this fashionable city have a special kind of bar. They are shrines to decay, homage to the old, hailing to the new, and utterly hip.

It's uncertain how long they will last, but for some time, I think, for Berlin still has a love affair with the ghost of its old decrepit East.

To make a bar like this you need time, money and a passion for eccentricity. When it's done, finished and ready for a customer, it will look like it has always been there; aged and ramshackle, just like a long forgotten warehouse or an abandoned factory. The only difference being that your bar won't just have been repaired; it will also be spotlessly clean: that quaint look of rural decay inside a city limit.

First, one needs to find a dilapidated shop in a cruddy part of town, preferably on a corner in an airy quiet street with trees and enough outside space for a few fair weather tables. Plane trees seem to be Berlin's favourite, tall and grand, offering a leafy seasonal umbrella to all. Big stare-through windows are a must; after all, this is going to be a pretend not to be gallery.

Next, clean out the crud and dust until there's a canvas; not a blank one but one that's surely more than half-complete.

Half strip the walls, knock off some plaster, expose brick, leave a little of the old wall paper hanging here and there, and do the same with the ceiling. A few essential repairs may be needed, but when it's done, it still has to look really trashed, yet beautifully clean – this is Germany.

Floors are always the same: wide and chunky old wooden boards, lightly sanded, stained and then polished, the wear and blemishes of age still clearly visible, or an old broken tiled floor, repaired with odd colours and textures before being smoothed down and highly polished.

Make sure the bar itself is made of some kind of discarded bric-a-brac like an old wardrobe, broken palettes or, even better, half a fishing boat. Again, make sure it's not too nice or in good condition.

The electrics must look bad. They are only good if it seems as if the wiring was done a hundred years ago: dirty hanging cables loosely wired into broken connectors with ancient lights casting spooky shadows. Silhouettes are good. Electrocution needs to be an option.

Just a few things left to add.

Tables and chairs, although functional, must be wobbly, eccentric and downright bizarre. They are cast outs found on the streets, in a dump or the poorest second hand shops. Nothing matches, no garish colours and if it breaks it doesn't matter (it's probably already broken, anyway). I even went to one that had a big old-fashioned bathtub just sitting on the bar room floor – for what? For everything – coats were lying in it when I looked, but I imagine kids would have a riot there, after all these places are civilised coffee shops in daylight hours.

One last thing: the toilets.

There are only two rules to follow. Obviously nothing will be new, that's a given. They have to be spotlessly clean and totally covered in graffiti, not the stylish arty type, but the thick felt pen of the urban yob. But don't worry if you're not up to the job, your clients will do it for you, soon enough and free of charge.

And now the staff:

Men must be wafer thin – no gym for them. Underfed and bearded, definitely not that unshaven macho type, casually dressed in bland clothes that are far too big. We're talking nineteenth century Norwegian fisherman or some kind of dirt poor Bolshevik farmer type. Women walk straight out of a Brueghel painting or a tragic Lorca play.

Open the doors and let the hip come in.

To enter such a place with awareness is like entering a church or place of worship. You may not be religious or even have religion, but you know that others entering do.

Welcome to the church of the urban hipster.

In the bar I had entered, music was playing but you could still hold conversation without raising your voice. I listened briefly: an American man with a deep-throated serious voice talked and half sung about life and the absurd. I stopped listening after I heard the word crucified, wondering who the hell had been crucified for the sinners of this holy place.

The congregation was out and the place was empty. We would pray alone tonight.

The barman appeared – waif like, bearded and very softly spoken. We ordered wine. I looked around, a piano stood in the corner and I wondered if it was ever played, or if it just sat there looking pretty, another piece of bric-a-brac from somewhere down the road.

There's only one Berlin now, no East or West, but the whole place is like a museum to both. You can see the divide in bits of the old wall with its famous graffiti along the Spree, and in the old check points, custom houses, gates and stations – even the tram lines only operate in the old East, for the West pulled up its tracks long ago. The miles of brain numbing apartments in the East at Marzahn-Hellersdorf and the old airfield at Templehof in the West, now a park and conference centre but still looking as if planes land every day, are all perfectly preserved and stating loudly – East, West or the line between.

These bars are something like that; a dividing line between the two – run-down, tired, malnourished and in decline – The East meeting the West with its ultra cool modernism.

And to be honest, they are fun and civilised places to visit. Not raucous and beer swilling, neither are they elitist. In fact, if you are dirt poor and turn up in shabby bland attire, you can just pretend deliberate and measured down dressing. You'll fit in just fine.

My friend and I sat down in this post-modern installation. I guess we were the only exhibits to anyone passing by. We talked about the day. We had hiked long and hard through a vast forest, whose floor had been a mottle of muted autumn colours glistening in the fine rain. The skies were overcast and moody, even at midday the tall beech trees, still considerably covered in leaf, created an eerie twilight. We walked in silence through a sea of grey and brown, the crisp air slightly stinging our faces.

In this empty tract near the Polish border, we had come to look for beaver. They frequent the rivers and marshland below the forest. Although we didn't see a beaver, there had been plenty of evidence of them in the boggy swamps and flowing streams. We saw the classic chewed up tree trunks where a trunk is left teetering and tottering on a tiny stem, and the log dams that make a beaver's lodge.

We had underestimated the time needed to return to the car, and had had to hike hard through fading light along confusing dark trails and increasingly dense mist, skirting around ghostly pools and gloomy lakes. We made it back just before pitch black enveloped the world.

There we were, happy and weary after a great hike through the forest, enjoying the surreal tranquility of this Berlin hipster bar. Out of the blue, my friend asked me if I thought she was a hipster girl. What the hell did that mean – being part of some phony transience, a small moment where you belong to some ephemeral elite, or just a modern thing deliberately showing difference? She was from another part of Germany, not a Berliner, but maybe that's the point – all hipsters are somehow foreign invaders. Who knows? Not me for sure.

That was about as deep as the conversation got, any deeper and we would be stripping away the wallpaper (or what was left of it anyway) to reveal probably nothing much at all – and that would have simply spoiled all the fun.

The American continued to deliver his endlessly dull word parade, and, I kid you not, when I went to the loo – there it was – the thick felt pen of yob graffiti covering every square inch.

As we were laughing together in this bizarre environment, another friend entered. Passing by, she had seen us through the windows and was now heading towards our table, beaming a huge smile that was almost lost in her mass of black hair, wild and thick like a Himalayan yak. She had just come from where half of Berlin had been; in fact, not just Berliners but half of the world's press and cameras.

This place was empty because it was November 9th.

Why had we been here and not there? This was no time to pray in an urban hipster bar, this was the time for celebration out in the cold crisp autumn air.

Was it?

Yes it was. The praying could wait 'till later.

Oh.

With all this talk about East and West reflecting in a hip bar's decor, we had somehow missed the point. Well not the point exactly, but what the majority had firmly on their minds.

It was twenty-five years to the day that the Berlin Wall came down, was breached, jumped and effectively finished – the day of re-unification, the day that difference died.

My friend and I had been deep in a forest unaware that a very long row of white balloons edged the old wall boundary, lit up and ready to be released into the night sky, cameras clicked and profound articles were being written. A night of joy – let's not forget we are one, once again.

Oh, sorry about that, but we were looking for beaver and the lesser spotted three toed earwig in a dark and vast forest that conjures dreams and spooky night time magic, while Berlin and probably half the world were celebrating the wall coming down.

But these bars are still lamenting this total loss of difference.

You may think I have a loose screw, am slightly unhinged with the door now hanging off, for thinking such a thing, but these bars are really crying such a loss whilst having a grand good time.

We spoke about our Jewish roots – mine shaky like thin cracked ice, but my black haired friend has an ice shelf under her, a thoroughbred, with Hebrew in her blood.

But wait, she had no real interest in the wall, that divide that toppled down, or the evening's celebration, that was all just something to do – to meet some friends and have some fun.

This was 9th November, Crystal Night. The night the Nazi's burnt the synagogues, smashed the Jewish shops – all that glass and fractured shards sparkling in the firelight or early morning sun.

No one in their right mind would celebrate a night like this.

Crystal Night 1938.

My Mother went to school next morning. She was six years old and living in Bad Homburg. It wasn't until school was out around midday that she first knew something had happened. Her class and a few teachers ended up about four minutes from the school, down a road everybody called Jew lane (it had been officially called Judengasse before being changed to Wallstasse). The synagogue was ablaze, flames coming from all the windows. The fire fighters were there, but only to douse the adjoining properties, not to quell the Jewish flames. The shop opposite the school was smashed and wrecked – it was a stationary shop for the kids, owned by a Jew who hanged himself a few days later.

No one asked questions and nothing was ever said. Soon after, my Mother remembers, two sisters in her class who had learning difficulties being taken away to a special school and being sterilised. It went on and on...

So, there we were – in a bar, hip or not hip, talking about a wall that was not a wall, and of a night the devil came and turned the world upside down. My Grandmother had come from Berlin and now I was not sure that I even liked it anymore.

Give me beaver anytime...

Here's a drawing that my Grandfather – Karl Trinkewitz – did of that very synagogue, sometime before it was burnt down to the ground:

MUMBO JUMBO

I have a very sensitive gag reflex. Put simply, it means that if I smell something extremely unpleasant it overpowers me. I start to gag and I need to vomit. Usually nothing comes out – I just retch and retch.

I remember the first time I visited Nepal. There were no proper toilets outside of the 'good' Kathmandu hotels; usually they were just pits, full and over-flowing. Boy, did I retch, as I half stood and half squatted, hand clasped over nose and mouth. It was foul and painful, so I usually opted for the fields in the dead of night.

Bear that in mind as you read this tale.

For me it all started in London. It's not a glamorous city or even a refined one. There's something very coarse about it; it has neither the sophistication of Paris nor the cultural decadence of Berlin, perhaps it did once, but not now. Neither is it New York, where money rules and the pursuit of it so brazenly displayed on everything and everybody. London is not that crude – it sits uncomfortably between Europe and America, being neither, but paying homage to both. It really is an island.

It was in this unattractive city that offers everything that I came across the perfect Mumbo Jumbo.

His name is Loof, not the Mumbo Jumbo but the guy who introduced me to it. I have quite a history with Loof and I like the guy, but his aloofness is exasperating. He's like a slippery fish that isn't slippery – you just can't pin him down at all but he has an easy air that says you can. He once admitted to me that he likes it that way. Well, that's Loof in a nutshell. I'm sure there's more to him, but he's just not letting on.

He had spent quite some time as a student of an Ecuadorian Amazonian shaman and healer, and yes, that involved ingesting copious amounts of various plants and toxins, as part of an enlightening and transformative process. He told entertaining and almost unbelievable tales of time spent in the jungle; the type of story that makes you feel you are missing out on something special.

Now, neither Loof nor I are interested in drugs – we both hardly drink, so it is a very strange thing indeed that we found an attraction in these strange plant medicines. In fact, the Amazonian Indians look at all these potent plants strictly in terms of medicine – nothing recreational here.

Two plants are used: ayahuasca, and Amazonian tobacco. Ayahuasca is drunk, and the tobacco is used in its fresh leaf form and is not smoked, it is sniffed as a terrifying strong liquid, or drunk in amounts that should just simply kill you.

Loof told me of drinking a full glass of crazily strong tobacco juice; he loudly and violently threw up, and then was able to see straight though a large rock. Now that just plain frightened me.

I turned up at his swanky west London apartment one evening to join a group about to engage in an ayahuasca ceremony – just a room full of people with dim lighting. I think it was all guys but I don't remember, as I was nervous.

Ayahuasca looks like black tar and has a stink that makes me want to gag immediately. And the taste? Well, that's just plain disgusting and left a gross aftertaste in my mouth. I didn't drink much, not more that a spirit shot or two.

So, what happened? Well, I felt weird alright, but it wasn't that strong. I didn't have a magical experience or anything like that. Actually, I suppose it was all quite disappointing on some level. I was either sitting on the loo or having my head down it retching and puking. Of course, others had done the same, so for me, in this room of holy porcelain, my gag reflex went into overdrive. I just couldn't stop retching. Half the night I spent in there, gagging, retching, puking and feeling nauseous. Boy, it was rough!

I remember Loof coming in and asking if I was alright – Jeez, what a question – between my shitting and puking and feeling pretty out of it, he asks this question! I laughed; actually, something in me felt fine and impervious to all this physical and external stuff. I looked at him and plainly stated: "There's absolutely nothing you can do to help me." I don't know what he thought, he must have been just as out of it in his own way, and he left me to it.

Back in the room, a guy was kneeling down with his head on the floor, Allah praying style, with no shirt and a naked torso. He was constantly knocking his head and neck rhythmically with his knuckles – like drumming. It was noisy, with me in the toilet and he drumming and vibrating the demons out of himself.

Such was the nature of this first time.

In the morning, I felt fine, as if nothing had happened – no hangover, no particular tiredness and no memory of anything bad.

Despite the lack of magic, I somehow found the whole thing fascinating. There is nothing pleasant about ayahuasca; you definitely wouldn't call it recreational. You can't socialise with it, you can barely talk, walk, think or function in any half-normal way. It's like being poisoned, taken close to death and towards whatever lies beyond. It is completely uncontrollable – it does with you whatever it does and you have absolutely no say, whatsoever.

So who was this healer that had led Loof to this other world? I wanted to experience the real thing as such, but lacked the spare funds for a trip to the high Amazon in Ecuador.

Chance is a strange thing. A few months later, I somehow learned that this mysterious healer was coming to Europe to hold a few small and discreet ceremonies. I wanted in.

Ayahuasca is illegal just about everywhere in Europe but legal in

Holland for religious ceremonies and purposes. Such are the Dutch. I found myself disembarking from the plane in Copenhagen, Denmark, and getting to a remote spot by train, bus and hiking. How the hell I managed to find the place I'll never know – no one spoke English, and after tramping along empty lanes in the freezing cold I eventually spotted a large Indian tipi sticking out above some small trees on the other side of a large empty field.

It seemed that I had arrived.

In fact, I was the first to arrive, and found myself sitting in a tiny house with a Danish couple who spoke scant English. He was a husky dog trainer and ran dog sled trips across Lapland's frozen wastes, and she was a local school teacher. I warmed myself against the inefficient wood burning stove.

The ceremony was to be held in the large tipi set behind the house in a wild garden sheltered by dense foliage and numerous trees.

People started arriving in dribs and drabs. In total, there may have been twenty of us, mostly Danes, but a few had crossed the bridge from Sweden. Thankfully, I could now disappear comfortably into the crowd.

Miguel arrived with Fish. Fish is a Mexican Indian now living in Holland. He had been a deep-sea diver on oilrigs and had a large barrel chest suggesting large and powerful lungs. Larger than life and very forward, he instantly stole the limelight.

Miguel is short like Fish, of slim build, handsome with shoulder length black shiny hair and a nasty scar on his right cheekbone, suggesting something had smashed into him. Unobtuse and quite discreet, Miguel was the opposite of Fish. He looked the classic Indian and was a Shaur from Ecuador and, of course, the shaman. He and Fish had come from another ceremony in Norway or somewhere equally as cold and were wearing full winter attire – I wished I were!

It was a pitch black and very chilly night. Damp cold air lingered in the sodden garden.

In the tipi, Miguel constructed a very impressive mud clay mountain, well sculpted and full of features, decorated with feathers and fresh leaves. A large branch with foliage was planted next to it, sticking erect like a flagpole. This construction represented the realm of ayahuasca or maybe where it took you to – I can't remember exactly, but it was something like that. Miguel was lost to us as he laboured hard on his magical construction. He was totally plastered in cold wet slimy mud. I dug and filled a few superfluous buckets out in the dark garden just to keep the biting chill at bay.

A fire had been built but not lit. People sat and lay around close to it in hopeful expectation of a spark. Most people had sleeping bags – not me of course – Denmark in winter, why would I have thought of that.

Miguel had disappeared and on returning was in full Indian regalia. His elaborately embroidered dress, necklace made from shells and seeds and his classic headdress decorated with dazzling dark blues feathers, made him look marvelous, quite formidable and downright scary.

I'm not exactly sure what Miguel did next – stamp his foot, clap his hands or make a large sound, but whatever it was, the room hushed.

The ceremony had begun.

He spoke Spanish, which Fish translated into English. It soon became obvious that this was going to be a serious affair and there were strict rules to follow. First, he checked that no one had eaten onion or garlic or drunk coffee (and a few other things I now forget) for the last week or so, as they would react badly with ayahuasca and one might feel terrible and the ayahuasca was unlikely to work. On top of that, no one should have eaten that day because vomiting was expected and an empty stomach would make things easier.

He explained that ayahuasca was alive, a healer, teacher, peaceful and simultaneously wrathful. It would do whatever it needed to help you. On top of that, its DNA is so close to humans that it could repair it and change it.

The rules of the ceremony were as follows:

1. If you needed to leave the tipi for a dash to the bushes, you had

to walk behind everyone going clockwise Even if you sat by the door, you couldn't exit if it wasn't a clockwise walk.

2. Vomit towards the fire only – fire dispels all negativities vomited out – we are not talking about digestive juices here, we're talking about demons and negative energies.

3. Everyone had to sit upright – no dozing, slouching or lying down – that would make you passive and might attract ghouls and monsters to your cozy bed.

4. No singing, dancing, tai chi or chanting mantras etc.

5. Behave yourself – no dramas and unnecessary antics.

Follow these rules and you'll be ok.

The fire was lit and the tobacco ritual started. Tobacco opens up the left and right channels of the body, works with and compliments the ayahuasca.

Miguel poured a copious amount of dark liquid into my cupped hands and I sniffed and snorted the burning potion as high as my body reactions would allow. Jeez, it hurt, like eating mustard or wasabi but a hundred times stronger. It infused into my head, eyes, nose and throat. My eyes stung and watered, everything burned, the back of my head was on itchy fire and my brain was tingling. Of course, it then ran down the back of my throat and into my lungs. Soon the whole room was coughing and spluttering. Some people were gagging and retching. Miguel laughed. Later, I learned to sniff and shut off my lungs so the liquid ran down into my stomach – a different kind of experience and a learned art which no one present had seemed to master.

We were all given plastic puke bowls and Miguel dished out the ayahuasca – a very small glass for each person.

We all settled down and waited for the inevitable.

The fire was great, warm with impressive flames reaching up. Sparks flew high to the very top of the tipi where smoke and heat, and probably demons, exited safely.

Miguel sang songs, played strange stringed instruments, told fantastic stories of the jungle and of his ayahuasca experiences.

During the various ceremonies I attended with him, I learned a little about his life. He had been arrogant, uncaring and materialistic, until he became sick with some paralysis. A shaman healed him. He then changed his life and became a shaman apprentice, living in the jungle, hardly eating, and drinking ayahuasca daily for a few years until the transformation was done. What transformation is that, you may ask? Tricky to say, but he looks great, radiating health and an abundance of energy – that's a pretty good advert to start with.

I vomited a few times, but it was a mild affair and nothing like my time with Loof, and I certainly had no need to dash to the bushes, which was a great relief. The ayahuasca created a weird feeling of course but overall it was a pleasant and fascinating experience. Some people had a hard time with it – crying, distressed, constant vomiting with plenty of bush runs.

Fish fed the fire and sang songs in his native Indian language whilst playing a drum. Occasionally during the long night, Miguel came around and 'cleansed' everybody by showering people's faces with a strong concoction he held in his mouth, along with some whispered chants while waving a reverberating feather fan. It was kind of spooky.

It was a nice night. In the morning, we recalled our experiences – some people's tales were fascinating. Others, like me, had nothing much to say.

We ate a healthy breakfast in the house and I retired alone to a caravan in the front yard. I couldn't sleep a wink and soon wandered down to the nearby coast to look at the fishing boats in the tiny harbour. The sky was grey and the sea rough, blowing a chilly onshore wind, about force four or five, if you know about such things. I soon returned to warm myself by the inefficient stove.

The ceremony was repeated the next night, but this time Miguel bypassed the ritual and clothing and went straight to the point. There were only about six people in the tipi besides Miguel and Fish, and Miguel seemed animated, immediately dishing out the ayahuasca after the tobacco splutter.

For some reason he gave me a glass, like a whisky glass but without the shot or two. It was a full glass. I heard him tell Fish in Spanish that it was really potent and Fish physically tried to stop him from giving it to me. Miguel shrugged him off.

I ended up drinking the lot.

Nothing could have prepared me for what happened next.

As I sat looking at the fire feeling most odd, a sound seemed to come out of nowhere – not just a sound but also a vibration, rising out of me and above the fire towards the open top of the tipi. It was almost like a helicopter taking off or rather, with that in mind, me taking off.

Then it happened.

I could see and hear the whole tipi – everyone in his or her own ayahuasca world – but it was hard to keep focused. Miguel was smiling.

I exploded from within.

I had a tube going straight through me from top to bottom. It was alive, full with vivid red energy, flowing and rising up. Within that, were zillions of fluorescent blue and green things, creatures almost, as bright and as colourful as anything can be, coursing upward and spilling out through my eyes. When I looked out at the fire, I could throw green, blue and red out into the room through my eyes in millions of bright flaming sparks. I remember being so aware of it all – I even checked to see how far I could throw them.

It just didn't stop – it went on and on. It was overwhelming and extremely physical. Then the puking started. That too was non-stop for god knows how long. There was nothing left inside me, yet small amounts of clear liquid came out, looking orange in the firelight. But not once did I have to run for the bushes. Miguel sang to me for what seemed like half the night, his stringed instrument reverberating and cutting through me, intensifying my already intense feeling. I wanted to let go, give in to it all, but something in me refused, hung on for dear life – it wasn't going anywhere, but I wanted it gone, whatever it was. God what a struggle I had between the two, and in the end, I couldn't sit upright anymore and flopped back, but kept remembering not to, and sat back up for a while, only to collapse again. I remember apologising to Miguel as he kept on singing.

Anyway, next to all the weird noises inside and outside the tipi, the commotion of people puking and dashing, I managed to resist the offer of another glass!

After that, I don't remember much, but did make it to the long breakfast table in the house with all the others some time after dawn.

I listened to a group of Danes talking about something in English, and joined the conversation by saying something appropriate. They all looked at me in disbelief and stopped talking. One of them apologised, a doctor from Copenhagen, and said they should and would now talk in English, as it was rude to be speaking Danish in front of me. I said they were already speaking English. They all laughed, saying they had been speaking Danish.

What?

I asked Miguel what he made of it and he said that in ceremonies while under the influence of ayahuasca he could understand other people's languages. I forgot to ask him if he heard it in Shaur or Spanish.

That was real by the way, believe it or not.

I went back to Copenhagen with Fish and then home to the UK where everyone told me how well I looked. I felt trashed.

The next time was in Holland. It was a mad rush to get the Euro Star, as I had only heard about the ceremony one day into the ceremony. I had missed the first night and was determined not to miss the next. It was being held in Utrecht. I had the usual delight of walking around in the freezing dark, not really knowing where I was going and asking people the way to a small community centre. I did eventually find it, and walked into a modern but small community hall that had a kitchen and two changing rooms with plenty of toilets and a shower – no bush runs here.

Obviously, this was no tipi and there was no central fire. It was a decent sized room – perhaps the same size as the tipi, but not round – with a long line of windows and a double glass door overlooking what I suspected to be a garden. It was now pitch black. On the opposite end to the doors was a small raised platform, a stage, and on that was a wood burning stove, already alight. Many people sat and lay in and on sleeping bags around the edges of the room – maybe twenty or more – it seemed a lot for some reason. They were relaxed and warm. This was five star compared to Denmark.

At all ceremonies, it is easy to be invisible, discreet and ignored if that is what you wish – no one bothers you at all. However, there is always someone to pay, someone looking, checking and hovering until your cash has been delivered. Then you are free to disappear.

This was a church affair. The Santo Daime church has its roots in Brazil, and kind of combines Christianity and Amazonian spiritual practices. It officially uses ayahuasca in Holland, and its founding member used it in the jungle, having visions that led him to practice and form a church – something like that anyway, but please – don't quote me. Now it was time to pay, and a slim Indonesian woman took my wad. Interestingly, she did not attend the ceremony.

I found Miguel in the kitchen cooking up the foul smelling ayahuasca. I almost gagged. He kind of remembered me but he must have done a shed load of ceremonies across Europe since Denmark, and seen a thousand like me. Yet he was friendly enough.

The translator was a stick thin Dutch guy whose command of Spanish and English was probably not up to the job, and he looked like he cared more about what he ingested than the task at hand.

Miguel sat by the double doors, which were slightly ajar so people near the door could make a dash to a pit that had been dug in the garden. He was facing the small stage and fire. In the middle of the room was a table with flowers and other decorations, but no mountain this time. The participants seemed uninterested in what he had to say, and chatted as he spoke. Miguel was not in any kind of special regalia.

The ceremony proceeded as before – tobacco followed by ayahuasca. It was a very uninspiring matter of fact affair. Unlike Denmark, there seemed no rules to follow – people lay, lounged, joked, smoked and some drank many glasses of ayahuasca. It was more like a party – only the music was missing.

I wondered what had happened. How many ceremonies had Miguel done? Had he learned that Europeans don't care for his ways and only come to drink the magic potion? Had he got the taste for money that these ceremonies bring? Only he knows the answer to all that.

I sat next to a German guy who had driven something like twelve hours to join for just one night – just like me, except I had caught a train.

I needed to puke. That was easy but afterwards my guts ached and I had nausea. Between nothing coming out from either end I had no choice but to kick-start my gag reflex. I had had my hand over my mouth and nose in the toilet but now removed it and inhaled. Boy, the reaction was fast and I was soon chucking up gloriously followed by explosions on the other end. That's a tricky manoeuvre to get everything down the pan and not across the floor. I felt that all the filth and garbage I had ingested through dirty food and drink from working in Nepal over the years was coming out.

Success, and I wobbled slowly back to the ceremony. Of course, many others were making a hasty dash to the garden or the toilet block.

The German guy had long disappeared and I had concerns that he was not okay. I went and looked – he had locked himself in a toilet and was moaning and talking to himself or having an animated conversation with someone or something else! With difficulty, I just about managed to tell the skinny Dutch guy of the German's plight, but he was too out of it to do a thing about it and the poor German spent the entire night locked in his hideout. By first light, he had disappeared. I hope he didn't drive in that condition.

At some point in the night, the skinny Dutch guy produced a saucepan full of disgusting black liquid with what looked like a huge rotting mushroom sitting in it. He exclaimed it was a mescaline carcass and we were free to help ourselves. No one did. It looked like the devil's brew itself.

The 'cleansing' ritual was brief, and before long, the ceremony finished. Miguel gave a long lecture and told everybody off. This was not a drinking party – where was the fire and place to make a mountain? Of course, no one answered. He made a big thing about the importance of the cardinal points – the fire, shaman and entrance, which all had to be lined up in a certain direction with Miguel facing a certain way.

Anyway, he was pissed off, or so it seemed.

I got a lift to Rotterdam with a seasoned hippy and caught the train back home.

The time between my first ayahuasca experience to the last in this story was about a couple of years at the most. Not long after Holland, I had an invite from Fish to join him in southern Spain. Once again, I found myself travelling alone, but this time both Fish and Miguel met me at the airport. A woman called Patricia drove us through the concrete coastal towns the Spanish so seem to love, to a beach cafe surrounded by hotels and apartment blocks. I wasn't friends with any of these people, and found it odd to be sitting there and listening to stories of people I knew nothing about.

Soon we set off again, driving up a steep track to the top of a hill and a half finished concrete house that overlooked the town of Malaga. The view was strange – the sorry looking treeless countryside that swept down to the town was dotted with lots of unfinished concrete houses. Over the top of the hill was the major coastal highway. Then a man appeared with more than one hundred goats. There was nowhere to herd them anymore; all the pasture was taken up either by plastic poly-tunnels growing tomatoes or the walls of crumbling concrete building plots. I watched him lead the goats between structures right up to the highway so they could find what was left to eat. This was an ugly place with an ugly feel and I was glad to hear that the ceremony would be held elsewhere.

I spent a boring night in the house. Everyone was friendly enough. The owners were an Argentinean couple with two small boys. He had had an accident whilst welding on a building site, and no longer worked.

I shared a room with Miguel who constantly drank what I thought was ayahuasca from a plastic bottle.

The next day was oh so tedious. There wasn't even anywhere pleasant to walk. Fish made calls, things were discussed, and in the middle of the afternoon, a blonde woman came by and drove Fish, Miguel and me many miles east along the coast. The Argentinean couple followed later.

I had worked in Estepona on a micro hydro-project on a private estate, and soon recognised the landscape. We drove into the hills along dirt tracks and stopped at a hidden log cabin set among pine trees. The views were great, and below the house was a steep and deep rocky gorge. In fact, there were two houses owned by a family, and we were all welcomed like old friends. This place still held onto some of its original beauty unlike the concrete coast from where we had just come.

The place was busy, and a fair amount of people arrived. What I quickly learned was that an eastern European 'shaman' was conducting a ceremony there as well, and it was going to be a two shaman affair with all of us in a big circle – the hippy European doing his thing with his people and Miguel doing his thing with his people. Two different kinds of ayahuasca were to be administered. I would drink Miguel's.

Pretty screwed up I thought, but I had come a long way and the place was great.

In fact, it was better than I had first thought. We walked up to a vantage spot, completely isolated from any neighbours or tracks, and surrounded by a fair amount of pine. A large clearing with a ready-made fire greeted us. The air was warm, and soon a quarter moon was clearly visible in the cloudless sky. We could see it glisten in the sea far away and way below. Miguel sat with his back to the west towards the fire facing an opening, where no one sat, to the east. I guess this is how a ceremony should be set up. I sat alone on the anti-clockwise side of the opening and Fish on the clockwise side, both of us facing Miguel. There was no Indian regalia, no introductions. He just got on with it.

The son of the owner cried out. He was no more than ten and started howling. Something had got into his eye and he was inconsolable. His mother thought it was an insect bite but Miguel said it was some negative energy or spirit. He said some chants and rubbed ayahuasca on the boy's eye. He soon fell asleep under a blanket and much to my relief did not drink the ayahuasca.

Besides being a very weird spilt ceremony between the hippy and Miguel, it followed the usual pattern. Some people were very sick, some slept, some looked traumatised, but that's how a ceremony is – business as usual.

The next morning, we all slept in the house, although I find it near impossible to sleep after drinking ayahuasca, and repeated things the following night.

One guy lay down moaning and puking all night, one woman had a fit and had to be restrained until she calmed down and Fish did more than his fair share of bush runs. I felt ok – not too many visits to the pines and nothing dramatic. However, I did fall asleep towards the end of the night, and woke to hear Miguel speaking English, which he couldn't at all, by the way. I heard him laugh and clearly say I would catch light as my feet were too close to the fire. Once I focused on it, I only heard Spanish. I then checked with Fish and he confirmed that Miguel had indeed been saying what I thought he had – in Spanish, not English!

Soon after, the hippy was trying to put some small pieces of wood together in a cross-like shape as a last quarter ritual for the end of the ceremony, but he was so out of it he kept falling over and Fish asked me to do it. I simply placed the pieces of wood together in a cross-like shape to complete the ritual. I forget what happened to the wood – maybe it was burned.

Fish and Miguel suddenly got up and I was whisked off with the blonde woman to her car. Before long, we were driving in the dark down the dirt track. It really was that fast. How the hell could the blonde drive? I asked her if she was ok to drive. I actually don't think she answered or was in a fit state, but drive we did down the Spanish coastal highway to the airport where Fish and Miguel hurried to catch a plane to another ceremony.

I was still on ayahuasca and had about six hours to wait. All the lights and commotion of a busy airport were too much and I slunk off to find a bench in a quiet corner to sit it out. Four hours I sat undisturbed, waiting for my plane and waiting to feel normal once again. By the time I checked in, I was fine and heading home once again.

I wondered how big Miguel's bag of money was when he returned home to Ecuador.

The next day I had to go to work and teach a bunch of energetic and bored teenagers English. I don't know how I did it, had been worried that I would still be off my face and rather strange, but I gave three days of lucid teaching where the whole class was engaged. After that, it reverted back to bored unruly teenagers causing havoc, but that really was the norm.

I had yet another invite from Fish, and once again travelled alone to be met by him at Oslo airport.

Four of us drove a long way through endless forest to a lake somewhere near Sweden, I think. I talked about wildlife, but no one was interested.

I'm not sure what kind of place we arrived at, but it was almost like a deserted holiday park. It had that kind of feel about it, but there was only a small house on a hill and a long drive, a road really, down to a huge lake surrounded by dense pine forest. There was a group of people in the house but they were not going to the ceremony – just hanging out. They seemed normal, or rather not hippy-like, and I couldn't quite work out what brought them to this isolated spot.

I walked down towards the lake and saw a large roundhouse like a massive tipi but made from wood and metal. It was impressive and could hold around eighty people. I was told it was a Viking replica.

I was already a day late and Miguel had already had a night of ceremony. He was sleeping near the fire.

On the walk down the half-mile or so drive, I had had one of those odd feelings – you know – the ones you just can't ignore. There seemed to be a black cloud around the top of the tipi and I had a sense of real evil lurking there, like the devil was lying in wait to do whatever the devil does best. Devilry, I suppose.

I made the decision not to join the ceremony but kept it to myself. I was in the middle of nowhere – didn't even know where I was – and knew getting back to the airport for my flight could not depend on a non-existent rural bus service.

I learned that Miguel had been terribly sick all night, as he took in the negativities from the ceremony to transform them into something not negative, I guess. Now he was sleeping it off. I knew then that I had made the right decision – always follow that first gut feeling.

A North American Indian was walking about, a little lost-looking, and I started chatting to him. He lived in Switzerland, but was a Sioux tribal chief from Dakota, and was proud to be one hundred percent Indian – I guess that must be a rare thing these days. He was not joining the ceremony; he had been invited to give a talk about his Indian culture but was not interested in drinking ayahuasca. He invited me to join a four-year Sun Dance programme in Dakota on his tribal land. This involved just four days a year where you dance around a pole to a slow drumbeat under a baking sun all day. At some point, you have sticks pushed through the soft flesh of your chest muscles that are connected to the pole by cords. And yes, towards the end of the ceremony you rip them out in a bloody mess using your own weight and volition. You can't eat or drink for four days, and I guess after that you would do just about anything. Of course, I was tempted, but as I was already heading down another path, declined. He told me that his tribe never used mind-bending drugs, and kept things pure. I liked that.

It turned out that a few people, including the two I had driven up from the airport with, had also decided not to join the ceremony. Independently from me they had come to the same conclusion – something dark was going on and they wanted no part of it.

In the house, I met Eva. She was some kind of psychic, and knew Miguel because he had stayed at her house a year before and had performed a ceremony in her well-being centre. It had been a very small affair and was at the beginning of Miguel's visits to Europe. She did not care for ayahuasca or for the Shaur way. Now I knew why she and the two guys were there – they had some sort of connection, but like me were having second thoughts.

There were four of us in the house and we had a pleasant evening. We could even look down onto the roundhouse from the large windows. It looked cold, dark and very uninviting.

The next morning there was to be a sweat lodge sauna with the Indian, and the two guys and I headed down the drive. There must have been seventy people milling around. It had obviously been a huge ceremony and there was yet another night to go. The only time I had been to a sweat lodge was in the UK. Ironically, that sweat lodge was held by a guy who had been through the whole Sun Dance ritual – he had the brutal scars to prove it. That sweat lodge was so hot that I thought I would expire – everyone was lying on the grass floor gasping and panting, and for me, having just come back from a very cold trek in the Himalayas, it was pure torture!

However, for very good reasons, this Norwegian sweat lodge never happened for me.

There was a lot of tension and people were arguing. It was about money, of course. There was Miguel, Fish, the Norwegian organiser, the roundhouse guy, the drivers, the cook, the guy who brings the ayahuasca into the country, and who knows who, all wanting their share.

If it averaged out at fifty clients each paying, at the very minimum, one hundred and twenty Euros for one night, then for three nights it would be 18,000 Euros at the very least – probably much more. Not bad I say, and plenty for everyone. But no, there were huge tensions and arguments and things looked aggressive. Not my problem and I wandered back up to the house taking one last look inside the Round-house. I saw a guy with a shaved head preparing the next night's wood. We smiled and exchanged a wave. He was a bit tough looking, but I later realised he wasn't at all. His name was Vince and we would meet many times again.

We left this ugly scene and the four of us drove to Honefoss where Eva had her centre. It was a long drive and we arrived in the dark. The centre was large: four nice treatment rooms, a shop selling candles, crystals, spirit catchers and things, a small coffee shop, a kitchen and dining area and a very large clean basement room, which served as an art gallery and a workshop space. It was really impressive, professional, and right in the centre of town. Its togetherness suggested the opposite of what we had just left behind.

Eva invited me to come back to hold my own energy workshops.

Great I thought, and it was even well paid!

I soon returned and started working in the centre, holding Tai Chi classes for the elderly in the morning and giving Tui Na, a Chinese type of massage, throughout the day. I really enjoyed it.

Miguel had left a small coca-cola bottle of ayahuasca in Eva's fridge, a very strong and pure concoction he had said. She offered it to me – take it or it would be thrown away. Well, I did not want to take it and mess a few working days up, but I didn't want her to throw it away either.

That is how bloody seductive this stuff was – it had a kind of magi-cal property that most probably played with my romantic notion that anything natural, pure and indigenous must somehow be good. Malaria is natural, but there is certainly nothing good about that – unless you are the parasite itself – but who knows how that feels, eh?

So, what did I do? I drank a little every day before going to work.

Mad? Yes and no.

It made the twenty minute walk to work a bit tricky but I could function and everyone seemed happy with what I did. However, one day I drank a little too much and had to struggle to keep my feet on the ground. The ayahuasca induced internal visions and made me feel weird. I forced myself to be normal and successfully engaged with clients at work. I got away with it, but decided to call it a day; work was work, and the black stuff didn't belong there. Losing my job wasn't an option I could afford.

I went to a cold lake in the middle of who knows where to have half a glass or, most probably, more. I just couldn't resist, and lay alone in a tatty old van, having visions of a group of men milling around nearby and waiting for me – ghosts from another time. I decided to jump in the lake. It was freezing. There was even some ice still around the edges. There's nothing quite like a cold shock to send a bunch of spooky ghouls on their way!

On the evening of the sixth day, the black tarry looking liquid went down the sink.

It is interesting how things are connected; soon after this, Loof headed to Honefoss to give workshops and healing in the centre. I'm sure ayahuasca was history for him by then.

What bugged me about the whole ceremony affair was that I never learned to let go and relax inside the powerful Mumbo Jumbo it produced. I was over having the delusion that it was somehow a magic fix for anything, but what I really wanted was to be myself, not have it push me around and beat me up, as was my experience.

I was not really over it. That's how stubborn I was.

Of course, I went again. I arrived in Amsterdam and made my way to a subway stop where I made a call. 'We are here, just opposite in an apartment' was the response and the phone went dead.

Jeez – that was clear then! But I was used to it now – find the apartment or go home.

Opposite was a sleazy entrance and I guessed it was in there. I was right, and was soon in a small and unfriendly flat that looked more like a squat. A guy called Midas had replaced Fish and I immediately sensed he took an instant dislike to me – I guess that was his gut feeling! Miguel was there with his son Ivan. They were all indifferent to me.

I was just another paying customer.

I knew this story well by now, and I too was indifferent. It can be strange how things change.

Vince picked us up and we drove south to a small town called Teuge. Miguel was already drinking small amounts of what I assumed was ayahuasca.

I learned that Vince was the driver on Miguel's various trips to Europe and attended most ceremonies as a fire keeper and general helper. He drank the magic potion as well of course, and had had several trips to Ecuador. He was a seasoned and dedicated ceremony man and followed a strict diet and an abstinence from sex, and god knows what else. He was truly on the shaman path.

We arrived at a strange place – a gated, dead end track on the outskirts of town set among pine trees, unruly bush and weeds. Fair sized houses dotted the rough road, and all of them were in a bad state of repair. It had been built by the Germans during World War Two as an officers' quarters and command centre, but was now a hippy squat. Lots of old abandoned vehicles sat in the grounds of the various houses.

We stopped outside a decrepit double storey dwelling that looked like an old military store, which it may well have been long ago. In the garden was a very large tent, more a yurt than a tipi. It had bales of straw stacked around the inside edge to keep the wind out and provide back support for ceremonies and workshops. A fire smouldered in the middle.

There was loads of room in the tent, and it could hold about forty or fifty people at least.

The squat was run by an interesting couple, and I saw the man unload about six plastic jerry cans full of water from his car. I soon learned the house was not on the mains supply. He proudly and a little aggressively told me that he did not want to pay for water or to be involved with society 'out there'. So where did he get the water from?

'The tap from the local graveyard...'

Maybe his justification is that the dead are no longer in society.

Incidentally, the tent burnt to the ground soon after this – no water to quell the flames...

There was a freezing cold house, which looked like a junk yard inside. Upstairs was a large, empty, ice-cold room, which had the feel of an abandoned farmyard barn, whose only access was a rickety wooden staircase up the side of an outside wall. The kitchen was in the garden next to several puke pits, which were dug inside a makeshift wooden shack. The toilet was something else altogether and was to be avoided at all costs. The hippy was a good artisan and numerous objects d'art in wood and metal adorned the garden.

It was the perfect place for a ceremony.

You may wonder why I refer to ceremony types as hippies. Well, that's because I have a cropped or shaved head, am a bit of a brute, have lived a tough but fairly normal life running adventure trips and expeditions, working on a fishing boat and various similar things. For me, many of the people I met at ceremonies were hippy types – soft, sensitive, alternative and definitely not brutish. Some were nice; some I could have done without, but that's just people in general – hippy or not.

So there I was, once again – at a ceremony, in a wild garden around an outdoor fire, impatiently waiting for the night to take the day. Miguel was on ayahuasca up to his eyeballs and Midas held court in a thatched gazebo like a modern Svengali, collecting money and writing down emails and phone numbers. He was the kind of guy who knew a good earner when he saw it.

The garden soon filled up with clients, and I started talking to a good friend of Vince's – a Dutch Canadian woman called Bianca. She was fun, talkative and seemed perfectly sane, much to my relief. She lived nearby and it was a simple affair for her to come along – her husband just drove her a few minutes up the road, unlike me for whom every ceremony was some kind of logistical nightmare.

Bianca had seen Miguel help a very sick friend of hers and, like me, it was Miguel she had now come to see rather than taste the sickly black potion, which we both drank as well, of course.

She would later spend time in Ecuador with Miguel and Vince – such was the pulling power of the shaman…

The evening came and we took our places. The tent was full up, suggesting a very busy three-night affair. I sat by the opening on the clockwise side – in Denmark that would have meant a long tricky walk around the entire inside of the tent, wobbling and stumbling as I tried to get behind everyone, even those half unconscious lying back against the straw bales, before desperately making a dash into the night. However, those rules were long gone, complete history, and all I had to do was turn right to be instantly in the pitch black of the cold garden.

There were no straw bales by the entrance and the chilly night air crept inside making it freezing. On top of that, I was a long way from the central fire. However, all that was preferable to being wedged between projectile vomit and perhaps a frenzied freak out or even two.

By this time, I had learned to close off my lungs to the burning tobacco juice, and understood why Miguel laughed at those who couldn't. He even said the coughing was some negativity leaving the body. I too would have spluttered without that closing art. I never heard Miguel splutter once – just blow his nose, clear his throat and make those all too familiar noises: the ones that anyone would make if their mucus membranes were on fire.

When the coughs and splutters had subsided, the ayahuasca was administered.

Now, as I have said, this was a three day affair, and I won't bore you with ceremony details – they are all pretty much the same; different locations, different people, different dynamics, but the essence always remains the same – tobacco, ayahuasca, more ayahuasca and tobacco followed by 'cleansing' – which actually translates to us mere mortals, as puking and crapping. All these harsh antics are serenaded by Miguel's strange music, soft singing and entertaining stories. During this, one is full of the magic potion racing around one's blood causing havoc and semi psychosis. I guess the more you take the more you get used to it and the more you can consume. For Miguel and others like him it was not like this; the ayahuasca is a spirit called Tsunki who heals and teaches, transforms and is soft. If you are tense, ayahuasca may beat you up to teach you something and if you are too soft, you may literally and frighteningly melt away. There's neither rhyme nor reason to all of this – it dishes out the lesson and you have no choice but to take it.

As I have said, the difference with this ceremony was that I no longer had an agenda or some delusion that there was any magic here. All I wanted was to drink, engage and let go, not by force but by just letting things be.

That changed everything.

I felt the ayahuasca of course, puked up a few times, sometimes felt pretty rough and had visions – but visions seemed like a trap, an endless cul-de-sac of hard-core, never-ending Mumbo Jumbo. There was all this ayahuasca stuff, superficial but dangerously seductive, and then there was me, somehow not really affected by any of it.

However, the biggest thing of all was the cold; I was numb with cold. Every time someone made a dash to a pit or just simply went outside to get away from the madness in the tent, I caught the biting chill. For three nights, there was hardly any time and space where the tent flap opening wasn't being used.

And a good job too – the numbing cold kept me sane, real, and totally grounded.

This was not hell for me – I like the cold. In the Himalayas, the Arctic or on a tiny fishing boat in the English Channel, cold is just the norm. I even sleep with my window open whatever the weather. Don't get me wrong, I feel the cold, add layers to fend it off, but so long as

I'm not getting frostbite I really don't mind it at all. Maybe it is because I grew up without heating or insulation – who knows, it's just how I am.

So, back to the ceremony – a lot of people had the usual hard time, moaning and groaning all night, endless runs to the filthy pits, one guy even had an aggressive freak out, not that anyone did much about it of course. Some people sat upright like stone statues with serious expressions on their faces, while others looked totally traumatised and transfixed with fear. Some people seemed fine and chatted away, but between all the commotion and constant noise, I failed to hear what anyone said.

Vince later told me stories of aggression, psychosis and even coma on his long, exhausting journeys across Europe and Ecuador with Miguel.

Bianca had sat near the guy freaking out and next to some serious vomiting folk. I laughed at her predicament and she smiled back – who knows what she saw when she looked at me!

It's all a question of perception.

The days and nights are a bit of a blur, all mixed up, but there was always a decent breakfast in the kitchen and some lunchtime food prepared by a beautiful Dutch model, who incidentally had her fair share of distressing pit runs.

In the daytime, I tried to sleep upstairs in the freezing barn. This place was even colder than the ceremony tent, and seriously tested my metal. I had brought a sleeping bag this time, but as it was a thin summer one, it was of little help.

Some people joined me on the floor nearby, but no one stayed for very long – they soon returned to the tipi with its fire and bales of insulating straw.

I lay motionless like a sack of ice-cold winter potatoes. What for, you may ask; after all, there was a cozy fire in a warm tent down the stairs across the garden. That's because I like my solitude and I like my space – even if I have to freeze to get them.

Bianca's husband had picked her up, and I imagine she had a shower, some home cooked food and a warm relaxing bed to rest in before returning for the next night's onslaught – so very different from my austere experience.

One funny thing I remember well about this particular ceremony was the puke pits. There were about five of them, round dug holes no more than a foot wide and half a foot deep, set in a thatched shack between the house and the tipi, at the back of the garden to keep the endless retching and gagging as far away as possible from the from neighbours' ears. It was poorly lit by dull candle light, and the flickering gave it a spooky and quite sinister feel. Add to that the madness of the ayahuasca and you get a place you want to spend as little time in as possible. With all those demons being puked up, creating strange psychic activity, it felt like you were at the gates of hell itself. Something inherently dangerous was going on.

So there I was, in the puke pit on my hands and knees with aching guts trying to chuck up whilst simultaneously laughing my head off as others came and went as fast as they could. Someone was laughing with me and I turned from my floor position to see Bianca retching and gagging between fits of laughter. Christ did we laugh at the absurdity of it all, us being in a puke pit, the ceremony and Christ knows what. Back in the tipi we laughed some more. It was great!

Midas offered me some San Pedro, another plant from the Amazon. It reminded me of the skinny Dutch guy with his mescaline in Utrecht, and, as I had already had enough, a belly full so to speak, I politely declined.

Miguel is a great storyteller and his stories during this ceremony were a pure delight. He told a fantastic tale about the origin of salt, which I can no longer remember as it was complex and full of imagery I cannot reproduce. He told of going to the hell realm and meeting the darkness and then going to the light; both things were different flavours of the same thing and he told it in a beautiful and clear way. In a ceremony, he was a true raconteur.

In the morning after the second night, after some great story telling and after the first light of dawn had illuminated the tipi, Miguel offered people the disgusting, burning, instant retching, potent tobacco juice. I drank a small glass and my reaction was classic and instantaneous – I immediately retched and violently threw up before I had even got halfway to the puke pits. On the morning after the third night this tobacco ritual was repeated, except there was no one brave or perhaps foolish enough to come forward and take it.

But I did.

I drank my small glass with the obvious expectation of an instant puke, but nothing happened. I got worried – surely something should have happened? Where was the nausea and burning? Where was the vomit? This stuff would be in my blood steam soon. I went and found Miguel and he gave me some more to drink. I did so quickly hoping to be heading to the puke pit to spew out all the demons but also to puke out the tobacco – it would be in my bloodstream any moment. I don't know how much time passed and I became very concerned. Miguel just gave me a third glass.

That should do it. But that didn't work either.

Miguel was generally unavailable as a human being, far more aloof than Loof had ever been, and this third glass seemed the only way to engage with him. Outside of magic potions, he was very uninterested in anyone. Perhaps that's just his Shaur way. Who knows? I guess I was trying to connect with him for one last time – through a death defying magic potion.

Vince always had a problem puking and suffered terribly at cere-monies with nausea and gut ache, wanting to puke but never able to. He used to drink copious amounts of water until his body rejected it and he puked a small lake. He now told me to do the same, and I did – so much that I had stomachache and couldn't drink another drop.

Nothing happened.

Maybe two hours had passed since the first glass, but instead of being worried, Miguel told me it was perfect – the ayahuasca and the tobacco were working together in my body.

Oh great! That was not reassuring at all.

But I didn't feel ill at all, and my worry was just knowing that the toxic tobacco was freely running through my veins.

Puking would just be psychological, of no use whatsoever, but I needed it.

There was only one thing for it, and I headed to the toilet.

It defies description really – a wooden box on a raised platform with a seat, set in another thatched shack off the front driveway. It was a full pit where the evidence of a three-night ceremony was desperately splattered everywhere. To say it was disgusting does not do the mess justice. I had been lucky enough not to have needed this facility, but obviously many others had.

I took my hand away from my nose and mouth and breathed.

My body convulsed, I retched, gagged, sweated, nearly passed out and ran to the fresh air.

I had not puked.

So I tried again and a tiny amount of water came up.

I didn't try again – it was too traumatic.

I asked Miguel one last question: how did he get that nasty scar on his cheek? None of his regular entourage had ever asked, and I listened intently as he told the story. He had been taking a small herd of horses from one location to another and was riding behind them shooing and shouting commands. His horse kept aggressively biting one of the others in front until that one got so pissed off that it kicked its rear legs up to strike Miguel's horse. It kicked Miguel in the face instead and he was badly injured.

Game over; I walked up the road to find a bus to a train and a train to the airport.

I was done with this ceremony lark.

On my return to England, I went straight to bed. Sometime that night I had a lucid dream. Actually, it was not really a dream, more a direct experience.

I woke up in my dream. I was in bed, awake. Somebody was in the house and I got up. It was still dark. I went to my bedroom door and saw two men trying to get into my room. I knew immediately that some beings or energy had followed me from the ceremony and were up to bad mischief.

I immediately woke up, and said some words I had been taught for this sort of thing and in a flash, the bad things were gone. It was similar to my experience in Norway before I jumped in the freezing lake, but this time I was not on ayahuasca, believe it or not.

I did return to see Vince in Eindhoven, Holland many times but have always refrained from any offer to drink ayahuasca.

He lived in a caravan on the Belgium border, in a forest with a few lakes. It had once been a thriving holiday park, but was now near deserted with rotting caravans and overgrown plots. It was wild and ramshackle and had a great feel to it.

Vince had drunk ayahuasca almost daily for several years, followed the strict diet, and was now getting to the end of his tether. He had spent a small fortune on going to Ecuador, buying his own personal ayahuasca, constantly driving Miguel and Midas around Europe for little or no reimbursement and had, of course, paid the shaman and his friends for their services, which turned out to be rather scant indeed.

He felt hard done by, and was now questioning the integrity of his quest.

How things change; Loof's tales in the high Amazon and Vince's couldn't have been more different. I was glad I never went.

As we chatted about his dilemma, he offered me a glass. I drank a ceremony's worth and lay back in front of the wood burning stove, warm and cozy for a change and drifted off.

I had the most extraordinary experience. I travelled to Ecuador but couldn't properly actually arrive or get in. I saw the cloud forest and the mist above the jungle. I even saw Miguel, but the gate was closed so to speak.

I then went to the hell realm just as Miguel had told it in the ceremony at Teuge. I saw lots of bones and bodies of creatures going down a conveyor belt thing to be delivered to hell and recycled. It was so lucid that I clearly remember it today. There were the bones of one creature, huge and powerful like a giant ape moving towards hell. However, power and strength meant nothing here; everyone was the same.

Suddenly I was taken off and appeared in a black universe where stars and life were born. Rainbow arcs and brilliant white light appeared and consciousness was born. I saw billions of stars as blobs of brilliant white consciousness. I could be reborn or join them. I joined them.

All this time I had been aware of Vince, visiting the small caravan toilet to sit and make an array of trumpet noises. He didn't puke of course, and I opened my eyes smiling.

Fortunately, I didn't have to make the same visit as him and just lay there enjoying the tranquil moments beside a burning fire.

That was that, no more Mumbo Jumbo for me.

But is it Mumbo Jumbo?

Well, one thing is certain – it sure showed me how much Mumbo Jumbo I had in me, how many delusions were clouding and influencing me.

It helped me a lot. Helped me see my own nonsense, and helped me to do something about it.

But don't take my word for it. I suggest a long slow drink of the most foul tasting, black tar potion you can find – or not!

*   *   *

TOBACCO CHUNDA

Muscles laced with treacle sauce

Fresh lamb with sock and knicker stew

Rabbit's pooh and honey dew

Washed down with a glass of fresh tobacco juice.

Now relax
Perhaps two, three minutes at the most
Before the churning and the pain
Sends you running for the porcelain
It won't take long
Before you spew that black disgust
In torrents down the loo

Now relax again
Oh what elation
You may now wonder why you never tried the wonder
Of tobacco chunda

PSYCHO GALLERY

They might live down the road from you, opposite to you, work with you or even socialise with you. You could be staring them in the face and be oblivious to the fact that these men are men of unfathomable violence. Not old-fashioned stereotypical tough men who like to fight and hone their skills to show they are true men. No, these are men without the obvious physical attributes of a hard man, that have a thing inside them you never want to meet, an undiluted horror that doesn't need respect, has no care of consequence or any form of moral code.

However, I did meet a few and for some bizarre reason they told their tales and shared with me their unhinged worlds. I never witnessed their violence or even experienced their violent worlds – they simply showed me their deranged psyches; on reflection, it was a very odd privilege.

To cut to the chase, I'll introduce them one by one.

Psycho One lived on my street in the house right opposite mine. I was about fourteen, maybe younger when we hung out for a bit. He was a few years older than me but had already left school. We went fishing together far out on the low tide sand after having dug lugworm for bait. He knew all about fishing the sea, not me and I went along like a boy does, looking up to an older boy. The fishing sucked, nothing ever took the bait as was common in my fishing ventures, but the sea was wild and the weather always stormy and I loved that. It didn't last that long, his mother called mine and told her to keep me away from him; only trouble would come from such a liaison, she said. I only waved and said hi from across the road after that, I can't even remember the sudden halt in socialising. He had said a few crazy things to me, like asking what it would feel like if a steel needle were pushed through an eyeball; I remember thinking he said it like a Gestapo officer from a TV-movie I had watched. One time, on the low tide sands with the cold wind blowing hard in our faces, he said some weird sexual stuff. I laughed, not having any clue what he was on about or what was in his twisted mind. Fortunately, nothing menacing or untoward ever happened. Looking back, I had a lucky escape – this guy was a monster in every sense.

I left school and went to college in London. Meanwhile, Psycho One cut logs in his front garden joking with passersby that he was getting his axe ready for some dire deed. He'd call the police and say he was about to use its sharp and heavy blade but when they arrived, nothing had happened and they left thinking he had wasted their time. He made threats by phone to various women and was arrested for blackmail when he said he would harm someone's daughter unless a package full of money was dropped off in a nearby litterbin. The police were waiting. He even called my mother and said he was going to marry my sister. That's all I know but there must have been a whole lot more.

One day he called the police, he was twenty-two or twenty-three. He said he had done it and they went around, probably thinking it was another hoax, and found he had used the axe on his father's head. I don't know the gory details but he is now a permanent guest in an asylum for the criminally insane.

Be careful whom you fish with!

As a teenager, **Psycho Two** lived two miles down the road from me at about the time I lived right opposite Psycho One. I didn't know him then, as he was older than I was and into completely different things. Nor did I recognise him when we later met in London at a mutual friend's house. When Psycho Two realised we were originally from the same small town, he called me brother and seemed to want to be my friend. Now, no way was I wanting to be his friend, he had a bad reputation for taking drugs, anything that would change his reality, probably selling them as well and I had no interest in sweeping myself into the gutter or engaging with such a dumb vocation; add to that, his gaunt skinny looks and gaudy dress, much like a cartoon pimp gangster, I would have been embarrassed just to have been seen with him. However, red shoes, green pants, sporty spiv jacket, flat cap and cravat weren't the problem – he was the problem. He just looked wrong – not the cool eccentric he might have imagined in his psycho head, but a fraud, illegitimate and dangerous. It was rumoured he had killed three people in moments of rage connected to his 'industry'. It was also rumoured that he would inject just about anything to get high; in the event his favoured highs were not available and feeling desperate, even whiskey and coke – I never asked if that was on the rocks or not! It was joked that he frequented hippy festivals, not as a punter but as a travelling salesman, smartly dressed with a fashionable briefcase full of goodies for the needy and half-baked. Never staying too long, he swiftly sold his wares before moving on to the next lucrative event.

Face on he didn't scare me, I could have broken him to bits with ease, but as it was obvious he was dangerous and deranged, I usually stayed well clear of him.

One day he insisted that I accept a lift to the subway and I stupidly agreed. He drove up Hackney Road in his nineteen fifties Chevrolet, fast and dangerous, running red lights and swerving to avoid the other cars, heading straight towards us. He was on the wrong side of the road. I'm sure he was high, probably permanently out to lunch, and such reckless antics may not have been that unusual in this semi-derelict part of town at that particular time. Suddenly, he pulled a handgun from the car's centre console and waved it around like a start flag on a racetrack. Anyone close by and looking in would have seen it clearly. He was paranoid and everything about him had a sudden urgency. He couldn't focus on the road, kept looking at me for a response, which I didn't give, and then he started babbling gangster talk, telling me he was the 'man' and no one messed with him. I don't remember exactly what he said as the road ahead was a bad dream quickly turning to a nightmare with every yard he drove – I needed to wake up fast. I looked hard at him and he stopped his rant and looked straight back at me. God knows how we didn't crash – the desperate sound of honking hooters so filled the car that I had to shout over the din:

'Slow down!'

The gun hadn't really bothered me – it was his driving that was freaking me out. Not wanting to upset his psycho sensibilities, I tried very hard not to swear at him. He put the gun away and stopped outside Bethnal Green subway station. Feeling relief to have made the mile or so journey from Hoxton Square without a major accident or provoking an armed police response, I got out, slammed the door shut and briskly walked towards the subway. Without stopping, I glanced back to see him staring at the road in front, transfixed, blocking the traffic and lost in thought or some paranoid delusion. Needless to say, I never got into a car with him again. Later, I heard all sorts of second hand stories of appalling violence. I don't know what happened to him but I'm sure he didn't last long; after all, they never do.

Be careful whom you get into a car with!

When I met him, **Psycho Three** lived with a woman in the same small town as Psycho One and Two and worked around the corner from where I lived. He was an alluring and diverse character into animal rights and liberation.

One morning before school, he heard his mother scream and found her laid out on the hallway floor. She had fainted. Sometime during the night, his father had hanged himself and his corpse now dangled from the banister, the horror of his dead eyes silently greeting her as she headed down the stairs. Never quite recovering from this tragedy, she withdrew, grew quiet and distant from her son. Cursed, his troubles now began, festering slowly as the years rolled on.

Much later, after a lost and misspent childhood where he stole bikes, cars and generally terrorised his local East End London neighbourhood, he joined the military police and did time in Northern Ireland and Aden. He had been wounded in Aden when the jeep in front of his was blown up and a flying wheel nut smashed into his thigh. On leaving the army, he was fit and able but very angry. Not angry in the usual sense one might associate with old-fashioned army life; he was not a drinker, had never been drunk in his life and didn't get into bar room brawls or stupid fights. He had charm, good looks and curiosity but it was his volcano, smouldering and in acute need of release, that now forged his path.

He joined an animal rights group. They went to demonstrate against an illegal badger-baiting meet, where a dog and a captured badger would fight to the death in a pit dug into the forest floor. Nasty, blood thirsty men would place bets on which creature would win, as they desperately fought and ripped each other apart. The animal rights group were demonstrating where the badger-baiters had parked their cars. Psycho Three was not aware of demonstration protocols, the way right-on fringe types did things, and had just imagined some kind of military manoeuvre where the opposition were sent running with their tales between their legs. He arrived with a club hammer and charged towards the cars expecting others to follow – he even screamed as he made his charge (maybe that's an army thing). No one moved as Psycho Three smashed up an expensive Jaguar, holing the windscreen and denting the body. Everyone was in shock, especially the car owners. Psycho Three had misjudged his fellow demonstrators and they now just stared aghast. It would be mere seconds before a bunch of angry violent men turned on him to seek revenge. Knowing he was outnumbered and on his own, he fled the scene. Later, under the cover of darkness while the baiters did their vile business, he returned and finished off the cars.

After that, he left the demonstrations behind and went solo, burning labs, releasing animals and destroying machinery that was intended to cut trees and develop pristine places. But it was not enough, he needed more and craved for action.

So, what does a man like this do?

On the advice of his old army commander, he went to a pub in Waterloo, ironically called The Volunteer. Inside were double-dealing men who fixed up dirty deals. Representing government and enterprise, they used men like Psycho Three in their business of cash and war to secure regime change and mining rights. He spent the next seven years going from one African country to another, fighting and killing whomever he was told to fight and kill. He never knew whom he was working for, whom he was fighting against, why it was happening or who paid him, but paid he was, in huge quantities of cash.

It was the nineteen sixties and his first job was in Nigeria to fight against the Biafrans. He was thirty-four years old. After a while, his unit was offered more money to fight alongside the Biafrans, the ones they had just been shooting at. They shot their commanding officer and turned against their former colleagues, lost the war and spent six weeks on the run, hiding out in thick jungle during daylight hours and moving on at night. He was in a group of six who managed to get across the border into Cameroon. No one seemed to care which side he had fought for, the money was paid and he had enough to buy a detached house outright back home. But he didn't go back to the UK, instead he went to Paris and spent the money on whores and hotels. He loved sex with women, had girlfriends, telling me he even had sex with his girlfriends' mothers sometimes. He had so many children that he had to ask sneaky questions when they called him up so he could work out who their mothers were.

When the money dried up, he went back to Africa.

He told me that he had killed people, once close up and gruesome, but not the details and I didn't ask; as he said it, his sideways glance and edgy look spoke a tacit silence. He was wounded in Chad when a bullet hit a rock behind his position, the ricochet striking him hard in the back. For three days he was laid out, losing blood; the rule was, if you couldn't walk, you were left with a pistol to shoot it out or shoot yourself. For four days, his small group of seventy were pinned down in a boulder field, vastly outnumbered and without any hope of backup. They lost four men. The siege ended on the fourth day as the assailants inexplicably left. Psycho Three had recovered enough to continue with the group so they could fulfil their contract of orchestrated havoc and earn their bloody cash.

He told me many stories of many countries, and not just in Africa. Sometimes, the money earned was simply divided evenly among the men who returned. The less men that returned, the more money each man would get. On a job like that, after the job had been done and the group were returning to a designated pick-up spot, men were murdered under the cover of darkness. Throats were slit whilst men slept; others simply disappeared along the trail. Psycho Three said he almost never slept, hid in a ditch under debris at night. He couldn't go it alone, none of them could, it was far too dangerous and they had to stick together in their dwindling group.

On the eve of Angolan independence, a recruitment drive for hired hands was launched. Psycho Three's old commander told him not to go; the writing was clearly on the wall, he said. Out of all the men he knew who went, not one of them returned alive. He reflected that they were all despicable, unleashing violence without any measure of restraint. In nineteen seventy-five, foreign interests with a stake in Africa had little care for scruples and I'm sure, at the time, he too didn't give a damn. He quit just in time. The world was about to shrink and change, and those who instigated such crimes were now more likely held accountable. Men like him had no place left to go, no place left to discharge brutality without redress or retribution. I asked him if he cared about the things he had done but he said it was just a normal thing for a man like him to do in those lawless, money grabbing African times. I don't think he did care – he probably loved every debauched moment, now keeping his darkest secrets buried deep within himself. When the shooting started, he said he kept his head down low, unlike most others who charged into the affray like demons full of plague. He didn't think any of his former colleagues were still alive and joked there were no reunions, as he would be the only one not to be a ghost.

When I met him, he was still good looking and soon met another woman, drifting off to some place else, as he probably always did.

Be careful whom you sleep with!

It was clear that **Psycho Four** was a psycho from the very first moment I met him. He was on the run, living in London squats, pretending he was some kind of ultra hip dude, although there was nothing cool or dude like about his dark dead eyes. He told lies, so who knows if his story is real. His fiancé died in a plane crash and his parents in a car crash, perhaps it was the other way round, I don't remember. Newly deserted from the British army, he had beaten people up, stuffed bottles in people's faces and who knows what, even bragging about his active participation in mob violence and frenzied attacks at Millwall football club. I realised he was on the run when the police turned up at the house next door for some minor domestic incident. Psycho Four panicked when he saw flashing blue lights illuminate the street. He scurried into a bedroom whose occupant was out at work. After a very short time, he emerged wearing a 'borrowed' suit. It was far too small for him, the sleeves stopping about four inches short of his wrist, the shoulders so tight that they were at breaking point and the trousers stopped way above his ankles. On top of that, the suit was cream coloured and looked ridiculous against his pallid thug face. God I laughed. To make matters worse and even more absurd, he picked up a briefcase and went outside, marching conspicuously down the road. He looked as mad as a hatter, which he was, by the way.

Psycho Four had a momentary fling with a girl I knew. I remember her kneeling on the floor, sitting on her own feet, looking up at him with her cute pretty face and doleful eyes, complaining about being broke; not just complaining, she actually started wailing, imploring him to do something about it. She wanted money for a visit to the zoo. He picked up a huge carving knife, left the house and returned a while later with a stash of cash. Imagine a six-foot, broad shouldered man with jet black, swept back hair in an open Russian brown fur coat staring right at you with demonic eyes, brandishing a carving knife and demanding cash in the dead of night. He looked like a Victorian hoodlum or worse,

Jack the Ripper. I don't know how many people he robbed but I can't imagine they put up much of a fight. Fortunately, on return, there was no blood on the knife. After that, I kept my distance. I told my new friend Psycho Five about him, who coincidently lived on the same street about a two-minute walk away from Psycho Four's front door. Without my knowledge, Psycho Five and a comrade in arms went around to where Psycho Four was staying – they didn't want him on their patch. Fortunately for Psycho Four, he was not in, but they terrorised the household to such a degree that my friends who lived there banned me from visiting the house. If Psycho Four had been in, he would have quickly become Psycho Four No More.

Be careful of scary men at midnight with demon eyes and carving knives!

For me, **Psycho Five** was the most interesting psycho. I met him at work. We were painting and performing safety maintenance on a massive portable stage that was to be used at an outdoor rock festival. There were four of us and we were working at a famous rock band's studio complex in north London. There was me, Psycho Five, a Rasta who permanently smoked weed and a nasty tough young boxer from a French speaking Caribbean island – but nasty, tough and boxer doesn't make a psycho.

Psycho Five and I did all the work, the Rasta was too stoned and the boxer was just angry and didn't like to get his hands dirty. On about the fourth day, the boxer wanted money and demanded his pay from the receptionist who got frightened as he was threatening and making unreasonable demands. I don't know what happened but he returned to the warehouse fuming and didn't do any work. I told him to help out as we had a deadline looming and the stage needed to be finished before we loaded the hefty sections onto a huge lorry in a few days' time. He picked up a large spanner and threatened me with it. As he stepped towards me looking for someone to vent his frustration on, Psycho Five intoned, 'back off'. It was almost inaudible but cut through enough to make the boxer turn and glare at the person who had dared say such a thing to him. It was short lived as the boxer immediately dropped the spanner and hastily walked out, never to return. I looked at Psycho Five – what had the boxer seen?

I became friends with Psycho Five, although I'm not sure if friend is the right word; perhaps Psycho Five gave me life coaching while he was briefly in remission from being a psycho. I'm not sure what really happened between us, but he sure did teach me some useful things. He had the words love and hate tattooed across his knuckles, had some teeth missing from violent encounters.

At 16, he had joined the army for a few years. On leaving, he rode with a Hell's Angel gang, living rough and dangerously before becoming a bodyguard to a drug dealer. Yes, he was tough. He had had several stints in prison for unspoken violent crimes. When I met him, he was signing into a police station several times a week for another violent crime; he had beaten up seven policemen on Camden high street. They had then thrown him into a cell, beaten him badly, putting him in hospital for many weeks. A deal was done, an arrangement of sorts was made and the charges watered down to insignificance. One time, when I accompanied him to the station to sign in, he so intimidated the desk officer, that the officer went pale and began to stutter as his shaking hands slid the book across the counter. Psycho Five had crushed him by his presence alone, turning into something so sinister that I felt as if I were watching a slow motion horror scene unfold. I saw it clear as day, an apparition that had total disregard for everything, and felt myself go cold. Another time, he let slip that he had shot at people standing at bus stops. They were jobs, political – he said – and pertinent to those troubled times but got vague when I asked questions about the Baader-Meinhof Gang, ETA, IRA and others in the London news.

He was another one who loved to have sex with his girlfriends' mothers – funny thing that was for me! Once he saw me looking at a woman in a pub, young like me and he said rather loudly –'I suppose you'll be hanging out in her guts all night now'. I didn't, but his couldn't-care-less, brazen attitude, where everything was a game, was so damned appealing that just being his 'friend' was exciting. He lived in Somers Town, a rough and tough central London estate, long before it was hip and trendy, with his brother, mother and father. From the outside, it was what you would call a completely normal family.

In prison, he had written poetry and read extensively. I don't think he wanted to be a psycho – but he was, for sure.

We went for a great hike across Hampstead Heath in a heavy snow-fall once – a complete whiteout, silent and empty of people. We both got wet and our feet were freezing. Crows laughed at us from their perches high up in the silhouettes of bare birch trees – that's what it seemed like and we both laughed. Years later, I wrote a poem called 'Crow' about the walk.

You can't trust a crow

They laughed at me freezing in the snow

Boots all frosted, wet and sodden

Fingers and toes, iced to the bone

Laugh crow laugh

You wouldn't help me if I fell

Frozen in the snow

Even if you could, you wouldn't

You're a crow

A shiny black hearted crow

Looks good in the snow

Flies with the wind

And laughs at those below

You can't trust a crow, you know

To show what it was like to hang out with him, here's a little tale, a small snippet of his world. One evening after work we went for a few beers and then to a Greek restaurant in his neighbourhood. He entertained me with articulate tales of his adventures as we were eating our kebabs. Suddenly he stopped, put his knife and fork down and said that this food wasn't really Greek. He got up and marched into the kitchen. The kitchen was clearly visible and there was a big pot simmering on the stove. He opened the lid, said a few words and came back to the table. I guess they knew him; they must have because they did exactly what he asked without ado. A steaming sheep's head was lifted from the pot and the next thing I knew I had an eyeball on my plate complete with optic nerve. With his fingers, Psycho Five picked up his eye by the nerve and, with some difficulty, bit through the hard slippery ball. Gooey fluid oozed out. I didn't even attempt to eat mine. The restaurant owners and staff were looking on nervously, hoping not to disappoint – they obviously knew better than that.

There were implicit lessons in everything he did and it took me years to comprehend them. He showed me how not to live my life.

I suppose Psycho Five cleverly taught me to walk on the wild side while avoiding all the bad stuff – bad stuff by accident, bad stuff through choice and bad stuff through naivety and idiocy; but most of all, avoiding the bad stuff because it's just plain bad. Good advice and I took it.

Psycho Five moved up the road to Kentish town. He moved in with a woman who was the ex-wife of a gangster with whom she had a bunch of kids. The gangster was well known and had a gang. Psycho Five was very white and the gangster very black – in those days there was still quite a clear-cut division between criminals and they tended to stick to their own kind, mistrusting any kind of difference. I don't know what happened but the police wanted info on a bunch of people I knew, including my friend who knew Psycho Two – they were barking up the wrong tree, grasping at straws, as I knew nothing about anything, of course. It was complicated, my friend was in hiding, deep in the forests along the Welsh English border; the gangster was now after him – money, of course. What made all this mess worse was that everybody lived around the corner or down the road from one another; add to that, Psycho Five now lived so close to the gangster that he could look out of his front room window and straight into the gangster's kitchen and the gangster could look into Psycho Five's new home and see his ex wife.

It was a mess, a microcosm of a much bigger picture. This was London in the early nineteen eighties – everything was up for grabs, nothing off limits and greed knew no bounds. Psycho Five was in custody, very bad things had happened. I never learned what and I never saw Psycho Five again. I took his advice and stayed well away from him, from psychos in general and the utter chaos they always have to make.

Be careful of making friends with Psychos – there're a lot of them about!

Down Hill Racer

I t looks good on You Tube, and great to watch for real.

But you try doing it for real, without fantasy to cosset and protect your vulnerabilities. It will bash you, throw you, crack you, and if you are lucky enough to still be in one piece at the end of it all, you can go back up and do it all again.

So, what is this thing, I hear you say?

Nothing less than downhill mountain biking. Not the gentle Sunday afternoon in the woods type but the hard-core steep downhill one, with jumps and obstacles like rocks and tree roots on tight twisty-turny tracks, at a speed where one miscalculation ends in broken bones and titanium plates.

So why would you do it? And why would I do it?

Firstly – I like to turn fantasy into reality. Otherwise, it just remains fantasy. For me, something is either real or unreal, useful or useless. So there's no point in fantasy, unless it becomes real. That's just how I see it.

I liked downhill biking – it's a lot of fun, but I had yet to experience the hard-core version. I was definitely up for it.

Secondly – now, this will take some time to explain, so bear with me as I take a little detour before we climb up the hill and reach the top; whereafter, it is all too easy to go downhill, let go of the brakes and begin the helter-skelter descent to the bottom once again.

It was the end of a wet and cloudy summer in southern Holland. I had been seeing clients, the life coaching and energy work kind of thing.

That's what I do. All had been going well, nothing special to report. However, a guy, whom I will just call Black Gloom, came to the house interested in coaching. He was tall and good looking, had the features, eyes and hair of James Dean. He looked great – like a classic film star. He suggested that we go and walk in a beautiful heathland spot full of lakes and wildlife. Great, I thought, the perfect spot to walk and talk.

How wrong I was.

It was a fair drive out of the city, along the busy highways.

I had no idea where I was. I had not paid much attention, only to Black Gloom's increasing tales of woe. This did not bode well, but I tried to keep a positive outlook.

After a lot of small, single track, pot-holed roads we parked the car and started walking – he talking and me just listening. We stopped by a lake whose waters were a sinister murky brown from the local peat soil. I sat on a bench and gazed across the tranquil water to some rushes on the other side. Above us, dark and gloomy clouds suggested rain.

Then it began – a non-stop rant and barrage of life's unfairness and misfortunes. This happens from time to time, a verbal vomit, an explosion of pent up feelings, but never like this. It went on and on, an articulated sermon of doom and gloom. I couldn't get a word in edgeways, tried to be polite, tried to bring things to a halt and back to ground, but no, it was useless and the tirade continued, only breaking as he struck a match to smoke his endless cigarettes.

Now, this is not what I do! I'm not a therapist, a sounding board for childhood catastrophes. Perhaps therapists deal with the echoes of ghosts, but not me. I deal with what is staring you in the face right here and now.

And staring me in the face was Black Gloom.

This was tricky, he appeared semi-psychotic and I was trapped. He could easily leave me stranded if I pissed him off, and walking back to the city did not appeal. I had to play it cool.

Damn this, I was in a tight spot and kind of helpless, as if I had been tricked and hijacked to be at his mercy.

He took me up on the idea of moving when I got up from the bench and started to walk. Around the lake, he had said – eight kilometers later, we reached the car, wet through from drizzle. However, as I was now in the car, it seemed progress towards getting me back.

Black Gloom then suggested a 'session' at his home around the corner. What exactly had I just endured if not a 'session'? Anyway, I agreed – keep is smooth, keep it happy. After about fifteen minutes, we arrived at a large suburban house. He then suddenly proclaimed that he was too tired to continue and shouted across the garden fence to his neighbour, demanding to be fed. It transpired that dinner was to be served sooner rather than later, so I found myself being raced back to the city. The barrage continued, but this time I tried not to listen or look at the road in front of me, where everything was coming towards us at incredible speed.

It had been six exhausting hours and I wasn't even paid – raising that as an issue would have meant prolonging the torture. I just cut my losses. (Interestingly, he proceeded to call me every day after that, until I left to go back to the UK a few weeks later. I didn't answer once).

That evening I walked along the city canal. The moon was full and the water clear and shallow, full of plants and an abundance of fish. Pike lay just under the surface above the weeds, still and serene. Then I saw one of those out of the blue and out of this world sights – a very large Koi carp, orange, white and black, just meandering through the water, slowly going back and forth. A few years before, I had put about forty goldfish from an over-crowded garden pond into this canal and now I stood wondering if this was one of them. It was far too big to be bothered by a pike.

Fortunately, a moonlit Koi carp is quite an antidote for an afternoon spent with Black Gloom.

A few days later, I had another strange encounter, but this time, instead of Black Gloom, it was Wide-Eyed and Frantic. Another session of non-stop talking, but instead of woe, it was of how wonderful life is and how God is great. She was flying high on the non-stop wonder train. That's all fine, but it went on and on, again I hardly said a word – I couldn't get started, there were no spaces to say anything. Ironically, just like Black Gloom, she looked great – pretty and vibrant, in fact, I could say fantastic.

Never judge a book by its cover. Old and corny I know – but oh, how true it is.

What I hadn't known at the time was that she and the friend I was staying with had arranged an afternoon out to follow the session. Now this was tricky. The session had ended, thank god, and now I was faced with the tricky predicament of going out with her. Did I really want to go out with a client? So far, it had not been on a Black Gloom scale, and I foolishly thought that it might be fun. I agreed to go along.

Never mix business with pleasure.

We went for a country drive to a café in the woods. I sat in the back of the car to avoid the conversation, which went on unabated in the front. At least a café in a wood would provide great scenery, and with other people around, I could avoid direct verbal bombardment. However, things never quite work out how you think they will – my friend and Wide-Eyed and Frantic, fell into a full-blown argument, half in English and half in Dutch. I didn't get the gist, didn't want to, but there I was in the middle of this affray. We soon left and the bitching continued on the way home. To make matters worse, we took a wrong turn and ended up on a motorway going in the wrong direction. That was cause for a blame war. I tried to sleep amongst the furore. It didn't work. Later, the two of them parted on very bad terms.

Black Gloom and Wide-Eyed and Frantic were different flavours of the same thing – people who talk incessantly with little heed for the sensibilities of those in front of them. It doesn't matter whether they are riding high or in a black hole – they are essentially the same.

The following day, I took another walk along the canal to look for the Koi. It was late afternoon and the sun had broken through the clouds at last. The water was still and brilliantly clear. Three rather large, jet-black friends had joined the Koi. They all swam together, meandering across the weeds. Occasionally they would stop with their backs and fins out of the water enjoying the sunshine for a moment before swimming off again.

I don't imagine Koi having much psychological drama in their lives…but you never know a Koi, eh!

The calm and languid nature of Koi carp helped me make the situation later that night funny, rather than another trying time.

Right across the canal, in the industrial wastelands of Eindhoven city centre, is the city scrap and recycling yard. Between this and the canal is a 'house', not a normal house but a house belonging to an artist who opens his ramshackle space full of found objects, bric-a-brac and scrap yard inventions every Friday night.

It becomes a bar – well, not really a bar, but more a place where social dysfunction can flourish and be played out without hindrance every a Friday night. The working week is over, no chance of staying sober – have that in mind as you enter a long room, completely glazed on one side, looking out and over the city scrapyard. It's full of mad objects, tables and chairs from the yard over the fence and a counter dispensing drinks. You don't have to pay upfront for your drinks, there's kind of an unspoken tab, which you negotiate at the end of the night, if you can still walk and talk that is. Upstairs is an open terrace with a fine view of the city dump. It was near impossible to get a seat on the terrace – it was coveted ground.

You can order pizza in this bar. The catch being that you need to make it yourself. There's a ticket system and when it magically transpires that is it your turn, you do it yourself from the ingredients provided, which were plentiful I have to say. A stoned hippy cooked the pizzas in a homemade wood burning oven.

There's also a small garden and a cat.

Sounds quite eccentric and fairly pleasant so far – right?

However (of course there was always going to be a 'however'); the bar's clients were the type who chain smoke strong reefers, drink beer by the gallon all night and most probably enjoy the effects of scrap yard waste! Now, I don't smoke weed at all, don't care if others do, but before long, this place was a smoky weed gas chamber and I needed to get out. The place was crazy; rock music blared, everyone was laughing and screaming – totally shit-faced, people could no longer talk properly, and the pizza production line had ground to a halt. I saw a young guy trying to make one, even I started to laugh – he was making an effort, all the right moves but his brain and body no longer worked well enough to flatten the dough and lay on it a few ready chopped vegetables and grated cheese. The pizza cooking man sat in front of his fire, grinning like a Cheshire cat with bloodshot eyes, doing nothing.

I tried to settle my bill. That was tricky, conversation was hard – it wasn't even late, so who knows how things were settled later on. It cost me four Euros and I left. The music slowly faded as I followed the canal back home.

So maybe you are getting the picture a little – two very tricky customers in the space of two days, both of whom would talk and suck the very life out of you given half the chance. Along with this, I had had a multitude of hiking and coaching clients, some of whom had the idea that hiking begins with getting out of bed at midday and going for a cappuccino and leisurely brunch! I kid you not.

All this adds up, until downhill racing just seems like a damn good idea; the freedom of letting go of the brakes…

That took me to Italy. The high and steep hills around Lake Garda make fantastic biking trails. I have a good friend there, an enthusiastic and slightly obsessed off-road biker. He had already snapped his pelvis in two on a mountain trail, but this hadn't dampened his high-octane drive for adventure. He had had one of those dumb accidents that should never have happened. His front wheel touched the back wheel of his friend's bike. He was wearing shoes that clip into the pedal, and the speed of his fall was much too fast for him to get his feet free to deflect and cushion his fall. He fell hard, with his pelvis taking the full brunt. It took a very long time before he was back in the saddle.

Having recovered, he was still a demon on the bike and as fit as anyone could possibly be. Now I am fit, but not that fit. I have a slow engine; it doesn't get tired easily, is good in the cold and uses minimal fuel. Let us say that I am a tractor whist my friend is a formula one racing car.

I could get up the hills okay, only having to push it once on an eight hundred meter, thirty-eight percent gradient hill climb. My friend almost raced to the top. But what goes up must come down.

I was on one of those mad descents where I had to negotiate ridiculously steep tiny forest paths, full of loose rocks, small drops and tree roots. I can't say I was quick, but I did okay.

Previously, I had tried the clip-in shoes but had slipped and fallen several times on loose rock during harsh but slow uphill climbs, ending up on my side with my feet still clipped in the pedals. No harm done, but I soon had the spanner out to change the pedals from clip-in back to normal.

I exited the woods and turned onto a small concrete road full of dry gravel and small stones. My front wheel slipped away and my reaction was to squeeze hard on the front brake. Next thing I knew, I was snowballing and bouncing down the hill. Fortunately, tractors don't break very easily – just a scraped knee and leg, banged hand and slightly twisted ankle where my foot had braced my fall. I wasn't wearing those clip-in-shoes, thank goodness! Fortunately, the bike was okay, and together we continued downhill. However, for the next few days I improved on the uphill but remained slow and very cautious on the downhill.

I like my body!

Later, my friend took me on an official mountain bike racetrack. The downhills were so steep and treacherous that, even going slowly, I could hardly believe it was possible to finish a race without an accident or a hospital visit.

If you ever watch professional downhill racing, the type with extreme jumps, you may notice something: almost everybody is well under twenty-five. Not sure you can ride after that with a twisted body and a few kilos of titanium.

And the moral of this little story…?

Going uphill is hard, you may break a cog or two or often never make it to the top, and, if you are one of the few that does, then what? Stay there and view the world from your castle? Maybe it's time for some fun, an adventure. Go on, let go of the brakes, pick up speed, the faster you go the more fun you can have, but the chances are you'll hit a rock and become a broken wreck forever.

It's so very easy to go downhill. You really don't have to do a thing, just let it all go and life will do the rest.

So before you go turning fantasy into reality, make sure you can handle it, 'coz whatever it may be – it's gonna hurt!

A DIFFICULT PLACE

I like difficult places. But, before you go wandering to a difficult place in your mind, let me put you in the picture a little.

The top of a mountain or a steep rock face, they can be difficult, downright dangerous in fact; however, no matter how difficult that may seem – it's just not what I mean.

A difficult place to me, is a place where it's not only hard to get to but one that no one is interested in getting to either. Well, not too many that is.

So, in my world, what's a difficult place?

Pyrenean Brook Salamanders live in difficult places. They need to, just to be out of harm's way, away from pollution, pesticides, hungry trout introduced for sport fishing, snakes and, of course, inquisitive and destructive people.

Now that doesn't leave much space, especially as they live in shallow pools and are visible and vulnerable. Luckily for them, nature has given these beautiful amphibians a home in a most difficult and rather tricky place.

A canyon is a difficult place, but for some that difficulty becomes a challenge and an adventure sport. Canyoneers go anywhere where water flows from deep pools into sheer waterfalls in an adventurous, steep and perilous cascading descent.

I too have done this; abseiling down vertical walls, water gushing all around, pushing you left and right, so noisy that you can't hear yourself think. At the bottom of a vertical canyon wall, there's usually a deep pool whose current quickly pushes you towards the next precipice as you struggle to get off the rope and grab some slippery rock for imaginary safety, before you pull the rope down, to do it all again.

You need your wits about you; you need gear, equipment, and loads of experience. I was, and technically still am, a canyoning guide and instructor, having obtained all my bits of paper in The Blue Mountains of Australia. That's what I did – canyoning, lots of it. It got me to difficult places. I needed ropes, a wetsuit, and like-minded buddies, which was fine and a lot of fun, but what I was missing was any connection to the canyon – to the actual place itself. It was all about sport, adventure, one-upmanship and nothing to do with the canyon itself – that was just the arena where these things could be played out.

Places where a canyon is too high and too small, too boring and no fun for canyoneers, caught my attention. In these places which are so very hard and dangerous to access, without the fun and thrill to lure the daring adventure sports enthusiast, I found a most interesting and difficult place.

All over the world, you can find these places and not just in canyons. It is here that small plants and creatures survive and thrive away from man.

Some years before writing this journal, I was in the Pyrenees canyoning – yes, old style for adventure and sports. Some local guy dropped us off at a high point, which I will just call Big Mountain. We had left a car on the French Spanish border by an old pilgrims' rest house for our return journey, once we had completed our canyon adventure.

We were a small party and had no clue where we were going. We just knew that the watercourse was far below us in an impossibly steep valley, and to get there we had to negotiate a near vertical gully of unknown proportions.

The ferns and gorse dropped steeply down, growing out of loose rock and mud. We were at the head of a very steep and narrow valley, the source of the river evident in the soggy ground and reeds beneath our feet. We had the gear, the will and the gall, but it sure looked daunting. There was no solid rock to fix rope anchors, only loose crumbly boulders. A few lone oak trees hung on for dear life where the ground had allowed the odd acorn to sprout. This wasn't canyoning; this was downhill scrambling on loose chaff (a climber's term to describe dangerously loose and crumbly rock) into something that would also not be a 'real' canyon.

No one comes to this place – it's dangerous, out of the way with nothing there at all.

We thought we were still in France, but actually, we were in Spain at a time when Basque separatism was still rife, with cross border contraband runs and hideouts in the lonely woods and steep valleys. I was told later that even the police were too scared to venture this far.

No wonder this place was so empty!

I won't bore you with technical details, but it was a long steep descent in a tiny gully where we occasionally needed ropes. When not using ropes, great care was needed to avoid a non-stop tumble to the valley floor. From a canyoning point of view it was a bore, uninteresting – in fact, beside the danger, it was not fun at all.

But at the bottom of the gully, where it met another slightly larger gully and formed a small canyon, were a series of beautiful, shallow rocky pools smoothed out by millennia of running water. Above us on all sides, the ferns clung onto the impossible steep slopes, hiding the top somewhere way above us.

Here was a tranquil paradise, hidden from all but the accidental adventurer or clandestine Basque (although I am sure they had easier routes than this one).

It was here that I first saw a salamander, then another and another, some dark, some grey green and white and some black with bright yellow stripes on their backs. Undisturbed, they barely moved at our presence, safe in their salamander haven.

Time was pressing. We hiked fast and hard, as we safely could, down the rocky river, until a barn appeared in a small field. Here we left the river and hiked for what seemed an age, up through an ancient dark green mossy forest along a tiny muddy track to a lone stone farmhouse. A small weather beaten farmer stood staring at us, perplexed. We told him, in French, that we were lost and he exclaimed in Spanish that this was Spain and sent us down the valley where we later found the car.

Some years later, when I was guiding a client around the green hills of the Basque Pyrenees, I had the strong memory of my old trip and an inclination to return and visit the salamanders I had so briefly encountered.

It was strange because local people had no real knowledge of these creatures and could not answer my questions. In fact, no one I asked had ever been all the way up the river. It was only after some research that I realised how lucky I had been to see so many salamanders, and that they really could only survive in the most difficult to reach places.

I returned with a like-minded friend and set off, not from Big Mountain but way down the valley, so we could hike up the river all the way – if that was at all possible. Six days supplies we carried, huge packs weighing us down, for the season was autumn and rain could be expected any day. I prayed not.

Given time, things always change; the separatist issue had now been 'resolved' and things had remained relatively quiet for the last four years. That would probably mean less tension, more tourists and more development. How would the salamanders be coping with such a change? Would hikers and adventurers now be in the valley?

The idea was to hike and explore the whole river valley all the way, from where it meets a big river in a broad valley with a main road and rail track, right up to its source on Big Mountain.

We arrived at the confluence of the two rivers and followed a small road upstream through a pretty Basque village, with its white and oxide red houses standing proud in the sunlight. The mixture of heat and rain makes this country so green that, even in autumn with leaves turning brown and chestnuts dropping, the fields and gardens still show lush and full.

I had been told, that in July, there had been the biggest river flood recorded in history – five metres it had risen, and the evidence was still apparent. Debris from the torrent was still caught and displaying high in tree branches – old grass and reeds, grey with age and decay, hung alongside ripped black plastic bags that I imagined must have been old farm sacks. Low-lying houses had been flooded out and the railway was still out of service due to landslip and mudslide. What did this mean further upstream?

Later on, we waded across the river to set up camp on a small patch of sand above the river, under an old chestnut tree. Boiled chestnuts became our after dinner treat each night.

We examined the river – plenty of small trout and a frog – there would be no salamanders here, for sure; and anyway, we were far too low – they prefer the high ground above 700m. No chance of a sighting until the river became too steep and shallow for hungry trout and reptiles.

Lying in our tent, listening to the endless rush and gurgle of water over stone and the soft wind on leaves above, we knew nature was still firmly in control here – not a human noise, besides our own, throughout the long dark night. Just the strong hoot of an owl kept us company for a while.

Although the days were still hot, the autumn morning light rose slow and late and it was well after ten by the time we were wading back across the stream to scrabble up a steep vegetated bank, onto the road again. Surprisingly, as the empty track switched back and high across a steep rocky gully tumbling down to the stream below, we passed a recently large squashed yellow and black striped salamander. What was it doing so low and so far from the stream? Had the flood washed them downstream, leaving the survivors to seek safety in the dense under-growth high above the stream?

I had no clue at all.

A few hours later, we were at the pilgrims' house, where another tributary rushed out of a narrow and very steep inclining valley, heavily wooded and very understated. It would have been the easiest thing to walk on by, continuing up the stream we had been following, where a small but powerful waterfall makes a pretty feature, and head on up the back road to the very top of Big Mountain.

But we didn't, and were soon heading up this deep cut valley along a track that served the last farm, where the farmer had told me we were in Spain, not France.

Vultures soared and dropped low above us, crying a sound I have no word for. We then saw another squashed yellow and black salamander. As there was virtually no traffic here, it was either very unlucky or there was an abundance of these creatures living in the wet, dense undergrowth. The river was right by us, flowing swiftly over and between smooth boulders, looking brown, which was the colour of its bed.

The valley is very narrow here and cut very steeply. Before long, we were hiking uphill with a great view back to where we had come from, and another towards the maze of rock and forest of where we were about to go.

We passed the farm and said hallo to the same farmer standing by his front door gate. He still looked perplexed, but smiled on hearing were we English. Perhaps it's still not good to be on either side, a Spaniard or a Frenchman, inside these tricky hills.

We left the track and entered the dark forest, old and undisturbed, dropping down towards the river on an overgrown stony path.

Every shade of green you could imagine was here, from the vibrant to the sinister, and soon we were standing on a piece of brilliant green pasture only just big enough to set a tent. The valley is so steep that flat ground is a rare find and we decided to set up camp. I noticed a small bridge, nothing more than a newly cut log really, that left the rocks by the pasture and ended up against the near vertical sides on the other side of the stream – a bridge to nowhere by the looks of it. I crossed over. Below was a deep pool where I saw an eight-inch trout dart to safety, as soon as my shadow hit the stream. On the other side was more pasture, a sandy area where patches of grass grew, now the water levels had receded from the incessant rain this place receives. We saw some Basque ponies, but no way was this bridge cut just for them to munch a few mouthfuls of the sporadic grass.

It was truly fortunate not to be Spanish or French in this place right now, I thought.

We could sleep in peace.

We set the tent up across the log bridge on a sandy patch and cooked food over a wooden fire. Then the rain came. All night it hammered down. The noise on the tent flysheet was loud, but the river was louder and I hoped it would not rise. Cutting through this hullaba-loo was an owl, clear as anything, and then there were two owls talking to one another.

I listened to the owls and worried about the river.

The water level was the same and the rain had stopped. We hiked up the rocky stream along the same side as our camp. The flood torrent was violently evident here; trees had been uprooted, broken and washed downstream. Anything growing along the streambed had been ripped up and cast aside. There was no room for water to spill anywhere – no fields to flood, no riverbanks to breach – just a gorge to fill up.

We waded across the stream and rejoined the stony path. Trout were still evident, although they were fewer and smaller now.

As the valley slopes became steeper, the path zigzagged high above the stream, yet we could hear it clearly, as it crashed and pounded over the rock below. Deer scat and what looked like grouses' littered the path.

Down we hiked, through an ancient hazel coppice grove, and brief-ly joined the stream again by a steep flowing rocky gully, before we hiked back up. Soon below us was the spot where I had left the stream some years before, but the barn was now a house.

I picked up an ancient broken horseshoe – maybe my luck was in – and put it in my bag.

Crossing gullies on our ascent, I thought about heading down and walking in the stream – but the heavy packs and tricky river terrain made the task near impossible.

When the trees allowed a view, I looked over to the other side of the steam; the trees were thinning as the slopes were so very steep, and, in a fold in the valley sides, I saw a very long thin cut of rock, slicing the fold from the very top to bottom – the canyon I had first descended. God it looked unfriendly!

Up we went until daylight filtered through the trees – a ridge or pass must be right ahead.

What a surprise I got: Basque farmer types with guns hiding out for a newfound prey – pigeon, so they said. However, none were flying overhead today, and not a shot was ever heard.

They said there was no way down into the canyon, no path at all, and sent us on a trip around the head of the valley to Big Mountain which was now right opposite us.

I knew they were mistaken; I knew the canyon I wanted was right below us, and once out of sight, we headed straight down through the trees. We were virtually at the very end of the valley – there was nothing left to walk, and I didn't want to get into another near vertical gully without a rope.

Backpacks can be great things; you can carry a house, larder, stove and wardrobe, sometimes with ease, but I had eighteen kilos and my friend had twenty-one – not a great idea when descending these slopes, hanging onto trees, making huge zigzags so not to take a fall – one tumble and you would be on the canyon floor. Taking great care, I slowly eased myself down. My friend was somewhere behind – I could hear him slip and slide.

Suddenly I saw his pack tumbling and thumping down the slope and coming to rest deep in thorns and ferns.

I looked up and saw him edging down after the pack. At that moment, I thought he had just let it go as an easy option – not a great idea I said aloud. However, after we had retrieved the pack, he said he had been slipping, desperately hanging on and would have fallen if he had not released the load.

Such is the nature of these trips.

We reached the canyon. We were high up, near the point where to go much higher would be too steep to walk. The spot was a large deep pool under a little waterfall. Paradise, my friend said then.

He was right – two huge grey salamanders were suspended motionless before my very eyes. I counted four in this pool – the water was dark and there would be more for sure.

I didn't want to head up canyon – that would have been very tricky and we needed to find a campsite long before dusk. We just had the time if we moved on fast but not too fast, as I wanted to look in every pool.

A small drop, too high to jump and too slippery to climb down, lay directly before us. The damp rocks were like ice under our feet and, to minimise the risk, I climbed up the steep bank and traversed the canyon around at about twenty feet above. It was slippery and loose, I had to take my pack off and push it in front of me through the ferns and brambles, eventually rejoining the canyon floor about a hundred feet ahead. I waited for my friend.

Nothing.

I left my pack and wandered back up the canyon floor to under the tricky down climb I had just avoided. He was above me at the start of the traverse, not moving an inch.

I didn't see a problem at first, I guess I should have, but I just didn't twig at all. He was scared of heights and unable to proceed. He hadn't told me that, and I had yet to cotton on.

From this point, it was easy for him to lower me his pack. Once it was safely down, I helped him jump across a gap in the rocks. He grabbed my hand and lunged hard, nearly pulling me off balance. Take it easy, I tried to joke.

I can't remember if we saw more salamanders, for the way needed thinking about, sizing up; one slip and a head would surely crack.

Another drop on smooth wet rock, not much water, but steep and wet enough for me to shy away. The choice was between a traverse on one side or the other. One side was so steep, that getting back into the canyon would have needed a rope, but even with a rope, there was nothing but ferns, no anchor points at all. I opted for the 'easy' side, heading up past two oak trees onto the ferny slopes. I had to traverse high up through tall bracken to keep away from the steepness below. I could see another very steep gully tumbling down towards the canyon, just slim enough in places for me to step over but a death trap to be inside. I stopped and looked behind. My friend was not in sight. I called but no answer.

Traversing back, I caught sight of him struggling to get up past the oak trees. He did not answer my calls. When he was at the last tree, he sat down. He didn't really give me answers, just vague replies about the pack and straps – nothing to explain what was up.

It seemed like an age before the penny dropped.

'If you are freaking out, you'd better tell me right now so I can do something about it'.

A simple yes came back at me.

I guess these things have now become automatic in me. I didn't need to know what was wrong or why. We were in a difficult place and needing to find a camp fast.

I dropped my pack and went over to him. Going back was not on my list – ahead is where I wanted to be. I took his pack – god it was heavy – and battled through the ferns a few hundred meters and dropped it down. I then went back for mine to do the same, telling my friend to follow close behind me. I set off.

When I arrived and dropped my pack, I turned around and saw only ferns.

I shouted to him and soon an answer came back at me, but he was nowhere to be seen. Then I saw the bracken move – he was down on his hands and knees crawling through the dense and wretched stuff. His head quickly bobbing up like a frightened rabbit to take a bearing, only to disappear again.

Just before he arrived, I was off again with a pack to the small gully where I just managed to step across and throw the pack to the ground. I was hot and sweating.

Returning to collect the other pack, I saw my friend sitting there amongst the ferns. I couldn't believe it – he was wearing a T-shirt and shorts and his hands and legs were lacerated, cut to ribbons by the brambles and gorse lying under the ferns – a proper bloody mess, superficial perhaps, but more scratches than I had ever seen. I mumbled something about the first aid kit, and he mumbled something back about washing in the river. I then just ignored it and focused on a way to get back into the canyon and relative safety.

It was far too steep to climb down the edge of the gully with these packs, and straight ahead was gorse and brambles – not an option anymore. I backtracked thirty feet or so and dropped down steeply to where the gully met the canyon. Here was a short vertical drop. I released my pack and dropped it down – it rolled a little way down the gully before stopping on a big flat rock. I then jumped the few feet down to meet a dry smooth piece of rock. To my surprise, my friend was following with his heavy load and did the same.

We were down, safe, and didn't need to mention what had just occurred.

It's not really a canyon, but a smoothed out narrow rocky stream bed with continuous small drops and large boulders. The sides were crumbly rocky vegetation leading onto the impossible steep fern slopes. However, it was quite easy to walk and negotiate obstacles on the canyon floor.

A few trees grew out of the crumbly sides, where the ground allowed – oak, beech and ash, large mature trees still full of leaves. Once out of the canyon only ferns could cling onto the steep slopes. The flood had obviously not been so severe here – no sign of the destruction that had occurred further downstream. The high water mark was no more than three or four feet above the very low level it was now.

This place was hidden from the world, hidden from the Basque farmers above, hidden from the view point on Big Mountain, three hundred metres or so above, and hidden from the forest further downstream – we couldn't see a thing above the fern slopes and nothing could look down into here.

Here we saw salamanders in the shallow pools, just a few of them at first, mainly green/grey with white dots and stripes on their backs. Some were dark, almost black, but no yellow anywhere – the ones we had seen squashed on the road were not here.

And then a pool, maybe four feet deep with shallow sides and plenty of small stones and boulders on its bed – Salamander City – I stopped counting at twenty. Now all the pools revealed a similar treasure. We had found our salamanders!

The strange thing was, no yellow ones were to be seen anywhere.

We made camp under a large old oak tree. In fact, the tent sat on the only flat ground around – a rough grassy patch sticking out into the canyon. Our tent was directly under a huge low-slung branch, which my friend swung from to check it wouldn't fall on top of us in the dead of night. It was the perfect spot, right at the juncture of two small canyons – the one we were in and the one I had canyoned down from the top of Big Mountain previously.

I explored the other canyon. Perhaps it was too steep and small or perhaps too open and exposed – whatever the reason, there were no salamanders here at all, and I knew further up between the steep drops there would definitely be none.

My friend had an Indian girlfriend and, as today was the Hindu festival of Diwali, he had promised her to eat boil-in-the-bag chicken tikka whilst dancing around the campfire. I was to take a photograph.

OK, so we had the chicken tikka, but to make a fire in this pristine place was like sacrilege to me, yet I didn't want to stop his fun. Oak is not the best wood to start a fire and he struggled to get a flame. When he did, by catching dry ferns, the wood would still not burn. I refrained from pointing to the ash tree in the shadows opposite our camp.

But I can vouch he tried and did his best (just in case a split is on the cards!).

The following morning we broke camp and packed our bags. We left them under the oak tree and wandered downstream to have a look for more pools. There was an old stone building above the stream junction, dilapidated with no roof. The timber supports could have been one hundred years old and the open floor was littered with large rough-cut slate tiles, half hidden in the ferns. I couldn't imagine anyone herding sheep down here – what a nightmare – and so very dangerous to round them up again. I fantasised it had been a safe house, hidden from view, allowing a clandestine escape down the canyon and into the dense forest below – who knows?

This time there were so many salamanders that we didn't even try to count them. We even saw a pair mating in six inches of water. This was October 24th and the day was balmy, as had all the other days been, the summer hanging over far too long this year – had the fauna and the flora been tricked by nature? The weather could turn any day now, forcing the salamanders to leave the streambed and hibernate above the canyon under rocks and logs.

Fresh deer scat and tracks were evident on the canyon floor – at least two different animals, and we saw what looked like cat and martin scat.

It was safe down here from men with guns and a liking for blood.

The canyon dropped steeply, and we climbed down until the forest started on the right hand bank. The Salamanders were scant here and, as I had already once walked down this stream, I knew that soon there would be no more. We turned and went back to our packs.

It would be fair to say that the salamanders live in a stretch of shallow canyon no more than six hundred metres long, with the main concentration being in a three hundred metre stretch. There is no evidence of them living in the steep gullies feeding the main stream.

In the bustle to transport the bags across the ferns, I had somehow lost the maps and compass. Damn! Maybe they wished to remain in this difficult place, hidden forever!

There were three ways out: back up the stream – that could mean traversing the fern slopes again; down the stream – that meant a very hard descent on slippery boulders and then a long walk up through the forest; going straight up to Big Mountain – nearly a thousand feet of very steep hiking through ferns and crumbly rock. Big Mountain seemed the best option and a route I knew – also the route was visible, and I remembered a track on the top, which would take us back around the head of the valley to where the Basque farmer pretended to shoot pigeons.

Off we set, up and up, slipping on loose rock, grunting and zigzagging to find the safest path. Our packs made it hard and I had to stop to catch my breath, often.

I looked back, saw my friend sitting, not moving up at all, and knew we had to turn back and try another way.

Back at the canyon floor, we had two choices left – up stream or down – he chose to go back up.

On arriving at the junction of the steep gully and the stream, we found a huge dead slowworm floating in a pool.

Going up a canyon, as long as it is not vertical, can be a lot easier than coming down one. I chose to try to ascend rather than face the ferns again. It was tricky and very slippery, and more than once, we had to pass the packs up after I had climbed up without one. I nearly fell back once, just managing to thrust and jam a hand into a crack in time. Fortunately, there were no snakes getting ready for hibernation. We passed a deer skull and were soon back at the oasis pool.

Back up the route we had come down, the way where my friend had released the pack – this was going to be a tough one for sure. I offered to relay both packs to the top, but he declined, much to my relief. I took his heavier bag and set off. Even zigzagging up the slope it was slippery, and with the weight constantly moving from side to side, it was tough not to succumb and take the unthinkable tumble to the canyon floor. My friend was slow, desperately grabbing at tree roots or the odd clump of grass – a complete mistake and a basic rule of trekking. I kept shouting down not to trust anything underfoot or in his hand – check it first.

I waited at the top, breathing hard and happy to have the pack off my back. Wild boar scat lay near my feet. He arrived some time later.

Finally, mission accomplished, we had to find a different and interesting way back home.

We camped by an old stone barn – this was luxury camping now – no hurry or pressure, as we had enough time to get back to our village and catch our flight home.

Owls kept us company once again that night.

There is one funny thing that happened that evening. We needed water, and there was a bath with a pipe-feed and ball-cock for some horses in a huge field. My friend disconnected the pipe, drank and washed. However, the fitting would not screw back on and the water powerfully gushed out all over the field, so he turned the screw valve off.

The horses drank the bath dry in no time. We were a bit concerned that some angry Basque would accuse us of breaking his pipefittings or worse, allowing his horses to die of dehydration – there were no houses up here, no 'farming' as such, just sheep and not many of those – so there would probably not be a person up here for days. Finally, he managed to bodge the pipe fitting, with half the water running into the bath and half onto the already wet quagmire field. The horses would get the blame no doubt!

The next morning the shooters were back – no pigeons they said, and when I asked about pheasants or grouse, they said they had all long disappeared. In the year 2000, the last Pyrenean ibex was found dead in a national park. They had systematically been shot out over hundreds of years.

Having no map or compass now, I had asked the Basques to point the way back. I had opted for a long traverse across the valley top – a high ridge and plateau directly opposite Big Mountain. The vista was magnificent; to our left we could see the whole valley from start to finish except for the small, discreet and well-hidden salamander canyon. To our right was a continuous huge drop down to the main river valley and rail track.

It was one of those hellish, non-stop hikes across an undulating rocky plateau that never seemed to end. At the top of every small escarpment, where we thought the path would drop down into the main valley, we saw yet another escarpment to traverse. So it went on, and, under a warm low sun and heavy packs, we forged on, hoping the end would soon be in sight. Eventually it was; a steep rocky descent taking us down hard and fast – it was an effort not to stumble. We rested for a while on some grass knowing there was no water anywhere near, no campground, and probably no hotel. We forced ourselves to get up and go on. We had long run out of water – there's almost never any water on top of a mountain, and we were now really parched.

Eventually, there was a hotel and bar, which had outside tables overlooking a church and the high hills we had just descended. We took our well-deserved place and rested for a moment. Water and lots of it was needed to quench our burning thirst; however, if anyone reading this has ever seen the movie Ice Cold in Alex, you will know what is coming next. In the movie, the main cast had just finished a gruelling truck ride full of peril across the scorching Sahara desert and arrived in Alexandria, Egypt – hot, exhausted and very, very thirsty. Water was badly needed. But no, not water but an ice-cold beer drunk and savoured slowly before any real hydration. You'll never taste a beer like it. All you need is one to taste and feel the cool nectar, the reward for all your hard work. It just doesn't taste the same or have any effect if you drink water first.

We ordered our beers and had the Ice Cold in Alex experience. One was enough, for we then had to trek another two miles to find a piece of flat ground alongside the big rushing river, where we set up camp and cooked in the pitch black of night.

Yes, it's fair to say we were spent by then!

A few days later, after we had returned, we were sitting outside a café in a splendid French Basque spa town, under the shade of an ornamental plane tree. The waitress sat on a stool, plucking birds. I strolled over and she seemed put out, slightly embarrassed, and I'm not surprised; she was plucking a green woodpecker and had two more besides, waiting their cooking pot fate.

Now for the moral of this story: If you are green or yellow, interesting, cute or tasty, I suggest hiding and hanging out in the most difficult place you can possibly find!

COSTA RICA

Rincon de la Vieja roughly translates to – The Nooks and Crannies of the Old Witch – and this active volcano in the Guanacaste highlands was where our small party was heading. Just before we left the Ranger station, a handsome coati (looking like a mix of badger and raccoon) suddenly appeared from nowhere and skillfully pilfered a pack of sandwiches from an open rucksack, much to my companion's chagrin and Ranger's amusement.

The forest here is lush, undisturbed and as humid as hell. It quickly enveloped us in a sea of endless green, as we followed the small wet and muddy trail up towards the swirling clouds we had seen from the car park. Wildlife is abundant, and, although we didn't catch a glimpse of the elusive jaguar, we did see huge tapir prints and many small animals scurrying and rustling across the forest floor. Three different species of monkey swung and chattered through the canopy high above. In the low forest, birds abound, but it is the brilliant blue of the amorphous butterflies, beautiful and dazzling against the hue of forest greens that is the jewel for all to see and wonder; occasionally they stopped to bask on a branch, catching a ray of brilliant sunshine that had somehow managed to break through the seemingly impenetrable canopy.

We finally broke out of the trees into the vast moonscape of the slopes of the volcano itself. Looking back from where we had just come was the magnificent view of the forest, sweeping down and reaching far below, to where the land flattened out and spanned the horizon to the Pacific Ocean many miles away.

Shale, gravel and broken rock greeted us as we stomped across a barren plateau, reminding us that not so very long ago Rincon de la

Vieja had violently spewed her wrath. We came to the crater: a deep gash in the Earth, whose blue water bubbled and steamed at the bottom of dangerous vertical cliffs. Streaks of bright yellow sulphur lined the vertical rock, blowing out the smell of rotten eggs. We had been told by the Ranger to stay for fifteen minutes maximum and, just as our time was up, we saw the clouds swirl, and then a flash of low lightning, not vertical but horizontal, at about our height, zigzag across the ridge mere yards in front of us with a huge accompanying crack and bang. Three of my companions were crouching down, having been 'sparked' and slightly electrified. As they looked nervously around, it happened again and the mist quickly engulfed us making visibility almost zero. I heard the crunching gravel as my friends dashed to escape the fury of the Old Witch, but I stood my ground, knowing one slip and I could end up in the bubbling cauldron below. Within five minutes, the air had cleared, the downpour stopped, and we laughed and hurried off the mountain before she changed her mind again!

A Camel's Tale

Raj was an unfortunate camel. I had tried to like him, be a friend, but under the circumstances, it was all rather hopeless. These days, being a camel in Rajasthan is to be born into a life of hard work and slavery; no camels roam free anymore to wander the gentle dusty dunes. A camel has to pull a cart, loaded, and more than likely overloaded, with people and chattel or bricks, sand and rocks; or dance in some cruel camel circus act; or more lucratively, be used to move tourists around the desert so they can witness its beauty before it evaporates into the modern world.

This good money earner for Indian business men requires complete submission, unconditional surrender, from the camels; of course, they are not born losers, it requires regular beatings, shackles and a rope threaded through the soft sensitive tissue of their noses, so authentic camel men can yank them anyway they choose by inflicting great pain. Then there is the whip, in case the camel forgets who the boss really is and has ideas other than a harsh life of enforced slavery.

If you don't care about camels then they are a great way to experience the Great Thar Desert. I didn't know much about camels and, wanting to see the diverse wildlife that the Great Thar offers, went into its beautiful lonely reaches with my girlfriend. Unfortunately, we needed camels and some camel men.

Every night under a vast twinkling sky I made chapatis in the burning coals of camel dung; an art the camel men patiently taught me. Desert nights were freezing, below zero, and any attempt to sleep under the stars was soon abandoned for the tent, where all night we would hear the gentle breeze and soft scratching of fine sand blowing on the flysheet.

I did not make a good camel commander and Raj would regularly stop at a bush or acacia tree to munch contentedly away, whilst the others ambled towards the horizon, leaving me to have an awkward discussion, which I knew was being ignored. I could get Raj to sit down and stand up, but due to my soft camel commander nature, could not get him to move forwards or backwards one inch, no matter how I reasoned. A camel man would soon return, shout aggressively, and whack Raj with a wooden club, wound with metal at its tip, on the neck or head and almost yank his nose clean off to get him moving again.

The blue bulls, Indian gazelles, black bucks, silver desert foxes and huge flocks of ugly vultures kept my interest, delayed my distaste for this camel cruelty for about a week or so.

The vast, still beauty of the Great Thar sets a style; a slow and tranquil pace, where every sound, every quiver and every breath is magnified, almost measured by an enormous silence; and reflecting such, people live a seemingly languid life. However, the Great Thar has a tacit cruelty, in metaphor and in fact, sands soaked in blood, well hidden and disguised from any passerby. Don't be fooled by this poetry, dazzle of its mesmerising light, slow swagger of some beauty's swinging hips, for the vultures wait as the culture stifles those within, beats those who disobey, shuns those without, and keeps those outside from coming in.

If you are born to the Great Thar, it will never let you go, and, if you're not, it will never give up its mystery.

Are you getting the picture? I rode Raj and got the picture.

Now Raj had a buddy called Rosie, a proud upstanding kind of camel, overflowing with oomph and verve, and one who really liked the girls. Nasty scars and deep gouges etched his strong body, where the camel men had clubbed and beaten him in their frenzied attempts to secure compliance and a Rajasthani set of morals; I'm glad to say that this savage re-education was a dismal failure.

One day as Rosie ambled along the endless track he became increasingly frustrated, wanted every female glimpsed or smelt; he would gurgle, salivate, dislodge his soft palette and hang the pink flesh out and down his neck for all to wonder and behold. Not a problem for some folk, after all it is something all men – real and fit – feel, like, and want to do; however, the camel men hated this display of open sexuality, perhaps it told them of their own true nature, made them feel uncomfortable. Surely they were not like this – they were men, not men like camels, camel men, oh my god what do I mean?

Meanwhile, as Rosie showed off and strutted his stuff, a storm brewed inside these tacit camel men; stony faces, muffled murmurs, the usual quiet before the first crack of thunder and lightning flash as the heavens open and all falls down.

Campsite fixed and Rosie won't play ball, takes offence at being yanked and pushed around, and rears up and tears around. No big deal, so I thought – letting off steam – give him space and he'll calm down. No way; the camel men jumped into action, pulled and pulled at the string through his nose, brought him down to his knees and clubbed him half to death with the metal tipped beating club; his head was clubbed, blood flowed as the club was whacked at full force – we'd be dead that's for sure. Then the club was forced down Rosie's throat and the metal ripped soft flesh...

After some shouting on my part, I managed to stop this insane cruelty. After all, they still needed me to pay them. I guess money was my club to bring these dogs back to heal.

So, beware of trips to lonely places with lonely thoughts of lovely things – it may force you to commit murder without regrets, well, only the regret of all that dull police stuff and hassle that ensues.

BIG TED

PART 1: SHARK FIN ROCK

Avocados sit in a small wicker basket, ripening in the sun. The basket in turn sits on a fairly high table in the conservatory glassed on three sides, catching as much autumn sun as it can.

On top of the avocados sits Big Ted. Actually, he's not so big, perhaps no more than ten inches or so, but he has a special power that makes him big.

He has a short coat – not the usual shaggy bear type – light, the colour of weak milky coffee or faded barley straw, cute ears and a little Ted tail.

Big Ted looks out to sea. He's on shark watch – I kid you not.

I'm not sure where Big Ted came from originally, but one day he arrived from Tajikistan – being a Teddy he had no problems with visas or immigration. He had been conscripted there, involuntarily of course, as a guard to ward off evil spirits and the like – you see he has this talent, some kind of special power. Day and night in the freezing cold he would sit on top of Mission Command's bed staring out, warning evil, mischievous spirits of big trouble, unless they scarpered fast. Such was Big Ted's life, it was all he knew – guard duty.

You may well ask – what's wrong with that? Just a Ted being a Ted in the way Mission Command wanted and needed.

But it's not that simple. I already had a monkey that Mission Command had given me – small, cuddly, orange and brown with a big smile to keep me company on long expeditions. I called him Monkey. My job was to look after him no matter what the terrain or conditions threw at us. Clients may have secretly smirked and probably wondered about my sanity. To hell with them, this monkey was going climbing and trekking, rain, snow or desert heat. Swamps were tricky, but a dry bag always saved the day.

However, there was a problem – I was just too rough for his sensitive nature, and besides, his fabric and insides were not robust enough to take my rough and tumble life.

It was decided that Mission Command would send me reinforcements. That's how Big Ted ended up with me.

Then there was problem: monkeys and bears just don't mix.

It should have been obvious really, as they don't hang out together in the wild. It was just a dumb move. They wouldn't sit next to each other, Monkey hadn't been trained for guard duty and Big Ted knew nothing about the big outdoors. It wasn't working and Big Ted started to get depressed.

Someone would have to go.

In the end, I called Mission Command and it was agreed that Monkey would be collected and flown to the Tajik capital, Dushanbe.

The deal had been that I would have to replace Big Ted, after all the Mission still needed a proper guard. Monkey was too inexperienced, unworldly and, quite frankly, in need of a hug.

It was just one of those lucky finds. I had been working in Eindhoven in southern Holland and had scoured all the toyshops for a tough and rough replacement who knew a thing or two about handling bad spirits. All I found were kids' toys, cuddly and cute, and all straight off the factory production line – certainly no personalities and definitely no risk takers.

On a cycle ride along the city canal to a small, pretty town just outside the city, my luck was in. Sitting outside a cafe (I won't call it a 'coffee shop' – this was Holland, where coffee shops only sell brain dead dope), I spotted a toyshop. Inside were the usual suspects, but amongst these toys was a very cheeky monkey sitting alone and out of place. He looked like an orphan rescued from jungle poachers, and was now imprisoned inside this Dutch zoo. It was just a question of time before he was sold off, probably to have his ears yanked off and stamped on in a temper tantrum fit. I couldn't take that risk.

I named him Vince after Vincent van Gogh, who indecently cut his own ear off – Jeez; ears are not safe in this place.

Vince happily packed his bags and headed off to the high Pamirs.

I'm told Vince makes a great guard but causes mayhem around the place. What do you expect if you have a monkey as a guard? I ask you! He gets on well with Monkey as well as Fred and Boris – but that's another story in itself.

What to do with Big Ted? Of course, there were a few issues at first.

When not on expedition, he didn't like lying in the bed – he looked unhappy and always ended up on his belly crawling towards the side.

I wasn't sure, but maybe he didn't like me. I mean he was in a different country now, a different culture. Maybe taking Teds out of an environment that they know and are used to is just darn right cruel. Whatever was going on with him, I felt bad.

So, I had a dilemma. Then the penny dropped. Guard duty – yes, that might work, and as my house is demon free (I think) the job would be a breeze.

Ted sat upright on the pillow in front of the wooden bedstead looking out at whatever Big Teds look out at.

Fine, or so I thought.

Although Big Ted is a shorthaired bear, he had rather a lot of tight curls hanging over his eyes. In fact, unless one physically parted this hair, his eyes were hidden. I often tried to get him to see 'properly' to no avail – the hair would always clump back over his eyes.

And what eyes he has – shiny obsidian, deep and enchanting.

After a call to Mission Command, it was decided that a very slight trim would be the best thing to do.

Carefully I snipped the very milky brown curls until his eyes were exposed and able to catch the light.

He looked great.

However, there was another problem.

All was fine until he sat on guard duty. Then I saw the absolute horror and trauma in his eyes. He looked scared stiff. My God, what happened, what had I done, and what had he been seeing whilst on Tajiki evil spirit watch?

He must have seen monsters in the room. Poor Ted, and I had cut the hair from around his eyes so he couldn't hide them from the terrible things that may still be manifesting. Maybe just being on guard duty was enough to trigger all these bad memories.

I needed to act fast, so I made him a little cave between the two pillows, where he could sit on guard but also be close to me and easily slip under the covers in case it all got too much for him.

This was going to take some time.

We have this thing called Child Line in the UK for children to call if they are having problems with adults; you know, all those wicked things adults can do. I did ponder calling Ted Line as I felt Big Ted had been abused – he was used as cheap labour really, being put on guard, a bit like a child working in a factory. However, I didn't think it would help much, as Tajikistan is so far away, and besides, it may be normal there using Teds as guards.

For a time he seemed fine, almost settled, let's say safe. But is just safe, safe enough? Probably not, because this is what happened next:

I was going to Berlin and had decided to take Big Ted on an adventure of sorts. Well, not really an adventure but a short work trip to Berlin. The weather was brisk and just right for his warm coat, I thought. I did mention it to him and he seemed fine. However, on the morning of departure he was face down on the sheet crawling back into his cave. It was a clear statement – Big Ted wasn't going anywhere by choice.

On return, the weather was nice; a warm sun cut through the chilly mornings, and there was no wind or rain. My bedroom is rather gloomy, north facing, sunless and empty. Not much fun for a Ted, I thought. I brought him out and sat him on the avocados.

Finally, he seemed happy, gazing out at the vast empty sea with nothing in between.

Big Ted had found his place.

There were no demons to chase away – I think he had realised that by then; only a few fishing boats their showing green and red night-lights at night. He quickly sussed that as he was facing south, green meant the boats were going west, and red going east. I told him that's where the idea of traffic lights had come from – give way to red and go on green. Stops crashes, you see.

There were also plenty of sunrises and sunsets turning the sky and clouds a multitude of reds, oranges and inky blues, along with rainbows, storms, lightning and thunder. He had never seen such wonders before, and now loves these things nature conjures up from thin air.

But he's not so sure about the seagulls or the cats. He sees those off fast before they get too interested in the fish swimming in the garden pond.

I always felt that there was a little more for Ted than the ever-changing sea and sky, as he gazed out into space. There was something out there that he liked; something that I couldn't quite put my finger on. Then one day I saw it: Shark Fin Rock.

I knew it was there – it had always been there as part of the low tide landscape. It looks indistinct, just a small black rock among the other ones dotted about the vast wet sand. Some of these rocks are covered in seaweed and mussels, with a few shallow pools where kids like to hunt for crabs. However, this rock you never give a second glance to unless the tide is rolling over it, half exposing it before it's either totally uncovered or submerged. It sits way out, close to the low tide mark, and, for perhaps fifteen minutes just before the tide is out, and for another fifteen just after the tide has turned to rush back in, the rock becomes alive.

You can't see it as it lies with no water on the empty sand, but once it starts to cover, you can see it clear as anything. The rock is about twelve feet long and not very high – maybe no more than two feet, and not very wide – so it looks like a long, black raised surfboard, with one exception – it has a fin at the rear, and when the water laps over the rock it looks like a sinister shark fin. In fact, the first time I saw it sticking out on its own with the water half covering the 'back', I almost shouted: 'Shark! Shark'!

I'm not sure what Big Ted thinks about sharks, but he sure enjoys looking out for them. Pods of porpoises and a few dolphins occasionally swim by the house looking very shark like and I'm sure he keeps a close vigilance on them.

As a lighthouse marks and warns of treacherous rocks, Shark Fin Rock warns Big Ted of sharks and other monsters, but they are out to sea and never set foot on land. He doesn't have to engage with these monsters, he can just observe them safely from on top of the avocados. At night, he often comes and sits in his little cave.

No more drama.

Such is the new life of Big Ted.

There is one more thing, not really a problem, more like a mistake I made. Foolishly, I thought that he might like a friend, well a girlfriend actually. I found a second hand, well worn, shaggy and, I assumed, previously loved bear, about the same size at Big Ted. I called her Mrs. Leens.

However, as soon as I sat her down on the table, not in the wicker basket with the avocados, but next to it, to introduce them, I knocked the table slightly with my knee. It vibrated and Big Ted moved and looked up at me. He was shaking too, especially his arm and head. Jeez – this was a big no, he didn't want her near him, this was his spot and Shark Fin Rock was clearly for him alone.

OK Big Ted, I've got the message. Mrs. Leens now sits alone in a chair with not much to do.

I feel sorry for her. Does anyone want a small shaggy bear to put on watch?

Oh, I nearly forgot, someone just reminded me…

For some time, I had been trying to find inspiration to write a short fiction story about Shark Fin Rock...I mean the rock is inspiration enough, but I just couldn't get a story out. I had the idea of two boys seeing the fin and then going shark fishing at high tide, but that didn't work out, just a few poor lines and no catch.

So thanks Big Ted – I now have a story for the rock, well, kind of anyway, and certainly not fiction.

I often ask him about passing sharks at night but he just keeps quiet and reminds me that that's his job – not mine!

Big Ted

Part 2: Goes to Sweden

I put Big Ted on the windowsill, gazing out across the deep flat snow towards the tall pines and light blue sky. He was no longer on shark watch, but on moose watch during the day and northern lights watch at night. It was the perfect spot for him, especially as I had seen moose tracks around the house as we arrived; add to that, a dark moon and clear night skies, which gave us a very good chance of an aurora display, Ted had a lot on his plate. However, he liked a challenge and I knew he could be properly relied on, unlike monkeys who would be off at the first chance to frolic in the snow and chase an arctic fox or two behind my back, and then pretend to have kept vigilance when I later checked up on them. Monkeys, eh!

The client had expressed her desire to see the northern lights flicker and dance across a starlit sky somewhere in a frozen wilderness without people, noise or lights. After some searching I found a place up in the Arctic circle, fifty miles from the nearest shop, with a near zero population. All it had was the hissing silence of endless snow and pines.

But there was another thing – she wanted to get fit, walk off the flab that office life so easily piles on. Lean times were ahead.

Lean times also meant frugal menus. After we had picked the car up from the small airport, we headed into town for a careful shop at the supermarket. We had to cater for eight days or more – running out or running low on food was not an option I could afford.

Quite frankly, I can't say that I was looking forward to a near zero calorie diet – I was starving already, but I could hardly eat roast potatoes and melted cheese to keep my oomph and enthusiasm up. That would have been downright cruel as the client munched on frozen carrot and Arctic muesli. I had to convince myself that this was good (it was my job after all), and embrace this lack of food, hoping I could last the course.

We headed north towards the frozen wilderness and an isolated lodge we would call home for a short while.

As the lonely drive north passed through endless forest, the tarmac slowly disappeared under a layer of solid ice. I was glad we didn't have to stop and fiddle around in freezing temperatures to fix snow chains to the wheels. Fortunately, the tyres had hard metal spikes, or nails as the Swedes like to call them. The little traffic we did encounter was mostly huge open-backed logging trucks stacked up with trunks, heading south to mills and ports. The chainsaw reaches everywhere.

We turned off the main road and drove slowly along an icy track through the darkening trees, until we crossed a bridge above a wide frozen river ten metres below us.

The instructions had been clear and we pulled up outside a white house. This was where the Hillbillies lived, two brothers, tall and huge like Viking lumberjacks. I don't think the top of my head even reached their massive shoulders. They were nice, friendly, warm guys who showed us to our lonely spot, five km up the road.

I got out of the car and looked around. It was an old abandoned farm or small settlement with about four dilapidated wooden houses and several barns. There was also another house – a modern log cabin with moose tracks all around. This would be our home.

Big Ted had arrived.

It was dusk and the Hillbilly who was with us looked high into the twilight sky above our heads, where streaky clouds had gathered, and proclaimed it would be a great night for the northern lights. He was more than right, for in less than two hours after arriving, after we had sorted out our chattel, rooms and modest food, we were outside in the cold night air watching one of nature's marvels.

It's hard to explain the phenomenon, even photographs don't come near to showing its full glory; in fact, most photographs of the northern lights only show a specific green – anti-freeze green, emerald green, fairy liquid green, or as the client pointed out, methadone green. I refrained from asking any prying questions!

That's the type of green our camera shot, the frames looked marvelous: full of green flickering and swirling above the snow and pines. The trouble is – that's not what our eyes saw at all. We saw a different green – soft green, lichen green, silver leaf green, soft and subtle with just a hint of emerald.

The display was bright and dazzling. It is said that the camera never lies, but as far as these northern lights were concerned, it told a huge fib. You can't trust even an expensive digital camera, and I wondered what real film would have looked like – who knows? One thing is for sure: you've got to be there to really experience its wonder.

It was like being in an upside down glass bowl with green light flickering and dancing from the zenith to the horizon in every direction – 360 degrees from the ground up to the centre of the universe above. The only place there was any black night sky was directly overhead – a small black circle at the very top.

It was a dark moon and a cloudless sky. The stars shone brightly through this green extravaganza. It's not two-dimensional; it's deep and layered, forever moving, sometimes with great speed, other times seemingly static and slow, but it's always morphing. Wherever we looked, it was different – different shapes, swirls, speeds and hues.

Then it faded and was gone as if it never happened.

We got lucky, and we would get lucky four nights in a row.

An owl had hooted constantly somewhere close among the dark pines, and, as the show faded back into a dark starry night, I walked towards the trees to have a look, only to sink up to my waist in soft snow as the icy crust gave way.

We would have been going nowhere without our snowshoes.

The Hillbillies had told me that we could walk in any direction for

70 kilometres through the snow and forest. They didn't know what lay beyond that – more snow and forest I suspected.

The first day of hiking was fairly gentle and undemanding, giving the client a chance to get used to the snowshoes. Actually, there is not much to it; snowshoeing is easy, non-technical and terrific fun. It's great for building stamina with minimal stress. Of course, the up hills require oomph and push, making you breathe hard and sweat a little.

The day was still, crisp and sunny with hardly a cloud in the soft blue sky. I didn't know the terrain and, in order to familiarise myself, I decided to follow some snow mobile tacks down a short steep hill through the forest. Before long, snow mobile tracks were going off in every direction, ensuring the return journey would be a confusing maze of tracks. As I hadn't brought a compass, map or GPS I would be doing navigation the old-fashioned way – remembering the route, the direction of the wind and the sun. A few other tricks and there was a chance we wouldn't get lost. Everywhere looked the same. The trees were all the same; well, I saw two types – silver birch and tal, a slow growing, tough Scandinavian pine. The small hills were all the same; the ground was all white, without any distinct geographical features, and it was a windless day.

There was one crafty trick left up my sleeve for the return navigation – I would very simply follow our tracks back in the snow! What great guiding skill is that you may ask... so I'm asking you to keep quiet – Mum's the word – don't want to blow my reputation!

I hoped snow wouldn't fall to fill our tracks. Spending hours going round in circles is not what people pay for.

The forest was crisscrossed with many animal tracks and we passed fresh moose scat. But today was not a tracking day – today was a 'getting used to it' day for me.

We ended up on a small barren plateau where we waded through deep wet snow to an isolated boulder to sit, drink tea and eat a solitary, calorie free sandwich (well, not quite). The view was pretty and interesting. We could see for miles in all directions; however, wherever we looked, it really did look all the same – small hills and endless forest, blindingly white to the horizon. Here and there, a few empty patches showed where the forest had been cut but not re-grown.

To the untrained eye it may all have looked like unspoilt forest wilderness, reaching out to every horizon, but it wasn't. This place was a gigantic Arctic tree farm. It may be devoid of people and housing, but it's totally managed, the trees being constantly cut and replanted. Tal is such a slow growing tree that a decent sized one takes more than ninety years to grow; therefore, the logging companies need this vast space to stay in business.

That's what I saw – wilderness existing just for business and commerce. The client may have seen something different – maybe just snow; after all, she had requested we build a large snowman near the house. I kept it quiet that my snowman building skills were near zero.

The temperature dropped and we headed back to the log cabin.

That evening's northern lights rolled over into another day of hiking. The Hillbillies had pointed to their local 'mountain' – a steep wooded hill with a near sheer drop on one side. It's probably not more than four hundred metres above sea level, and from the frozen river rises up less than two hundred metres. That's where we headed, across the frozen river and through a snow filled horse paddock. The Hillbillies had shown us how to trick the horses, to stop them from getting out and onto the small logging road when we opened the gate. We did this by feeding them along the fence away from the gate in a small enclosure. It gave us enough time to open and shut it before they could inquisitively return. The irony of this was that the horses were free to roam deep into the forest, over the hill and far away. In fact, we saw their hoof marks in the snow all over the place, and anyway, the fence that held the horses in ran out after about 100 metres!

It was impossible to get lost as the river was always in view, and if not, then the downward slopes would always take us there, as the river snaked around the hill. We saw lynx and a solitary wolf track along with a bunch of tracks I couldn't identify. Fox was abundant for sure, but all the small weasel and martin-like tracks were too confusing for me to recognise.

The slope to the top was very steep and I ploughed up at speed, but not so fast that I had to stop to catch my breath. The client followed valiantly – it was just what she had ordered.

The top of the hill was small, with the ground quickly falling away in all directions. We found the only fallen tree still visible above the deep snow and used it to sit, drink tea and eat. The cold wind blew hard here and we were soon heading down to explore some different forest.

That evening after our aurora display, I decided to have a sauna. The client had already expressed her dislike of these hot houses, so I was on my own in the little log cabin, next to the house, with a wood burning stove. After about an hour, the stove was hot enough to pour water on and create steam. I had had the fantasy that after a hot steamy session and dripping with sweat I would be able to jump in the wet snow, bask awhile as the heat dissipated and melted the snow. No such luck or luxury – the snow was as hard as ice because that's what it was – ice – it was night and the sun long gone. So I had to fill up a few buckets with water for an icy drench.

It's funny how things turn out...

The sauna was so hot that it was unbearable. I could hardly breathe because the heat burned my mouth and throat, and, when I went for a desperate cool down, the top half inch of water in the buckets was frozen solid. I cracked it open with a broom handle before drenching myself. I can't say it was pleasant.

I had once been to a sweat lodge; the native Indian type that was so damned hot that everyone lay on the grassy floor in pitch black, gasping. I had had my hand over my mouth to stop the burning steam into my lungs, wondering how long this torture would persist before someone expired or the tent flap was opened to let the hot air out and the cool rush in.

Back then, I wondered what the point was, and now I thought the same.

I needed Big Ted for some answers.

Back at the house, as he stared out into dark night sky, I knew good things lay ahead. Sod the sauna; I had the northern lights and fabulous hikes. What more could I ask, except a bit more food perhaps.

Obviously, there were more hikes, but two stand out. The first hike crossed the frozen track in front of the house and into the woods, where we followed a narrow track winding through the trees towards a small tree-lined ridge, which we had previously seen from the road. It had looked the perfect place to hike – but, when we arrived to where the gentle slope of the ridge began, we changed our minds. The way ahead looked much more interesting. It was a small, open, flat valley, more like a wide frozen river, almost treeless with steep wooded inclines on either side. The top of the hills to our left side was our original ridge.

The empty way in front was white to the horizon, and, with the cold crisp air on our faces, it really did feel like the Arctic. Of course, it was the Arctic, but the presence of so many trees had thrown up doubt, suggesting we were not quite there. Now in this stark white reality I could really believe it. Funny thing one's mind.

At our steady pace we could have hiked all day on this endless flat basin neatly nestled between two low wooded ridges. However, the client had taken a renewed interest in our original plan and was now admiring the left hand ridge, wondering if there were great views from the top down to the frozen river valley on the other side. We changed course and an easy uphill plod took us to the start of the steep rocky way to the top. No way could we hike up that, so we continued under the ridge until the steep slope petered out somewhat and the way up became more manageable. It was still steep, with massive boulders hiding deep holes where the snowdrift had piled up. I knew the dangers here, and I continuously prodded the snow with my hiking poles. Occasionally they disappeared deep into a dangerous void. Not wanting to fall six feet under and land on some jagged edge, I gave these places a wide berth.

Finally, we arrived on the ridge, not the high point, we still had some way to go to reach that, and turned left, back towards the direction we had come, hiking up through undisturbed forest and a maze of snowy boulders. The going was steep and slow, the route always twisting and turning around rocks and hidden holes. I had to check that every step was safe, and even with great caution, I sometimes broke through the snow up to my waist.

The client was nervous, kept telling me to be careful, take care, which I was, and I showed her the technique of checking for holes with her hiking poles. Even so, she didn't like it there in this steep rocky forest so I suggested we turn around and go back the way we came. But that was an even worse scenario for her.

Then she told me her real concern. She didn't mind about the snow holes – I was taking care of those.

It was the Bears!

The Bears?

Yes the Bears. They may be hibernating deep under a rock. To be exact, in one of those holes I was prodding. Her concern was that I might prod a sleeping bear on the nose.

Oh, I hadn't thought about that. The Hillbillies later told me that they had no idea where the bears go to sleep in the winter. Sweden has around 2500 bears, so what are the odds of accidently poking one on the nose? I had no clue. I later asked Big Ted about these sleeping bears, but he just smiled and kept looking out for moose.

It had been hard making a safe route through this complicated terrain, and now I had the bears to worry about as well! I didn't really worry, but from that point on, I did stay away from the very large boulders with deep drifts.

Finally, we reached the top. There was no view of course, as the dense uncut trees blocked out everything. The terrain was far too complicated and tricky for it ever to have been worth logging up here, and we stopped for lunch in this natural piece of forest. It was cold and the whole place full of unfriendly boulders, which were impossible to sit on. I reckoned that the forest floor abounded with fallen trees to sit and rest on, but right there and then, deep hard snow covered everything. After a little search, we found a broken tree and sat on its trunk to eat our scant lunch. I pondered taking off my thick gloves, a risky move because once cold, our hands would take an age to warm up again. However, holding a cup of hot tea and undoing a wrapper was near impossible so we both removed our gloves. Within minutes, we had them back on again. God it was cold, and soon we were heading along the ridge to warm up, reversing the route we had originally intended.

The trees thinned and finally vanished – victims of the chainsaw – as we steeply dropped to the valley floor.

The Hillbillies had invited us to their hideout in the dense forest above the sheer banks of the frozen river. They were cool guys, wanting us to share and experience their forest life.

After they had convinced us that the ice really was six feet deep, we hacked along the frozen river on snowmobiles. For those who don't have snowmobile experience and have some kind of fantasy of what it's like, I'll try to put things straight. If you are the sort who likes the loud aggressive noise of an old two-stroke motorbike screaming in your ears along with the smell of petrol fumes and dirty exhaust as you shatter the delicate silence of an awesome landscape, terrifying every creature in a five hundred meter radius, then this is for you. Perhaps it's less damaging than a 4x4 churning up the forest floor, it's probably a lot more fun, but not for me.

Anyway, we arrived at their place. It was a well-built, ramshackle, wooden lodge with an old kitchen, large social room and a room with some bunk beds. They were cooking us up some moose stew on an old wood burning stove. These two brothers were the sort of guys that could do everything practical imaginable – build their house, fix trucks, hunt and grow their own food (although the growing part seemed to start and end with mountain potatoes), cut timber and farm reindeer – they could also repair their own clothes and use the internet. Their family had been in these forests since at least 1700 and they still owned around one thousand hectares of trees, which they now fiercely protected. They were proud to have stopped all bird shooting on their land and the cutting of all big trees – that scored a few brownie points with me.

While the moose stew slowly cooked, we headed out to view a waterfall, a famous local landmark, whose powerful flow is so strong that it never completely freezes solid. The river directly below the fall was a turbulent black hole and the surrounding ice must have been thin. We drove the long way round to the top. The small river at the top ran steep before vertically dropping its torrent about forty feet into the menacing black hole below. An impressive new fish ladder zigzagged up the side of the falls.

Today this place was frozen, but in a few months it would be full of melting snow, turning the river into a dangerous high flood before the arrival of summer, when the river would slow down, become crystal clear and less than a meter deep in places, full of fish, beaver, otter and darting birds.

At the top of the falls, set back about thirty feet, was a flat picnic recreation area open to the small river on one side and surrounded by forest on the rest. In this spot and blending well into the landscape were some wooden buildings, which included a small wooden round-house with a central fireplace, some bunkhouses, pit toilets and a cafe lodge, which was closed.

The client and I peered through the windows of the cafe lodge.

In every country and place I have ever visited where people shoot for fun and sport (and by this I mean a place where there is not a desperate need to eat what is shot) I am always greeted with the same sight – a lodge or cabin full of well presented stuffed local animals. And here we had a splendid example: a lynx, a wolf, a bear, a moose head, weasels and the like, all proudly displayed on the walls and among the neatly positioned tables and chairs of the rustic interior. Later on, during our return journey back to the airport we would stop at a roadside cafe, another rustic lodge with friendly staff and great food; here they had a special room displaying the spoils of slaughter, including owls and huge hawks. Maybe one day these places will be like dinosaur museums, a reminder of what once lived but no longer does.

Oh well, back to the moose stew.

It was tough, chewy and strongly flavoured with a slightly rancid edge, but I can't say it was particularly tasty. I had to wait until my hands warmed up before I could hold a knife and fork. The icy wind whilst driving the snow mobile had gone right through my mountaineering gloves and now my hands were freezing and painful.

I had noticed that both Hillbillies had worn thick old-fashioned leather gauntlets, and later I bought myself a pair. Never again would I suffer from the debilitating pain extreme cold dishes out. My modern mountaineering gloves are now relegated to riding pushbikes and changing tyres in the snow.

We were plied with schnapps and red cowberries soaked in some kind of powerful alcohol, and by the time we were shown around the reindeer farm, I was quite merry to say the least.

I had no interest in reindeer farming, but the client was curious. However, the pitiful sight of these exquisite creatures tightly tethered or showing terror as they were herded around a small enclosure, soon had her hailing a cab back home. As we sat on the snow mobile just before I pulled the starter cord, a beautiful white reindeer trotted past; it looked delicate and softly magical, its warm breath steaming in the icy air. I had once seen a completely white stag in the Sussex countryside with huge antlers being followed by a herd of thirty roes – a lucky and rare sight indeed.

I pulled the cord and wrecked the silence. Reindeer scattered to the corners of the enclosure as I drove the snow mobile rather slowly away and definitely not in a straight line back along the frozen river to where I had parked the car.

By the way, there are no wild reindeer left in Sweden, every single one roaming the forests is farmed, their ears clipped and tagged in recognisable ways to show ownership. Bears, wolves, lynx and wolverines don't understand this ownership thing and suffer persecution if they dine on their natural dinner.

The following day it started to snow, lightly but steadily. We walked from the house and, although our snowshoe prints were deep and clear, I did wonder if after some hours they would slowly fill and become invisible. I tried to remember the twists and turns between the trees so we could get back to our lodge without getting lost.

Now, having seen the snow falling before we left the house, I reckoned it would be a great day out for Big Ted. I mean, he's a bear – right? Therefore, the snow and cold should be perfect for him, but I wasn't taking any chances; after all, he may have got a little soft with all the central heating and indoor living. I wrapped him up in a scarf and placed him in the top part of my backpack, so he was looking out behind me as we hiked.

When we took a break and I took the backpack off, it was good to see him looking out and covered in snow smiling at the world. Even the client asked how he was. He's a bear I said, and with a bear, we could never get lost or need to worry about poking a sleeping bear on the nose – Big Ted would fix it all.

There was one mishap on the trail – well, two really. The first was my tummy – it had been gurgling all morning, and the client's too. We deduced that the rancid moose stew combined with Hillbilly cowberry schnapps was now playing havoc with our non-Arctic sensibilities. When it got too much to endure, I threw my backpack to the ground and headed for the bushes.

What relief!

The client was also suffering but she never made a bush run. Perhaps she was too polite and cultured, or just had robust iron guts, to do such a public thing.

On returning, I found her dusting off thick snow from Big Ted's head. In my urgency, I had dropped him face down in the snow. Oh, maybe he was mad at me, but as the client quickly pointed out – he was still smiling and having a great day out.

Our snowshoe tracks had filled up and had mostly disappeared, but the way home was not so tricky and we arrived with hours to spare before the darkness brought the Northern Lights.

Apparently, it was snowman time. However, I had a good way out of this: the client had also asked to be shown how to dig a snow hole; an emergency shelter in case one is stuck out in a storm at night. She would build the snowman whilst I dug out the shelter a few feet away. We did this right by the house.

The snow was hard and icy, so no way could she gather snow to complete her work of art. To build a snow hole in these conditions required an ice axe and loads of grunt and toil. I had the axe but the client needed snow, buckets of it, as her plan was large and grand.

I went to the shed and found a large shovel. My job had suddenly become a whole lot easier.

Usually snow holes are dug into a slope, but here, with no slopes anywhere nearby, it had to be dug into the flat – a deep trench, big enough to shelter two people and their gear.

I started digging. God the snow was hard, and I smashed it up small enough for the client to create slowly her snow-white monster. I actually sweated as I dug non-stop to complete the hole. I didn't need to work so hard, but in a real life situation, that's what you do, work like the clappers to finish the shelter before you freeze to death or a storm batters the life out of you.

And there it was – three and a half feet deep, a yard wide and around seven feet long. I don't think I could ever dig such a magnificent hole on the side of an isolated mountain. I wouldn't have a shovel for a start, and I would probably be so desperate that I would only dig down far enough to lie flat and be out of the wind.

However, here it was – my textbook snow hole…trench.

Meanwhile, the client had been busy; in fact, she worked well into darkness using a torch to finish off the details.

It was impressive. It was a fat snowman with a big head. Charcoal from the sauna made his eyes and teeth, a big curved red chilli for his hooked nose, fir cones for his buttons, some light green lichen for his eyebrows and moustache and twigs for his arms. He wore an old baseball cap I had rummaged from the shed.

I filled in my trench the following day. I didn't want to risk the next guest at the lodge falling in, as it was very hard to see in the dazzling white landscape.

There's not much more to say about the trip. It was a great success and the client is now size zero and a stick thin international celebrity (actually not, she's far too robust and worldly to become such a vacuous thing).

On returning home, I placed Big Ted on the conservatory table looking out to sea. There were no avocados ripening in the sun that day.

Work had become scant, just a few jobs here and there, so I needed a plan, a helping hand, if you like. Instead of shark watch, I put Big Ted and Mrs. Leens on job watch, on the table hand in hand, gazing out to sea beyond the horizon and far away. A great plan I thought. I wasn't too sure if putting Big Ted and Mrs. Leens together again, after Big Ted had complained, was such a good idea, but I decided to take the risk anyway.

I wondered how far away the jobs were, maybe too far for even the combined powers of Big Ted and Mrs. Leens. Therefore, I needed another thing to make this job search more tangible, more accessible, or better still – more real.

Whilst in Brighton doing a small job on a roof, I heard an ice cream van cruise around the local streets playing its ice cream tune. What was that tune? I racked my brain but couldn't get it at all, knowing that's what Big Ted and Mrs. Leens needed – a tune, a song, a lullaby to entice and lure those unsuspecting jobs onto shore where they would flounder in the shallows by Shark Fin Rock. After that, it would be easy pickings for the two monkeys to go down and drag the jobs up to me. (I had two more monkeys by then who just held hands all day – they could do with a little exercise.)

Somewhere in my brain was this perfect lullaby, perfect like the deadly hymns of the Lorelei on the Rhine or the Sirens in Greek mythology. Then the penny dropped. That Brighton ice cream van tune was no other than The Teddy Bears' Picnic. I kid you not. No wonder it was driving me crazy. The next bit was easy – I played The Teddy Bears' Picnic to the two Teds and sang along. Being smart Teds, they got it in a jiffy. Now, all I had to do was wait.

However, life never quite works out as you plan.

Going into the conservatory the following day, I knew something was amiss.

Big Ted was gone!

Maybe someone in the house was playing a prank on me to show me how all this Ted behaviour was simply just absurd. But no, they all pleaded innocence.

I looked around and there he was, on the floor, sitting upright below the table looking very grumpy indeed.

What had happened? Had Mrs. Leens shoved him off over the edge? Had Big Ted jumped to get away?

I called Mission Command and she reckoned that Mrs. Leens was actually a male Ted. I had got it wrong and Big Ted had got it right. In my Ted world, they should never have been holding hands.

Big Ted had jumped.

I had forced them together like an arranged marriage and, as Mrs. Leens was a fully blown Rescue Ted full of who knows what drama, this was a disaster waiting to happen. I had turned Mrs. Leens into a Lady Boy. Maybe he or she didn't mind, after all he or she now had a nice home, and perhaps being a Lady Boy Ted was a small price to pay.

But Big Ted wasn't having any of it. What a mess, I had truly stuffed up. I should have let things be.

I kept Big Ted on the table gazing out to sea and put Mrs. Leens on some avocados looking out to sea on the other side of the room.

The natural order was once again restored. And you know what? After this, the jobs started coming in.

Time for Big Ted's next adventure overseas.

FRIEDA PAVLOV

First published in Literary Veganism: an online journal (Sept 2020)

People speak, dogs bark. Silencing a dog's voice is akin to not allowing a baby to cry: both are talking, communicating in their own way.

Frieda lives next door, a nice friendly dog that barks and wags her tail. But every time she barks in her back garden, her owners seem embarrassed, put out and take her inside and shut the sliding conservatory doors. I have said to them on several occasions that I don't mind the barking (it's soft and mild) and Frieda is welcome to wander into our garden if she so wishes. That said, she's still taken inside and the door to the outside world, firmly shut.

Adding to this injustice, Frieda is expected to be bilingual, not only speaking dog language but also the language of her owners. Have you ever tried learning a foreign language? It's hard and takes an age; in fact it's so hard that people never even attempt learning dog language.

I'm reminded of Pavlov's Dogs: Ivan Pavlov in the 1890's trained dogs to salivate when they heard a metronome because the dogs associated that particular sound with feeding time. Is Frieda being trained like a Pavlov dog? Forced to go inside every time she barks, until one day she has no voice.

Such is the life of Frieda Pavlov.

MY SWEDISH DIET

I knew I was in trouble when I saw the price tag on a cucumber in the cheapest supermarket in town at more than 2 Euros a pop.

That's a lot of money for a piece of cool green; maybe I should say royal green or 24 carat emerald green, but however I label it, it's still bloody expensive. A quick scan around the fruit and veg aisles told me I was in bigger trouble than I first thought; everything was outrageously priced.

I had six weeks to last on a food budget of 45 Euros a week. That's twenty two and a bit cucumbers a week, luxury for some perhaps but I was meant to be helping restore a small beach cottage where grunt and oomph were probably required. In England, 45 Euros would have been enough to eat nutritionally without too much supermarket aisle anxiety.

Generally speaking, Swedes are tall and slim; slim does not mean skinny and tall does not mean lanky – they are a fit people whose diet does not revolve around some watery cucumber cuisine. Sweden is expensive and, on my budget, I was going to have to be creative or go hungry. I ended up being both.

Symbolically, I had a pocket full of washers rather than a bag of gold coins. In a dilemma and at a total loss of what to do, l left the supermarket and went back to my room with an empty bag. I needed to think.

This trip had started off with good expectations; six weeks in Sweden helping my friend's builder restore a cottage in exchange for a room and food budget. Now, one may say, quite rightly, that I was getting a rough deal and my friend a rather good one but there was no particular expectation from either side and I could check out Sweden in the summer as I had always been there in winter. By the way, I had paid my own travel costs.

So far, so good or so it seemed.

I arrived, met my friend, went to one of her several homes and put my stuff down. She was meant to be exchanging contracts and getting her beach cottage in a few days but there had been a hitch of sorts and there was going to be a delay. She already had another beach cottage, which she had yet to sell; add to that an apartment, a shop where she often lived, a busy responsible job, a needy dog and god knows what else that was none of my business, the word 'stress' comes to mind. This is what I walked into with nothing but good intentions, but the road to hell is often paved with good intentions.

I was quickly informed that we were going on a road trip to the other side of the country to price up a series of jobs. That sounded good, especially as it was a new bit of the country for me to see and the weather was unusually warm.

The dog came with us. It was a cute and very insecure dog; small and grey, I would put it into the rat catching terrier type. The dog would constantly jump from the back of the car onto me, stand up and before I knew it, was on my friend's lap moving around agitated, knocking things, obscuring the windscreen and distracting her so much that the drive became dangerous and terrifying. I managed to get hold of the dog and place it in the back again but moments later, it was climbing onto me and on to her again. She seemed unperturbed or unaware of the devastating consequences that flying through a hedge or flipping head-over-heels might do to us, let alone a head-on collision. Maybe this is what she always did – I don't know, but we weren't going to last very long swerving on a highway at 70 mph and, as canned sardines in tomato sauce seemed increasingly likely by the millisecond, I quickly took over as driver.

It was a long drive from town to town, down the coast and then across country towards Stockholm. A moose ambled across the highway in front, so slowly that I had to break and drive at a crawl until it sauntered off into the dense forest. I saw two magnificent Eurasian cranes and the reddest fox I had ever seen. That was the excitement of the drive, nothing more.

Now, my friend and I have very different culinary needs. She survives on frost-bitingly cold, frozen spinach and raspberry smoothies, blended straight from the deep freeze; and when hunger gets too much, she eats ravenously whatever is available. This isn't me being facetious — this is what I saw. I was a little tired, thirsty and hungry, but food and pit stops were not welcome. I struggled to be heard. It had been years since we last hung out and we no longer knew each other (if we ever did); so let me say, I probably wasn't what she had expected and certainly not the kind of guy she was used to or wanted around in any way, and she wasn't what I could be bothered with anymore. It was no one's fault, that's just life, but bad vibes quickly manifested between us; we were from different planets, needing different airs to breathe. When we were together, we both ended up suffocating. We both felt it, knew it, even spoke a bit about it, but as I was now in Sweden we decided that my going home was not an option — yet; after all, there was still a cottage to be re-built. We both held on to that, I guess.

I could have spent my own money but that was not the idea, not the deal. Three days later back in Gothenburg and in the apartment, I managed to get my food stipend. As there was going to be some wait for the contracts to be exchanged, my friend tried to get me to 'work' at other things like dog walking and poop scooping, laundry, shop duties, food shops etc. I declined and waited for the building work. Keeping out of my friend's way, not wanting to create more tensions, I decided to lie low, do my own thing until the real work materialised. We had a deal, and a deal's a deal until it's broken, but I guess we both broke the deal in our own respective ways, rather quickly.

As I said, I could have spent my own money on food but I like a challenge and I was determined to see what I could do on my anorexic friendly budget.

I had brought some kefir yogurt with me to Sweden and now, as I sat in the kitchen of the apartment trying to figure out a way to keep healthy, knew that smoothies were the answer; not frozen but defrosted. With that in mind, I headed back out to the supermarket.

Frozen fruit was affordable and I always kept a mixed bag of blueberries and raspberries in the freezer.

Breakfast consisted of a mug of whole milk kefir. To this, I added a handful of defrosted fruit, chopped kale, a banana and a teaspoon of 100% cocoa powder, whizzed it all up in a blender and hey presto, a breakfast that kept me going all day – so long as I didn't think about food. Now, I did vary the green stuff a bit, mixing in spinach, chard or cavolo nero depending on what was available and how cheap it was. I didn't use much quantity of anything except for the kefir.

So that was breakfast sorted, followed by a milky coffee or two. Maybe I'd do fifty push-ups if the mood took me and my arms could take it; some days my arms refused, especially as the days wore on and I started losing weight – my oomph just simply waned. After this macho fiasco, I headed out for the day. I had use of a funky looking bright orange bike; the old-fashioned type where one sits upright, has three gears to choose from and a back-pedal brake. There was a nice big basket at the front for my backpack. It was out of time, hard work and slow but it sure looked cool. I used it to the max.

Even on my limited diet, a glorious Swedish summer with a sci-fi hipster bike and oodles of magnificent countryside and coastline to explore was nothing less than luxury. I didn't complain in anyway whatsoever.

I waited for contracts to be exchanged…but in the meantime, it was time to look around.

Gothenburg has some nice parks, a wonderful botanical garden, cool cafés, a big port on a big river, loads of small islands and a superb craggy coastline – time to explore.

I could bike about forty km a day with stops, anymore was too much for the bike and me; we both had to last the daily course. That meant a twenty km radius around the city. I headed for the coast. It was still too cold to swim; well, I guess I could have swum, but as I had already had so many cold-water experiences, knew the consequences. Once, when in Sweden, north of Gothenburg in the winter months, I braved the sea. It was a beautiful spot: a large rocky inlet surrounded by forest, the sun was out and I couldn't resist. It took me an age to get in and then I stayed in far too long. By the time I reached the car, squelching through icy mud, I couldn't feel my feet, they were totally numb and I was shivering. I put the car heater on; yes, I warmed up but it took an age to thaw out! I then caught a miserable cold that lasted weeks. Another time in Maine, on a really hot beach full of people sunbathing, I noticed the sea was empty, yet there were four lifeguards perched on a tower looking out – at no one! The beach was a small cove and two lifeguards would have sufficed. I strolled up to them and asked if the water was dangerous. No, the water is fine and you go right ahead and swim. So why would I be alone then? Ah, that's because the water temperature is about 54° Fahrenheit; after some fun working the calculation, we figured it was 12.5° Celsius. The Atlantic Ocean doesn't catch the Gulf Stream in Maine, hence the water stays cold in midsummer. Sometimes, when feeling brave, I swim in 13° Celsius in the UK; it's cold and unpleasant and I never stay in very long. I braved the Maine Atlantic, the surf was great and I had fun in the waves, but again I stayed in far too long and on returning to the beach to sunbathe, listening to those around saying how hot it was and applying sunscreen, I uncomfortably shivered for thirty minutes.

I looked into the clear blue water of Sweden's North Sea with no intention of a chilly dip. However, the coastline is a delight, full of tiny islands, inlets and small harbours full of pleasure boats, all ringed with rock and pine. I spent days checking it out, occasionally parking the bike and heading off into the forest to find some rocks to climb. At the end of every day, I would return to the apartment, awfully hungry. It was always the same, two hard-boiled eggs and sautéed vegetables usually consisting of onion, red pepper, kale or spinach and tinned tomatoes; sometimes, later in the evening, I ate an avocado with lemon juice to keep the hunger pangs at bay. For some supernatural reason, avocados were cheap, I mean really cheap, even by English standards.

That was it, nothing more. Generally, with the odd exception, I don't eat wheat, rice, potatoes or refined sugar and here in Sweden I couldn't afford meat, fish or cheese. Twice I went out to watch the sunset outside a cafe, drinking two pints of beer each time, anymore and I wouldn't have been able to bike back home! I sat outside this pleasant cafe above a busy highway overlooking the main Gothenburg Park getting a sugar and alcohol hit. For some reason this urban landscape with its slow setting orange orb and endless hum of traffic was a very cool experience. I also drank a few café lattes on my travels, here and there.

And that, my friends, is The Swedish Diet; mine anyway. Now you have the diet and the daily routine of exploration (I won't call it exercise as it was slow and languid, even the climbing was toned down with no partner to hold a rope) but there is more to come – a slight twist in this tale.

I biked to Fiskeback, a small suburb of Gothenburg on the coast with a large pretty harbour. As with most small Swedish towns, it was clean and spread out, giving the air of a fairy tale environment where nothing bad ever happens. It's a very pleasant place to bike around. After the harbour, there is a bit of rugged coast that leads to where the Gothenburg river (the Göta älv) meets the sea. A path leads through some pine forest; on the left is a rocky coastline where one can sunbathe, scramble on the rocks and swim in clear water, admiring the view of islands and endless passing boats; on the right is a small rocky plateau where I played around on rocks and, at the very top of the plateau (not so high and easy to walk up), one gets a splendid view. It was here, in the still air and high humidity under the fragrant pines that I stumbled upon a small isolated pond. It was surrounded by dwarf pine, birch trees and smooth rock. It was kind of a paradise. It was right above the harbour and close to the path, yet there was no evidence or trace of people. On my travels through the forests around the city, I had found a few old camps, broken tents and abandoned sleeping bags with plants now growing through fabric, which I later learned were secret hiding spots where homeless and illegal migrants laid low at night. Nothing like that evident here.

The pond was full of beautiful flowering plants, lilies and an array of multicoloured dragonflies hovering and darting about; a few ducks sat motionless in the middle of this treasure. I wandered around the edge and back into the trees. The birch trees were small and old, many of them fallen, half-rotten on the rocky floor. I saw something unusual out the corner of my eye and looked hard at a broken trunk. In the shadow of the forest, the mottled light filtering through the canopy illuminated a small jet-black gnarly bole growing on the bark. I studied what looked like giant black fossilised fish scales growing sideways out of the trunk.

It was a Chaga fungus.

What was it doing in such a warm environment? They usually grow on birch but in arctic conditions, not here in sunny southern Sweden! They need hard-core minus degrees Celsius to thrive and multiply.

I asked around about climate change. Gothenburg used to get harsh winters but not anymore and this explained everything. The trees on which I found Chaga growing were old, probably much more than forty years – it was hard for me to tell, but they were all broken and nearly dead. There was no chance of a fruiting Chaga to reproduce in these mild modern times. Where there others to be found locally? The search was on.

Why, may you ask, was I interested in a rather ugly, rock hard piece of fungus? Because, if prepared correctly, it is a powerful medicine that two of my very ill friends may want to take. The preparation is no simple task; first, one has to smash the Chaga into small pieces, then heat it to a sub-boil simmer only, adding and topping up with exactly the right amount of water for four days, before freezing the liquid and solids; after twenty four hours of being properly frozen, it is defrosted and the liquid strained off using a hand press and put back in the freezer, the left over solids are then fermented in 90% alcohol (yes, the air locks do pop even at that level of alcohol!) for two months before straining and pressing again; finally, the water extract is defrosted again and mixed with alcohol liquid extract. Phew! On top of that, you try finding 90% alcohol in the UK that is not poison. It is taken by the drop, by the way.

The hunt was on and I spent my days before the contracts were signed scouring the forests. I found four spots and about ten trees in all and took home more than four kilos of dried Chaga.

Back to the contracts – they were signed and work commenced. There were issues between the builder and my friend; dry rot was found, the roof was in questionable condition and work ground to a halt rather fast. My friend was going on a course in Stockholm and wanted shot of me – I was just another unnecessary thing to think about. She didn't need me, had a string of her own pleasing, willing hands to call upon and speedily bought me a ticket home. I had a return ticket that could be changed, but that wasn't fast enough for her and told me in the most tactless and amusing way to sling my hook, scram, get out of here and never come back.

That's exactly what I did; leaving Sweden 4.8 kilos lighter than when I first arrived (I was away one month). My friends were horrified at the new skinny faced me, my trousers kept falling down and my shirts were like tents.

I didn't plan to lose weight, I didn't think about it, it just happened and I had a good time in the process. It wasn't hard, it didn't involve sweat, workouts or gruelling boot camp classes – it was only about what I put into my mouth; or rather, what I didn't put into my mouth.

The proof of the pudding is – not eating the pudding!

ANOTHER SUNDAY

As the last grain of pink sand falls, time's up: the hour glass empty. The temperature gauge reads 110 degrees C. It's said to be accurate, there about. Watching the grains of time drain away, I manage to hang on for the entire twenty minutes.

Alone in the small sauna, looking out at the pool where others are having fun, this is definitely not fun. Burning up and leaking sweat, I hold onto the bench, forcing myself to stay put, as the increasing urge to make a beeline for the door intensifies with the decreasing grains of sand. I wonder why extremes make me feel so alive.

Time's up. But I go nowhere. How much more can I endure? I had already been to a Spin class a few hours before, burning up the calories, pushing it to the limit, leaving a puddle of sweat on the floor.

I squirt the hot stones with copious amount of water. They hiss, steam quickly rising. My ears are burning. As I breathe, the steam heat in my nose and mouth becomes unbearable.

While I can still function, I need to leave.

Stumbling to the door, into the seemingly cool chlorine air of poolside, time is most definitely up.

Dazed and feeling stoned, I lean against the white tiled wall under a lukewarm shower. Within a minute, I come to, staring out across the pool.

It's the pool that cools me down, sitting in the shallows for five minutes or more.

The grains of sand are gone and living in this odd state becomes a natural state. I swim 25 metres underwater, slowly and methodically. Up for air at the other end; a minute or two break before repeating. In the end, the air just won't hold anymore. Today it is 32 lengths.

It's spring time and the outside air pleasantly warm. Rooks make their nests in tall willows and white poplars that edge the small road between the leisure centre and the single track rail crossing. Nest building is a noisy affair. I head for the harbour, where once I was a fisherman, risking all in a tiny boat amongst the wind, waves and terrifying swell. I never cared if I didn't catch a fish, it was the excitement of it all.

Now, it's time for tea and cake.

I'm in the ancient town or Rye, quaint with pretty streets; far from these sought extremes.

Such is another Sunday.

LIKE IT OR LUMP IT

Published in Poached Hare Journal (2019: Identity Theme)

'Dead cat, bad scene man'

And there it was, lying by the side of the road in the grass and the weeds below the hedgerow that edged a very large field of summer wheat. It was black and stretched out, having probably been hit by a recent passing car as it hadn't been there in the morning.

The school bus moved on having dropped off a kid who lived opposite the dead cat on this lonely stretch of road. Maybe it was his cat, we never knew.

The few of us left on the bus, the few that lived way out, laughed hard at John's joke, strange use of street language which we were not used to; for us a dead cat was just that, a dead cat, and there was nothing bad scene about it at all.

Someone had told me that John hung out with biker gangs and the like; all I knew is that he wore a tatty old leather jacket with the word LUMPIT painted low on the back in a faded, cracked white paint. I guess it meant 'like it or LUMPIT, I never asked. To me, he was an odd one – we were both 15 but as different as chalk and cheese. He lived in a children's home in the same town as me, but his sister, who had now left school lived somewhere else, I recall an aunt being mentioned. His sister was short with curly brown hair, carrying a basket which usually with some cigarettes lying on top. There were tales told at school – their mother some dysfunctional alcoholic, mentally ill, a prostitute; their father having gassed himself in the kitchen oven. Who knows if any of it was true, we were kids and nothing went as deep as another's troubles – they just simply didn't exist.

Returning from school the next day the bus slowed to make the usual drop off.

Suddenly, someone shouted:

'The cat's gone'

Owen, a younger kid, shrieked in excitement:

'The gypsies must have eaten it!'

Boy did we laugh at that, but John was furious, walked straight down the bus to the front where Owen sat with his sister. All the older kids sat at the back for some mysterious reason thinking it was cool, but actually we all knew that it was uncomfortable and as bumpy as hell! Immediately he had Owen by the collar of his blazer and pushed him hard against the back of the seat.

'The gypsies didn't eat the cat – ok?'

Poor Owen was in tears. John wasn't what we called a tough guy by any means, just rough and fairly tramp like for a kid of his age. Someone barked at him and he backed off to sit and sulk on his own with his secret memories or fantasies about gypsy cuisine, none of which he shared with us.

A few years later I bumped into John in the street. I was on my way to college and he walked past me without any acknowledgement or eye contact. Just as he passed, I turned and shouted out to him, and as he turned I saw an older man, still scruffy, but now almost vagrant, with a look that said he was into his own bad scene. We exchanged grunts.

I only saw him once again after that, on the seafront outside the entrance to the pier. In those days they still had rock concerts on the pier and perhaps he was going to one, or maybe buying a ticket. He was now a hippy, perhaps gypsy like in that traditional way; black curly hair and a hoop earring with some paisley shirt and an Afghan type coat. This time we spoke for a while. He was serene, had a soft look, was friendly but still somehow had that troubled aura about him. He was with a hippy girl, said he liked her but preferred someone else who he was seeing soon. The girl just smiled. He said he was travelling about from place to place, sleeping here and there and would soon be gone.

We were never friends, just two guys who, for a few years, travelled on the school bus home together.

I never saw him again, never thought about him; all the same, I never forgot those priceless few words:

'Dead cat, bad scene man'

THE DEALER

(a true story of an English lesson I gave to an EFL graduate class)

The dealer held the cards tightly in one hand and with the thumb of his other flicked across the top of the pack, making a sound that only a pack of cards can.

That sound told everyone in the hot, humid and oppressive room, the time had come. All fell silent, only the exaggerated slow whir of an overhead fan made noise. In a moment of unbearable suspense, the thumb flicked again, but slower this time, driving the silent onlookers towards an inner frenzy.

Before anyone cracked, the top card slammed hard on the table, face up.

Not a playing card, but a word card:

LANGUID.

The first person nearest the dealer picked it up and headed for the door.

Not a murmur as the next card slammed down:

PRUDE.

A disappointed looking woman picked it up and walked resignedly away.

Slam! And Jesus picked up the card:

DEMUR.

Not the Demure he knew, and he exited into the glare of low late afternoon sun. For the next week he would have to live his word, keep his word and be the word as faithfully as he could before the following week dealt another brand new hand.

At home, he went straight for the dictionary so he would know how to live his life as Demur as he possibly could. Before it had even been lived, his week had already been written; only the details, his inventions, were missing.

Yana got APPLES and an OLD BAG.

Anna got COLD FEET and A DARK WOLF.

Laura got BETWEEN THE DEVIL AND THE DEEP BLUE SEA.

Karolina got BEWITCHED and AWAY WITH THE FARIES.

Tomasz GOT LAID.

Viktoria got a YELLOW CHICKEN and a CONJURING TRICK.

AT THE END OF A RAINBOW

Ask Andy or Alice, they'll tell how it was; they were with, standing close – right in the middle of a rainbow's end.

You may well think this is fiction or fantasy, or perhaps just delusion, but it's not – this is real.

It was somewhere in Shropshire, I forget exactly where, but near to Ludlow on the Welsh border side, magnificent green countryside with rolling hills, small river valleys and big forests.

We were out in the open, in the fields on the kind of day that is pleasant and warm with nice sunshine. However, as this was England, it was cut by the occasional summer shower.

We'd had a summer of long walks with heavy packs, as we were all off to Nepal to hike to Everest Base Camp and thought it best to get some training in and spend time hanging out together.

So there we were, at the top of a small field surrounded by trees. The field sloped down in front of us, but it also sloped down to our left – it was like a bank, a kind of difficult and useless field if you were a farmer, but for the hiker it was a small hidden delight.

Across a gate, down in the left hand corner of the field, we saw a small rainbow go to ground – nothing we hadn't all seen a million times before. It shimmered against the trees, and went to ground on the short green, wet grass.

Nothing special and certainly nothing unusual so far, but then I suggested as a joke that we should stand in it and find a pot of gold.

You may think this is absurd, but as we walked across the field towards it, instead of disappearing or moving away as science tells us it should, it remained the same – it didn't move an inch.

We didn't speak until we were right close to it – maybe ten feet away, perhaps even closer. It shimmered mainly green and red, transparent like a giant soap bubble with all the colours of the rainbow moving and subtly vibrating.

Can you believe it? We could hardly believe our eyes.

So we stepped right on into it, all three of us. Maybe the rainbow was about four feet across, and we all fitted in it, looking at each other, wondering what was going on. It really was like being in a soap bubble – looking through the soft coloured hues at each other and the field and trees outside.

Bewildered, we asked each other – is this real? We all agreed that we were seeing and having the same experience. Stepping out we were in the regular daylight, looking at a rainbow's end, and stepping in again we were in a rainbow' end, a giant soap bubble.

It was bedazzling and as real as anything you experience in an ordinary day.

I can't remember what we said to each other, probably not a lot – what could we say!

We moved away to the end of the field a short distance away to cross another gate. I decided to return and have a reality check – there it was, still there and I stepped in again and looked at my friends looking back at me in a rainbow's end and me looking back at them through a soft soapy multicoloured rainbow.

I returned to where they waited in silence and we watched together as the rainbow slowly disappeared into thin air.

A scruffy man appeared with a boy, the gamekeeper; he had seen his pheasants rise up in flight and wondered if poachers were in the woods. We told him our story, and he looked and acknowledged he could see the fading rainbow and had seen it in the sky as normal not so long ago.

He looked at us and then back to the field and then back at us with a frown.

Then we continued on our way.

We still all agree on what we saw and experienced – not that anyone ever believes us.

I stood in the end of a rainbow with two friends. There was no pot of gold, but just being able to do such a thing is more treasure than you could possibly wish.

FICTION

ICE FINGER

Published in Scarlet Leaf Review (October 2020)

1.

Stockholm Airport, 2ⁿᵈ January.

Detective Sergeant Ryan Reeves sits at a small table looking through huge glass panes into the murky light of a bitterly cold afternoon. Outside, well-insulated crew stand on mobile platforms spraying de-icer over a waiting plane's wings. It's a time consuming job and he notices the frustrated looks from passengers peering out of porthole windows.

If it's cold here, what would it be like further north?

He had already had two shocks that day: the first was the call; the second, his sandwich, probably the most expensive sandwich in the world. For almost half the price he could be lounging in a ritzy London hotel, overhearing conversations from the rich and famous, smelling French perfume and admiring sun tans and designer suits, with exactly the same bread and ingredients sitting on a plate in front of him. But he's not: he's on a public concourse in a busy airport. The sandwich looks good. He takes a bite. It is good and he snickers: still not worth thirteen pounds.

Unable to raise a smile at the other shock, he ponders as he eats the sandwich. The call had come before dawn. It had never happened before, not to him, and not to anyone he had ever known. These calls were urban myths, until now.

Anxiety suddenly washes over him and he abruptly leaves his ivory crust to pace the long concourse, glancing into shops, feigning interest. In a few hours he too would be peering out a porthole window, waiting for the de-icers to do their job. The connecting flight would then fly north, to a job he knows nothing about in a country he's never been to.

The call had been brief. His boss, the reticent Inspector Charlie Mace, had told him to pack a bag with warm clothes, bring his passport and immediately come down to the station. He protested. It was his day off and he needed to prepare for his promotion interview: he was days away from becoming a Deputy Inspector. He had earned it, done his time, and tried to reason with Charlie Mace, but his boss got angry and the phone went dead.

In less than an hour he was at the station. Charlie Mace was not there and the desk sergeant handed him a folder. There wasn't much inside, just a ticket to Lulea, car hire details and destination along with a short note telling him the Swedes would pay for everything. His flight left in three hours. Asking for more information, the officer at the desk had just shrugged, meanly saying:

'You got the call, now don't mess it up.'

Was he jealous?

On the subway to Heathrow airport, the train had rushed out a noisy tunnel into the gloomy light of a winter dawn. His carriage was hushed and the few people sitting near him looked out from sleepy, empty faces. Maybe they were heading to work or, like him, to a flight to who knows where. He had to rush to catch his flight. It felt like exile.

He stops pacing the concourse as the penny drops. The promotion: they don't want him to get the job. Charlie Mace knows how much it means to him. It was his, now it's for someone more in favour. He had had the call that everyone wants: an international crime scene detective, glamorous, double time and an expense account. On return, he would be back to his old job, one he didn't want anymore.

With his stomach rumbling and anxiety waning, he returns to find his half-eaten sandwich and coffee cup still there. He sits and gloomily watches the de-icers. He had only packed a jumper.

The raucous New Year Eve's party, just two days ago, where he and friends danced vivaciously and drank too much, seems an age away.

Life feels bitter sweet.

2.

Ryan wakes from his doze as the plane lands bumpily on the runway. Although it's pitch black outside, he sees white, and lots of it. By the time the plane taxis towards the terminal, the landscape is illuminated by flood lights. Snow and ice is everywhere and the wind gusting, blowing spindrift right and left. Battling the elements, ground crew are wearing large gauntlets and thick parkas, hoods up and fastened tight. Ryan hadn't even bought a hat, let alone a pair of gloves. Maybe his shock of black hair would keep him warm. But as this was all new to him, he really has no clue.

Collecting the car keys from the desk, he nonchalantly exits the temperate terminal. The wind hits, driving cold into every part of him. He gasps at the shock, aware his temperature is dropping fast. By the time he reaches the car, his hand pulling the suitcase is numb and his thumbs are painful. It's unbearable. Wasting no time, he starts the car. Turning the heater full up, he waits for warmth.

As he drives off, the GPS shows fifteen minutes to the hotel. There's no tarmac to be seen, the car's headlights illuminating white sheet ice.

Stay on the right he keeps telling himself as he turns into a roundabout, gingerly taking the turn. The car broadsides and comes to a halt, banked up against a wall of snow. The car hire note had told him he would have full winter tyres, this can't be right. Are they trying to kill him? Nervously, he drives back to the airport, sliding into a parking spot just missing the adjacent car. He needs to change the tyres.

He tries to be calm but when the girl at the desk fobs him off by telling him he's just not used to these winter conditions, he loses his cool:

'I'm driving three hundred kilometres north tomorrow!'

That does the trick and he's given the keys to another car with brand new tyres: type Ice 2 with studs, he's told. Ryan feigns a confident nod.

Cautiously, he drives to the hotel, chilled to the bone.

Confused and exhausted, he crashes fully clothed on the bed, not waking until seven the next morning. Knowing his destination has good daylight from only 10.30.am until 12.45.pm, he starts his journey north. It's dark and freezing cold. Not daring to call Charlie Mace until he arrives at Gallivare police station, he still has hope of his promotion.

The empty road cuts through tracts of snowy pine. It's more than twenty minutes before he meets another vehicle: a logging lorry passing on the other side, sending up clouds of spindrift so thick it blocks his view. Unable to see the road ahead, he drifts into the path of another logging truck, its horn blaring horribly. Urgently he pulls the wheel, steering the car back, studs and tyres grinding in the ice. The girl was right, he's not used to these conditions, good tyres or not.

Jittery, it's with some relief that Ryan pulls into a siding with a lit-up neon sign. This must be a cafe, Ryan thinks as he hurries from the car to the front door. It's still dark and freezing cold. Standing opposite a pretty woman, she looks him up and down. From his first hello, she knows he's not a Swede and speaks in fluent English:

'Are you trying to kill yourself with those clothes, it's minus twenty six outside and dropping fast.'

Ryan feels a fool. Maybe the truth will help.

'I came unprepared, they called me yesterday morning, it's urgent I guess. I'm Ryan, a British Policeman, come to help out in Gallivare.'

'Oh, the murder of that Englishman, never off the news.'

Murder? Ryan was a specialist in drugs and money laundering. What use would he be to the Swedes? He really has been exiled.

'Sorry, I can't talk about it.' And he couldn't, he knows nothing.

'Well, buy some warm clothes, don't want another dead Englishman.'

Ryan laughs. Is that his case? Maybe, maybe not and his hand reaches for the mobile in his jacket pocket to look at online news.

Pulling out the mobile, he hears the woman asking for his order. Hungry, he leaves the phone and tells her he'll take whatever she suggests.

The place is empty. Lifeless eyes of wild creatures bear down from shelves and perches. An ancient collection of taxidermy tells him he's in an unfamiliar world.

Ignoring this display of hunting trophies, he helps himself to bread and coffee. Ryan drinks two mugs and tastes the unfamiliar black bread. Two steaming moose meatballs arrive with potatoes and overdone veg. Curiously, it's delicious. The cafe starts filling up with customers, outside workers in what seems like full arctic attire. They smile, momentarily staring; in his jeans, trainers and leather jacket he must really look a fool.

Drinking a third cup of coffee, Ryan looks at his mobile: no message from Mace. He decides to leave the news, not wanting to fill his head with something that may be distracting and probably irrelevant, and hurries to the car.

Passing an ice clad sign telling him he's now inside the Arctic Circle, the drive to Gallivare becomes increasingly stressful. Snow had started falling during breakfast and visibility is now dangerously low, even with full beam on. The road becomes soft and slushy as the car ploughs through the newly fallen snow. Ryan realises he can't see the sides or middle of the carriageway. Everything is white. With nowhere to pull over, he carries on, dropping speed to less than thirty. As dawn breaks, things become easier but the stark facts frightening: he's on a white road with white sides in a white landscape. A snow plough passes on the other side; no sign of any other vehicles.

Tense and knotted, he turns off to Gallivare. The GPS shows sixteen minutes to his destination. Bursting for pee, he curses as he passes a lay-by – it's full of snow, he'd get stuck if he drives in there.

3.

Ryan had driven into the first large supermarket he saw, used the toilet and now sits in the Co-op cafe with yet another cup of coffee. The drive had shaken him badly. He's a detective, meant to be level-headed, focused and professional, but feels a wreck. He had looked in the bathroom mirror and saw himself pale, unshaven and glassy eyed. They won't be expecting this, he frets.

Ten minutes later he's staring through the windscreen at a large, modern and very uninteresting building: Gallivare Police Station. He hurries through the snow and wind to the glass fronted entrance.

'Detective Sergeant Ryan Reeves, British Police.'

Shivering from cold, he tries to smile.

The woman at the desk just stares back; in fact, the entire office behind her stare. An uncomfortable moment is broken by a deep voice:

'Happy New Year Ryan, come on through, we are glad you're here. How was the drive up?'

'Err, different…Happy New Year.'

The office breaks out in laughter. The man speaking to him from behind the desk laughs too:

'Damned dangerous, you mean!'

Ryan manages a smile and goes through a door someone else is holding open.

The deep voice belongs to Chief Inspector Erik Olofsson, head of station; burly, fair headed with an impressive blonde beard. After jokes and concerns about his clothing, he's introduced to a woman who would partner him while he's in Sweden.

Special Investigator Captain Eva Strid is petite, slim with long black hair. A sallow complexion matches her shiny black obsidian eyes. She puts her hand out. Ryan shakes it.

'Let's try and work this out together. Did they brief you in London?'

'Inspector Mace didn't say…very much at all.'

Eva and Erik exchange glances. Erik speaks:

'Not your boss, this is inter-government co-operation, the request was made at the highest level. We need a specialist...we don't want to look like incompetent fools.'

Erik laughs but Ryan grimaces. He too will probably end up looking like a fool when they realise he's not special, just a detective working on low level money laundering cases. He chooses bluff as a defence.

'I am a specialist,' Ryan says, unconvinced by his own words. After all, that's what they're expecting. He starts to feel on edge.

Before anxiety gets the better of him, he's thankful when Eva takes him outside to collect his bag. He follows her down the street thick with snow to the hotel: The Quality Resort, right opposite the eloquent train station neatly painted in red and black. Eva studies Ryan and then tells him to get some rest; she'll pick him up at six. Ryan checks his watch: 12.45.pm. It's getting dark.

His spacious room overlooks the icy train station. Although pleased to be inside a warm hotel room, he just can't shake the cold. Standing in wet trainers with numbing feet, he heads towards the shower.

4.

Meanwhile, down the road at the police station, Eva Strid worries about Ryan. He's unprepared: has not been briefed and risks frostbite or hyperthermia in his urban clothing. She'd appealed for help and now she's got it. Having been assigned to work closely with him, feels responsible. With Stockholm overwhelmed with increasing crime and terrorism, most Lulea detectives have flown south. At Gallivare, the station has a skeleton staff, most of whom are not experienced for a case like this. She needs to look after Ryan.

Erik, seeing a concerned look on Eva's face, walks over to her desk. 'Think he's up to the job?'

Eva keeps her thoughts to herself. After all, Ryan is only here be-cause she put in a request for help to Lulea, which went to Stockholm and then became political. She has no idea if Ryan is the man she needs.

'He's a specialist, said so himself…he needs clothes though, we might be in the backcountry. The forecast says minus thirty five tomorrow. It's one of those winters.'

'I think the budget will stretch to some warm clothing. Brief him tonight.'

At the hotel, Ryan sits on the bed staring at his mobile: still no message. He's tired but with all the coffee he's drunk, just can't sleep. Clean, shaved and wearing new clothes, he feels respectable again. He dials London.

'DC. Reeves here Sir, I'm in Gallivare.'

'Anything to report Reeves?'

'No, just arrived.'

'Then why are you calling? You'll be some time out there I think. Send a report by email every few days or so. Is there anything else?'

'My promotion sir…'

'DC Coogan is now Deputy Inspector Coogan. You volunteered for an important posting.'

Ryan hesitates and the phone goes dead, again.

Ryan looks across the road to the train station. That bastard, he fumes. He never volunteered, press-ganged into service more like. Charlie Mace and Jack Coogan play squash together, their wives go shopping together, yet he's only been in the job for half a year. Is that why he'd been sent here, to remove him from the interview process? Add to that his lack of international experience and unsuitable clothing, he's bound to make a hash of it. At a time like this, only the bar could give him solace.

Later, outside the hotel, Eva sits in her car mulling over the situation. It's six o'clock but she hesitates. She needs to get this right, brief him properly so tomorrow they can work together. Hopefully he's had some rest.

The murder of a British celebrity in a remote cabin without clues, motive or murder weapon has so far hit a dead end. His name was

Fuzzy Smith, a famous British comedian. He and a Russian business partner were trying to develop pristine forest into a winter holiday resort. It had been met with fierce local opposition; however, it seemed likely the authorities would grant permission. She now needs to tell Ryan in a way that is clear to him. Eva leaves the car.

She sees Ryan in the bar. He's lounging in an easy chair behind a table of empty glasses. He looks different, more relaxed, clean and shaven. But he's still wearing inappropriate clothing.

Greeting her with a smile, he wobbles as he gets up out the chair, hand outstretched. Not shaking it, she momentarily stares. He's obviously drunk.

'Ryan, are you on duty?'

'I don't know, am I?' He laughs.

'I suppose not.'

There can be no briefing in his condition. But time is of the essence, more snow is due tonight; it's already hard to get about. Eva knows she's got to take control.

'Have you eaten?'

'This morning at some weird roadside cafe.'

'You're in no shape for briefing. You need to sober up and eat. I'll cook something at mine. I'll drive.'

This is hard work for Ryan, all he wants to do is drink himself into a stupor and forget about the lost promotion. Now he's been summoned to her house for food and work. Don't these Swedes relax, he's been on the go all day?

She's looking at him impatiently and he resigns himself to a sobering night out.

5.

They don't speak during the drive. It takes about twenty minutes down a pitch black road without any obvious signs of housing. The road's been recently been ploughed but is still thick with hard dense ice, reminding Ryan of his perilous trip north earlier that day. Considering the conditions, Eva drives fast.

Eva slows the car to a crawl, the headlights illuminating a small neat red house where the road becomes a dead end.

'They plough this just for you?'

'I'm resident,' Eva states emphatically.

Ryan, struggling with the effects of alcohol and increasing weariness, steps out the car as soon as it comes to a halt. The biting wind burns his face. Eva opens the house front door.

Before she takes the key out of lock, she points to a chair in the middle of the room.

'Take off your shoes and sit there, and Ryan…there's no alcohol.'

'Don't you drink?'

'I'm Muslim.'

Ryan does as he's told. The chair is comfortable and the house warm. He soon finds himself battling sleep. For distraction, he looks around. The room is modern, almost minimalist, the polished wooden floor partially covered by a large oriental rug. In another room, he hears the movement of plates and pots, a cupboard being opened and closed and the noise of a kettle warming up. Through the window he gazes down the dark and empty road, mesmerised by the fall of heavy snow.

'I'm vegetarian, so I hope this will do. I know it's late for coffee but I need you alert.'

Ryan glances up as Eva puts down a tray on the table in front of him. He studies his plate of steaming food and large jug of coffee.

'Ryan!'

He jumps as she shouts his name, instantly snapping out of his reverie. Embarrassed, he points towards the window.

'Sorry, it's snowing.'

Frowning, Eva looks through the window at the flakes.

They eat in silence. When finished, Eva produces a thick file, which heavily thuds down on the table between them. Disinterested, Ryan sighs softly. But instead of asking Ryan to take a look, she tells the story of Fuzzy Smith. He quickly perks up, taking interest in her every word.

Fuzzy Smith found on the 1st of January. No wonder Ryan hadn't heard, he was busy nursing a savage New Year's hangover; and then the call.

'Was the Russian laundering money?'

Eva looks hard at Ryan. So he is a real detective, she surmises.

'I don't know, he was in Russia over New Year and the Russians aren't co-operating. I'm sure we'll never see him again.'

She pulls a photograph from the file and shows it to Ryan. It's the murder scene with Smith on his back, eyes open pointing skywards, covered in ice and spats of frozen blood. His clothes are torn and bits scattered in the snow.

'I doubt it was the Russians, far too messy. Looks more like a brawl to me.'

Ryan studies the photo.

'Would you like to see more pictures?'

'I'd like to see the crime scene,' Ryan says, looking up at Eva.

She hesitates, looks out the window at the falling snow before looking back at Ryan.

'There is no crime scene.'

She says it so quietly that Ryan's sure he heard her wrong, but her look tells him differently. Perplexed, he just stares and listens to the story.

'Two days after Christmas, Fuzzy Smith wasn't missing but his hire car was two days overdue.'

Ryan learns that the hire company, not being able to get through to Smith, had tracked the car down to a remote cabin. It was an expensive car and they wanted it back. As so much snow had fallen, they had been forced to hire a snow plough to push through the last thirteen kilometres. It was dark by the time they reached the car. Not noticing the body, they simply drove the car away. In fact, it's now suspected that the plough drove over Smith while doing a U-turn to drive back out again. The car hire company then spotlessly cleaned the vehicle and hired it out again. Only when he hadn't returned on New Year's Eve did a member of his family call the police.

'But the photograph, it's a crime scene, Eva.'

'On New Year's Day, two local policemen and their dog went to investigate. They found Smith lying face up in the snow just like photograph, but contaminated the entire scene, even treading on the body in an attempt to stop the dog urinating on Smith. They failed. By the time forensics arrived, heavy snowfall had started and the wind blowing so hard that the body was quickly covered in snow. A tent was erected but that soon flattened and blew away. Conditions were impossible and the men so cold, it was decided to remove the body and take it to Lulea. Only the cabin had any real forensics done. That photo was taken by the first policemen on the scene. The nearest neighbour is twenty kilometres away and then they are only summer residents.'

Eva shakes her head.

'That's when I became involved. Forensics should be in tomorrow for the body, car and cabin. Besides that, there's nothing.'

Looking at the picture, Ryan feels somehow cheated out of an investigation and says, rather cattily:

'So this messy crime scene isn't a brawl, it's just a big mess made by your colleagues and their well trained dog.'

He regrets his comment.

'Sorry.'

She sits down opposite him and puts her head in her hands. Ryan hopes she doesn't start to cry. He can't cope with that.

She stares up at him with a worried, ashen look.

'Please help me Ryan.'

Of course he's going to help her, it's his job. Out of habit, he laughs. But this isn't England and his defence mechanisms don't work. She's still looking, nothing's funny, nothing's changed.

Ryan blurts out the last forty eight hours and his feelings of dejection at being shafted by his boss. Suddenly it's him who has his head in hands, wondering if it's he that's going to cry. Feeling like a mess, he can't quite believe what he's just said.

He feels her hand on his shoulder. Tensing, he looks up and says: 'Any of that coffee left?'

His voice sounds urgent and, as Eva heads towards the kitchen, Ryan feels ridiculous. Badly needing personal space, he yearns for the hotel.

She returns with tea.

'You need warm clothing.'

Snow had started freezing to the windows and Eva walks over to peer through. Studying the road, she speaks quietly without looking back.

'We'll never get the car through that, will have to wait for the early morning plough.'

Unsure of what she means, he waits. It's at least a minute before she turns around, and, as she can't see him, Ryan doesn't take his eyes off her. But his reflection in the glass tells her exactly what he's doing.

'There's a spare room upstairs but I think it best you sleep down here, I'll get some blankets. There's a small bathroom out the back.'

6.

Glaring lights and loud noises startle him. Panicked, Ryan sits bolt upright. Through the window he sees a large modern tractor pushing snow, its large protruding bucket scraping the thick ice on the road as it clears the area around the front of the house.

The unfamiliar surroundings have him confused and Ryan pushes back the covers and stands up. Illuminated by bright white light, he retreats into the shadows. Minutes later he watches red taillights and flashes of a yellow hazard disappear up the road. It's still snowing. He lies back down.

He awakes to the sound of a shower and footsteps overhead. Not wanting any more awkward moments, he dresses and tidies up the room. The outside thermometer fixed to the window ledge reads minus thirty seven. How cold is that? Ryan wonders.

The answer comes soon enough. Eva appears, dressed in warm clothing, woollen green slacks and a thick white patterned jumper. She looks like she's going skiing.

'Dressed for the weather?' He says, making light of things.

She looks at him oddly.

'My husband is about the same size as you, you can use his things. Follow me.'

He follows her through the kitchen into the garage where she searches through a pile of boxes, handing him pieces of outdoor clothing. Not waiting for a response, she starts dressing herself until she looks like an arctic explorer in a padded parka with a fake fur-lined hood. Remembering the airport workers at Lulea, he laughs but she doesn't, insisting he dresses the same. She hands him a pair of thick-lined winter boots.

Feeling absurdly overdressed, he follows Eva to the car. One step out the door has his ears aching so badly from the icy wind that he frantically pulls at the hood of his new jacket. Fumbling, as he had ignored Eva's pleas to put on gloves, his fingers don't work properly. Helping him, she straightens his hood and pulls the gloves up over his hands. A few minutes later they are sitting in her green police car. Ryan is breathing hard, almost in shock.

Now she laughs.

'Welcome to Sweden.'

As the car warms up, Ryan unzips his jacket and removes his gloves.

'I feel bad about using your husband's things…'

She cuts him off.

'He's in Athens. Familiar food, nice weather…'

She pauses, takes a big breath and continues:

'We were reporters in Iran but had to flee, run for our lives. He couldn't stand the cold or the Swedish language, loathed it when I joined the police… he left me.'

She glances anxiously at Ryan.

'At home we had terrible experiences with authority. I had to change my name, I'm Swedish now…'

Eva suddenly stops talking and Ryan, knowing how close he had come to crossing a red line last night, doesn't ask questions. They stay silent until they reach the hotel. When they arrive, it's still dark outside.

'I'll pick you up ten thirty, read the file.'

Ryan showers and then orders breakfast at the bar. The file tells him nothing, it's full of dull paperwork. Only the photographs are of interest. He reads the online news and learns there's nothing new.

For how long can he string-out this dead-end case: days, weeks, months? The last place he wants to be is home, working for that irascible Charlie Mace or worse, Deputy Inspector Jack Coogan.

7.

At the station, Eva studies the forensic report and, without speaking, hands it over to Erik. He reads it thoroughly and then seems lost in thought before putting the file down, asking:

'How good do you think Ryan Reeves is?'

'He's very to the point…don't think he's used to sticking to the rules.'

Erik looks hard at Eva.

'Then let him loose, and if it goes badly wrong, we can blame him before we kick him out.'

'Are we that desperate?'

'You tell me Eva, he wasn't at the hotel this morning when I stopped by.'

'Oh…'

Eva knows the sombre light of dawn will never pass. It will be dark in a few hours. She enters the hotel to find Ryan waiting in the foyer, dressed in all the clothes she had given him. He seems irritated.

'How can you bear living with no light, and when it comes, it's like this?'

He indicates to the gloom.

'That's what my husband used to say.'

Ignoring that, he points to the car.

'Where are we going?'

Not answering, she goes back to the car. Ryan follows. As she drives, she hands him the forensic report. He reads it twice.

That morning from the hotel, he'd asked the British police for more information on Fuzzy Smith, but they couldn't give him anything useful.

He's quiet for a while, mulling over what he's just read.

No forensics of any use, certainly no strange prints, DNA or fibres. And as there's no mobile phone signal at the murder scene, there are no phone records. Add to that no witness, murder weapon or obvious motive, Ryan feels Inspector Mace has sent him on a wild goose chase. There's nothing he can do.

He looks at the report again. Smith hadn't even been drinking before he died. A light blow to the head and death by freezing: at least that's clear. So are the dog, fox, moose and reindeer tracks. The fox had even nibbled Smith's frozen ear. And then there's the snow plough whose huge heavy chained wheels had reversed over Smith, let alone all the messy police contamination.

'Any other cock-ups I should know about?'

Blurting that out, it had sounded mean. Ryan instantly regrets his tone.

'Eva, I don't know what's wrong with me.'

'Nothing's wrong with you. You're in a strange country with no light at minus thirty seven and a half with no clues for a case you're expected to solve. And you lost your promotion.'

Eva pauses before saying quietly:

'I know exactly how you feel.'

Out of awkwardness, Ryan laughs.

'I'll try and help you solve this case, but I just don't think I can. By the way, where are we going?'

'To a crime scene that isn't there.'

Eva turns the car into a narrow single track road. At least it's been kept ploughed, she notes. She doesn't want 'no snow plough' added to Ryan's list of Swedish police incompetencies. As Erik suggested, they're desperate. In fact, she must be really desperate to be driving Ryan to this desolate place. She hopes he won't get angry when he finds there's only snow and nothing else to see. And what did Erik mean by "let him loose"? What kinds of pressure is Erik under to solve this case if he's more than willing to throw Ryan to the dogs if it all goes wrong?

Ryan breaks her thoughts.

'Is there any colour besides white around here?'

8.

After a long and slow drive, what light there is begins to fade. They have parked up where the snow plough stopped, about twenty metres from a large cabin on the edge of a dark forest. A piece of police tape, one end stapled to the front cabin wall, flaps in the wind.

'We don't have much time.'

Eva takes two pairs of snow shoes out the trunk and passes a pair to Ryan. He looks bewildered.

'Put them on, you'll get nowhere without them, in fact, you'll sink up to your waist.'

Eva watches and then follows as Ryan does his own thing. He's pulled the photos from the file and clasps them tightly, examining them and looking at what he assumes was once a crime scene. There's police debris, the remains of the flattened tent, torn and shredded in the wind and stuff he can't quite place. The cabin's locked and he refrains from asking why. In the last of the light, he stands awkwardly, trying not to let the wind rip the photos from his hands. He studies the front of the cabin. It's exactly the same as in the photograph. He makes a mental note of what he sees.

He can't believe how cold he is and sits in the car with Eva, trying to warm up. She's apprehensive.

'Did you see anything?'

'I don't think so. What was he doing out here on his own at Christmas?'

'We'll probably never know. The land they wanted to develop starts right here and runs back for miles, right up into those hills and more.

Eva points. 'It's full of lakes and creeks.'

'Environmental activists?'

'We checked the data base, anyone like that is just a lefty student type and anyway, they were all away for Christmas.'

'A wandering psycho, who took offence to his bad humour...?'

'Ryan, be serious, please.'

In the last of the light, Ryan looks at a photo and back to the cabin one more time.

'Have you found something?'

'It's not like that, I'm being thorough. Besides, I never found him funny. Let's watch one of his shows later, you can get a measure of the man.'

He turns and faces her and she's quick to answer:

'At the hotel, not mine.'

As they start to drive away, a gust of wind howls, shuddering the car. A second later, a fair sized tree branch hits the bonnet with a loud scraping thud before being pulled away with the wind. Eva stops the car. They look at each other.

Ryan says it first:

'What if it's not murder but an accidental freak of nature? Hit on the head by a piece of flying debris...makes perfect sense.'

'You'd have to return to England.'

Not liking that prospect, Ryan pushes it aside, gruffly remarking:

'Let's exhaust the murder enquiry first, there's still a lot we can to do.'

In silence they drive, Eva wondering how a murder case could make her feel so optimistic.

9.

Eva drops Ryan at the hotel so he can mull things over, come up with a coherent plan to move the investigation on. But in their hearts, the flying wood tells a different story.

At the station, Erik is curious.

'Nothing new, Ryan wondered about environmental activists. He's thinking it through. I'm sure he saw something at the cabin besides the endless white of snow.'

In the hotel bar, Ryan sits with a cup of coffee and a rather good sandwich. At least he's not paying for it, he muses. Having written a short report to Inspector Mace, detailing only the positive points of the investigation, he is now trying to get a grip of anything that might push the investigation forward. A dead-end would mean a flight back home.

Eva had told him that the proposed resort site lay in a buffer zone around a large National Park. Even with development there would be restrictions and limitations. To him, that ruled out environmental activists. Along with that, local hunting societies had long been banned from the area; so no recent grievance there. Nothing fitted, not even a piece of flying wood. Forensics had said nothing of wood in the shallow gash on Smith's left temple.

Knowing that they must get a breakthrough in the next few days, Ryan leaves the hotel and hurries through the cold to the station. Snow ploughs are busy, their flashing yellow hazard lights illuminating the streets. It's snowing again.

Having been buzzed through reception, he stands in the big open office looking at Eva from across the room. Sitting at her desk, busy with paperwork, she looks up and sees Ryan's cold, tense face.

A minute later she's in Erik's office.

'He wants what? We just don't have the staff. There's all the other regular police work to do. In these conditions there's a car accident every few hours. A farm gate was stolen last night. We can't even manage these things effectively.'

'We're desperate and it's the only idea he has.'

'We already look incompetent. Anymore mistakes and they'll send in a hard-nosed team from Stockholm. No doubt we'll be transferred, rural duties farther north…I'll have no choice but to blame it all on Ryan.'

'No, don't do that, he's doing his best, please Erik.'

'His idea, he'll get blamed. I don't want to spend my days chasing missing reindeer, do you?'

Eva goes back to Ryan, who is now sitting in her chair.

'Are you sure you want to do this, what if we find nothing?'

'We're at nothing now, can't see that changing, can you?'

'But every suspicious or unsolved case for the last twenty years…do you know how many files that is, some of them in other stations collecting dust.'

Ryan nods.

'I suppose I could ask Olaf to come out of retirement for a week or so and then there's that intern, what's her name…you don't read Swedish either, we'll have to translate everything.'

'No you won't. Focus on isolated rural cases, especially in winter. Start there and make a short list.'

Eva is impatient.

'What's on your mind, I'm your partner.'

'Something's not right with this case, I just don't know what. What did Erik say?'

'I'll be sent north to look for missing reindeer, and you, you'll be blamed for wasting police time and for all our…cock-ups.'

10.

Managing to get a small private room next to the hotel reception to watch a Fuzzy Smith show, Ryan sits looking through the window at the continuing snowfall. He's not in the mood to watch a crass comedian, but feels Eva needs to know something about the character found frozen outside a lonely cabin.

Mulling over the mystery of Smith's demise, Ryan blurts out his concerns as soon as Eva walks into the room.

'…if the snow plough had deliberately been sent to remove any traces on the road before they crushed Smith's body, along with all the other missing evidence, it starts to look like high level conspiracy.'

'Or it just might be a piece of flying wood,' Eva says.

'Think we'll ever know?'

Not waiting for a response he turns on the screen. In silence they start to watch the show. Neither laughs nor makes a comment. Before a minute passes, Eva pushes the off-button on the remote control.

'Graceless and tasteless, but bad humour isn't cause for murder.'

Ryan laughs at Eva's wit.

'Maybe Smith was in the wrong place, wrong time, witnessed something, something secret that goes on round here?'

'Is that why you want the files?'

Ryan, looking up to the ceiling, stretches his arms out wide and shrugs.

'If we don't spend time looking in the files Eva, I'll be sent home.'

They stare at each other for a moment.

'I know a good place to eat. They sell drink.'

11.

Sitting at a table by a window, they have been talking about the case.

'I still prefer the flying stick theory,' Eva says jovially.

How can she be so happy, she's not even had a drink, Ryan wonders.

'Besides, it's normal procedure to requisition an expensive missing car.'

'And the snow plough – thirteen kilometres, what did that cost?'

'Insurance paid it.'

'Flying sticks it is then.'

Ryan lifts his wine glass and downs the contents. He orders more.

'Does it always snow like this?' Ryan is looking out the window.

'Not like this. The last time it snowed this hard, I was with my mother. She smuggled us to Baku in an old boat. That's how we escaped. Holding my hand, she sung poetry, things I didn't under-stand…she…'

Eva breaks mid sentence, and Ryan, feeling she's about to say something personally revealing, deflects the conversation:

'Poetry…is she still alive?'

Eva nods, knowing he's not that interested.

'In Baku…can you swim Ryan?'

'Not in this weather.'

About to ask why she asked that question, his wine arrives. One more for the snow-ploughed road, he thinks, knowing he'll sleep well tonight.

12.

Gallivare Police Station, 7th January.

Eva had managed to enlist Olaf, Ann the Intern and Sharky from the basement archives. Everything had been collected and for several days now they have been meticulously sifting through old files. An upstairs room is full of them. Eva's compiled a list.

'Missing, disappeared, unexplained, suspicious, some murdered, in remote places in the dead of winter. Not so short, this short list.'

'Let's start with the oldest.'

Each file requires one of the Swedes to read before verbally trans-lating it to Ryan. Everyone is trying to find something that will link to Smith's case, no matter how tenuous. Photographs are put upon the wall. More whiteboards are brought in and they try to put a jigsaw puzzle together. But it doesn't work. The pieces are all wrong.

Ryan needs to narrow it down somehow. There are too many files, too many imaginary links. He looks at the heaps of files that are still unopened. They break for lunch.

Ryan suggests the hotel and he and Eva sit in the bar area eating expensive sandwiches.

'They really make the best.'

'Go to Norway, The Swedes call it Land of the Sandwich.'

'Don't you miss the food back home?'

'Of course,' she says, forlornly. Ryan changes subject.

'Who's the longest serving member of the police here?'

'Olaf until he retired.'

Back in the station, he asks Eva to quiz Olaf about any old cases that had seemed unusual: missing people, accidents in remote places, perhaps with property or resort connections.

There's a sudden exchange between Olaf and Sharky.

'They both remember a case, more than twenty years ago, on the other side of the National Park. A property developer went missing, he was later found by rangers outside a small fishing cabin by a frozen lake, with no obvious cause of death.'

Sharky and Olaf stare at Ryan.

'Which file,' he asks, looking around at all the files. 'And why the odd looks?'

'It's not here, last saw they saw of it was in a tiny police station, which closed down years ago…strange case, best forgot.'

A few minutes later, Eva is in Erik's office. He's unhappy.

'My predecessor lost his job over that. These things run deep around here. It was one of only two cases that station ever had to deal with. The other was a case of missing reindeer. I suggest you familiarise yourself with that one, Eva.'

13.

The Quality Resort Breakfast Bar, 6.15.am 8ᵗʰ January.

Too early for breakfast, Ryan sips coffee and gazes through a nearby window. The night sky clearly shows the falling snow. His tranquil thoughts are interrupted by bright headlights and flashing hazards of a passing snow plough. Turning away from the glare, he looks across empty tables towards the hotel lobby and main entrance. Eva should be here by now; it's not like her to be so late.

Meanwhile, down her lonely narrow road, Eva drives fast to make up time for her rendezvous with Ryan. Unusually, the snow plough had been late as all the unexpected snow made for lots of extra work. Her solitary house on an empty road is not municipal priority.

Her mind is on the case. Indulging Ryan's far-fetched theories is risky and just might end her career. But what else can she do? Admit to failure? Erik had clearly warned her about his intentions if things went wrong, but the only way to hang on to Ryan is to let him loose, let him follow his nose.

Having been briefed by Olaf, she worries nothing good will come of opening up an old police post to pull a dusty file, if it's still there, of yet another unsolved case. It had caused a lot of trouble in its day.

It was with apprehension that she had turned the starter key to pass the plough and drive the road to Ryan's hotel.

Distracted by her thoughts, she fails to notice a large moose standing in the middle of the road, nostrils steaming in the cold night air. Frantically swerving to avoid collision, Eva rams the car into deep soft snow piled high along the edges of the road. Stopping with a shuddered thud, an airbag triggers, smothering her face in an expanding hissing cushion. On deflation, she peers through her side view window, glimpsing the dark shape of the moose disappearing down the road.

Stuck, Eva waits for the flashing hazards of the snow plough to come back up the road. Minutes later it starts to dig her out.

At 6.45.am Ryan drains his second cup of coffee. Picking up the heavy parka, he walks over to wait by the hotel reception. It's pitch black and far too cold to wait outside. Last night Erik paid a visit, warning Ryan not to look too hard at the old unsolved case. It had caused much anger and resentment. Local Sami people claimed the casualty had raised the wrath of ancient forest spirits. The church was furious. There was uproar, with both sides defending faith and heritage. The provincial police, caught in the middle of this feud, along with a general lack of evidence, became embarrassed. Stockholm took control. As the cause of death was unknown and nothing obviously suspicious found, the case was quickly closed. Erik's predecessor was up in arms. A day later, he lost his job.

A cover up, that would figure, Ryan mused, or maybe just incompetence. If the cases are somehow linked, he would be way out of his depth and politically his hands completely tied. But for now he has a theme: wild nature, property development and suspicious police incompetencies. At least it takes his mind off things at home.

Eva's car pulls up with a buckled bonnet and a broken headlight. Putting on the parka, Ryan pulls the hood up tight. Instead of waiting in the car, Eva walks towards the hotel entrance. She's slow, and Ryan pulls the door open. As freezing wind blasts him in the face, he sees that she is shaking.

She avoids eye contact and her fragile face tells Ryan not to be a dumbass and ask a stupid question. Concerned, he takes her arm and helps her to a nearby table. Unsure of what to do or say, he orders coffee and breakfast for them both.

Some minutes later after coffee has arrived, she tells him of the moose and being half buried in the snow. Badly shaken, she drove straight to the hotel. Ryan offers to take her to a hospital but she declines.

Picking at her breakfast, she imploringly looks him in the eye:

'I don't want to lose my job. I'm a refugee with no ties here in Sweden.'

Knowing that plea contains a warning aimed at him, Ryan's gets the message loud and clear: if he messes up, he'll be taken down. There can be no real investigation. It simply isn't going to be allowed.

'Can I at least stay and do my best? Nothing has to be official.'

Eva nods. Is that a smile Ryan sees, he's not entirely sure.

14.

Reporting the damage to her car, they leave the hotel and hurry to the station.

Having lost time, Ryan starts his hire car as Eva picks up the key to the old police post from Erik in the office.

For his sake and for hers, Ryan drives slowly. These roads terrify him.

'How's Erik?'

'Not happy.'

'Is it a nice drive?'

'It's dark.'

What an idiot he must seem. Ryan doesn't even laugh.

Soon after leaving Gallivare, Eva falls asleep and Ryan follows the sat-nav, cautiously looking out for moose.

On a small and empty icy road, the gloomy light of dawn begins to show. Ahead, surrounded by thick snow covered pine is the silhouette of the police post: a large black corrugated cabin half buried in the snow. No wonder it was closed down, Ryan surmises, there's nothing out here.

Although the road has been recently ploughed, there's only room for one car on the narrow carriageway. Ryan stops outside the post.

Eva had put the key on top of the dash and Ryan takes it. She's still asleep. He softly clicks the car door shut. The snowy bank at the side of the road is more than three feet high and Ryan clambers up and over to sink thigh deep. As he pushes down with his hands to free his legs, his arms too sink down. He flounders, lies flat and tries to forge a path to the post's front door. It takes a full five minutes and he half sits, half lies, panting, wondering if he'll make the last ten feet. Turning, he looks back towards the car. Eva is staring at him. Embarrassed, he wonders for how long. The window of the car comes down and she tries to speak but starts to laugh instead, giggling at his predicament. Ryan doesn't feel like laughing, everything so far has been a disaster, so much so that he feels he'll end up covering up his own incompetence. But his seriousness doesn't deter Eva. She gets out, shouting:

'Every hire car has a shovel in the trunk.'

And she fetches it to start clearing a path to Ryan and the front door. On reaching him she hands over the shovel.

'Team work, partner.'

In silence, he gets to it.

Clearing the steps and the area immediately in front of the door he looks at her. She's smiling and he can't help himself.

'I love your smile.'

Looking down at the icy wooden veranda, he reaches in his pocket and hands over the key without catching her eye. Eva turns the lock. A dry musty air catches them by surprise.

'We've opened a tomb.'

'Then let's not disturb the dead, as Erik said,' Eva replies.

Ryan, taking a step inside, doesn't know if that's a joke or not. The lights don't work and the shutters are all down. Entering the shadows, Eva turns on her torch.

The wind blows in cold air and Ryan pushes the door shut. In silence they stand still following the light of the torch. There's not much left, most of the furniture has gone. Covered in dust and cobwebs, a large map of the area is on one wall. Below it is a simple metal filing cabinet. Eva goes straight to it, pulls open the draws and takes out just two files. Without saying a word, Eva closes the draws, walks over to the door, opens it and leaves. Ryan follows and Eva locks it and heads straight for the car.

Sitting in the car, Ryan warms up as Eva reads. It doesn't take long and she turns to him.

'There's not much here, a photo of the cabin but not the victim, a poor sketch of a suspect that led nowhere, and a name of an unreliable witness who was later deemed mentally ill.'

'And the other file?'

'It's an insurance policy.' Eva throws that file on the back seat and hands the old case file over to Ryan. As he studies it, she turns her head, glancing at the back seat.

'That's it, no forensics?'

Eva shakes her head.

Ryan studies the old photo, and then looks at the sketch: a fierce looking unkempt man with long hair and a beard. He tries to remember something he had seen at the Smith site, but nothing comes.

Shaking his head:

'Useless….who was this witness?'

Eva looks at the file again.

'A name but no address, it seems.'

'Someone really wanted this case shut down.'

'Please Ryan, don't…'

An open-back pickup truck brimming with cut logs stops in front of them. A bearded wild looking woodsman type stares at them through the windscreen.

'Ask him about that name.' Ryan points at the file. 'Then I'll back up.'

Eva gets out. The conversation is brief. As Ryan backs down the road, Eva speaks:

'Past his wood yard is one house only. That's where she lives.'

15.

As Ryan focuses on the dimly lit forest road, Eva eyes him. Had she heard him right outside the police post door?

They pass a roadside clearing full of ramshackle sheds and piled up logs. Fresh tyre tracks lead from a yard onto the road.

'It must be soon,' Ryan states, looking right and left.

But it's another twenty minutes before the snow ploughed road ends in front of a crooked wooden house with a black metal chimney, smoke churning in the wind. Outside, on a cleared veranda sheltered from the wind, is a bench. Sitting on it is an old woman dressed in what looks like black rags, stroking a black cat. Her feet are bare.

'She must be near frozen…mentally ill you say?'

Eva studies the file one more time.

'Yes…and totally unreliable.'

Ryan switches off the engine. The woman is staring at them.

'I have a bad feeling about this, Ryan.'

'Let's make it quick then.'

Eva nods. From the car she had looked wizened; but now up close, she's gnarly like the twisted bark of the old pines growing tall around the house.

Eva asks some questions. The woman and cat both stare at Ryan. The cat stands up in her lap, the dark fur raised on its back and neck. Ryan feels the need to leave but her deep gravelly voice keeps him rooted to the spot. She doesn't take her eyes off him.

'Her Swedish is poor, worse than mine.'

Eva shows the suspect sketch. The woman looks, speaks and points into the dark forest behind her house.

'Twenty three years ago, she saw him following the victim to his fishing cabin…he had a large dog with him.'

Eva, struggling with the language, asks more questions.

'He spoke to her.'

'That's not in the report. What'd he say?'

But the woman only laughs, her piecing shrill startling some birds that start squawking overhead.

Ryan and Eva exchange worried looks. Sensing some hysterical outburst, they turn and leave. The woman shouts, her words stabbing the harsh cold air. Ryan wastes no time and turns the car around. Neither of them dare look back.

Passing the wood yard, Ryan finally speaks.

'She spooked the hell out of me,' he jokes, letting out his nervous tension.

Turning to briefly glance at Eva, he sees her pensive face transfixed on the road in front.

'What wrong? She's just a batty old lady.'

'She said…'

Eva turns and looks deadpan at Ryan.

'…that he spoke to her, just one hour before we arrived.'

16.

At the station, Ryan studies the photos: Smith's cabin and the twenty three year old black and white photo of the small fishing cabin by a frozen lake. Spotting something, he shows Eva, convincing her to call Lulea Forensics.

A while later, after Forensics has sent a new report, Eva and Ryan are in Erik's office.

Erik doesn't need convincing, it's plain to see: both photographs show huge icicles hanging down the front of their respective cabins. But in each photo there's an icicle missing, snapped off from where it left the roof. No one has doubt that both icicles had deliberately been broken off.

'A big weapon, a meter I'd say and thicker than your arm, Eva.'

Eva agrees, passing over the forensic note. As Erik scan reads, he mumbles out the words:

'Ice embedded in his wound, frozen cells before Smith's actual death, etc, etc.'

He looks up, smiling.

'Not proof of anything but at least we no longer look like imbeciles.'

Erik's body language expresses ruffled excitement, making Eva wants to laugh but she still has more to say.

Hearing about the old lady irks Erik.

'That mad Sami woman was nothing but trouble, we'll all get fired. The old case is closed and stays closed. Do you hear me?'

Eva's nod placates Erik and he states that Stockholm will be pleased; they'll not be sending up a hard-nosed team.

Leaving the office, Eva whispers to Ryan:

'You have something concrete now to tell your boss, hopefully this will last for months, and I...'

But she doesn't finish, leaving Ryan wondering if she's hoping for promotion. No chance of that for him. Suddenly, he wants a drink.

He invites her to the hotel; they could have a bite to eat and he a drink or two. She declines; there's all the paperwork to do, she says. Ryan heads off alone, exiting through the big glass doors into darkness, bitter wind and snow. Eva watches him disappear across the road.

In his room, Ryan too has paperwork. Knowing Stockholm will send full reports to Inspector Mace's superiors, he hurries through it: bullet points of his own excellence should keep that bastard off his back. He won't bother with anymore phone calls; so long as Erik's happy, there's nothing Mace can do. Ryan heads downstairs to find a friend at the bottom of a glass and hatch a plan. He's on his own agenda now.

Eva leaves the station at 8.pm. Having been given a new car, she sits with the engine running, studying herself in the rear view mirror. The long fraught day, starting with the car crash, shows in her drawn and tired face. Glassy eyed, she cautiously drives out the station car park towards home; but she's unable to switch off her thoughts. Ryan had triumphed today, so much so that the office hadn't stop talking about him. They had made a breakthrough: a probable murder weapon linking to another case. But that case is off limits, she had had her orders. What will Ryan do next? Intuitive and creative, he's also unpredictable.

As the wipers take away the snow, Eva peers down the narrow icy road trying hard to get him out her head.

17.

The Quality Resort Breakfast Bar, 8.15.am 9th January.

Last night hadn't gone to plan.

Instead of a solitary session of self medication, Ryan was spontaneously joined by Erik and a bunch of people from the station, most of whom he'd never seen before. They wanted to party. An absurdly premature party, Ryan thought: the case wasn't anywhere near being solved and probably never would. However, it quickly transpired that he had unwittingly saved their jobs. As the Swedes hit the bottle, Ryan kept his drinking modest: no need to overdo it, he told himself, he was on full display.

With a clear head, Ryan now watches snow through the windows of the breakfast bar.

Things would start slow and late today. Erik and his drinking pals would be worse for wear, giving Ryan time and space to try and comprehend the secrets of this case.

He had missed Eva last night. But before thoughts of her start to blunt his focus, he leaves the hotel. He already has a plan of sorts.

Cold air jars him. Ryan gasps, hurrying to his hire car. In the police car park, he passes Eva's damaged car. Seeing that the driver's door is bent and misaligned, he stops. In the dark, Ryan tries the door. It squeaks open. Pulling the boot release catch, he moves to the rear of the car and removes a pair of snow shoes.

Minutes later on the edge of Gallivare, Ryan stops for gas. Filling up the car, he deliberates his plan. If he's fast, he won't be missed.

It's not even a hunch, more a sense of curiosity that has him driving round the edges of the National Park. Although the old case is off limits, experience tells him the two cases are linked by something more than icicles, but if the Swedes find out he's poking about, he's sure to lose the job. They just won't find out, he confidently thinks.

It's light by the time he stops outside the old police post. Eva had forgotten to take the front door key back; it sits on his dashboard.

Using the snow shoes, he's soon at the door, turning the lock. The place still smells musty and feels oppressive. Wasting no time, Ryan uses the light from his mobile phone to illuminate the map. And there it is, an X that marks the cabin by a lake, somewhere behind the cackling Sami witch's place. How far is that? The map's hand drawn, nothing's to scale, but it can't be that far, he thinks. Who in their right mind would walk any distance in an arctic winter to go fishing?

Twenty minutes later he pulls up outside the Sami woman's wooden house. She's nowhere to be seen. Putting the snow shoes back on, he heads around the house. The wind is freezing and Ryan hopes that his journey will be quick. At the back of the house, she stands there, holding the cat. Still dressed in rags, she's barefoot and her toes are grimy black. Ryan stops. Before he can frame a thought, her gaze and finger point to the forest. Not risking another skittish outburst, he follows her direction to the trees. According to the map, her direction seems right.

How can she be barefoot in the snow? But as she's out of sight, she's quickly out of mind.

Enveloped by tall trees, he moves as quickly as he can. Even with snow shoes it's a slow and tiring plod; sinking and pulling up with every step. Ryan focuses on the task: if he pushes hard, he should be by the lake around midday. He hopes to find something useful there, and make a concrete link.

Stopping to catch his breath, he listens to the forest. Increasing gusts of wind disturb the silence and blow around the snow. Realising that snow's been falling all day, he turns, looking back the way he came. His tracks are still there, but for how much longer? He forges on. Even with Eva's husband's gear, he feels cold; stopping is not an option now.

Tree trunks turn black and the bright snow underfoot begins to dull. Ryan looks at his watch: one thirty. Having lost track of time and fearful of losing light, he decides to turn back.

The forest suddenly feels menacing and Ryan feels the need to flee. His tracks are faint and filled with snow. In the fading light, they're soon lost from view.

It must be this way, or is it over there? Lost, confused and, more urgently, in pain from cold, he desperately keeps on moving. Drawn to a steep bank, he scrambles up among the rocks and trees. There must be a view at the top, he thinks, but thinking's getting hard. Everything's becoming numb.

At the top of the bank, he stops, struggling for breath in the cold air. There is no view, only eerie silhouettes. He's in a clearing and looks across to the other side. Is that a cabin or a shack? He's not sure as the dark sky has given up the day. I need to be out of the wind, he mumbles to himself, and lurches forward, towards the other side. Soft snow gives way to hard ice. He's on a lake and instinct tells him to skirt around the edge. Faster on ice than snow, he feels a surge of energy. Where the edge of the lake meets some trees, he pauses and looks hard at the dark shape: yes, it's a small cabin, less than fifty meters away, he thinks. His mind's going foggy and his hands seizing up, but the confirmed sight of shelter spurs him on. The hard ice beneath him turns mushy. Looking down, he sees dark swirling patches and hears a wretched crack. He's on a running creek and the ice gives way.

Ryan's down and under, surfacing with a gasping cry. Grasping at the icy crust he tries to pull himself up and out, but the ice breaks and he slips back down. Frozen, he hears the sound of bubbles and sees only black. Then the doom of silence comes.

18.

Gallivare, 10.40.am 9th January.

Driving to work gives space, time to think and ponder on events. Reflecting off the white road, the morning light is harsh. Eva puts on her sunglasses and listens to the radio. She smiles when she learns it's minus forty one outside. Even her husband's gear won't cope with that temperature, especially as the wind now blows from the north east. That will keep Ryan indoors and out of trouble, although he's probably still asleep, waking up to a thick head. Erik had texted her last night telling her to come in late: there was a party at the hotel, a celebration for the breakthrough in the case.

The endless excuses to celebrate the dark winter months, is something she had learned to accept. There was no breakthrough in the case, just a possibility that Smith was wacked over the head with an icicle. It could never be proved, she was sure of that.

The police station is near empty. Besides the Smith case, which is Eva's only job in Gallivare, nothing much happens in the dead of winter: crime goes to sleep. She's usually away, working in Kiruna or Lulea at this time of year. A drunk driver in an overturned car in a snow filled ditch or some high-spirited kids booting a football down an icy urban street scaring a bored pedestrian, is the extent of it round here.

Having completed all the necessary paperwork last night, she's at a loss of what to do. There really is nothing to investigate, no leads to follow or questions to be asked. Smith's finances are in order; even the Russian's money seems to be legitimate. Maybe Ryan has a way forward, she's sure he does: he seems desperate to string this out and not go home.

Ryan's mobile doesn't ring and Eva walks over to the hotel. On arriving she's almost in shock from cold. Reception calls his room: no answer. Eva takes the lift to Ryan's floor and door. She knocks three times before calling out his name.

Hurrying through the police car park, she notices her battered police car's boot is half open. About to bang it shut, she sees an empty space: a pair of snow shoes is missing. And there she was, a little while ago imagining Gallivare as a winter crime free zone. They had been stolen. A present from her husband, the only useful thing he had ever given her, was gone. They were meant for Ryan; something hurts inside her.

Seething, she heads towards the main entrance, but stops. Ryan's hire car is also gone. The tyre marks in the snow tells her it left not so long ago. She just knows Ryan took the shoes.

Erik arrives but takes no interest in Eva's questions to where Ryan might have gone. She scowls: he's always disinterested after a drinking session. But she does learn that Ryan left the party early, and sober; he must have had a morning plan, she thinks.

Wherever he is, there's no mobile reception: the phone still won't ring. And, if he wants daylight, he'd be there by now. Smith's cabin or the old police post – where else does Ryan know? Smith's has no mobile reception but the old post must have some. Eva opts for Smith's cabin and drives to pick up gas. The cashier remembers Ryan, the only Englishman in town. She points to a newspaper on the counter. The headline reads: 'The Icicle Murder'. That's just plain wrong, there's no proof and who leaked it to the press anyway? The cashier points towards the main road out of town. That's not the way to Smith's cabin. Eva ruffles through her pockets. Where's the key? Had she left the key in Ryan's car?

Heading for the old police post, she turns on the car's blue lights. This has started to feel wrong.

Eva pulls up outside the old post. Although it's been snowing most of the day, she sees the vague outline of snow shoe tracks leading from the road up to the front door. So he's been here, she deduces. What for? Then it clicks: the map, the cabin by the lake. What's he going to find there after twenty three frozen winters?

The road is full of snow and it takes more than half an hour to reach the house; the plough won't be back 'til the morning. She parks behind Ryan's car. It's one thirty: she's almost lost the light.

Even in full winter attire, Eva feels the cold. She must find Ryan: he won't last long out there. She sees his tracks disappearing around the house. Full of snow, they're almost gone. Putting on her own snow shoes, she starts to follow what's left to see. A small gust of wind blows spindrift in her eyes and nose. She stops, sneezes and wipes away the snow to see the old woman standing in her way speaking a language Eva doesn't know. She's pointing to the tracks. Inside each of Ryan's large prints are others: a bare human footprint and what looks like a large dog. Eva suddenly feels terrified.

The woman then speaks in broken Swedish:

'There's nothing you can do, the Nightmare will choose.'

Before she faints, Eva sits down on the veranda bench. She feels the cat's tail swish across her face.

When she wakes, it's dark. Numb with cold, she drags herself off the bench. The front door is wide open. Stopping in the opening, she leans against the frame. Warmth from the wood burner draws her inside. The door slams shut behind her. The only light is from the wood burning stove. As Eva adjusts her eyes, the old lady commands her to sit. There are no chairs, just large cushions on the bare wood floor. Sitting down next to the old woman, Eva notices her black feet and smell like old milk mixed with fresh cut hay. Not speaking, Eva gazes through the burner glass, mesmerised by flames. She's so cold that it takes some time before she can take off her gloves and coat. Her mobile falls out. The signal is strong and she calls Erik.

'It's two o'clock in the morning Eva.'

'What, oh…'

Ryan would be dead by now.

Explaining the situation, she keeps any reference of the Sami woman to a minimum. Erik doesn't have much hope as the temperature is near minus forty five in Gallivare. It must be lower in the forest. A search and rescue team would be there in the morning, but morning still means darkness. Ryan might have found an old cabin to take shelter, but Eva knows he's only trying to be nice.

On the boat to Baku as they fled Iran, Eva's mother had sung poetry: beautiful words that wove mysterious tales. Eva had laughed, enjoying the distraction, especially when told that she would meet a man in a foreign land who would later fall into the freezing waters of a winter nightmare. Then, listening to that melody helped take away bad thoughts. Now, it's just plain frightening.

19.

The Wooden House, 10.15.am 10ᵗʰ January.

Cold, Eva wakes. The fire's out and the room full of sombre shadows. It must be near ten o'clock, she thinks. Breathing in, a weight on her chest feels uncomfortable. The cat sits staring at her before stretching out and scratching at her woollen jumper. Standing, it arches, turns around and displays herself right in Eva's face. Charming, Eva frowns, as the cat jumps down.

Arctic wind bites as she heads towards an outhouse she'd noticed by her car. Having left her coat and gloves, she's tight and pained by the time she's returning to the house. The old woman sits on the bench, still bare foot in rags. Eva hurries past and goes straight to the stove, opening the door to blow any embers that might be left. A glow of red and Eva stokes the fire.

The old woman is behind her offering a steaming bowl of food. In the other hand is a mug. Eva takes them and sits down by the fire. She can barely see in the gloomy light and doesn't understand the food she eats: a stew made of things unknown and a drink that tastes resentful.

The woman just stands and stares. Eva stares back while eating and drinking alien cuisine. She looks like a fairy tale witch. Superstition is not something Eva wants or needs; back home it meant believing in things you couldn't understand. She had her facts: Ryan had gone looking for a cabin by a lake to get some clues to connect to Smith's murder case. The old woman just lives here with a cat and has remarkably tough feet. That's all. Nightmares are just things that disturb your sleep, and she had slept very well last night.

Where's Ryan? As Eva feels the rise of fear, the woman's raspy voice says things Eva doesn't understand. The moment is broken by a helicopter passing overhead, and then by someone knocking at the door.

'Sorry we're late, got stuck and had to call the snow plough. Only this woman and her grandson's wood yard ever use this road.'

Erik explains that they had to break down the police post door. Olaf had confirmed that the lake Ryan had headed for was indeed the old murder site. But it's a day's walk without the snow; Ryan couldn't have covered even a third of the distance. Police skiers would make their way from here while others would be dropped by helicopter at the lake.

'Has she said anything?'

'I can't understand her.'

'It's a Sami language.'

Erik talks to the old woman who says a few words back.

'Twenty three year old trouble…she's barking mad.'

Erik and a dozen police officers ski into the shadows of the forest. A van with two officers sits outside the house co-ordinating the search. Eva spends her time between the van, her car to listen to the radio and the house where she warms up and drinks tea the colour of black tar.

It's late by the time everyone returns. They had found no trace of Ryan. More men will come tomorrow to broaden the search area, Erik says, before he and everybody heads off home.

Feeling no need to ask permission, Eva stays.

It's past midnight. Not having exchanged a word, the two women stare at the fire. Headlights illuminate the room, giving Eva hope that a rescue party has returned. On hearing noises, bangs and thumps, she heads outside with her coat and gloves.

There's no police search and rescue team, just a white pickup truck being unloaded of cut logs. The old woman's grandson walks past Eva without a glance. He's carrying two shopping bags of food. Eva stands at the open door staring in. The two are in conversation. He must speak Swedish, Eva thinks, blurting out a question:

'Where's Ryan?'

'At the bottom of the lake,' he replies.

'But there was no trace of him anywhere around the lake.'

Eva knows she sounds desperate.

They both stare at her. The sound of spitting wood from the fire fills up the room. She feels like screaming.

'Wrong lake.' Looking out the window, he points: 'It's dangerous, full of fast creeks and tiny lakes, that's where he went down.'

Not saying another word, he leaves. Eva hears the pickup start, reverse and turn before driving away.

How can he know Ryan broke through the ice? That's not possible. Back arched and fur on end, the cat is hissing at her. She turns and looks at the old woman who puts a finger to her lips. Woefully resigned and not wanting to hear things she doesn't understand, Eva stays quiet.

20.

The Lake, 11.am 11th January.

The lake is completely covered in snow, except for one small area of thick translucent ice: a self-evident and recent hole. Through it, the ominous murk of deep water shows.

Eva had pointed the way to Erik and his team. It turned out to be only five hundred metres from the old woman's house. She hadn't dared tell what the grandson said; she kept things simple and told a lie, saying the old woman had seen Ryan heading off that way.

The team is large. At least twenty five people had skied ahead of Eva. She followed in her snow shoes. Arriving, she saw the team spread out along the lakeside, all focused on one spot: the hole.

No one speaks. In the hush, she hears the wind swishing through the swaying trees. Battling the cold and holding back tears, Eva can't imagine a scene more solemn. It's obvious what had happened.

No one really knows what's next: divers in the lake perhaps? Eva alone knows what the grandson said, but all the others only guess. Is Ryan really at the bottom of the lake? Unsure of what to think or do, people start to look around. Someone points and shouts. Across the lake, leaning against the cabin door, is a huge icicle shaped like a bent finger. Some distance from the door, between two large hanging icicles, is a gaping space: an icicle is missing. The ice finger had been snapped off and deliberately placed against the door. Looking from the ice finger to the black hole in the lake, Eva spots a trail of disturbed snow. Something had been dragged from the lake to the cabin's front door.

21.

The Lake, 3.15.pm 9ᵗʰ January.

Retching and disgorging water full of icy lumps, Ryan flounders in the snow. Foggy and disorientated, he recalls empty darkness before rough hands yanked him to the surface. Someone had then slung him to the ground where he now lies.

As cold spikes every fibre in his body, he starts to uncontrollably shake.

Cabin by the Lake, 6.am 10ᵗʰ January.

Orange shadows flicker, something cracks and fizzes. An oppressive presence fills his space.

It's the growl that rekindles his senses. Ryan gulps for air, a huge inward gasp. Throwing off a blanket, he bolts upright in a state of panic. Breathing hard, he takes in his surroundings. Ignoring the wood burner and his clothes hanging on a lean-to branch, it's the massive dog, bearing teeth, that has his attention. A huge man, strong and powerful, stands next to the dog holding a piece of ice. More than a metre long and bent like a crooked finger, it's pointing straight at Ryan. In a dream like state, he tries to scream but nothing comes out. The man is speaking but Ryan can't hear him. Nothing makes sense. Then the dog lurches forward and bites Ryan on the hand.

The pain is real, the blood feels warm, oozing and dripping on the blanket. Forced to listen, Ryan can't understand a word. A rhythm and a rhyme keep turning round and round until he recognises the man's face as the suspect from the old case. Seemingly satisfied, the man stops speaking and leaves the cabin with the dog. Intense cold blasting through the open door has Ryan down on the hard board bench, pulling the scratchy blanket over his head.

The cabin rocks as the door bangs shut and Ryan shivers into sleep.

22.

The Lake, 11.15.am 11th January.

There's a dilemma. No one wants to cross the ice. Having seen the dreadful hole where the creek flows into the lake, the team don't want to risk the hundred metre crossing. The ice could be one metre thick or a mere centimetre; no one knows. The team, apprehensive, opt to skirt around the lake's long perimeter to get to the cabin.

They hit a snag: dropping out the lake into the forest is another creek, full of cracked and broken ice.

The Lake, 12.45.pm 11th January.

Eva stands shivering, her hood tied tight against the wind. It had seemed an age waiting for a chainsaw to be fetched from a vehicle parked by the old woman's wooden house. She now feels irritable, watching as a makeshift bridge is cut from nearby trees and laid across the creek.

It's tough keeping up with the skiers, but for some unknown reason Erik, at the lead, takes it slow. What's wrong with him? Eva fumes. He's wasting precious time.

Erik arrives at the cabin. Instead of forcing the door open, he starts taking photos with his phone. Furious, Eva barges past the police team and demands to know why he's not pushing at the door.

'I've never seen one this big,' he says, pointing at the finger.

'What…?'

How many has he seen? She eyes the grotesque weapon, its frozen crooked joint set in a ghastly smile. Erik can't fool Eva. She sees that he's scared stiff, delaying finding out what lies behind the door.

'Ryan,' she yells, before banging the wooden door with her clenched fists. The door swings open and the ice finger falls, breaking clean in two.

Cold air quickly fills the cabin. Half conscious, Ryan hears the yell, thump and cracking sound of ice. Under darkness of the covers, he curls into a ball. Not that dog and man again, he silently pleads.

The cabin's dark and Eva hovers in the doorway adjusting to the light. Recognising her husband's parka hanging on a branch, she says his name again, quietly this time.

He knows that word, it sounds familiar and the soft voice not foreboding. He tries to speak, to say that he is here, but nothing seems to work.

Eva pulls the blanket back. Facing her, eyes shut and curled up, she wonders if he's dead: ashen skin, cold to touch and a hand crusted in dry blood. As she kneels to see if there is any life, Erik enters, blocking out the light.

Eva turns and looks back at Erik. He moves into the cabin. On seeing Ryan's hand, the deep holes of the dog's incisors clearly visible, proclaims:

'He'd be better off dead at the bottom of the lake.'

Horrified and perplexed, Eva is transfixed.

'I told you not to mess. You've no idea...'

Without hesitation, Eva picks up half the ice finger lying on the floor. In one fast ferocious move, she's on her feet smashing it into Erik's face. With a crack, the finger shatters into flying shards of ice. Erik groans and stumbles back.

Back home, she'd hurt a man like this before: he'd pushed his luck too far.

Confused and concerned, Olaf and some men rush in. Erik barks an order and then leaves the cabin, nursing a bloody wound across his cheek.

She hears Erik tell the team that Ryan must have pulled himself out the icy water, valiantly crawling fifty freezing metres to the cabin; a remarkable feat in these conditions. That doesn't explain the ice finger or Erik's strange behaviour, Eva rages. No evidence has been collected or other ideas explored. Would she ever get to the bottom of this?

A medic arrives. A few minutes later, Ryan is on a stretcher, being carefully carried back towards the wooden house.

Aware of movement and his throbbing hand, he opens his eyes. Squinting in the harsh light, he briefly sees the lake. Recalling the taste of its peaty water in his mouth and throat, he starts to gag and shuts his eyes to make it stop. He hears a language he doesn't know and feels something softly touch his head. Then he feels a sharp pain in his arm.

The man and dog: this is all he remembers. Helpless, he falls back to oblivion.

When she knows he's alive, she doesn't show emotion. Stay strong, she tells herself, this is far from over: unprovoked, she had violently attacked her boss. She would have to deal with that later; for now, she needs to stick with Ryan. He's not safe, she feels.

23.

The Wooden House, 2.45.pm 11ᵗʰ January.

In the deep gloom of arctic twilight, they enter the clearing by the house. An ambulance had been called from the cabin, and Eva now sees faint blue flashing lights on the dark horizon. The saline drip in Ryan's arm had made the journey through the dusky forest slow and difficult. The team are packing up. It's a large crowd, gear is everywhere and their vehicles, jammed together down the road, are making space for the ambulance to pass.

Eva spots Erik talking to the old woman and her grandson. He's speaking Sami, she realises: of course he is – he is Sami! How could she be such a knucklehead? A large makeshift lint plaster covers one of his cheeks. Even in the dimness, she sees the dark spread of blood.

Although she knows she will probably lose her job, she won't back down and plead forgiveness. Ryan would be better dead than found alive, he'd said. What's wrong with that man and what's he hiding? Still enraged, she marches over, confronting Erik.

'What aren't you telling me?'

Erik stares but doesn't answer back. His frightened face tells Eva that he doesn't know what's going on. He might know facts, but not the truth. Realising this puzzle won't be solved by asking questions, she turns away to watch the ambulance arrive. As the door opens and Ryan placed inside, his wounded hand clearly shows.

'Nightmare,' the old woman gasps.

'What nightmare? Eva seethes.

The old woman lets out a deep raw cry, forcing Eva to hurry to the ambulance. Once inside, the closing door shuts the madness out.

24.

Kiruna Hospital, 11.00.am 15th January.

For three days now Eva's been visiting Ryan in his room. Each morning and afternoon she tells him things about her life back home, and other things she wouldn't dare if he were wide awake. Not regaining consciousness since briefly waking at the lake, she wonders if he ever will. Dehydrated and hypothermic, he'd been in a state of total shock. Considering the lethal low temperature, icy water of the lake and length of time spent inside a freezing cabin, it's a miracle he'd survived, the doctor said.

For the first two days, Erik had phoned twice a day. Initially demanding her return to Gallivare, she'd refused. He hadn't asked again and never mentioned the assault. Relieved, she'd then been foolish, asking awkward questions about the case. 'Call me if he wakes,' was all he said.

Eva had booked in at the Scandic Ferrum Hotel, a short walk from the hospital. She'd paid with Ryan's Swedish expense account. Angry, with scant regard for protocol, she'd even bought some new clothes. Right now, there's no chance of going back to Gallivare: it's feels risky, something's very wrong.

The doctor had told her that, although Ryan may not seem conscious, his hearing may still function: any words of comfort might help him wake up. Sitting across the room, she's telling tales from Iran. Ryan stirs, a slight movement of his head. Watchful, Eva keeps on talking. Making soft noises, he breathes out with a sigh. Instead of calling for a nurse, she calls his name.

That word again, is that me? It is me, and who's that voice. Ryan opens his eyes and stares blankly across the room.

'Ryan, it's Eva. I'm here.'

He knows that name. Almost inaudible, he answers back:

'Eva?'

She leaves to fetch a nurse.

Barred from the room as two doctors and a nurse attend Ryan, she calls Erik. He'll be there in two hours; he'll meet her at the hotel. Peering through glass at the movement in the room, she could do without a fraught and potentially explosive meeting with her boss right now.

Allowed back, she's self conscious. What if he heard all those things she'd said? He's very much awake and she sits close to him. For a short while, they don't speak.

The words the man had spoken in the cabin keep going round and round. As their vibration slowly starts to settle, Ryan tells his story. It's brief, there's not much he can remember.

'He was the same man in the photo-fit, hadn't aged a day.'

She stares out the window. Looking back at Ryan, hoping for a reasoned explanation, he's fallen asleep. This case is now ineffable, she fears.

25.

Scandic Ferrum Hotel Lobby, *1.00.pm 14th January.*

When Eva arrives, Erik's sitting on a sofa near the fire. Finishing a large glass of beer, he doesn't bother greeting her. He must have put his blue lights on to get here this fast, she derives. Not wanting to look him directly in the face, she stands watching the amber liquid drain from his glass. She listens to his gulps as a few drips of beer run down his chin, dropping onto the wooden table top. He no longer has a beard but she still doesn't dare look him in the face.

'Want to eat?'

Eva nods. Badly needing food, she sits down opposite and studies the menu.

'I'll put it on expenses along with everything else, won't be questioned; be assured of that.'

She knows he's looking directly at her but she still can't meet his gaze.

That's not like Erik, he's a stickler for detail: he's got something fishy up his sleeve, she's sure of that. What the hell is coming next? As Erik orders food and another beer, she finds the courage to look directly at his face. The plaster's new but still covers half his face. Without a beard, he looks formidable, young and strong and not the man she's used to seeing at the office every day. Above his cheekbone near his temple, Eva uncomfortably views the knotted end of stitching protruding from the plaster.

Feeling less on edge, she starts to settle. Sensing that, Erik takes a file from his case.

Reading out a lengthy report, he doesn't finish until the food arrives.

For the first time, Eva meets his gaze. Perplexed, she tries to comprehend what she's just heard.

'Ryan chased a suspect through the woods before falling through the ice?'

'We have a suspect, although he's now twenty three years older, and a possible murder weapon we think was used in both cases.'

'The Ice Finger?'

'Just like the one that broke off and whacked me in the face as I opened the cabin door.'

Now she knows he's really lying.

'I've recommended you for promotion and a medal. Ryan would have died without your vigilance.'

The bastard wanted Ryan dead and now he's trying to buy me off. What will Ryan think?'

Eva tries to tell Ryan's story but Erik shows no interest; in fact, he cuts in as she speaks, causing Eva to erupt:

'God damn you, you wanted him dead and have a report full of fabrication and downright lies!'

Unfazed, Erik puts his hands up, palms out, and shrugs, as if to say: okay, I'll listen if I must.

Eva knows he's heard the words but couldn't give a darn.

'Hallucinations, quite common in these extreme survival cases…this is the report Eva, Ryan's report. He can sign it later.'

Unable to fathom the confounding mysteries of the case, she says no more.

26.

Kiruna Hospital, *3.00.pm 14th January.*

Ryan is sitting up in bed looking at the two of them sitting across the room. There's a frosty silence, Ryan notices. Erik reads the report aloud and then shows Ryan a sketch of an older man, not recognisable at all.

'This is your photo-fit description.'

About to say he hadn't done photo-fit and besides, the man he'd seen looked exactly the same as in the original sketch, Erik continues:

'Inspector Mace is mighty pleased with you, spoke to him myself. There might be a promotion, rural Shropshire.'

Ryan almost laughs but he's feeling too strange for that.

'Chasing lost sheep, you mean.'

'I've been speaking to my boss. A lot of foreign money laundering is buying up resorts, paying off corrupt local officials. It's getting too much…a nightmare job. We could do with a man like you.'

Ryan doesn't say a word. Eva knows he's trying to buy Ryan off too.

'We could put you on salary, paperwork will take some time, three months or so, you could both do with a holiday.'

'He'll take it.'

Eva is up out of her seat, energised, and then Erik has the report in front of Ryan, handing over a pen for him to sign.

He just signs, knowing he has no life at home and the pack of lies written in the report is how it's got to be.

Ryan's hand itches.

'What happened to me?

But Erik's already leaving the room. Pausing, he turns:

'It's all in the report, you said it yourself.'

The door clicks shut and Eva is immediately up and over Ryan.

'I'm going to Baku, come with me.'

Her eyes are shining. He feels changed but a small part of him remains the same, the old Ryan. It's that part which speaks:

'Now you've got me spooked.'

MADE IN AMERICA

The summer breeze ceased to blow in from the ocean before them, leaving the evening balmy and still.

'It's a place where crime and police are the same thing.'

Danny stared out to sea from the wooden veranda and took a slow drink from the beer bottle he held loosely in his hand, whilst waiting for Chima to respond.

She too looked out into the dark calm behind the soft lapping waves on the sandy shore, and pondered the odd statement before asking:

'What's that supposed to mean?'

Without looking over to her sitting on the other end of the worn couch, he said:

'How many people are there in jail?'

'Here?'

'Right here in the land of the righteous and free.'

He turned and studied her looking at him, her legs crossed and her dress hanging down so low he could see no tantalising flesh. He wished he could, and she wished he'd stop trying.

'About two million – give or take.'

'How many people does that employ?'

'Police, judges, lawyers, prison staff and all?'

Danny nodded without looking over.

'That's a very big number.'

They were both beaming big smiles, her white teeth showing like faint pearls from the glimmer of the clear night sky, and his eyes speaking a mischief she just loved to hate.

'So what would happen if crime stopped?'

'They'd be an awful lot of people out of work – they'd have to make a whole heap of new, stupid laws just so people couldn't help but break them.'

'Just to keep their jobs, pay the rent, have a holiday…holidays dependent on crimes being committed; now that's a weird idea.

'This place needs crime – right?'

'Sure seems that way.'

'Criminals are doing society a favour.'

'Sacrificing their freedom, so others can earn a buck, be able to lie on a beach for a few weeks a year.'

'Saints and Martyrs!'

'How the hell did it become such a screwy mess?'

'It's a mess alright, and what the hell are you going to do about it?'

'Me?'

'Yes you!'

'Watch it burn!'

They both laughed loudly before swigging their beers.

After a minute's pause, both staring deeply and blankly towards the dark horizon with its passing ships, Danny casually remarked:

'Igbo Lita, now he did society many great favours.'

'Except, he never got caught.'

'Ah, but imagine how many people he kept in work as they chased him, searched under every stone until they gave up and attended to new work.'

'That was decent of him.'

'Ought to give him a medal, after all, he must have paid off so many mortgages, given so many a few weeks on the beach.'

'What happened to him?'

'Probably went south.'

'All criminals go south.'

'Must be a lot of crime down there.'

'Nah, with all that money they took with them – they're now lawyers and judges.'

'We could do with a good lawyer.'

They both eyed the bag of money sitting by the end of the couch, next to Chima.

'A good lawyer would know how to hide and wash all that swag.'

'Do you think Igbo's a respected banker by now?'

'Let's find out.'

Danny looked over at Chima just like before, and she quickly cut him dead.

'Go to hell – I'm your step sister.'

'Gina always lets me.'

'She's a wicked sister – twisted like you.'

'You're right of course. Maybe I'll go find her tonight.'

'Be my guest.'

With that, Danny left the veranda, dropping onto the sandy beach and turning around the house to the front. A minute later Chima heard the car start and drive away.

Danny and Gina had been at it since teenagers, probably before, but she only guessed at that. He had always tried it on with Chima, except he never actually touched her, just asked, always asking and she always telling him where to go. She blamed it on the devil, must have got into both of them for Danny to get into Gina and for her to let him and like it. Their mother never cared; she was always out – probably with her own brother or something. But it was the noise of the pair at it in the next room that was unbearable – all those sleepless nights with the devil doing his dirty work – and everyone wondering why she had flunked school!

Soon after dawn, the car arrived back and two doors slammed shut, waking Chima from a comfortable slumber. The soft murmurs of Danny and Gina, along with the smell of coffee, had her dressing and coming out into the kitchen.

'Hey Sis want some coffee?'

Chima sat at the table looking over at Gina. She smelt of sex.

'You're disgusting.'

Both Danny and Gina laughed.

Gina disappeared into the bathroom, and soon the shower was going at full pelt.

'When did you first know I was not your brother?'

'When I realised we were black and you were not! Mum used to tell us you were our special brother.'

'Gina knew I was just the kid next door living with you, like some kind of stray cat.'

'Tom cat.'

'Hey Gina, when were we first at it?' Danny yelled.

The shower had stopped and she shouted back:

'Down in the old wood shed behind the junk yard, I don't think we were even at school. Hey, whose idea was it?'

'Yours, twisted sister.'

'Yes twisted brother!'

As they cackled, Chima knew they were trying to rile her, but she couldn't help smiling.

'God I must have been a dumb ass – I even asked Mum why you were crying out like that.'

'What did she say?'

Gina was back from the shower wearing some of Chima's clothes, smirking and waiting for the answer she had heard a hundred times before.

'That the devil had got into you and that you were crying out to the Lord for salvation.'

The room erupted with laughter, even Chima enjoying the moment, before adding:

'But it was true!'

'So Sis, it's another screwy mess – what the hell you gonna do about it?'

'Watch you burn!'

They sat drinking coffee around the wooden table, the sea slowly brightening as the sun shone over the front of the house.

'Why couldn't we have an east facing house?'

'Because we wouldn't see *those* Californian sunsets, idiot!'

Chima broke the banter:

'The money – what are we going to do with the money? The police might come asking questions – we're meant to be poor remember.'

'Gina and me went down to the moorings last night – Old Man Toot told us Igbo stole a sailing boat about a month ago. Toot didn't know Igbo was still about, scared the hell out of him. Forced him to pick a decent yacht and they stole into the night – heading south of course.'

'But he can't even sail!'

'The old man said Igbo had a tough looking white guy with him – looked mean and nasty – he sailed the boat, had a gun too.' Gina answered.

'Let's follow him.'

'We can't sail either.'

'So we need a tough and mean looking white guy too.'

'Unlike your over-sexed brother here.'

'He has other talents.'

They all chuckled together again.

Down at the moorings, with its broken pontoons, abandoned boats and collapsing sheds, the few boats that still worked looked out of place, showing up new and bright against the ramshackle decay of the old fishing harbour.

Old Man Toot was in his shack working on an engine, ignoring them as they entered.

Danny spoke:

'We need a boat.'

Still without looking up, Toot replied:

'You too eh? I don't reckon you kids could even afford one of those half sunken wrecks hanging off the old pontoons.'

'And if we could – what then?'

'Then you better learn how to sail.'

'Show us a boat.'

Toot had always liked Chima, called her the sensible one of that clan – the family, or was it two families, that still lived in the old fishing houses after everyone else had upped and left.

'There's one in the dry dock – be ready for a long journey in about a weeks' time for forty thousand bucks.'

'Forty thousand!' They all exclaimed.

'Fifty if you want it kitted out with electronics and spares.'

Toot chuckled to himself and finally looked up at the kids, except he saw they weren't really kids anymore, and they had that look which said – we mean it.

'Fifty and it will get you round the cape and through the canal. I'll even buy it back off you – if you ever make it back that is!'

The boat was magnificent and standing under a large gantry. It looked finished and ready to go. They touched it, got on board, examined every detail and decided they wanted it.

Soon the threesome were back with Old Man Toot, Danny clutching the bag to his chest as Chima rummaged around inside counting the money out loud before thrusting it towards a shocked and pale Old Man Toot.

'Fifty thousand.'

Old Man Toot was nobody's fool, but it took a few moments before he had fathomed what was happening and how he should respond.

'Don't suppose I better be putting this in the bank?'

'Guess not, old man.'

Toot smiled – he wasn't really old but realised he looked ancient to these kids, who suddenly seemed very grown up.

'A week then – you want me to do all the paperwork, kit it out for you and all that?'

'Of course we do – what the hell do we know? Can you find us a boatman?' Chima answered, with Gina blurting out:

'We want to buy our house, well, both of our houses actually – who owns them?'

'The town – they've been trying to sell the harbour plot ever since the fishing collapsed.'

'So, why haven't they?' asked Gina.

Toot sat down on a threadbare chair and stared at the money in his hands.

'What have you kids been up to?'

'Went to the drive-in.'

'Shopping at the Mall.' Danny and Chima replied.

Toot smiled, knowing he'd better cut to the chase – might be a good thing, these kids with their bag of money.

'This is useless land, too soft for development and now useless as a harbour since the fishing collapsed and the new marina was built up coast – on top of that it is too shallow to get big boats in. No one wants this place – especially as you lot are sitting tenants on controlled rent.'

The three siblings looked confused.

'Are we?'

'They'd probably sell all one hundred acres for the price of a boat – give or take.'

'Can you buy it for us?'

Toot eyed the bag.

'If I can have a quarter of it – I'll buy it for you.'

The siblings got excited.

'Our own harbour!'

About a week later, Chima was sitting on the veranda looking out across a clear blue sea to the ships on the horizon. The day was calm and warm with only a few lazy white clouds occasionally blocking the sunshine. She was on the couch, day dreaming of sailing south, when a voice broke her trance.

'I'm Mark, Toot sent me.'

Chima looked up at a clean cut college kid, neatly dressed and inno-cent looking; not the tough looking white guy she had imagined – he was white alright, but there was nothing tough about him by any stretch of the imagination.

'Have you seen the boat yet?'

'The Igbo Lita?'

'They called it what?'

Chima was already up and walking fast along the shore towards the old wharf with the boy following.

They arrived at the dry dock to find Old Man Toot, Gina and Dan-ny in a heated conversation.

'But I've already registered it.'

'We never told you to call it that!'

Chima joined in:

'But what if someone gets suspicious?'

'Nobody knows him by that name – only us right here.'

'Danny's right – besides, he might spot it in one of those harbours down south and come find you.'

Chima nodded and pointed over to their new boatman.

'Meet Mark, our boatman.'

Gina studied him, looked him up and down, as the others knew she would, and asked:

'How old are you?'

'Twenty three, Miss.'

'Gina to you.'

'He's the same age as you Gina!' Danny bellowed.

'And you too Danny!'

Looking at Chima, Gina said:

'An older brother for you.'

'I'm Danny – these two are my sisters.'

Mark looked at the two girls and seemed confused.

'Complicated wildlife down here – you'll get used to it.'

Mark smiled at Danny's remark as Danny asked:

'How much?'

Mark looked at Toot and Toot spoke:

'Mark only wants expenses, he's looking for the experience.'

The three siblings looked at one another, and Chima said:

'What, no money?'

'No, it's a fantastic opportunity to be skipper of your boat. I hear you might even go through the canal.'

Danny wasted no time in convincing Mark otherwise and held out his hand, which Mark shook.

'How many rooms on board?' Chima quickly asked.

'One double and two single berths – so Danny, you and I will have to share or your sisters can,' Mark answered.

The three siblings burst out laughing and Toot looked away, slightly embarrassed.

Mark came by almost every day over the next week or so, arriving at the old port at around ten, parking his parents' car among the debris and long discarded junk that littered the quayside. A few of the old sheds that made up the small wharf were still in use by some die-hard fishermen who came less and less these days, but mostly everything was ruined and wrecked. Chima had got into the habit of being there when he arrived; she got the bug for boats and lapped up everything Mark told her, as Danny and Gina lay in bed, only turning up on the odd occasion to check on progress, and to make sure that the money was being well spent.

'Your brother and sister don't seem that interested in the boat!'

'It's not the boat, it's the journey that interests them – anyway we grew up with motor boats, fishing boats, so it's only the sail bit that they don't get. Danny's smart – you'll see.'

'And Gina? I mean is she smart too?'

'Oh sure, she'll out-smart you any day.'

Being poked by Chima embarrassed Mark. She saw it as he busied himself with the radar installation.

Chima was on deck looking up onto the wheelhouse roof where Mark sat connecting some terminals, as she broke his tension by asking:

'You want to go to the drive-in tonight?'

He didn't look at her, pretended indifference by nonchalantly asking in a mumble:

'What's on?'

'The old man and the sea – sorry, the grumpy old man and the sea.'

'Hey, I'm not grumpy!'

He looked down on her smiling face.

'Who cares what's on – makes a nice change. You got the car – got a girl?'

'No.'

He was embarrassed again.

'So no one to make jealous then – but don't get any ideas – where do you live?'

'Cedar Ranch – know it?'

'If we can't see it from the wharf then I guess not.'

'Two miles – right at the diner towards the hills – only one down there – I can pick you up around eight.'

'No, I'll see you at the house.'

Danny and Gina sat on the veranda watching Chima step lightly towards them.

'We're going to the drive-in tonight.'

Gina let out a long high cry:

'Halleluiah! You want to borrow some of my sexy drawers?'

'They're all in the back of Danny's car – it's disgusting!'

Chima left the pair laughing on the veranda as she went in to decide what to wear, but was soon out again with a pleading look to Gina.

'You got nothing to wear – is that it?'

Danny jumped up and left the house heading to the dry dock. Spotting Mark as he was making his way to the car, he yelled over:

'Hey Mark – hear you're going to the drive-in?'

Mark was caught out and embarrassed yet again.

'Should I have asked you if it was ok to take your sister out?'

'Hell no, Chima's the twisted one – she'll pounce before the interval!'

With Mark looking and feeling slightly troubled, Danny left and wandered into the small cabin that Toot called home.

'Got passports?'

'Sure – we always had those in case Gina and Chima's old man ever took us down to Mexico.'

'Did he?'

'No – all talk – that loser couldn't even catch fish properly.'

'That was the booze – they're well rid of him.'

'How come you're still around old man?'

'Got my life down here, everything I ever did is wrapped up in this place.'

It was almost dark when Chima passed through the wooden ranch gates and strolled down the long drive towards the imposing country house. The fading sunset behind her was still bright enough for her to see manicured lawns, a row of stables and some fancy cars in their full polished glory, before the shadows dulled and hid them as she knocked hard on the oak front door.

Mark answered; he was slightly dressed up, had shaved, combed his hair, his jeans looking new and pressed, his tight t-shirt clearly showing his half man half-boy torso. He looked pleased to see her, and she just stared as he looked out past her around the front of the house.

'Where's your car?

'I walked.'

'Walked? But this is America – no-one walks.'

Chima was wearing shorts, pale cream with a nice large green flower pattern, although Gina had tried to get her to wear a short skirt telling her that boys needed good and easy access at a drive-in. She wore sandals and a pink sweatshirt; her frizzy hair untouched as always.

Chima thought she must be the only girl in America to have a natural Afro these days. Gina spent hours getting rid of what was, to Chima at least, their greatest natural asset.

Mark took her through the large entrance hall with its grand sweeping staircase into a long room full of windows that ran the length of the side of the house; it had a bar, a pool table and lots of comfortable chairs and sofas. Before she could really take it all in, she was being introduced to his parents who reminded her of waxworks, so plastic looking and scrubbed clean that she found herself out of sorts and in a trance. She saw a moose head mounted on the wall and a TV screen so big that it seemed pointless going to the movies, and she wondered why she had never had a television. She came to when Mark nudged her saying:

'My parents want to know what you graduated in.'

Chima knew it was useless to pretend and answered in the only way she could:

'I kind of left school at twelve and worked on Pa's fishing boat down at the wharf after Mum left…that is until he upped and left too. Guess I was fourteen then, so I started working at the diner until they found out my age, and ever since I help my brother Danny look after the port, you know, the rubbish, fences – except the town hall never comes to look so we don't do much, just get paid to loaf around most days.'

The brief silence, which showed Chima she had shocked the lot of them, was broken by Mark's swift intervention:

'She's pulling your leg – this girl manages the whole port with her brother – amazing really considering the plug was nearly pulled on the place.'

On the way to the drive-in, Mark shook his head, beamed a huge grin and let out a sigh of relief.

'That was some story you concocted for my folks. Boy were they impressed by you – loved the humour.'

'It's all true.'

Mark was silent for a time before asking:

'Are you going to pounce on me before the interval?'

Chima laughed hard and loud and didn't stop, which made Mark laugh too, half out of nervousness but also because he just loved her humour, even if he didn't have a clue.

When they had settled down again, Chima looked at Mark and showed her teeth with her smile, saying:

'God, my face aches – I guess Danny or Gina told you that – right?'

'He did.'

'Just don't get any dirty ideas – ok?'

'OK – just like brother and sister then.'

Chima didn't say a thing to that, she just turned on the radio and hummed along to some old rock n roll song.

Mark dropped Chima off just after midnight; Danny and Gina sat in the front room curled up into one another, listening to the radio with the light off. A large waxing moon illuminated the couple, Danny looking ghostly white and Gina a shadow with bright gleaming eyes.

'Any action down there sister?'

'I wouldn't tell if there was – and why did you have to tell him I'd pounce?'

'I live in hope!'

'The film was boring – thanks for asking by the way! And it got me thinking – now we have a boat and are buying the wharf – what the hell do we need Igbo for?'

Danny pondered before replying:

'You're right, we don't need to find Igbo after all.'

Gina curtly cut in:

'So why are we going then, what for?'

'So, Chima and Mark can fall in love of course.'

'I hate you sometimes!' Chima yelled.

'No you don't – you love me – just don't know it yet!'

'That's like holding out for the Virgin Mary,' said Gina.

'She's not a virgin – there was that fumble with Igbo's brother on Halloween – remember?'

Danny burst out laughing as Chima stormed out. The couple soon heard the bedroom door slam shut.

'Ouch.'

'Hey Gina, do you think she really did it with Igbo's brother?'

'She wasn't drunk – Toot found her pinned up against an outside wall with her skirt hitched up and that bastard about to force it – Old Man Toot put his shotgun right up against that Nigga's head – we ain't never seen him since.'

'Why didn't you tell me?'

'Toot reckoned you'd only do something stupid.'

'What's it got to do with that old man?'

'Dunno, but he sure looks out for us ever since all our folks upped and left.'

'Weird eh?'

'After our Pa left he used to give me money for the shopping, right up until you left high school and started working around the wharf – did you know that?'

'I suppose so, but I never really knew who was supposed to be looking after us – we ain't normal Sis.'

'Quit lamenting – we going on a boat trip?'

'Never done it on a sail boat before.'

'Might take a lot of practice to get it right!'

'That's for sure – damn, I'd better make it up to Chima in the morning.'

Chima was watching the grey ocean slowly brighten up as the sun rose on the other side of the house; she had a blanket wrapped around her and held a steaming cup of coffee.

Danny spoke from inside the kitchen through the open door.

'Why doesn't our house face east?'

'Because we'd never see *those* Californian sunsets, idiot!'

Danny chuckled and Chima turned and saw him standing in the doorway.

'I'm sorry Sis, Gina told me last night about Igbo's brother and Old Man Toot.'

'Old Man Toot – I don't get that guy – I'm sure he was about to pull the trigger – for what?'

'Gina said he used to bang your Mum – is that right?'

'Maybe, we don't know for sure – all the same, he saved…'

'Your cherry.'

'I hate you sometimes.'

'No, you don't….'

'Has Toot asked about the money?'

'No, and he won't.'

'Good – now let's get that boat in the water today. Mark said it's ready.'

It took a lot of care and precision to hoist the boat out of the pit, across the wharf and into the deep channel by the old loading dock without scratching or knocking it, as it swung about as they moved the gantry across the wharf.

Before Toot had finished dropping the boat, a car drove down the long track and pulled up beside them. Igbo Lita got out from the passenger seat.

He looked desperate, scrawny and drawn, moving with nervous tension.

'Going south I hear.'

No one spoke.

'I know what you done and you better give some right now.'

He was menacing, and to make matters worse the tough white guy also got out of the car. He had a nasty scar across his forehead and had that look that only meant trouble. A handgun was stuffed into his belt, on display for all to see.

'I know you took that dead man's money – so where is it?'

Danny spoke:

'He was dead, stinking for days in that hole he called a home. Why didn't YOU take it?'

'He had a gun and I was in enough trouble – and how was I to know he was dead.'

Gina spoke:

'We got there first'

Igbo looked at Chima.

'My brother should have nailed you bitch.'

Toot walked away towards his cabin.

'Where're you going old man?'

'To get your money.'

The tough guy pulled his gun, saying:

'Where's the other guy?'

Mark had disappeared.

'So how much did the dead man have?'

'Nothing, he had nothing – we took the risk – it ain't your business.'

Gina helped Danny, adding:

'It weren't stealing – he had no family – the state would've taken the lot.'

Igbo sneered:

'I'll take the boat as well, as it's got my name on it.'

Toot came back with the bag.

'So, he had nothing eh – show me old man.'

Toot pulled a small shotgun out and had both barrels cocked and right up against Igbo's chest.

The tough white guy leveled the gun at Toot.

'You ain't got it in you, old man,' Igbo sneered.

'I have.'

Mark had returned with a handgun from the boat, pointing it at the tough. His hands were shaking and he found it hard to keep from squeezing the trigger.

'You said it would be easy, now we have two guns on us – let's quit – we got enough trouble.'

'They're pussies, shoot the old man.'

Mark couldn't control his hands and the gun went off, the bullet narrowly missing the tough guy and shattering the windscreen.

'He don't miss, so that was a warning.'

After saying that, Toot pulled the gun away from Igbo and unloaded one barrel into the side of the car, blowing a hole in the driver's door.

The tough lowered the gun and stuffed it into his belt.

'I'm gone.'

He slowly got into the car, aware that both guns were now on him.

Igbo followed, but before getting in, looked at Danny.

'You know he's your Daddy don't you – he used to bang your Mummy when your Pa was at sea.'

No one spoke.

'And he used to do your Ma too – that's why you are lighter than Chima and tall and thin like him.

Igbo turned away from Gina and got into the car. They all watched it reverse up the track to the road and quickly disappear.

Toot spoke:

'They won't be back – not now he's said that.'

However, no one cared about Igbo just then.

'Is it true, you're our old man and we really are brother and sister?'

Toot unloaded the unspent cartridge, put the shotgun in the bag again, and replied without looking at them as he returned to his cabin:

'Half brother and sister.'

'So that makes it half alright.'

Chima chuckled.

She went to Mark who was shaking like a leaf, took the gun out of his hand and laid it on the ground. She hugged him long and hard.

Danny and Gina stared at each other.

'Feel any different twisted sister?'

'No twisted brother.'

'Makes me feel even better – what about you?'

'I need reminding – got the time.'

'Now I can really say yuck!' Chima shrieked.

Sometime later, they all sat on the veranda watching the sun setting over the ocean.

Mark had recovered from his ordeal but still hadn't said a word to any of them.

Toot appeared along the beach to join them.

'Don't change a thing does it?'

'That all depends on one thing old man,' Gina replied.

'What's that?'

'Answering one simple question.'

Danny asked the question:

'Why doesn't the sun rise in the west and set in the east?'

Toot knew everything was going to be okay as he replied:

'Because we wouldn't see *those* Californian sunsets, idiot!'

They all laughed, except Mark who asked them all:

'Is there anything else I should know about you lot?'

'No twisted brother,' Chima replied.

#The National Sex Consensus Board

(Part One)

Published in Scarlet Leaf Review (Nov 2019)

The slow moving river sparkles here and there in the moonlight. Two men sit at a wooden slated table, staring out beyond the water into darkness, listening to the chorus of a hot summer night. Behind them, the house, flanked by an immaculate cut lawn. They drink whiskey watered down with copious amounts of soda.

'I'm telling you, we're not decent.'

'Speak for yourself, not for me.'

'If we were, you wouldn't need a front door lock, that terrible car alarm that shrills half the night scaring wildlife, or that rude light and camera peering over your manicured lawn.'

'That's not me being indecent…dam, I mean not-decent, it's all the others, anyway it's not manicured…'

They both laugh.

'Remember that girl?'

'Can't you just drop it – she slapped me round the face, so what?'

'Guess you're not so decent after all.'

'You know, hot summer night, few drinks, seemed right.'

'For you, soon fell apart when you grabbed her ass and kissed her lips hard. Look at the trouble it got you in.'

'Lost me my job, ended up at the station half the night. God it was embarrassing, had to say sorry a thousand times, beg forgiveness, blame it on the drink…and then move house. I just wanted her. Is that so indecent?

'It is now.'

'Trouble is, we don't have rules, real rules on the correct way to date.'

'We need laws to stop this indecency, otherwise I'll be forever moving house.'

They burst out laughing, pour another drink and raise a toast.

'The rules!'

'Let's take the boat into the swamp, might see fish spawning under moonlight. Grab the whiskey.'

At the end of the lawn, where the ground gently falls away to the water's edge, lies a wooden canoe. Moments later they are paddling through small vegetated channels under the canopy of tall trees. Here and there, moonlight cuts a beam and shimmers in the gentle ripples. The noise of insects, birds and frogs drowns the whispers.

'What was that?'

'Just saying that it's me and you who need to write the rules…for our own protection.'

'If it becomes law, we'll never have sex again!'

They laugh some more, passing the bottle between them.

'It will have to start with an interview – both interested parties.'

'How will they meet?'

'Not sure, something online, like a government app.'

'Then a blood and genetic test to make sure you don't have plague or related to Frankenstein.'

'References…'

'Do you think anyone will go through this twice? Imagine the stamina you'd need!'

'Of course it will cost, after which a date can be had.'

'A controlled meeting, maybe a drink or two, no more. Would there be a handler to make sure the rules are being followed?'

'Probably, then the next phase could be initiated after a feedback session.'

'Consent to go ahead.'

'Yeah, but no touching yet, that would come after a few more re-views.'

'So when do we get to have sex in all this?'

'Not sure, they'd have to be a meeting, a panel of experts, could take months.'

'Oh, you mean: The National Sex Consensus Board.'

'Hey, that's brilliant.'

'Who would go through with it? Who would actually ever end up having sex?'

'You know, these kids with all their apps, no real life, end up having sex through mobiles.'

'OK, here we are – see any fish?'

'No, they didn't pass the test. Maybe next year.'

#The National Sex Consensus Board

(Part Two)

It's tricky, this sex thing. I wonder if anyone's really doing it anymore. If not, that's a problem, because everyone out there, including you, comes from sex: good sex, bad sex, interesting sex, boring sex, abusive sex, gang rape – that's how we're all made, like it or not. What kind of sex made you? Do you know? Have you asked? Maybe you should, learn why you're the way you are, or not.

I wanted to have a date, you know the kind of boy girl thing where no one mentions sex but it's on everyone's mind. Normal stuff, you may say – but you just wait; these days, this is how it has to happen.

It's an App, of course. I found a nice looking girl with all the right box ticks and I guess she must have said the same about me. We both had to fill in a consent form and agree to the terms, for this date.

A few rules:

1. A meeting in a coffee shop, in public view and open to scrutiny.
2. No mention of sex or any flirting allowed.
3. Etc

We send off our consent forms and get a response to proceed. We meet. She looks pretty just like in her photo. Nice dress, makes her body look sexy. I want her now. Alas, I can't, there are the rules, so I pretend I am some sort of bore and ask dumb questions about her job and family. She does the same with me. I can't flirt, it runs the risk of incarceration, a month of correction therapy.

We have permission for a twenty-minute chat. After which, we have a discussion about the next phase, if we agree to a next phase, that is. Of course, this requires another form, filled in by the both of us. We agree to flirt but there can be no touching or any suggestion of sex, whatsoever. The forms sent off, we have permission to proceed for thirty minutes more.

We flirt. It's a body language thing, some laughter, a few mild innuendos. She goes to the bathroom and comes back wearing bright red lipstick. I love red lips. She does a twirl before sitting down, the dress rising, showing her legs. I could do a twirl but that would show me bursting out of my trousers and she may shriek. I don't want to run the risk of being dragged off, drugged and kept out of harm's way for six months or so. Is she feeling it? I daren't ask.

Thirty minutes is up. We now discuss if we want a third phase. By the way, there's no choice in all of this – these are the rules, like it or leave.

We agree, more forms, sent off and approved. It's coffee at her place. Now, that means coffee and chat, perhaps some more flirting, I'm not exactly sure. When we arrive, she reports in, all is going to plan, sorry, I mean to the rules.

We have coffee and some lesser type of flirting. Maybe she's unsure. There's another form to fill and send off. At last, we can kiss. No tongues and no fondling. We get ten minutes.

She's unsure but agrees to some kind of touching. It seems her bum is in limits but breasts completely off limits.

More forms, another permission.

She has to check in after five minutes. Her bum is nice, soft, not hard sinew like those over toned athlete types.

I'm going crazy.

She decides to remove her bra. I have to keep all my clothes on, even my shoes. This form is a long one. Her bra comes off, her dress still on but I'm not allowed to touch. Approved, we kiss, tongues this time.

We're still about ten forms away from being naked and then many more before sex.

I make my excuse; have to be at work early.

Back home, I feel exhausted. My flat mate looks at me and laughs.

'Been on a date…how many forms did you manage?'

'A few, left before I went crazy, did something stupid or fell asleep. Have you ever managed to get to the end and actually do it?'

'Don't have the stamina. Apparently it takes up to six hours to get all the paperwork done.'

'Exhausting – is it true, there was a time…?

'Still is…around the corner, next to the fried chicken shop, there's a red door. Knock twice, someone will answer. You get handed a menu. Everything has a price and a time limit. You choose, cash only…and forget that kissing stuff, it's just yucky. No forms, no prison and no review board.'

'Feeling hungry?

Tales from the Marsh
Part 1: The Flying Bass Man

The small fishing boat hit the drift net a hundred yards outside the harbour entrance. The motor whirred unhealthily and skipper Bronx cut the power before cursing and switching on the deck spotlight to assess the damage. The big drift boat came slowly towards them, its flashing orange light indicating work.

Bronx shouted over:

'You're not meant to net the harbour entrance and where the hell are your dan-marker lights?'

The two large men on the drift boat said nothing about that, one of them asking:

'Did you cut the rope?'

'No, but I'll have to cut the net out of the prop.'

Bronx pulled a knife from his overall and leant over the back of the boat to cut the nylon mesh twisted around the propeller. The drift boat turned about and Bronx turned to his mate sitting on the port side:

'Bastards must have thought all the boats would've have left by now.'

He knew he should report it to the harbour master but that was not what any of them ever did – they all broke the rules and he was no exception.

They had left Rye dock just after midnight, only just catching enough water before the receding tide left the harbour boats stranded on the mud until the next flood of tide. The harbour had been deserted as they slowly motored down the dark river with its shadows and silhouettes of old jetties and ramshackle pontoons where the cheap yachts were moored alongside long abandoned boat restoration projects; it looked more like a sorry junk yard than a working port. Past the skeletons of rotting boats lying high up on the muddy river bank, then the long coaster wharf with its mountains of unloaded ballast and piles of new timber, more old pontoons, and finally the Harbour Master's tower before the long, narrow channel that led out into the muddy bay. It was here, as Bronx opened up the throttle towards the black open sea, they hit the net.

After this small mishap, they slowly took Sato about a mile out, to drift with the tide until first light showed. They would then motor fast and fly across the rolling surf into the shipping lane where the bass lurked and the fishing was good. Sato was a seventeen-foot open deck Portuguese fishing boat, the kind you see in corny tourist posters of some idyllic Mediterranean scene, whose powerful outboard motor raised it up and planed it fast across the water.

Bronx wasn't much of a talker, said it broke his concentration; out here in the endless blue and green of the day, the hissing wind and lapping waves were company enough for him.

They looked out and waited for the day. As the stars faded and the eerie hue of twilight suggested the imminent break of day, first light showed as a gloomy cold white line on the horizon to the east, soon cutting through and chasing away the shadows of the night. This was dawn, and moments later the rising red fireball of a brand new day illuminated the sky, burning away the remains of the night until it was a glorious sun sitting on the edge of the world.

With a huge full sun hanging low over the sea, Bronx fired up the motor again and propelled Sato into the middle of the busy shipping lane where the soft light of morning rippled in the ebbing tide.

The work was always the same – they'd find an old shipwreck, of which there were hundreds in the Channel, drift over it with the tide, and fish for bass with live mackerel, which they'd have caught quickly and easily on the edge of the wreck. Depending on the speed of the tide and wind direction, the drift was usually over within five minutes and then Sato was taken up tide and the drift started over again. There was no telling when the bass would feed; sometimes things kicked off immediately and the bass were taking the bait in a frenzy, other times nothing and they had to change wrecks several times before any fish were landed.

The mate could see Bronx was distracted that day. Usually he had his eyes on his rod as well as the computer screen in the tiny cabin, showing the seabed and wreck. He also had an eye out for the huge tankers and cargo vessels bearing down on them. It was this part that unnerved them most; not falling in the sea, but being demolished by one of these monsters. Usually the big ships caught them on the radar or by the steely eyes of a Watchman, and the ships slightly changed course for avoidance. Frequently they were sandwiched between two colossal ships, so close you could see the buttons on a sailor's shirt. Occasionally a ship didn't make the change – Bronx always said if you can't see the sides of the ship as it bore down on you, it's on a collision course.

The mate had watched the ship for a while now, no sides showed, no whistle blew – perhaps no Watchman or they just didn't care.

'Hey Bronx, that boat's not changing course.'

Bronx looked back but didn't do a thing. A minute passed and the huge mass of cargo boat bore down on them.

'Bronx!'

Bronx cursed and fully opened the throttle, raising the front of the boat high as it flew through the surf, throwing the mate hard to the deck, as The Star of Panama cut the water not fifty feet away, sending a huge wake wave to batter them. Bronx waved a fist, but the bridge was too close and too high for them to notice.

'What is it with you today?'

Bronx said nothing and returned the boat to the top of the wreck to have another drift. It was only yesterday that Bronx seemed light at heart. They had talked, albeit briefly, about food and sushi. Before the mate knew what was happening, Bronx had a mackerel on the line, slapped it wriggling onto the cooler box, filleted one side clean off and dipped the fillet into the sea, cut into two, ate his part and gave the mate the other, which he ate although he didn't like the bloody taste it left in his mouth. Bronx then cut the other side off the still flapping mackerel and did the same before returning to his fishing duties as if nothing had happened. The mate threw the half skeleton in the sea, watched it spasm and mimic life, before a black headed gull dived in to finish it off for good in one huge greedy gulp. Anyway, that was Bronx.

The bass were now feeding and money being earned, when Bronx suddenly said to reel in as they were now going to head for Wreck 101.

'That ain't been fishing so well – what's wrong with here?'

'Just wanna give it a go.'

With that, they motored slowly up the Channel towards another ancient wreck, lying a hundred foot or so below the surface of the deep blue sea. The summer mist was rolling in from the west making visibility poor, and by the time Bronx cut the engine it was thick fog.

'Let's get out of the shipping lane.'

'Give it five and then we'll go,' Bronx replied.

He knew Bronx was acting odd, because usually they would have been heading towards the shore by now in these conditions.

The shadow of a small boat drifting near them was just visible through the fog, then it was gone and the sound of a chugging motor was just audible amongst the numerous foghorns the large ships were now blasting.

Bronx checked the GPS and steered slowly to a spot marked by a small bobbing orange buoy.

Keeping the boat steady, Bronx said:

'Pull it up.'

Hooking the buoy with a wooden gaff, the mate hauled it on board pulling the short rope up that lay underneath. On the end, a lobster pot with a blue dry bag was firmly stuffed inside. It lay on the deck and he looked at Bronx.

'What's this?'

'Nothing for you to worry about.'

'Sure there is.'

The mate pulled the bag from the pot.

'Don't touch that!'

Bronx looked furious.

'Screw you.'

Undoing the clips of the dry bag, the mate emptied the contents on the deck.

Looking down in disbelief, he studied the gems, mainly diamonds, spread across the deck.

'I told you not to open the bag.'

'Where are these from?'

'Best you don't know – put 'em back.'

'And then what?'

'Deliver them.'

'You shouldn't have taken me out today.'

'It makes it look normal – the two of us fishing – now you've spoiled it'

'What did you expect – me not to look in the bag?'

'You'll get some cash.'

'Better do, I'm pretty pissed right now.'

He knew the fishing had been lousy recently and making ends meet for Bronx meant a lot of long hours at sea – but smuggling? That's not what he had signed up for, but, besides throwing the gems overboard, he was at a loss at what to do, and nothing could be done until they touched dry land.

Without any more words being exchanged, they headed back to the harbour. The mate had scooped up the gems and secured the dry bag again before tidying up the boat as was normal on a return trip.

The fog was clearing, and only a few wisps of sea mist remained to be burnt off by the late morning sun. They could see the point jutting out with its dead looking, grey block power station and the vast empty shingle banks sweeping back towards the harbour. Huge white wind turbines turned lazily in the breeze showing strongly against the light blue sky, just before the sandy dunes joined the shored up channel of the river mouth. Just past the choppy sea of the inner bay where the strong current of the incoming tide pulls up towards the point, Sato entered the muddy swirling water of the narrow channel and Bronx cut the motor to six knots. The trawler boats were leaving on the flood, the crews waving at Bronx as they passed close by with the occasional greeting shout.

Bronx had hidden the dry bag in a locked cabin drawer. They proceeded on as normal, delivering the bass to the harbour fish market, a stone's throw away from their pontoon. Bronx collected the dry bag, threw it into the boot of the car, and the two men drove away, the mate badly wanting to be dropped off at his usual spot, never to return to the adventures of Sato.

Bronx spoke:

'No one knows you down the harbour, you're just a face with no name – I don't even know your last name – if this goes wrong you gotta lie low until it blows over.'

'What the hell are you talking about?'

Bronx seemed nervous.

'Just see this out and I'll see you alright.'

'See what out? Just give me some cash and drop me off – we don't have to do this again.'

'I'll pay you five grand.'

The mate hesitated.

'Five grand, for what?'

'Just come with me today– something don't feel right.'

'You done this before?'

'A few.'

'Jesus, what's different about today?'

'If you don't know then you can't tell.'

'Just drop me off.'

'Ten grand.'

'To get killed or banged up?'

'Fifteen, today in cash.'

'No one pays that sort of money.'

'I promise – in two hours you'll have it and that can be that.'

The mate said nothing more, he would go along with it and hope for the payout – Bronx had been pretty good like that when it came to the fishing.

They headed inland, turning away from the small town and into the marsh, passing the old sandstone sea cliffs that ran alongside the river. They crossed the river and followed the canal to the Isle of Oxney, which had once been surrounded by sea, but now stood high and proud in the endless green of the marsh. Bronx turned here and drove to the top, where the views were magnificent. On the way down the other side, he indicated another island, very small and gentle, jutting out of the flat landscape; it was a smooth mound, much lower and smaller than the one they were crossing.

The mate knew this place – Chapel Bank – an old graveyard on a mound that the Vikings used to row to. Now it was some kind of amazing secret spot, lost and hidden in the nothingness of the marsh, with its ditches and dykes. The local church still did the occasional burial and once a year hosted a small pilgrimage to the top.

They stopped by a farm. A few old wrecked lorries lay about; small shrubs and trees grew through them.

Bronx got the dry bag from the boot and they walked in silence towards the mound along a chalky track. It was too late to complain or change a thing now and the mate hoped all this would soon pass like a bad dream, where everything was just fine once you had woken up.

The few trees at the top of the mound swayed gently in the breeze as they passed between two ditches full of water, before veering off up through the bright yellow rape fields, which surrounded the entire mound with their sweet smells and endless insects.

Near the top where the rape gave way to long grass and nettles, the first indication that something was up showed – a helicopter whirring in the distance.

Bronx stopped briefly and then continued, but immediately stopped again, saying:

'Find the tomb opposite the yellow stone and drop the bag in and take whatever is there.'

'What about you?'

'I'll watch out.'

The mate hurried to the top where the mound levelled off. Old dilapidated gravestones littered the top. Some tombs had trees growing right out of them, but one stone was painted bright shocking yellow. He had no time to ponder this, looked opposite and saw a tomb behind some ancient rectangular metal fencing, hidden amongst some trees. He dashed to it, heard Bronx curse, and quickly pushed the flat top stone to one side; inside he saw a holdall in the shadows, grabbed it, threw in the dry bag and shut the top again.

Bronx had seen a police car down by the farm coming up the chalky track, and then another at the Ferry Inn straight below across the marsh by the old drainage sewer.

Bronx arrived quickly, he looked ashen and slightly out of breath from his run to the top. He took the holdall whilst urgently hissing:

'Quick – police!'

The mate hesitated, but Bronx grabbed his arm and they speedily headed to the other side of the mound. They could see the sewer as it wound its way around the mound, another farm and a church, but also more police below and some kind of village fete in a field near the lane with scores of people everywhere. They dived into the rape and crawled downhill hoping the helicopter, which was now somewhere above, hadn't spotted them. They heard dogs and desperately tried to increase their speed whilst scrabbling and scuttling to get below and into some good cover.

The dogs appeared, went straight for Bronx, pulling him down. As he tried to fight back, he dropped the holdall. The mate scrambled back to help but there were shouts nearby, so he grabbed the holdall, leaving Bronx to his fate, and hastily headed down the hill to where the rape petered out. He looked out and across a short piece of open grassland over which lay a ditch. If he could use the ditches then the dogs wouldn't get a scent, but it left him exposed to the heat sensor of the helicopter. The whirr was away slightly to one side and he made a dash across the grass, keeping low. Soon he was shoulder deep in water. Squeezing the holdall with one arm tight against himself, he submerged completely as the helicopter sounded close again. He held on to the weeds, keeping himself down until, gasping for breath, he surfaced, panting as he watched the helicopter move away towards the north, where the sewer wound its way around the mound.

He knew they weren't stupid, knew that they knew he hadn't gone far – couldn't have gone far – and would limit their search to the immediate area whilst cordoning off all the roads.

He thought fast as he snaked through the shallow water towards the people that he had seen from the top of the mound. Cows were on the banks and some were even lolling in the ditch; this was his chance; the dogs were barking in the rape and, as the helicopter came back high, he crawled out of the ditch and hunched up in the reeds amongst the inquisitive cows. No way would they spot him with the sensor amongst this lot. He was right, and as soon as they had passed overhead, he again made a dash, heading towards the Isle of Oxney. Soon he was travelling along the hedgerows up towards the top. If the helicopter came by, he got inside a hedge or under anything that would shield his heat.

It was late afternoon, the sun still hot and the sky still when he finally got off the isle and back onto the marsh.

He wondered if Bronx had been right – no one knew him at the harbour. As long as Bronx kept quiet, he ought to be ok, but then Bronx didn't even know where he lived or who he really was – just an early morning pick-up on the edge of town. He had got the job by asking around the boats. It had all seemed so casual and easy, but now it seemed crazy and on a knife-edge – would he be lucky and the trail go cold?

The rest of the overland hike went without a hitch and after a few hours, he was home.

Emptying the bag on the kitchen table, he couldn't believe the amount – all in Euros, looking used and still soaking wet. Bronx was in much deeper than he thought.

The local news had the incident covered in some detail, it was an exciting story – they had recovered the gems, had the ringleader behind bars and were looking for an accomplice whose identity was unknown. Apparently, there was a dirty trail from Africa to Moscow, across Europe to here – some bad things had happened and some bad people were involved.

He learned Bronx was not his real name, In fact, the name Bronx was never even mentioned – so who the hell was he and why the hell had he got the mate involved?

His pondering was short lived and quickly broken by a gentle knock, which set him panicking, but on recognising familiar features through the netted window, he soon calmed and went over to the door.

He left the bag and contents sprawled out across the table and some of it on the floor.

A pretty, smiling face greeted him, full of excited gushing fervour:

'Did you hear all about the palaver at the port?'

He came out onto the driveway, closing the door behind him, saying:

'Sure – it's all over the news.'

It was a marvelous still evening with a slight breeze, refreshing here inland, but which he knew would be strong at sea, making peaks and troughs and the going rough – but that stuff was all over now, he wouldn't be going out there again in a hurry.

He tried to smile, hoping it would somehow be convincing.

'Did Bronx know that guy?'

'Don't think so – but as I told you – that guy doesn't say much about anything.'

And right there and then he knew Bronx or whatever his name was wouldn't be saying a thing about him or anything else.

'Did the police ask you anything?'

'No – we were gone by then – you know, it's best not to mention my working down the port.'

'Why not?'

'Well, I get paid cash – don't want any questions asked – could mean trouble. After all, we're trying to save up.'

'Oh, suppose you're right.'

He was still in a bit of a fix with her and needed something extra.

'Do you want to go to France this weekend?'

She beamed hopefully:

'Can we afford it?'

'Had a good haul.'

She threw her arms around him and kissed him.

'I'd love to.'

He had to get her away from the house, so added:

'Come on – let's go to the country and have a drink and get something to eat.'

As they made towards the car, he said:

'Be nice to buy a boat – you know down on the Med somewhere.'

'You'll need more than a few good hauls for that!'

TALES FROM THE MARSH

PART 2: THE DESECRATION OF CHAPEL BANK

'**C**hicken.'

'Not – it's just stupid.'

'Chicken!'

Jenny held onto the hem of her skirt with both hands and twirled, dancing around the dusty farmyard chanting and goading Johnny, who sat in the shade on an old straw bale that was holding the large swinging barn door open.

He was flummoxed. Jenny had this way of making him feel bad about not doing something, even when he knew it was her just being her usual mischievous self.

'Well, I'm not doing it and that's that.'

She stopped herself in mid spin and said:

'You can have a peek.'

She lifted her skirt so he caught a fleeting glimpse before pulling her hands back down quickly, shutting off the view.

She knew he liked it, had learned to get her own way with him like that ever since she caught him staring goggled-eyed one day as she sat showing all, albeit accidently, at the village fete. She had felt embarrassed then, but smiled at him before getting up and hence out of her predicament, and saw him grinning back. She had been twelve then and now, two years later, she was still smiling and he was still grinning right on back.

'I'm still not doing it – you can't get me like that this time.'

Jenny smiled widely showing her metal brace and half whispered as she turned and skipped towards the dark interior of the barn:

'I'll show you more.'

'It won't work you know – no way am I doing it.'

But before the words had finished leaving his mouth, he was following her into the cool shade.

A silent moment in a new landscape, she grabbed the moment, twirling like before, but this time had her skirt held high in her hands as she loudly hummed a tune. He just grinned and stared, and lapped up this show for his eyes only.

He very nearly cracked but just managed to hold on, saying confidently:

'I'm not doing it.'

She stopped and faced him, hands and skirt still held high, coyly smiling and saying softly:

'Do it and I'll dance like this with nothing underneath.'

He cracked, exclaiming excitedly:

'You're on! – now promise me.'

'Oh, it'll be so much fun Johnny – we'll show them – won't we?'

'Yes, and you'll show me right?'

'Oh yes Johnny – everything.'

She dropped her hands and twirled some more, humming the same tune which Johnny knew to be her favourite song.

She grabbed his hand and pulled him out into the bright sunlight of the summer's day. She was gay, happy that they were about to get revenge, some kind of sweet payback against those beastly Slaters down the road by the pumping station. She never thought much about her promise to Johnny, who could now think of nothing else at all.

'It's nearly lunch time, we'll have to be quick.'

She grabbed his hand again, leading him urgently through the open farm gate and down the narrow lane, to where some highwaymen were painting yellow lines on the road right next to the footpath, which led up the mound of Chapel Bank. The men were about to break for lunch. Jenny pulled Johnny into a gap in the hedgerow where they wouldn't be seen and where they could safely wait until the road was clear. Squatting down, they peered through the twigs and dark shaded foliage at the men packing up and preparing to go. He could feel her breath warm and close and, as she looked him in the eyes, smiling and squeezing his hand, he sensed her daring and excitement at what was about to happen next.

As soon as the car door slammed shut, she was up and through the hedge. Johnny had remained behind, watching her enthusiastically dash and swipe a small pot of yellow highway paint and brush, before running back to his side so fast that the car had barely driven up the road. She was giggling with delight, and without a word, they turned and looked up at the mound with its few scant trees on top and magnificent fields of rape sweeping down to where they stood.

With no time to spare, they hurried up through the warm bright yellow fields, avoiding the footpath so as not to be noticed. After about fifteen minutes, they arrived at the top, sweaty and panting for breath. It was deserted and silent around the old dilapidated tombs and gravestones, which had quietly sat for hundreds of years on this tiny island gently protruding from the endless flat fields and still water of the marsh.

It was too hot for anyone to be out and they both set about the task with speed. Johnny went and kept lookout, scanning the landscape across the rape, down to his father's farm and village church right next to where the men had broken for lunch. Jenny's house stood opposite the farm, behind some old, fine looking cedar trees near a large stone house, which sat back from the road near the pumping station. This was where the Slaters lived with their oodles of unused land, pots of money and antique car collection.

Jenny had made a bee line to a large stone, standing more than four feet tall with the name SLATER just showing amongst the crinkly lichen with the date of seventeen hundred and something barely visible below.

With spiteful glee, she started painting the stone yellow, trying not to miss a spot; when she was half done, she whispered to Johnny on the lookout.

'Psst…your turn.'

They changed roles, with Johnny furiously splashing on the paint to finish this daft idea of Jenny's and to secure his twirling dancing show.

By the time he had finished, his hands were covered in paint. Jenny was standing by his side, marvelling at their magnificent piece of sweet revenge. She made a squealing noise and momentarily tensed her body with excitement and satisfaction. Johnny marvelled too – they had done it and there was no going back now, and he stared at the brilliant luminescence shining like a beacon to the stars amongst the drab stones and dull foliage on the mound.

'We've really done it now.'

'Oh yes Johnny – I can't wait. Can't wait for them to see it – that'll teach them, won't it?'

Johnny felt nervous now and just said:

'We'd better go.'

The pair hurriedly left the top of the mound. By the time they were being bathed in sunshine and losing themselves in the rape, they burst out laughing, splitting their sides and rolling about on the dry hard mud ground. It was a few minutes before they were able to carry on down the hill, both still giggling and talking incessantly about how old Ma Slater would shriek as if she'd seen a ghost the next time she went up the mound.

At the bottom of the hill, where the rape petered out and the field joined the road by the hedge, they both stopped dead in their tracks.

They had forgotten the paint.

'You used it last.'

'It was your idea, not mine.'

They bickered for a few moments, blaming each other for leaving the pot and brush behind when the men returned, quickly silencing them both. Jenny looked helplessly at Johnny who took her hand and led them alongside the hedgerow, past the gap in the hedge, and along to where the footpath stile crossed the road near the farm. He speedily led them through the open gate and towards the barn where she pulled her hand free and stopped before going inside.

'I'm not doing it, I've changed my mind.'

'You promised me.'

'That was before you left the paint behind.'

'I didn't – we both left it behind.'

'Now there'll be trouble.'

'No more than if we had returned the paint.'

'They'll know it wasn't the highwaymen but someone close by.'

'They won't know anything – come on Jenny.'

'No Johnny, it's not right – I'm not doing it.'

'That's not fair.'

'You didn't really think I'd do THAT did you?'

'And you really didn't think I'd do THAT for nothing do you?'

He pointed up to the mound.

'Those Slaters have spoiled it for everyone – for you too Johnny.'

He knew she was right, those Slaters had ruined everything for the whole village and he was glad they had done it, but he still wanted his promise.

But before he could say another thing, she had turned and left the farmyard, stomping up the lane, passing the men who were looking around for a missing pot of paint, towards the cedar trees of home.

Johnny felt angry, seething that he had been tricked and was probably now going to get into big trouble, maybe be grounded for the whole summer. He'd noticed that the paint on his hands was very visible and went to the yard tap to rinse and scrub them with the old brush, which they used for cleaning boots. Nothing budged and he knew he was really in trouble now.

He would tell them everything – that it was her idea and she had promised him...but he couldn't say that, and, no matter how angry he felt he couldn't stop thinking about her.

Damn her.

Jenny arrived back home and sat in a garden chair next to her mother, who was chopping apples on the outside table for the pies she was making for the village fete, except the fete was not going to be happening this year. Those beastly Slaters had refused the use of their nice ample unused land. They had fallen out with Johnny's father over the noise of the animals and the smell of the silage, dung and whatever else they could complain about, because Johnny's father had complained about the roar of their antique cars around the lanes being dangerous and scaring all his livestock.

Damn those Slaters.

Jenny's mum lived in hope that all these small-minded people would learn to get on and she could sell her pies and cakes to raise money for the church.

As Jenny sat there chatting away about mundane things and helping her mother with the preparation, she regretted falling out with Johnny, and tried not to think about her promise which she now felt so confused about.

The trouble came sooner than later. In fact, it was that very same day that an almighty shriek reverberated across the dusky sky, breaking the early evening peace around the village and sending the rooks cawing and flying up from their tree top roosts.

Jenny and Johnny silently understood what had happened, as half the village tore up the mound to find some furious Slaters ranting and raving about devil worship and insult and that there would be hell to pay for this. Both Jenny and Johnny had decided to stay indoors and away from the furore, feigning indifference as people their age could. They later learned that some villagers had laughed at the yellow day-glo, while others were perplexed, the vicar was upset and overall it was an eventful evening, which kept the village gossip fuelled for many months.

However, Johnny's mother had already seen his yellow paint stained hands and was now in the farmyard, talking to his father who had returned from the fields for the day. She held her hands against her hips, meaning she meant business, but Johnny soon saw his father smile, nod and look up at the mound, shaking his head in total disbelief.

It was only after his father had looked at the Slater stone himself that he came and found Johnny sitting sheepishly in front of the television pretending to be watching some programme.

His father asked if he wanted to drive down to the harbour and watch the boats from the grassy banks opposite the moorings coming in with the rising tide. He'd imagined a long lecture before being grounded for the entire summer and having to apologise and grovel to the Slaters in some public humiliating ceremony. This offer of one of his favourite trips was mind-boggling. He wondered if it was some sort of trap to get him to confess everything, even Jenny's promise.

His mother joined them on the trip. As soon as they had driven out of the village, his dad said that getting paint on his hands had been a really dumb thing and did that Jenny girl have anything to do with it as she was a bad influence on him. He had better give her a break for a while, let this all settle down a bit, at least until the paint had washed off and he could go out in public again. He then laughed, much to Johnny's shock, who looked towards his mother sitting beside his father, and she too was smiling. Then all three of them were howling with laughter, with Johnny's dad exclaiming that he wished he'd thought of it himself.

They ate fish and chips sitting on the grassy bank as the boats returned quietly from the sea with the lapping tide. Watching the fishermen unload their catches on the small commercial dock, Johnny felt a power, some kind of self-sufficiency with what he had done. He knew he would have to keep it secret, knew it was Jenny's idea, that she had tricked him into it with the irresistible lure of that promise, but he had nevertheless done it, and there was no doubt or going back on that.

He stayed inside the house and around the farmyard for a few days, hiding his hands until the paint had all disappeared, waiting for the heat from the incensed Slaters to cool off a bit. The highwaymen had been grilled about the incident as the paint pot had obviously been found on top of the mound. They had threatened to go on strike and boycott further work around the village, so questions were asked of others and soon the trail went icy cold. The Slaters, who still suspected half the village, were left clueless and without a hunch. Even the police were of no help, saying it was a local issue that was best resolved amongst themselves.

Jenny had not seen Johnny for about a week, not even in passing, and she put him and the entire incident to the back of her mind. There was not going to be a village fete that year and she and her whole family, along with the entire village except for the Slaters, were utterly disappointed. Even the yellow painted stone was of little consolation for her – the fete, which she had been to every summer of her life, was not happening that year. The villagers held a meeting in the hall and it was agreed that one of Johnny's father's fields at the far end of the village, where the water meadows started, would be dry enough in high summer to hold the fete next year. There was a big cheer and many of the men went off to the pub to celebrate. She'd seen Johnny across the crowded room but they never spoke; in fact, it was a whole year before they were to speak again.

It was at the fete the following year that they met again. Down the lane, at the end of the village where the lush water meadows began, there was a commotion. A helicopter buzzed overhead as a score of police searched the lanes and rape, their dogs furiously barking somewhere out of sight. Jenny learned that two gem smuggling fishermen, who had stashed their swag at the top of Chapel Bank, were on the run. During this distraction, which took most villagers towards the hedge by the lane at the bottom of the mound where they could easily watch the spectacle, Johnny found himself standing next to her.

'Do you think they've seen Slater yellow yet?'

'Stop it Johnny.'

'Fun though, wasn't it?'

She looked at him carefully; it was the same old Johnny, handsome and full of life and turning into a man.

She smiled and said:

'Fantastic fun.'

She was older too, and had grown like a young woman does.

He continued:

'My parents saw my yellow hands.'

'What happened?'

'Nothing – my dad thought it was a great laugh.'

'Oh, he would.'

'What's that supposed to mean?'

'Fickle like you.'

'Me fickle? Look at you!'

'Stop it Johnny.'

'You owe me a promise'

'Don't.'

'We had such fun – you never minded then.'

'It went too far that day.'

'Not far enough!'

They both laughed, and Johnny blurted out:

'If you were my girlfriend would you twirl like before?'

Jenny went ashen.

'What are you talking about?'

He felt sure now.

'If we were friends like before, but you were my girlfriend…'

'I don't understand.'

But she did understand alright and felt things move inside her. She was suddenly wanting him to say more, but as she couldn't twirl just then as she used to, to make him do as she asked, she was stuck.

He couldn't say it again, so she said it:

'Twirl and things?'

'Yes.'

He paused and then finished.

'Yes, if you were my girlfriend, I mean….do you want to be my girlfriend?'

As the police brought down a handcuffed gem thief to the lane, Johnny and Jenny were kissing somewhere in the hedgerow.

YELLOW GRAVE STONE ON CHAPEL BANK

THE GOOD LIARS

'The trouble is, good liars are just that – good liars!'

Now that made Kay ponder and there was a short silence between them.

It had been one of those mundane chats about some romantic deceit in a trashy novel they had both read, and before the silence became too long, she left the flat and her flat mate, to amble across the hot, still and empty square to a table outside a cafe, under the shade of an old and faded awning.

Even on a still day like this, the square's impressive palm fronds somehow managed to catch a subtle breeze and sway a little, as if to say: we are the only midday life here. And they were right; every living thing had retreated into deep cool recesses and were nowhere to be seen, except for Kay and a reluctant waiter who had shown himself only for her brief and usual order.

Her habit had been the same every day for nearly a month now; a couple of hours of quiet solitude in a still and empty square, where she could write productively in peace.

Well, that had been the plan at least, but, as she looked out across the bright square to where her flat sat a couple of storeys above the stone facade of an old bank, lost in deep shadow, she knew it wasn't working at all; in fact, it was pretty much a disaster. Sure, she had a story, a good story. It was all there, no problem with that – it would probably sell, well-done old girl and all that nonsense that had once flattered, but now seemed such boring rubbish.

Fuck it – novel number three by numbers by a predictable boring formula; yes, what boredom it had become. Where was the excitement she first felt putting pen to paper. How old fashioned is that – pen to paper and not finger to touch screen.

She slammed her pencil hard down on the table, the brief thud momentarily cutting through the stillness of the day before it fell onto the stone slabs below, rolling to a stop a few feet away.

With her writing tool lying slightly out of reach, and now feeling quite lazy from the midday heat, Kay stretched out both legs to try to roll it back towards the table with her feet. She tried several times before succeeding and then bent down to snatch the pencil up.

Impatient, she quickly sat back up catching her head on the edge of the heavy wooden table. She cursed, and slammed the pencil back down hard again. It remained motionless as she breathed in hard, feeling the angry pounding of her heart.

This wasn't like her, getting angry and having a total hissy fit. What had she been thinking? Being a writer was like having an illness, some affliction whose demon drove her on and on. She was fuming and alone in a baking hot square, in a country whose language she could barely understand, let alone speak.

This was now hurting and any more pencil to paper would be certain torment.

It had to stop no matter what – she had lost and that was simply that.

She hurried back to the flat and slammed the door shut behind her. The cool shadows of the hallway were a welcome relief after the burning heat of her frustrations on the other side of the deserted square.

'That was quick!'

Kay let rip, told her story in a flood of tears and fury before collapsing on the sofa.

Her flat mate was silent, looking at the manuscript that had been banged down onto the table and then at Kay who was now sobbing uncontrollably, her head hidden by her hands.

He hadn't known about her woes; they just shared a long summer let together – he merely hanging out and being lazy, while she seemed focused and intent.

He tried not to laugh, but a snort came out, and a glance between her sobs caught his obvious smile.

'You bastard!'

She was up and out, again slamming the door shut behind her, leaving him with the empty echoes of her fury.

He felt a little bad, but not too much, after all, he hardly knew this woman except by reputation, and what a high reputation it was – she was a name you sometimes read in the paper.

He looked down and lightly touched the manuscript.

Kay had called a friend for some consolation, and now sat on a bench under the shade of a large poplar tree, overlooking the town's lazy river shimmering in the afternoon sun at the edge of town, feeling a little better. Her friend had suggested coming straight home, but perhaps she would do some sightseeing first, relax a little before she had to face her friends, agent and publisher and disappoint the lot, let alone herself.

Not blaming her flat mate for his insensitive laughter, she knew she would somehow have to make up for her rude remark; after all, he had always given her space and had never asked a personal question.

It took some time for Kay to wind down and just be able to sit and be in this tranquil spot she had accidently found whilst pounding the streets to find some reprieve. Only when her angst had gone, did she dare risk going back to town to face the flat.

It was late afternoon, and she hugged the long cool shadows opposite the sunny side of the narrow cobbled streets until she reached the busy square, now bustling with shoppers.

Kay closed the front door gently. Only the soft click of the latch told of her return, but her flat mate hadn't noticed as he was on his knees and totally engrossed in the manuscript, which was now spread right across the living room floor.

Stopping dead in her tracks, she viewed him scribbling notes and re-arranging a page or two.

'What the hell do you think you're doing? That's my private stuff!'

Taken slightly aback, he looked up.

'I didn't see you there.'

Kay immediately started to pick up the papers, trying to put them back in order while staring right at him, hissing:

'Well?'

'I can do it for you – it's a great story, just missing some, um…'

'Excitement you mean.'

She quickened her efforts to put it all back into the proper order once again.

'Yes, but not just that, all of it needs working on – it needs to go to hell…'

She stopped dead and looked right at him, wanting to hear more.

'…and stay there.'

She just stared in horror at his smiling face. What was he saying? She couldn't do that – it was so outside her experience, and besides, it would be far too horrible and sordid for a girl like her. But he was right, and she knew it too – that's exactly what it needed.

As shock and some kind of realisation gripped her, she quickly sat down on the sofa as the blood began to drain from her head.

She awoke to the rude awakening of a glass of water being thrown over her head and face. She gasped, dizzily stood up and walked shakily to her bedroom where she shut the door and turned the lock before getting into bed, soaking wet and fully clothed.

It was evening when she woke, feeling parched, hungry and rather weak. She showered, changed and was back in the living room where the same shocking sight greeted her once again. However, this time, the manuscript was spread everywhere, even on the chairs and sofa, as her flat mate worked on his secret plan.

Kay feigned indifference, merely asking:

'Shall we eat?'

They walked in silence across the evening glow of the square and along dark narrow streets to where the river met the sea. They sat together outside an old wooden ramshackle restaurant, which had once seen better days. It was a good spot to eat, as the sea breeze eased the humidity of the long hot August night.

The tide was out and the river mostly mud, with only a narrow channel in the middle flowing out to sea. The silhouettes of a few small boats lay along its grassy banks.

As there was no beach here, just rocks and a wild sea that never slept, even on the stillest of days it was free from tourists and the incessant hum of cars. With the sound of pounding waves echoing her own heart, Kay tried to ponder her next move.

They had eaten here together once before, although she didn't really like to keep his company that much; he was on a long break, getting drunk and sometimes staying out all night, not that that was a concern for her, as she had had to focus and work towards her goal. But that was gone and out to sea, and now she needed him or at the very least to hear him out.

She viewed the stars brilliantly shining over-head and looked out towards the dark horizon, where lights of passing ships clearly showed against the night, and asked:

'Why?'

'Because I can,' was the dry reply.

She agreed that he could do a review, not an edit, some sort of revision of the text, and then perhaps she would see what she could do with what was left.

But she never did a thing, just did as she had planned – went sightseeing and started to relax. She even spent nights away in different towns with real beaches, where she could sunbathe and take a dip.

To hell with the book – she didn't want to know right now.

And he did the lot. What fun he had. They barely spoke, and he even insisted she hand over her laptop to get it done.

As August disappeared and the deadline loomed close, she came and found him in a bar drinking alone, looking pale and washed out from all the late nights working on the text. He saw her slim, nut brown, with little care for a thing called book.

Yes, he was done and it was ready to read.

It took her three days to get through it, absorb it, until she understood what he had really done.

It was early morning and, as she lay in bed turning over the finished book in her head, she shot up and walked naked into his bedroom, demanding that he change the lot.

He woke and looked at her naked body, brown all over except for where her bikini had stopped the sun.

Suddenly realising what she was doing and what he now saw, she gasped and grabbed his bed sheet, pulling it hard to wrap around her modesty. When she saw him naked, morning stiff and waking up, she ran back to her own room dropping the sheet midway in her flight.

There was no time left – just show them back home what he had done, or walk away for good.

Stuck between the devil and the deep blue sea she let out a scream, and kicked her feet and legs wildly on the bed. On hearing her, he laughed aloud, threw on some clothes and headed for the kitchen. He needed coffee to soothe his drinking head.

The smell of coffee soon lured her out and they met in the living room. She had pulled on a dress and nothing more.

'It's disgusting – I would never write such filth!'

'You didn't! Anyway I think it's rather good myself.'

'What will they think of me?'

He just shrugged.

'Who cares – it's all made up anyway.'

He clearly saw her dilemma as she screamed:

'You're abhorrent!'

She was about to storm out of the flat, was at the front door, as he loudly shouted back:

'It's exactly what the public wants.'

She knew that he was right; he had given it that and much more – too much in fact, and no matter how she deplored what he had written, it was affecting her right there and then; aroused and wet and aching for sex she turned back and stopped in front of him. He had sensed it before she blurted out:

'Fuck me like you wrote.'

He pushed her back into the bedroom and she flopped onto the bed and pulled her legs right up showing him her wet and aching everything, but he didn't want it like that, and rolled her over, plunging deep inside her. She moaned, didn't want to, hated him, but wanted that kind of sex right now. He whispered that he liked her shaved; it reminded him of a little girl. Stuck somewhere between the devil and another devil, between loving the moment and an absolute disgust for him and herself, she tried to pull away from him, but he had her by the hair and was now painfully twisting one of her arms as she felt him push up against her other hole. She shouted no and tightened against penetration but she was too physically weak to stop his twisted urge. His excitement was too much and he shot his load over her tightly squeezed sex. He groaned and flopped allowing her to escape his weakening grip.

Looking at the monster lying on the bed that was half smiling at her, she let rip:

'You lied to me – it wasn't some fantasy – it was you on all fours with your head down some filthy public lavatory at midnight being banged by another completely twisted stranger – wasn't it?'

He said nothing.

'Wasn't it?'

'So what?'

'Get out and don't come back, or I'll tell the police what you just tried to do.'

She grabbed her bag and ran out of the flat without her shoes, knowing exactly what she had to do.

At the clinic across the square, she was a sticky mess, but the doctor was sympathetic, reassured her it would all be fine, offered to call the police, but she didn't want that. All she wanted was the morning after pill and a post exposure prophylactic to be rid of any monster disease. Six weeks of feeling rough was a small price to pay, but a big hit on her credit card. The doctor said it was lucky that she came straight away. Lucky! She wasn't lucky, only stupid. What had come over her? Something so dirty all locked up inside her just waiting to burst forth.

He escorted her back to the flat and entered while she stood in the square below. The monster had gone, had even left his keys, and she went inside and locked the door.

She had the finished book and would use it – tell them it was all hers and pretend she was that sort. If it made a hit, she would have the cash to walk away, be free to do exactly as she pleased. No way could she 'write' another one.

But what of him? He had written all that damned stuff that people want to read – not her. To hell with him.

Kay packed up what she needed, stuffed the altered manuscript into a plastic bag, having checked she had the lot on her laptop, and left the flat for good. Dropping off the keys at the letting agent, she forwent her deposit and headed to the river mouth.

At the river mouth there was always a smouldering fire; a kind of rubbish tip the fishermen used to burn anything they didn't need. The smells of burning nylon rope and nets was taken by the off shore wind, and soon the smell of burning paper joined this lot. Page by page she fed the flames until nothing remained except black ash.

It was done and she could lie and lie…that's what the world wanted from her, a story so vile that they would be up in arms, tell her she was a monster, shouldn't be allowed – but they wouldn't put it down, and read the whole damned lot.

The Other Side of Midnight

Published in Dead Mule School of Southern Literature (July 2020)

"Witches raise the wind," the captain cried.
"The ship will break, lower the sail," the first mate replied.
"In the cauldron, water boils, turns us 'wards the rocks and reef."
"Only Heaven helps us now."

The dreams had been getting stronger, alive and more lucid; downright annoying. Throwing off the covers, the smell of night-sweats and dreamtime drama sent her quickly to the shower.

The streets had a jubilant air, the party not yet over. It would last some time, she suspected. A nationalist victory in a fraught and desperate election where old ghosts and tacit retribution lay low, waiting in the shadows until today. Now they would show.

At work she couldn't hide her foreign accent or the colour of her skin. From a near-by country, she was pale and sallow skinned. But today, felt it not quite pale enough. Showing difference, she felt a creeping new found fear.

The looks from men, always confusing and unclear, were now a threat.

She was second class, chattel for a trade.

Hurrying home before shadows took the day, she double locked the door. It felt safe to be inside her make-shift cage.

Her grandmother had told her how the Nazi's shouted loud:

"…it's their fault…"

The finger pointed, the blame so clearly laid. The rest is history, shame, shame, shame.

That night, the dream came quickly.

The captain was frantic, beside himself.

"The fury of these howling winds steers us to a rocky ruin. We'll splinter there, like firewood. Tell the men to abandon ship."

"Nay Captain, they will not, won't stand a chance in those flimsy rafts, get swamped and overturned, thrown to the deep."

"What chance then? Do as ye wish, the moon shows shadows of the closing reef. It's nearly midnight but the ship clock will never make that strike. We'll be done by then and the ticking stopped."

"Witches trap us with their dismal spell, they've raised the winds, we're doomed I say."

"Abandon ship I say!"

"Nay Captain."

"Lower the raft, I'll take my chances with the fury of the sea, not the anvil of the reef."

Bathed in sweat, she awoke with a start, her heart beating to the rhythm of the dark and stormy sea.

The day had urgency. She had heard some whispers, broken sentences and knew that soon it would be out-loud and bold: foreigner, go home.

Her grandmother had had to run, abandon ship for a distant shore. Those who stayed hit the reef, dreams all sinking in the deep.

The need to leave, abandon ship, a risky move and a lonely one.

She didn't tell a soul, packed a bag and left her home. The plane would land before the clock struck twelve. She dozed at thirty thousand feet.

On the shore, the captain sat on a rock, staring hard at her.

"You made it though the tempest, that's good to see. Almost had me that foolish crew, too scared to risk the fury of the sea. Had no choice but abandon ship, the clock was nearing midnight's strike, the witching-hour, to you and me. Crew went down, look around, no chance of surviving that, the perils of the reef and windy wild sea."

She wanted to talk but could not. Bits of ship-timbers lay strewn about the shoreline. The storm had abated and dawn approached. She gazed into the fading night. A star briefly twinkled, before a band of cold light cut the horizon out to sea. Desperately wanting to know where they were, she turned back towards the captain.

He had gone but his word echoed through her over and over again.

"Safe".

GETTING STONED AGAIN

London in the late '70s was a pretty run down city. It was the financial hub of Europe and an epicentre for music, art, theatre and ideas, but none of that was reflected in anything you saw on the streets or in the buildings. Only the years of neglect showed.

This wasn't decadence, this was decay, and the rot had set in.

Take Covent Garden for example, now full of designer shops, overpriced apartments, expensive bars and hip nightlife. Tom remembered whole streets empty, tattered and neglected just a few blocks from the Royal Opera House. So neglected and devoid of care that it was possible to squat there and not be out of place. When his Basque friend Sebastian threw a brick through the grand window of a Spanish bank late one night, no one seemed to blink an eye.

Such was life back then.

Even Notting Hill, now the domain of media, film and pop stars living in their central London rich kid haven, was half derelict – grand Victorian and Georgian houses falling down, squatted, empty and on the verge of ruin. There were streets you didn't want to walk down because your colour wasn't right and dark alleyways full of graffiti with bad people doing bad things to themselves and others.

The docklands, now expensive glass and concrete, had vast derelict spaces, crumbling warehouses, old cranes and burnt out cars. There were people who needed money fast and the crime that goes with that.

Those days are long gone, replaced with modern things designed by those who want to keep urban decay far away.

Berlin 2014.

Its modern centre with grand buildings, good design and an urban park full of trees, ponds and monuments pays homage to important things. This is the Berlin you see in films and adverts. Between this and the old East with its dull grey flats cut through by large main roads – the kind of place that drives a person to despair – lies an area a little like London in the 1970's. Berlin's not so miserable or neglected, but there was something in the old factories, the endless train lines with their empty depots and a nightlife that was still sleazy enough not to give a damn that took Tom back to the grey but exciting times of London.

It won't last long of course; soon the old becomes the new and this gloomy urban landscape, will be gone for good.

But today, Tom felt the old London in Berlin. There were no real punks of course, no ideas of revolution, no squats by the thousand, no Baader-Meinhof on the run and in the shadows, no communists and certainly no Basque separatists. That was London way back then, a safe house for radical ideas. This was Berlin now, modern, hip and tediously correct; however, it still somehow clung onto something dark, unruly and disheveled, refusing to be named or tamed – it was there alright, not much of it, but he could sense it in the air, in the pavements and in the concrete itself. The ghosts of Berlin's dark past still linger in its shadows.

As he walked down Emserstrasse from the sunken garden of Korner Park, where he liked to sit on a summer's night, towards the old West Berlin airport at Templehof, passing new bars and restaurants, he knew what was about to come. Once across Hermannstrasse, the decay was not hidden or disguised – it was on display with hideous pride. Smashed bottles and endless throw-outs littered the streets; dirty old clothes, bric-a-brac and broken furniture, useful only to the desperate, were scattered about between neon brothels and drinking parlours, some of which you couldn't even call bars – just someone's front room spilling out onto the open street.

Tom wasn't fooled by any of it, he saw no glamour, and everything this place was, was in the dog shit, supernatural amounts, like a museum collection, piled up around the trees, which were numerous. German was a second language here as swarthy macho men and headscarf women, herded kids from one block to the next in this very other Berlin world. You see a few young with-it things, maybe poor, but more likely living the bohemian life – what fun this is!

Tom watched the floor, dodging what dogs had done and do, and, outside his apartment block, he held his hand over his nose and mouth. The ground floor flat had open windows covered with chicken wire to stop the hundred rescue cats from jumping out. Through the front door and along the public corridor, stands the rescue cats' front door with another flat opposite; there the stench was at its strongest, in summer, unbearable. Tom thought about that other flat – they must love the smell of a hundred cats or have no sense of smell at all, have heavily discounted rent or just be generally desperate and grateful to have a place called cat pee home.

Up the stairs, away from the dirty street and cat smell hell below, another front door was home.

The girl was sitting in the kitchen as always, legs pulled up on the comfy armchair and indulging in her usual evening habit – getting stoned and puffing away at a small and strong smelling reefer, getting on with whatever she usually got on with – nothing much he suspected.

The washing machine whirred, spun, stopped and whirred again as she just stared at the drum of colours after giving him a courteous grin.

Damn Berlin, it had woken up the London in him – living on the edge, living hand to mouth – different times but simple times. How did it ever get so complicated? Modern life was a string of passwords and endless technology that never gave him any time, space or empty days where nothing could possibly happen. The worst thing was – it all felt perfectly normal to be crammed full and planning the next day or moment.

Maybe she had the right idea.

'Give me some of that.'

She looked puzzled and somewhat taken aback, before slowly stretching her arm out in front for him to take the smouldering incendiary from her feeble grip. He drew the smoke into his lungs, instantly coughing and dribbling saliva down his shirt.

She laughed and pulled a handkerchief from her sweater pocket. Still coughing, he caught her throw and mopped up the drool. He too was laughing now and, between splutters, took another drag.

He eyed her sitting there in that chair in that usual way of hers. She looked sexy – did she always look that good? He felt the sudden urge to pin her down and bang her hard right there and then.

Instead, he pulled on the reefer once again to distract himself.

What was she thinking now – the same thing? God, how was he to know? Was he getting stoned?

He coughed and she beamed a smile, as if to say this smoking thing somehow brought them close, but he knew that was all bullshit. He recalled the dope smoking at Art College many years ago, and all the useless talk and false feelings it aroused; for when it passed it was like it never happened – just the smoke of delusion. He could now feel it coming on strong.

He sensed the room was getting smaller, or was it getting bigger? The annoying whir stopped, allowing the shouts and traffic noise to filter in from down below. Then the machine spun again, reverberating, making him tingle, filling him up to an explosive point, until it stopped and he could hear the traffic once again, so close it was in the room.

This feeling of unreality, which was a kind of reality of course, started feeling good.

Then endless thoughts started pouring through and overloading his mind. He shut his eyes and saw vivid colours moving in kaleidoscope.

He tried to stop it, knowing it was near impossible to do so, but also knowing that all he was experiencing was nothing more than a toxin rushing through his blood and brain.

He plonked himself down on a wooden chair.

Somehow, he managed to cut the babble from his mind and listen to the magic sounds around. He could smell the girl but had lost the urge to do whatever it was he thought he might like to do to her, and sat for what seemed like an age.

'You ok?'

'What? Yes.'

Was she worried? Was that really his voice answering?

It was nice to have all his tensions wash away. He could get used to this.

He tried to stand, only managing it with some focus and by holding onto the kitchen counter. He was wobbly and woozy.

God, they call it dope for good reason.

The whir now irritated him – it was far too loud and rude, and the girl was far too real, still in the same position and grinning like a fairground doll, rolling another joint.

Where was the other one? Had he smoked it all and stubbed it out in the ashtray?

'Did I smoke it all?'

His voice was too loud and seemed to echo. It made him laugh and she laughed too, not giving him an answer, and he knew this was how it was and would always be – stoned is stoned, no matter where, when or how you do it. This was as good as it would ever get.

I'm drunk he thought; a different drunk, but drunk I am for sure.

How was he going to get to the bedroom – it seemed miles away and full of obstacles to negotiate.

Ignoring the girl, he stumbled and fumbled his way out of kitchen through the open door into the dimly lit hallway. Not daring to turn around and see the brightly lit reality of the girl and the sounds of her still rolling a joint, he lunged left and into safety.

It was dark. Silhouettes and strange shapes that he could not recognise lay like a maze in his path.

Tom stood still, caught between the world of a smoking girl where nothing but confusion lay and the black door of his bedroom where he would be alone with all this mad stuff running through his brain.

He could hear his heart pound and the sound of blood rushing through his ears. He didn't dare plonk himself down in this no-man's land of a dark hallway. Yes, it was safe between those two awful realities, but what if she came and asked him if he was all right, touched him – wanted something, anything...?

Tom suddenly found himself on the floor, melting away into the floorboards, the warm wood pressing against his cheek. Had he fallen?

'What happened?'

She was touching him, talking to him, seemed concerned. Was he damaged somehow? He could not talk, only managing to mumble something even he didn't understand.

Oh my god – no, please go away...

She was the last thing he wanted to deal with.

While she was talking and trying to get him up, he lunged forwards towards the black door and knocked it open. On all fours now, he herded his clumsy body inside and spun around to catch sight of her shocked face, bemused and full of night shadows and ghostly glare, transfixed and staring right at him.

She was the devil – he was sure of that, and Tom used his foot to slam the door shut tight.

Christ...what happened just then.

He heard her shuffle back to the kitchen, and then nothing. Only the hum of the Berlin traffic told him he was not in hell.

But it felt like hell.

The only solution lay somewhere above him, amongst the sombre and melancholic shadows of the room. The safety of his bed urgently pulled him up. He flopped fully clothed on the duvet, struggling with it for a while, turning and pulling at it until he was hidden from whatever it was he was hiding from.

Safety.

Just switch it all off now please...

He heard himself breathing, loud, fast and very shallow. Deep breaths were needed and he obeyed this inner command whilst feeling and hearing the thudding of his heart that shook the bed. Can they hear it down below?

There was nothing more until the morning light and early birds had him waking up. Strangely, he felt normal. Did that really happen?

Tom lay looking out of the window at the autumn leaves on the high trees, still and catching the first rays of sunshine.

A different world; so peaceful that he didn't get up, just drifted between sleep and a waking blankness where all his thoughts were gone.

Bliss.

Sometime passed like this. He could have stayed like that forever had it not been for a noise. Not any noise, but the noise of her doing the things she always did before she left for work.

Damn. Tom shot up. Dizzy, he fell back on the bed.

God, I'm drunk…no I'm not…I'm…like hung-over without pain or any discomfort.

Jeez. It was hard to walk. Wobbly and slightly floppy, he left the room.

The hall was light and no longer full of menace. Pausing before the kitchen, he tried to make and memorise a speech, an apology of sorts for his behaviour last night, but he could not remember much, let alone the feeling.

Had it been as bad as he now imagined?

Before he could say a word she burst out laughing, sitting there as she had done when this mess all started. It was a cup in her hand now, not a joint, and the tea slightly spilled over and down her pants. She didn't care, she had seen what she had expected to see and it filled her with joy. He knew it too.

He was a shocking mess, clothes all crumpled, hair unkempt, and that look of washed out drama in his face.

'Don't say a word – it's always like that the first time.'

She had cut him dead but as it was not the first time, he kept quiet, let her have the moment, for it gave him the perfect excuse to connect with her. After all, she still looked good.

Damn that stuff. Tom laughed too, and hoped that one joint would be enough.

A Day in the Garden

Through the keyhole of an old wooden door at the end of an overgrown gravel path, I see something. The shed should have collapsed years ago but a tangle of twisted creepers and sturdy shrubs hold it firm, its slow decay hiding behind dense foliage. All I see is green, from plants obscuring the window to the lichen covered wood and mossy ground. Somewhere, under a maze of creepers reaching high up into the branches of overhanging trees, is the roof.

It's early, dew still soaking the ground. Soon, the sun will turn this wild garden into a humid jungle full of buzzing bugs.

One kick and the wooden door would surly fall. However, that's just wrong. I look again and see that something showing in the dim light coming from the window. This shed is not my business, but I'm making it mine.

Unsure, I turn and look towards the house. It's lost from view, obscured by trees and hanging leaves. I feel safe in this forgotten spot.

The owner's dead and the house empty, cleared out by greedy relatives who had waited impatiently until the morning of his death. I had looked through the windows at first light today; everything is gone, nothing left at all. The man had been a collector, a hoarder of high-class junk and wonderful treasures that he had accumulated through years of travel. It had been the talk of the village. To the relatives, this junk and treasure meant money. Within days, the house emptied, the booty looted and the doors locked. I don't think they knew about the shed, hidden from view, dilapidated and full of creepy crawlies, no doubt.

The garden had been well kept, a gardener keeping order, holding back and taming nature's onslaught. He had done a good job but I prefer it now, a year on, still a garden but overrun and in decline. In a few years, it will be lost, waiting for discovery. There's an abandoned orchard full of apple, pear, cherry and other fruit whose names I do not know. Between the orchard and the house is a large ornamental pond full of beautiful lilies and plopping frogs. In the centre of the pond stands a large stone two-tiered fountain, beautifully carved, its urns full of moss and weeds. Only in a heavy downpour does it flow again, the rain loosening and pushing the weeds over the urn lips.

I know this place; I live close by. Occasionally, on a stroll through the fields behind the grounds, I saw him carrying things to the shed, always boxed or wrapped. Over ten years, I had only seen him half a dozen times, at most. We had never spoken.

What had I seen through the keyhole? I don't want to break anything, force my way inside. On the ground around the shed, is a line of terracotta pots smothered in vegetation. Could it be that obvious? On my hands and knees, I pull the pots free from their entanglement and look underneath each one. It's getting hot, the air thick, and by the time I finish looking, feel flushed and wet. Nothing found. There's just one more thing to try. On what timbers I can see, I scour the surfaces looking for a hook. Stepping to the rear, pushing the creepers apart, I force my way behind the shed, the vegetation so thick I can barely move. Reaching out, my hand goes through the dense creepers to feel along the wooden side under the roof. Then I feel it. In my hand is a large rusty key.

Why I'm doing this? Curiosity, to know what the man was storing; my own greed; or to salvage something before the roof collapses and all is flattened, soaked with rain? I'm not sure, but I want to know before it's gone for good.

I hesitate before putting the key in the lock. It turns effortlessly and clonks. The lock is free. I pull the door towards me. The tight hinges creak as I yank the door through hanging vegetation. Through the wide open door a wet musty smells appears followed by a wasp and then another. I take a step back. Wasps don't like change, movement, vibration, unwelcome light or nosey people. Other wasps soon follow. They fly around and investigate me. I don't move. Somehow satisfied that I pose no threat, they fly back in.

This is tricky. There may be a thousand wasps around a nest inside the shed. I step into darkness and move to my right, leaving the open door, free for flying wasps. My eyes adjust to the light. It's warm and humid, the buzzing intense. The shed is not as full of bric-a-brac as I had imagined. In a neat row, some ancient looking farm tools lean against the back wall. Standing by the wall opposite me is a vividly painted classic rocking horse, its wild mane and bushy tale covered in dust and cobwebs. Wrapped around the saddle is an enormous nest, crawling with wasps. Fortunately, they are sedate, toing and froing from a small hole in the roof where creepers have broken through. In the back corner, near to where I stand, is that thing I saw spying through the keyhole – a slim wooden box, about three feet tall and nailed shut. Through the keyhole in the dim light, I had seen the glint of a stainless steel nail.

Farm tools and a stinging rocking horse aside, the box holds my attention. I don't feel comfortable here, doing this, and grab the box, speedily exiting before gently closing the door. I turn the lock and pull the key. Leaning the box against a terracotta pot, I move behind the shed, battle with the creepers and put the rusty key back on its hook.

Is this stealing or reclamation salvage? Nervous, I pick up the box and walk under the canopy along the overgrown path towards the house, knowing I'm never coming back.

I see the house and abruptly stop. The old gardener stands by the pond, looking at the fountain, his back towards me. One more crunching footstep and he'll turn to see me with my old shed swag. I dare not move. This is his place and might soon sense a foreign presence. He's a big wasp now.

Fighting panic, I lean and stretch, placing the box behind bunch of hollyhocks and tall exotic grass. Is it lost from view?

He turns and stares. I haven't planned for this. Act normal, but this is not normal and he must know it too. I wave and smile. He returns the greeting and I stroll towards him smiling, hoping it's not a scowl.

'You're the chap who lives in the cottage by the stream? What brings you here?'

'Well, it's all closed up now, thought I'd take a peak, is that ok? You still work here?'

'No, just take a look now and then, see the sad decline, worked here half my life. Good year for fruit, you should help yourself. Hell knows what they're going to do with it, arguing among themselves, I hear. There's a court case going on. Enjoy it while you can.'

I'm in the clear.

'Did you come over the fence by the old shed?'

'From the field, didn't see a shed.'

'It's overgrown now.'

Not so clear. I need to distract him.

'What a great fountain!'

'He had it commissioned, famous sculptor, focal point of the garden when it was running and everything neat and tidy. Still works, there's a switch behind that bench. They never turned the electric off. Want to see it running?'

I smile and he goes to the bench to press something on the back of the top rung. There's a splutter but nothing happens.

'Dirt in the spout.'

He walks to a flowerbed, pulls a long wooden rod out of the ground, goes to the edge of the pond and leans out over the water to swish the top of the spout clean. Still nothing happens.

'Can you hold onto me, can't get the lean.'

I grab his shoulders as he stretches to the max and pokes about the spout. Another splutter and pieces of dirt spit into the air before the fountain comes to life. We hear the gurgle of the first urn filling up. Saying nothing, we watch. The water spills over to the lower urn. Pieces of moss follow. Soon the water splashes in the pond, the sight and sound mesmerising. Frogs start to jump.

'That's more like it, like it used to be.'

'Leave it on, no one will care.'

'Think that's alright?'

'Sure.'

Nodding, he stares at the fountain, nonchalantly remarking:

'I'll show you that shed.'

He walks away before I say a word. He's on the path. I move fast to catch him up. He's near the hollyhocks. Opposite are some pretty pinkish flowers poking out of grass and weeds.

'What are those?'

He stops, turns away from the hollyhocks, looks at the flowers and then to me, bemused.

'Foxgloves…'

He says nothing more and continues to the shed.

Stopping at the shed, he looks it over. I notice the fresh earth around the bottom of the terracotta pots I moved. I hadn't put them back exactly as they were.

'Missed that on the way in…all those creepers….'

'He liked it hidden, used it as some kind of storehouse…never been inside.'

He pulls the creepers gently away from the window and rubs the dirt away with the sleeve of his jumper. Peering inside, he stays quiet and motionless. I can't bear it.

'See anything?'

Still peering, he softly speaks.

'Agricultural tools, antique…look in perfect condition.'

He steps away.

'Don't think they'll be missed now the house is cleared and they're fighting in the courts for all the money left behind.'

'Want me to help you carry them home?'

'Got to wait 'till autumn now, there's a big wasp nest…only a fool would walk inside…'

He points to the maze of creepers hiding the roof. I see the wasps crawling through the foliage to enter and leave their home. He's staring at me in a peculiar way.

Feeling uncomfortable, I need to get away.

'I'll be on my way, then…'

'Let's go out the front, not a soul around.'

He leads the way along the overgrown path, walking right past the hollyhocks and around the side of the house to the front. A long weedy gravel drive takes us to the tiny road. We both live along this stretch and stroll together.

'Do you miss the garden?'

'It was just a job, a good one at that, paid well and I had free reign. All he wanted was an outdoor place to entertain his weekend guests. Every month I got a bonus, often more than my wages, what for, I'll never know, discretion, I suppose.'

I want to ask questions but dare not, but I don't need to as he quickly carries on.

He walks slowly. I'm next to him. The day is getting hot but the huge trees behind the hedgerow shade us.

'He had parties, lasting days sometimes. I'd find bodies crashed out in a flowerbed, bottles in the pond. Sometimes they had a fire on the lawn, burnt the grass and ground, takes months to put a mess like that right.'

I laugh, half out of nervousness and half out of fascination.

'I can't tell you how many times I saw people doing it in the garden, in broad daylight too, sometimes in the bushes, sometimes on the grass, not caring, not embarrassed, I didn't know what to do.'

'What did you do?'

'After some years, I just looked. Ever seen people…?'

'Only on the internet.'

'It's boring, pointless…especially as I couldn't join in.'

Now I'm laughing.

'Why not?'

'It's not Lady Chatterley.'

I'm still laughing.

'I realised how dull my life was, it made me go and…you know…?'

'Find your own garden party, did you?'

Nodding, he's laughing too now. Somehow, I feel vindicated.

We laugh together until the stone bridge over the stream and part company. I don't go inside my house but around the side to the garden at the rear, past my own shed and into the fields behind where I hurry back to the garden.

It's still there behind the hollyhocks. I pick it up, retracing my steps back home.

In my own shed, carefully prizing the box open on the worktop, I can hardly wait to see what lies inside.

Disappointment must be showing clearly on my face. What had I expected? I don't know, but it surely wasn't this.

I'm gazing at a painting. It looks a little dirty, the colours muted and the thick brush marks rough and crude. Out of the box, I stand it upright on the worktop. Drenched in morning light, dull sunflowers in a crooked simple vase stare back at me. It might look good on my toilet wall, as the colours seem to match. There's a bold black signature on the vase.

Vincent.

I laugh. I already have a copy of something similar in my house, a poster, nicely framed, the colours clean and bright. I could give this to a friend, perhaps. Or would it be an insult to gift this dirty little fraud?

I take a photo on my phone and start a recognition search. Easily found, there it is, in a national collection, worth the most obscene amount.

It's missing, stolen, subject to a huge reward.

If it is the one, I stole it too. What to do – put it back or hand it in? I need a plan to fix this mess.

Leaving the painting on the shed worktop, I walk across the field behind my house to follow a line of trees along the stream. Entering the old forest, I feel safe among the shadows of tall and broken trunks. I try to think, hatch a plan but nothing seems to come. I push on, further from the troubles of my curiosity.

The stream drops down between some rocks. I follow. The water is fast and shallow, the streambed full of rock and gravel. Around me, lush plants grow. The air is still and humid, as the canopy hides the sky.

I stop, concealed in this little magic world. Smelling wild garlic, I look towards its source. The stream banks gently flatten out before the crumbly escarpment rises to the forest floor. Before the rise, among the garlic, is an ancient bottle dump. Earth and plants have mostly covered it, but here and there, old glass protrudes. A rusted water tank, resting on its side, half-buried in the ground and half-hidden by ferns and other plants that love the damp, tells me I have my plan.

On the phone, back in my shed, I do a little research. There are two numbers to call and one place I have to visit.

First, it's the gallery. They are somewhat suspicious, asking questions about the rear of the piece. I put the phone on speaker and turn the painting round. A photograph seems best; I click and send. Moment later, there's great excitement on the other end. I leave my name before rudely hanging up and turn the ringer off.

Next, I call the insurance company. Compared to the tens of millions in insurance compensation they must be facing, my reward is pittance. Of course, they're not friendly, so I become difficult to ensure commitment in handing me the reward. It seems to work. I leave my name and hang up once again.

I've recorded both these calls.

Placing the painting back inside the box, I shut it, carefully pressing in the stainless steel nails with my thumb. Taking dirt from my shoe, I smear it around the outside of the box.

I need to run before this becomes front-page news, a swarm of reporters heading for my door. On the drive, inside my car, I place the box on the front passenger seat and secure it with the seat belt. Nervously, I head towards the nearest town.

My thoughts run wild as doubt creeps in. Have I really thought this through? Although I didn't steal the painting from a national collection, I did remove it from a derelict shed in the garden of an abandoned house. Is that stealing? Under these circumstances, maybe not, but it may void my reward.

I soon find myself inside the station.

The police seem friendly, amused at first, as it brightens up their sleepy day. Efficient, they record every detail that I say. They take my fingerprints.

My story is a simple one:

It was this morning (not early in case the gardener spills the beans) that I took a stroll along the streambed through the overgrown forest to the bottle dump. They don't know about the bottle dump so I enlighten them that it's a fine spot to hunt for glass in the wilds of the English countryside (of course, I don't actually have any bottles and hope they won't do a bottle check inside my home). The box lay inside a rusted water tank, hidden amongst the ferns. Before today, I'd never looked inside, I say.

Retracing my every step, they insist I take them to the bottle dump. I have to wait around as they muster up their troops: a forensic specialist, photographer, two detectives and a PC. Rather I lot, I think.

Fortunately, I had messed up the inside of the rusted tank, kicked around the dirt and ferns a bit. I hope the scene looks genuine to their professional eye. They're asking more questions, making a plaster cast of my footprint in the mud and want my shoes to check that they are mine. Leaving the others, one detective goes back to my house with me. He looks bored, peers around the house and shed a bit, asks me for my shoes and leaves.

I'm not sure exactly what I've done. It's too late now and the only thing to do is drink a cup of tea. Passing time, it doesn't really help.

It's three o'clock. My phone has at least a dozen missed calls. I'm glad I left the ringer off.

The sound of cars and a walky-talky radio has me to the window. Down the road, outside the old man's house, there's a commotion going on. Police are everywhere. Feeling butterflies yet totally ignored, I wander towards the house. The sight of flashing lights and a large forensic van tell me more is yet to come, from opening the box.

The house is big, situated where the road turns into a dirt farm track. At a cordon of yellow tape, I stop to join other village folk peering towards a row of tall Scot pines, behind which lies the house. I fail to see anything that's going on.

The gardener is next to me, he too peering down the road. Without turning, he starts to speak.

'Created quite a hoo-ha by opening that box.'

'You know…?'

'Everyone knows now. Police came by, asked a thousand questions about the old man, asked about you too…'

I'm sweating.

'…said you didn't know him, only me and Mrs. Brown from down the village shop. I just kept the garden but she did other things, suppose.'

I need to keep this light.

'Show her his etchings, did he?'

'Sunflowers, kept her warm on chilly nights.'

I chuckle. What else can I do?

'They told me you found it in the bottle dump, in a rusty water tank…box would have rotten through by now.'

He turns to face me. His look is wry and wily.

'Except there is no bottle dump, never was, just a place the farmer used to dump his farmyard junk.'

A pained smile is all I muster.

'The police wouldn't know a bottle dump from farmyard junk, didn't contradict them. In fact, said it was the old man's favourite stomping ground.'

'Was it?'

'Mrs. Brown was stomping ground…your phone been ringing off the hook?'

'Ringer turned off.'

'Suggest you turn it on, sell your story to the papers, make a tidy sum.'

He's still looking in that peculiar way.

'How much is the reward?'

'Enough to pay the mortgage and whole lot more.'

He's still looking.

'Three hundred and fifty thousand.'

Sometimes I'm so dumb. With my head full of money, I never thought to ask.

'What are the police doing in his house?'

'Thought you'd never ask – the old man was dealer, crooked one at that, police said, had had their eye on him until he died. You found the painting near his house, so they think they'll find a clue, the thieves, another painting, who knows…'

'Will they?'

'Relatives had the lot. All that art they took will be confiscated, and checked to see if it is kosher. They'll never sell the house now, not for years and years. Think of all the hanging fruit that's ours.'

'Tell about this morning?'

'What, and risk having to pay an electric bill for turning on the fountain. No way, you and me were never here. It's just between ourselves, a few hundred wasps and some very indiscreet purple hollyhocks.'

'You can't trust a hollyhock,' I try to parry back.

'I've been thinking: need a new pick-up truck, one of those fancy types.'

'Want me to lend you the money?'

His look has not changed.

'Indefinitely,' I add.

'With a trailer,' he's smiling now.

I feel the tension leave my body.

'I'm just scared of wasps,' he lies.

The Seven Million Year Itch

Published in Literary Veganism: an online journal (May 2020)

'Conservation starts with extinction.'

'That's a bit late!'

'Well, maybe conservation starts when extinction looms close.'

'That's still a bit too late.'

'There's just no money to be made in conservation.'

'No, it's all in the destruction.'

'You're not wrong there!'

'Cut the trees down for wood, make way for development and agro industries – unused wilderness is such a useless waste!'

'And kill off all the wildlife too – kill it if it tastes good, has big teeth, eats your crops or livestock, or is just too darn big.'

'And hunt what's left for sport.'

'It's got to be small, cute and vegetarian to be safe.'

'What about rabbits? You told me you like the taste of rabbit.'

'I did, until you told me they taste of piss!'

'Guess you must have liked the taste of piss then.'

'Guess I did. What about all the fish?'

'Hoover those up – the rarer they get the more money they're worth.'

'Blow up the mountains for rocks and minerals. Pump the toxic waste into rivers and out to sea.'

'Then eat the polluted fish.'

'And dam up the rivers to destroy an eco system.'

'Electricity – money to be made there!'

'What's left untouched?'

'Certainly not the air we breathe.'

'When I was in Phuket I visited the last big unfelled tree, and in Hokkaido I found some of the last magnificent giant trees on an impossible ridge where the chainsaw couldn't reach.'

'Do you think we'll have tree museums one day to remind us what used to be?'

'Only if they charge an entry fee. What about any indigenous people still lurking in the forests, keeping that entire wilderness to themselves?'

'Not right – should be rounded up and put into zoos – that way people would pay money to see them.'

'Good idea – incorporate them into the economy.'

'What the hell is wrong with us?

'We're possessed by a hungry ghost that's never satisfied.'

'You think the Earth has feelings?'

'Maybe. We're like billions of parasites eating away at its surface.'

'A skin disease.'

'Exactly that.'

'I guess one day the Earth will shed its skin and all that goes with it.'

'And start again without us?'

'Well it sure won't wanna feel that itch again!'

The tree stood alone in the parched landscape without company or any other greenery.

Looking out at this scene from the pleasant shade of the veranda into the vast sea of a rust coloured desert, the woman listened to the two men's conversation – out of sight by the pool nearby, until a splash put a halt to their witty discourse.

She liked these two men, holidaying or taking time out, didn't know their names yet, but knew she would sleep with one of them – which one she didn't care, hopefully the best. But that was a nighttime thrill and she left her longing to step down off the veranda into the garden, whose life depended on a constant supply of water delivered by a very slow moving gardener.

Another splash and brief laughter reassured her as she left this artificial paradise and crossed over into rust.

The sky was cloudless and brilliant blue, the air hot and heavy and her slow steps, rhythmic. The sounds now were her breathing and the soft shuffling of sand underfoot, seemingly exaggerated in the silence. She felt self-conscious as the tree came closer and closer.

The heat scorched her bare legs and she was wet from the blazing heat. She welcomed the shade of its thick chewy leaf canopy and the subtle breeze that appeared from nowhere.

Sun bleached animal bones were strewn around and one gave a loud crack as she stepped right on it, making her jump in fright and bump into the hard gnarly bark. The coarse texture grazed her arm and she immediately broke out of the daze the short hot walk had given.

The hotel staff had told her that once a lush forest grew here with many wild animals, some dangerous and some good to eat, but that was a long time ago, before the gun and chainsaw turned it into this beautiful desert.

Now only this strange tree grew, alone and full of life, as if all the missing nature had fled into this one magnificent majestic thing. It was protected of course and the hotel built just to marvel at its beauty.

Something always survives and this was it, a reminder of what was and could be again. But that was just too big a thing to ponder and she turned towards the hotel in the distance, feeling that longing once again.

THE DARK SIDE OF MONEY

At a civil dinner party, family silver cuts and scrapes fine cuisine; heirlooms that have made and witnessed history. Not that anyone remembers or even has a clue; it's all invisible now, secrets long concealed.

One sharp and polished knife is a small example of such masquerade. It would not be true to call them lies; however, it's near impossible to see what sparkles right into the eye.

This knife saw action: two bloody revolutions; went through the shoulder of a screaming wife, the drunken husband far too drunk to stab again, slipped on blood, falling to the floor; the wife later cut his throat, same knife, midnight Halloween.

"It was a witch, she cried, "I know the one, go find her, burn her at the stake."

She paid for the poor girl's cinders to be buried near the church, praying hard for her own redemption, paying for it all. This church got rich through this wife's guilt, burning up a dreamed-up witch, a pretty girl who turned men's heads while muttering to the breeze.

One day, this knife and other swag come knocking at your door.

The knife looks good, as it joins the rest, sitting polished in your draw; it's only silver, after all.

The money, clean, washed and laundered new, no longer dirty, just stained and bloodied through.

Cut your food

Spend the money

Enjoy the time

As the curse comes around

To put you in the ground

Russian Criminal Tattoo

Inspired by an exhibition of Russian criminal tattoo photographs at the Saatchi Gallery, London

Poison or cure, you tell me. Here, in this palace of thieves, it may well be a cure, administered by a royal surgeon wielding a tool of trade: the dirty needle.

To be safe, protected by the keepers of this place, or, more importantly, its inmates, you need a mark, valid credentials, to show belonging, position, no matter how lowly or pathetic.

You may be a common thief, notorious murderer or political idealist, in favour or out of odds. It makes no difference. Without this mark, you are vermin to be hunted, to endlessly scurry in imaginary shadows, waiting for a ghastly end.

The king of thieves has spoken: it's time to show pathetic deference, obedience and bared skin for a royal seal of criminal approval.

The tool etches flesh, foul ink stains. Poison runs deep, amok. Can you hold if off, keep the demon at bay, have the dice rolled your way, or will the rot take root, like all the hollow apparitions looking on?

Poison or cure: it makes no difference. They have ruined you, and if you ever make it back to sunlight, this cut, criminal tattoo, is a scar for life.

Ten Gallon Reef

'B ail!'

The desperate cry was almost drowned out by the driving wind and powerful surf that crashed and spilled over the jagged reef and stacks sitting no more than one hundred yards out from the dark, imposing cliffs.

With the wind behind them, it would only take another large swell or two for the small boat to smash up against the reef, before being dragged into the back pull of a retreating wave and pushed up once again, until just shards and splinters remained and the two men were lost forever to the hard blue below.

One man bailed furiously with a small bucket as the other pulled hard on the oars into the back pull, before the swell could push them closer towards the frothy violence of the reef that lined the entire west side of the island.

It was a hopeless task delaying the inevitable, as they inched closer to the pounding white waves breaking over the black barrier, now no more than ten yards ahead.

The boat was swamped and the bailing too slow and inadequate, as the next lashing of white water sunk the boat deeper, dangerously filling it inches from rim.

The boat, heavy from flood, slowed, allowing time for the oarsman to push away against the reef and into the pull of a retreating wave; it gave some grace before the next wave threw them forward once again onto some submerged rocks in front of the stacks. They bottomed out and breeched. Seconds later, another wave ripped them off and tossed the boat behind the jagged rocks into the swirling eddies between the reef and cliffs.

Around and around they went as one bailed and the other kept pushing off the cliff or reef with the oars. For some time this cycle continued, and, though exhausted, they kept up this tedious task into the twilight, where the only hues were steel grey and eerie white. Fulmars dropped off their perches, chuckling and swooping, indifferent to the two men weakening in their fight to save themselves.

It was a little after dusk when the wind dropped and the swells abated somewhat, allowing the men to sit and shiver as they drifted between reef and cliff.

They started rowing at first light, the sea now calm, its fury spent, and the reef passive in the welcome light of morning.

It was a mere mile and a half to their inlet mooring where the others were waiting, their drawn faces relieved to see the two return, full of questions as no one had really expected them back after such a violent blow.

'Was fishing the stacks when it came.'

'What stacks?'

'I don't know – those where we got swamped.'

'Ten Gallon or more came with each wave, we was nearly done – spent the night against the cliff.'

They all drifted off, leaving only an old man to ponder the empty stillness of the sea.

A boy approached.

'Where they been all night?'

There was a pause, and then the answer came with a certainty as he pointed north.

'Ten Gallon Reef – don't you ever be going there now.'

STAR MAN

A beautiful, cold crisp and clear starry night.

A man is fishing (FM) from the shingle beach, the high tide rollers gently crashing and sucking back like a living thing.

In the starlight, a stranger (SM) approaches, feet crunching on the mottled blanket of stones.

ST: Nice evening for it.

FM: A perfect one.

(glances of camaraderie)

ST: Caught anything yet?

FM: Not yet – but they'll come, always do.

ST: Surf looks good, what ya after?

FM: Stars, always stars of course.

ST: Yeah, on a night like this they're magnificent. *(looks up at the night sky)*

FM: Bright and full of mystery – do you ever wonder what they really are?

ST: Err… what kind of fish you after?

FM: No fish here at night, only stars, millions of 'em.

ST: No fish uh? Just passing the… err…time of night, like me then? *(smiles)*

FM: And what a good place for that! *(turns and looks at the stranger)* No rod?'

ST: No fish, no rod!

FM: Stars, I catch stars.

ST: Up there? *(points up)* Maybe in our dreams, but you're fishing the sea.

FM: I catch stars in this black and endless sea – wishing stars I call them.

ST: So no fish *(slightly irate)*, just stars in there *(points to the dark sea)* – is that what you're saying?

FM: Stars at night, fish in day, but fish ain't no use to me.

ST: Why not?

FM: I'm a star man.

ST: A star man eh…? *(shuffles nervously)*

FM: It's my job, see – to catch a star now and then – catch a wish, catch a dream.

ST: Whatever.

FM: Forever.

ST: Nice talking to you star man… *(starts to leave)*.

FM: I've got one, strong, out there in the breaking surf.

(he points, and they both look out – the rod bends and the line goes tight and starts to sing)

FM: See it jump? Wow, it's a good one alright!

ST: That's no star, that's a big, mean looking jumping fish.

(large fish leaps out of the surf – fighting the fish, the fisherman moves into the sea a little and the stranger follows)

ST: Anyway, if the stars are all up there, how can they be in here? *(Points up and then down to the sea)*

FM: They only come out at night, rise up – look at the horizon – you know a shooting star ain't no different from this jumping fish, just that stars can't swim, just like fish can't twinkle in the night sky, they have to change you know, and anyway not all fish become stars at night, too damned many of them – it would be permanent daytime! *(laughs)*

ST: Whatever, it sure is a nice fish though. Here it comes! Wow, look at it sparkle!

FM: Star, it's a star – not a fish.

ST: Star fish you mean.

FM: You trying to be funny? Guess it is funny *(laughs)* – make a wish, quick, quick, you've got your chance now.

ST: Wish – what wish?

FM: How should I know, but be careful, don't wish for too much, last guy wished for peace and crashed on the way home – he got his peace alright.

ST: You're a nut.

FM: Wish! Wish!

ST: I wish! I wish! I wish!

FM: Hey! That's three!

ST: So what? You're totally freaking me out!

FM: Here it is!

(the fish swims around the shallows right by the two men's feet leaving a swirl of white surf and green sparkling fluorescence in its wake)

ST: I wish I could have some of whatever it is you've had – because I just don't get you and all your crazy talk!

FM: Aaah a good wish.

ST: The fish is off, gone – why didn't you land it?

FM: Land it? What use would that be – you've heard of meteorites right? Best leave it as a fish star

ST: You mean star fish.

FM: No I don't.

ST: Who do you think you are – God?

FM: The star man of course.

ST: And I suppose you become a fish at daybreak?

FM: Don't be daft, I just disappear and turn up some place else with my fishing rod and line – catch a wish, sometimes two – you were really lucky tonight, that was one hell of a fish to wish on – you'll see – it's done now. Won't get two like that in a night.

(reels the line out of the water)

ST: Fish must have swallowed the hook. *(examining the dangling line)*

FM: There weren't no hook or bait, but I do use a weight to cast into the surf.

ST: So how did you hook it? *(looking perplexed)*

FM: I'm a star man. Well, I guess I'll be seeing around you then, show you a few tricks sometime.

ST: Sure, whatever.

(the two men part and we follow the stranger across the shingle to his car. He looks troubled as he glances back at the empty beach, fading stars and the coming dawn)

(the following night we see the stranger on a different beach with a rod and line ready for casting, looking up and then out to sea, not exactly sure of what to do — he is soon joined by the star man)

ST: Did I really wish upon a star?

WHEN THE NORTH STAR FALLS

Published in Fear of Monkeys (Dec 2019 – The Moor Macaque issue)

C old wind gently hisses at the cabin door. Inside, through an old wooden window, two people stare at a clear night full of stars.

Dave: 'Do it right, or you'll do it wrong.'

Rex: 'Feels like trouble.'

Dave: 'Trouble only comes when the North Star falls out the sky…still there?'

Rex: 'Still there…'

Dave: 'Sure it is, now pass that box.'

Rex: 'Junk…'

Dave: 'Once upon a time, when nothing bad ever happened, this junk was someone's treasure…my mother's before you ask…my job to save it or dump it.'

Rex: 'This her house?'

Dave: 'Walked out one day about a year ago, never came back…sent a letter asking to give it closure.'

Rex: 'Letter…?

Dave: 'Lvov postmark, looked it up, there's an opera house, loves opera, listened to it on the radio, that radio there, taught me more about the world than any book… could be anywhere now, over the hill, far away, that's for sure…

…had a lodger, not that he paid a cent, drifter type, lived in the woods, scavenged trashcans at night, scruffy with a big black beard, turned up when first snow fell, desperate. She took him in, still strong, not wasted like those scrawny tramps you see down town muttering to ghosts, became her handyman, chopped logs…guess he did the other thing, never asked and she never told…took him with her.'

Rex: 'Her lover?'

Dave: 'Wouldn't say that exactly, makes it sound romantic, can't see it myself, maybe they were co-dependent and sex part of the deal. It's anyone's guess.'

Rex: 'Your old man…?'

Dave: 'Threw him out when I was five. His drinking got too much. Useless and wasted, every night sat in that chair looking for the star that had long fallen from his sky, so she said.'

Rex: 'Sad story…'

Dave: 'Sad in the fairy tale of your mind…she taught me to fish, gather mushrooms, everything you need to be self sufficient in these lonely woods…know how long it took me to walk to school…in summer, hour and a half, over the mountain…winter, skied the frozen river down to school…if wind blew hard and the drifts too deep, couldn't get back, slept in a shack, wreck down there, right where the steep track ends and the river meets the sea…planned for that, had a stash of food, logs and stove, even had a bed… freezing cold 'less under blankets huddled by the stove. Morning time, back at school, everybody knew, didn't say a word…least I learned to read and write. Got a girlfriend, half moved in the winter shack, must have honked like a pair of rotten skunks…her folks the type who married their offspring, better off with me…ended up moving to this cabin, got on great with Mom. What did I need an old man for, telling me what to do…anyway, what sort of person tells another what to do…things were fine.'

Rex: '…don't think trouble's coming?'

Dave: 'Still up there in the night sky, told me yourself.'

Rex: 'Doesn't feel right…'

Dave: 'Not for you.'

Rex: 'Feel responsible.'

Dave: 'Lost you mean. She's having the baby, not you.'

Rex: 'Aren't I?'

Dave: 'Don't be a dumbass, you're concealing a six-pack under that jacket, not a sprout. Grab the kerosene lamp, want to show you something.'

The following afternoon, through a gap in the cliff top trees, the wild sea shows. Gazing at spray lifting from tops of rolling waves, all around him tall pines hiss and sway.

The hillbilly was too worldly. How could his Mom, who lived half way up a mountain with no road, take a tramp across the world? Nothing added up. Had he really skied to school? It was bloody miles away and the winters long and savage.

Walking along the cliff, Rex drops steeply down to the river mouth. Just before the slopes flatten out he sees the shack, tumbled down and full of weeds. Inside is an old stove and a rotting sodden bed. Kicking a rusted can, he turns, following the river back inland. High above, low grey cloud warns of snow. The mountain's already impassable.

Still unfrozen, the only way to cross the river is by a footbridge at the far end of town on the other side of the mountain. An old canoe solves this problem. Untying a rope from a rickety post, he pulls the canoe down the steep bank, into the river racing out to sea. Jumping in, he paddles hard across the current to the other side. Dragging the canoe out of the water, he leaves it high, far from the reaches of the tide.

The walk is long, a winding path between trees bending from relentless wind. It won't be long before this too is full of snow and the frozen river the only option left.

The crack of a breaking branch makes him stop. A storm is coming and he hurries on, trying not to think. It's dusk by the time he reaches the boundary gate, its red sign warning not to trespass. Slightly out of breath, he arrives at the road leading into town. Distant lights pull him on.

The store is empty. Rex hands over a piece of paper to the store-keeper.

Storekeeper: 'Going to carry everything on this list up there by yourself?'

Rex: 'It's the job, what he asked.'

Storekeeper: 'Take it from me, that's two good runs, you'll be exhausted, end up stumbling back in the dark, it's risky…you are coming back?'

Rex: 'Do my best…make up two loads, here's the pack for the first.'

Storekeeper: 'You're one of those new college kids, what made you come up here to study?'

Rex: 'Free room, free food, free fees, no free money so I'm working for…'

Storekeeper: 'Dave, his Mom gave him an unpronounceable Indian name, just like hers, so someone called him Dave, just stuck…'

Rex: 'Rex…pleased to meet you, I mean…I've been coming here a while now, but you know that…'

Storekeeper: 'How old fashioned. Storekeeper to you, folks here like to keep things discreet…many kids in college?'

Rex: 'Twelve, meant to be hundreds, maybe next year, we'll see…'

Storekeeper: 'Revive the town, good for us, boring for you, can't see it with our winters…what's your girl's name?'

Rex: 'You know? Of course you do, Anastasia…tell me about the drifter?'

Storekeeper: 'Gone.'

Rex: '…must know something, he, Dave, mentioned him.'

Storekeeper: 'Like the rest, turned up one day looking for work, no past, no questions, didn't get work…either freeze to death in winter, or leave town, head south, he did neither. Didn't see him for a while, then he was here, six feet four looking like he could wrestle a bear, snap you right in two, had that toxic look, dangerous. Hell knows what she did to him…anything else?'

Rex: 'See you in the morning.'

Pushing the glass door open, Rex leaves. Stepping into cold night air, he hurries home to Ana.

Ana: 'Two hours!'

Rex: 'Snow closed the mountain.'

Ana: 'That's four hours a day, every day you work for him, the river won't be frozen solid for another month…be exhausted, skin and bone…'

Rex: '…get a six-pack.'

Ana: 'Only idiots at the gym get six-packs.'

Rex: 'We need the money, besides, needs me with his broken arm, there's a lot of lifting, said something about cutting logs, wants gas and oil…gave me a list for the store.'

Ana: 'Logs, thought he was closing the place down?'

Rex: 'Said so, got a month max before weather shuts the forest route. Reckon your Dad will lend me his skis?'

Ana: 'Even he couldn't get up the mountain with skis, slept in that broken shack you saw, with…what was her name?

Rex: 'Didn't say.'

Ana: 'I'll ask Mom, she knows everyone, still left here.'

Rex: 'How's the little bump?'

Ana: 'Find out for yourself…'

Long before dawn, the rude clank of alarm wakes them both.

Ana: 'Still pitch black…'

Rex: 'Early start, long day,'

Ana: 'Don't go, not yet…you will be back, won't you?'

The town is hushed and dark. Each cold morning for the next month or so, entering or passing the store will become routine for Rex.

Storekeeper: 'Seven o'clock, you're half an hour late, it'll be light by the time you reach the gate. Here's a torch for getting back, take it, I'll put it on the bill. With this heavy load you won't be at the cabin until ten so don't hang around, I'll have the other pack ready for twelve…now get going and don't forget to bring the money down…did you eat?'

Rex: 'Thanks, no…'

Storekeeper: 'Doesn't that girl feed you? Take this, it's my lunch, I'll put that on the bill too…be sure to make some noise, bears are on the move.'

The pack pulls him down. Dragging his feet, he hears his heavy breath. Twilight shows shadows, just enough to mark the way. He drops the torch into a pocket. At the gate, daybreak breaks.

To make the sign clearly visible, Dave had asked him to close the gate. The clonk breaks his dreamy thoughts and he hikes slowly to the soft hiss of wind and crunching snow. The storm has left a sprinkle that has frozen overnight. Although it's around freezing, he soon becomes warm, near hot as he pushes hard to make up time. Hiking in the dark couldn't be an option.

Tired, he drops the pack by the canoe and watches the river race towards the sea. Dave had warned him of the rush of tides, told him how to gauge them but, more importantly, know when not to cross. Placing the pack behind the seat, he pushes the canoe to the river's edge and lets it slide into the water. Yanking on the rope, he drags the canoe upstream, a hundred yards at least, and jumps in, the current taking him downstream as he furiously paddles to the other side. His heart racing, he hurriedly steps out, hauling the canoe to safety.

By the time he passes the shack, an inch of snow is underfoot. His tracks join bear prints. Under the load, his pace agonisingly slow, he starts to hum, whistling in the wind.

Dave: 'Storekeeper tell you to wake the neighbourhood? Thought so, winding you up, reminding me he wants his money…the bears have already left, gone high…except for the ones that seem to like the winter here…you're the last thing on their mind, besides they're too fat now to give chase, if that happens, run downhill…won't take the risk of falling head over heels.'

Rex: 'Run? This thing must weigh thirty kilos!'

Dave: 'Did you secure the canoe? Good…let's empty this, get you some food before we think about the next load.'

Rex: 'Gave me sandwiches, putting it on the bill, he said…second pack ready at twelve.'

Dave: 'Got you on a time trial, has he? You won't be back by twelve. Throw the sandwiches, I'll cook some fish, caught this morning….in fact, forget the second load, too much with this limited daylight unless you want to stay the night again…didn't think so, we'll do it tomorrow…now the fish…'

Rex: 'Those maps you showed me yesterday…so carefully detailed…'

Dave: 'Took us years, precious…if you want mushrooms, the month to pick, it's there, everything's there from the other side of river, over the mountain to the miles of forest right up to the national wilderness boundary, round the coast too, winter and summer maps. For survival, living here, marks where I caught this fish…not that knife, this one, the bendy one, use that to fillet…slowly now, let it curve around the bone…even shows where bears like to sleep….good, that's it.'

Rex: 'What about the heads and tails…and those little markings on the maps, the yellow ones…?'

Dave: 'Soup, don't waste a thing. You noticed uh…old mines, shafts, some covered with debris, wouldn't want to fall through, some sixty feet deep and full of water, tells you where not to tread, especially in the snow…men disappear up here, fools looking…use this pan, we'll fry it, add the mushrooms at the end.'

Rex: 'That was fantastic…'

Dave: 'Better than a lousy sandwich, usually smoke the fish in that shed, it needs a good clean, proper sort out, start tomorrow…you can always stay…'

Rex: '…have to get back, she…Ana…'

Dave: '…needs you, if you don't do it right…'

Rex: 'That's so obvious…three years before I finish…what was I thinking?'

Dave: 'You weren't, that's how it works. In three years, unless you make another, it'll go stale. On the other side of town, out in The Boonies, some make six or eight, keeps them together until they finally run out of steam, then they just stay put…'

Rex: 'Boonies…for real?'

Dave: 'Broken down homes, broken families, teeth are optional, only cooking done is in meth labs, sheds like my old school shack, blow themselves up sometimes…not from The Boonies, is she?'

Rex: '…not inbred, and Anastasia still has her own teeth…'

Dave: 'The Petrov kid?'

Rex: 'Is nothing secret?'

Dave: 'Secret yes, private no…only one Anastasia in town…went to school with her Mom, she married a Russian, engineer who jumped ship…nothing's private here…already making up stories 'bout you.'

Rex: 'Oh…asked about your shack friend from school, didn't mean to pry.'

Dave: 'No secret…came from The Boonies, never went back, this place was…everything. Come on…go back down together…

…you're good with the canoe…remember what I said, never cross if the small waves have white caps, end up out to sea or half way to town…chanced it once, never again…incoming flood pushed me way upstream, not a thing I could do, couldn't get it out, steep walls, got stuck between boulders, had to wait hours for the tide to turn…repaired the bridge after that.'

Dave banged the gate shut.

Rex: 'People trespass?'

Dave: 'Occasional poacher…one shot, whole town wakes up, gets the jitters…gives Sheriff and his dozy men something to do…hemmed in between the river and the sea, why would anyone bother…different story on the mountain.'

They head for the store.

Storekeeper: 'Three hours late…you'll never make it back…oh, didn't expect you so soon…how's the arm?'

Dave: 'Cast comes off in a few days, lucky not to need a pin…got to take it gentle…why I need the kid here.'

Storekeeper: 'Sheriff made enquiries, routine, shows he's trying, asked if I'd seen you... course I had, around the time that guy disappeared, right when you broke your arm slipping on ice outside my store.'

Dave: 'Shouldn't have been on the mountain, fool, like all the others, it's dangerous, bears, mine shafts...saw a pack of wolves swimming across the river this year, three weeks later ran passed the cabin, yelping, enjoying themselves, counted fourteen...don't worry Kid, you're safe...what I owe you?'

Storekeeper: 'Sheriff says it's the bridge...no bridge, no access...you're not finished yet, pay me at the end...those the maps you want copied, laminated?'

Later, at the house:

Ana: 'How's your day?'

Rex: 'Hardly managed the first load, was terrible, think he knew that...god my shoulders ache...ended up showing me the tasks, little jobs needing done, walked back with me... asked after you...know him?'

Ana: 'Know his face, who doesn't, everybody knows every face around here...Mom says the kids were mean to him at school, especially The Boonies, coz the colour of his skin, called him names...cracked open an older boy's skull one day with a lump of wood...boy was picking on him, had stitches, was an uproar, parents wanted to press charges but Sheriff wasn't having it...blew over quick enough, was left alone after that, no one wanted to be his friend except some half-baked misfit, sat right next to him in class the following day, real close, they'd never even spoken...Mom say she was a Boonie, girl who moved into the shack with him...just turned fourteen!

Taught her to ski, 'came so good was nicknamed Ski, no one said her real name after that...been forgot...'

Rex: 'From Boonie to Ski, that's funny...'

Ana: 'Half the town are Boonies...alright, long as you don't go asking questions, poking in their business.'

Rex: 'What a place to put a faculty, what were they thinking…'

Ana: 'Regretting it, are you?'

Rex: 'It's so out of time.'

Ana: 'This place is home for me….Mom says we can live here while you study and the baby is still small…after that…'

Rex: 'Move far away…'

Ana: '…won't leave me, will you?'

Rex: 'Will you want another…?'

Ana: 'Don't ask that, not over the shock of this one…there's more to your winter job…Drifter spoke fluent Russian, English broken bad…came around when I was small, don't know what they talked about, maybe Russia…Dad refused to see him after the disappearances…'

Rex: 'Storekeeper said a man disappeared recently on the mountain, when Dave broke his arm slipping on the ice…'

Ana: 'Slipping on ice, did he say that?'

Rex: 'Storekeeper did, outside the shop.'

Ana: '…been at least six disappearances, maybe more, cars found abandoned near the bridge, no trace except one body found at sea, lungs full of river water, shot right though the heart, high velocity…took Drifter in, checked ballistics, nothing, had to let him go…no guns at the cabin except an old shotgun…wild goose chase, another unsolved murder case…something with that Sheriff though…know how gossip goes…long tales, passes idle time, suppose…'

Rex: '…already doing that to us, he said.'

Ana: 'Oh don't…it's the gold, the disused mines shafts…people go looking, snooping…if there was gold, you'd think Dave would be rich and gone.'

Rex: 'Likes it up there…never seen anyone more at home…maybe Drifter cleaned the mines out, found new ones…?'

Ana: 'Why the secrecy, it's legal to have gold on your land…'

Rex: 'Would be nothing but trouble…maybe it's not their land…think Drifter killed those people, ran off with a horde of gold?'

Ana: 'Ran off with Dave's Mom to Ukraine, Dad said…never thought before, but Dad paid off the mortgage in one big lump after Drifter disappeared…was an engineer doing small repairs in the saw mill before they it shut down…how could that be?'

Rex: 'Specialised in gold…disappearances…'

Ana: 'Dad's far too peachy…we're as bad as others, making stuff up, stories…anyway, what's he paying you?'

Rex: 'Didn't ask…'

Ana: 'Rex! We need money.'

The following morning, Rex, half asleep, creeps downstairs to the kitchen.

Rex: 'Mrs. Petrov…up early…anything wrong…?'

Mrs. Petrov: 'Feel like a walk.'

Rex: 'Pitch black and freezing, you sure…?'

Mrs. Petrov: 'Made coffee, join you, far as the gate, today…'

Not speaking, they walk carefully on icy streets towards the lit-up store. From behind the glass, Dave and Storekeeper watch them approach.

Storekeeper: 'What brings her out on a dark frosty morning?'

Dave: 'Supplies…'

Storekeeper: 'That's what you call it these days…'

Opening the door, Dave steps out.

Dave: 'Mrs. Petrov.'

Mrs. Petrov: 'Kei…Dave…'

Dave: 'Grab the pack Rex, got quite a day today.'

Trailing behind, following the torchlight, he tries to catch the murmurs. They are waiting by the gate.

No one speaks, only the familiar sound of the closing latch tells him to move, follow the light towards the forest. Pausing, he turns. Just visible, her silhouette stands motionless. He's sure she's staring back.

Dave: 'Damn tide racing…need to sit it out, wait for it to slack.'

Rex: 'You know Ana's Mom?'

Dave: 'Small town…watching out for you, nothing funny 'bout that…'

Rex: 'Says her Mom often leaves before first light…returns late, sometimes not at all…Dad says it's fine, what she does, walk.'

Dave: 'Go stir crazy stuck indoors all day…he must also have a thing…'

Rex: 'He hunts, at night.'

Dave: 'Catching shadows…come on…let's get it in the water.'

Sometime later, outside the cabin:

Dave: 'Good day's work…better get going soon, plenty light still left.'

Rex: 'Ana wants to know…how much?'

Dave: 'Two hundred a day…pay you for a month, regard-less…sound right to you? Good…you smell that…?'

Rex: 'Smoke…?'

Dave: 'Grab the bag of shot, you know the one…I'll get the gun.'

On fresh snow, they move fast uphill.

Dave: '…long way off, near the mine cluster, north side of the mountain…keep up.'

Rex: 'It's strong now…'

Dave: 'Shush, stay low, we'll creep up.

See him, there, behind the fire. Load, that's it, both barrels…when I say, snap it shut, hold it steady…fire into the trees, blast the twigs above his head.

Now…!'

Rex: 'Jesus!'

Dave: 'Where is he…?'

Rex: 'On the ground… got a rifle!'

Dave: 'Quick, load…ready…'

Rex: 'What was that…?'

Dave: 'Hit the kerosene, pack's on fire…load again…come on…'

Rex: 'He's running off…'

Dave: 'Heading for the pass, stay close.'

Rex: 'It's closed, you said.'

Dave: 'Closed, not impassable...need to get around the mountain, sitting ducks if he shoots from the top.'

Rex: 'It's tiring...up to my thighs, snow's too deep...'

Dave: 'Keep up...see him?'

Rex: 'Down there, looking back...heading for the bridge...'

Dave: 'Hold it, steady...ready...

You ok, Kid?'

Rex: 'Blast knocked me off my feet...'

Dave: 'Let's finish the job.'

Rex: 'Shoot him, you mean.'

Dave: 'With you around, dumb...scare him witless, that's what....'

Down at the river, before the last of dusk hides the view, they step onto the bridge. At the far end, across the dirt road, a yellow car stands, engine running.

Dave: 'Across the rail...steady...'

Pellets hit the rear of the car, the resounding bang echoing down the river.

Dave: 'There he goes...nearly missed the bend...'

Standing in silence, they watch dark shapes of crows cawing in tall trees opposite. Mist rises from the river. Minutes later, everything is black. Rex leans against the rail, shaking.

Flashing lights of the Sheriff's car round the bend. It stops. The lights cut. They hear the door open, click shut. In the darkness, the voice speaks softly.

Sheriff: 'Got a call from a man scared half to death...said someone trying to kill him on the mountain...heard the shots myself.'

Dave: 'Trespassing...was out shooting...how was I to know he was hiding behind a tree?'

Sheriff: 'Take the bridge away, you never use it anymore...'

Dave nudges Rex and they move to the far end of the bridge where they can make out the Sheriff's face.

Sheriff: 'Got him with you, have you?'

Dave: 'Be dead without the Kid…loaded up, four times at least.'

Sheriff: 'That's a serious offence…'

Rex: 'Didn't shoot anyone!'

Sheriff: 'Loaded the gun, four times, I heard.'

Dave: 'Both barrels, Sheriff, snapped them shut, held it steady, like a pro…I just feebly pulled the trigger…couldn't do much with my busted arm.'

Ana: 'That's it, nothing more?'

Rex: 'Drove us both to town, Dave still holding the shotgun…could smell the burnt powder. Pulled up outside your door, said: 'tomorrow at the store'…not a word more, I swear that's what happened…'

Ana: 'Come on…wrack that big brain of yours…'

Rex: '…your Mom started to call him…Ka, Kei, something…changed to Dave, fast.'

Ana: 'Why would she use his Indian name? You're shivering, freezing cold, have a hot shower…I'll have a word…'

'…that woman, blood out of a stone…knows nothing, just walks, all night sometimes…Dad's gone hunting, never brings a thing home …'

Rex: 'Only shadows…Dave said…'

Ana: 'What does that mean…parents are weird, never known them to share a bed, let alone a room…is it me, or is this town somehow off the compass? What yours like?'

Rex: 'Find out next break, if I live that long…I wish I'd…'

Ana: 'Don't say that, I need you…did you ask how much?'

Rex: 'Two hundred a day, every day for a month…regardless, whatever that means.'

Ana: 'Great! We'll have money, keep us going while you study. You can do it… not too difficult…is it?'

Rex: 'Physically, near impossible.'

Ana: 'You wanted a six pack…'

Rex: 'I'm not an idiot…someone may die next time…'

Ana: 'Please Rex, the baby…my job pays peanuts….Mom says he likes you.'

Stopping the alarm, Ana pulls Rex back to bed.

Ana: 'Can't go…scan, remember? Need you there…'

Rex: 'Forgot…god I'm tired…have to tell him, he's at the store…back soon.'

Ana: 'Be waiting for you…right here.'

Rex: 'Good morning Mrs. Petrov, Mr. Petrov catching shadows in the night?'

Mrs. Petrov: 'You sound just like him…become like him if you keep loading shotguns on the hill.'

Rex: 'How could you know…forget it, this place…'

He hurries to the store.

Storekeeper: 'Too late, he left an hour ago.'

Rex: 'I'm not late…he didn't wait…?'

Storekeeper: 'The clinic…she told him, was here at six…pack's ready for tomorrow, be early…'

Rex: '…Mrs. Petrov…can't be…she's in the kitchen, didn't say…
…who told him?'

Storekeeper: 'She did…
…canoe still this side of the river, where you left it…he went over the mountain this morning…'

Rex: 'Thanks…would never have thought, of that…'

After a three-hour drive, they both look together at the screen.

Ana: 'Rex, our baby…I'm so happy…'

Rex: '…not again…turn it off Ana…I didn't sleep a wink'

Ana: 'Mom's doing breakfast…long day, she said…'

Rex: 'What would she know…?'

Rex: 'Good morning Mrs. Petrov…Mr. Petrov…how's the night?'
Mr. Petrov: 'Dark…'

No sooner has he left the house, the unmistakable shadowed gait of Storekeeper comes towards him.

Storekeeper: 'Ice on the road, fresh snow on the trail…stay out the forest 'till day breaks, might slip with this load…one broken arm's enough around here…'

Later, passing the gate, everything's still black. The torch barely lights the frosty trail. Stopping at the edge of the forest, he drops the heavy pack, cuts the light and waits in the cold. It becomes unbearable, forcing him to pace, stamp his freezing feet until twilight breaks the night. In gloomy light, he moves towards the shadows of tall trees.

On the icy riverbank, the canoe sticks hard to frozen grass. He wrenches it free.

At the top of the steep uphill trail, hissing wind blows hard and cold. Relieved, he drops the pack outside the cabin.

Dave: 'Glad you made it…thought you might leave town after all the excitement…'

Rex: 'Between the Sheriff, Storekeeper and those loony Petrovs, feel I'm public property…she tell about the scan?'

Dave: 'Daughter's having a baby, one you put there…looking out for you both…'

Rex: 'Snow's getting deep…how much longer…?'

Dave: 'Once the river starts freezing, break it with the paddle…if it doesn't break, leave it, don't cross, you'll be through…current runs hard under the ice, remember that…forest be impassable any-way…week later, hard enough to ski, let you know…you cross-country?'

Rex: 'Badly…'

Dave: 'Good enough… don't worry, no more heavy loads.…warm up, coffee on the stove…need to move the outhouse before the ground freezes solid…feeling strong?'

Later, in the afternoon:

Dave: 'Grand job, can't see that filling up…let's grab another coffee, have a bite…walk back with you, cast comes off in morning…'

Rex: '…that jersey, one neatly placed over the chair, wasn't there before, looks like…Mrs…'

Dave: 'Last night, North Star shone pretty in the sky…if it falls, you'll never get it back…darkness ever more…'

Rex: '…trouble…'

Dave: '…doesn't have to come…you loaded the gun, remember…'

Rex: '…feel set up, trapped…'

Dave: 'Smart kid, University, got a girl, pretty, no Boonie, that's for sure…crazy about you, her Mom said so herself…you're her ticket out…what you feel when you saw the scan?'

Rex: 'Nothing, felt nothing…damn you…'

Dave: 'There was a time men didn't know their fathers, slept with their mothers…'

Rex: 'That's disgusting!'

Dave: 'Unless you're a Boonie…it's not the baby you want, it's her, all silky…felt good uh…still feels good, keep it feeling good…leave this place, take her with you…like her, don't you…like…'

Rex: '…you liked Ski…'

Dave: 'Not wrong there…losing light with all this talk, have to go over the mountain now, yesterday's tracks should still be good…come on, need haste…'

They cross the bridge in darkness. Rex turns on the torch.

Dave: 'Long hike back to town, sorry Kid, no chauffer today…'

Rex: 'Drifter shoot the man…found out to sea…?'

Dave: 'Questions lead to trouble…Drifter looks like Bigfoot's cousin but wouldn't harm a fly…river rises in the snowy peaks we glimpsed from the pass…winds round Boonie country…have their own wars, laws, missing people aren't reported, maybe the body floated down…'

Rex: 'What if she wants another?'

Dave: '…stop asking questions none wants to hear…'

Ana: '…why would he say that…river doesn't go near The Boonies, they live on the other side of town, miles out…'

Rex: '…maybe mixing things up, was a horrible day, digging a six foot hole, ground full of rocks…helped with the barrow, can't do too much…cast comes off tomorrow…make my life easier, at least…meeting at the store, ten o'clock…glad when this job's over…back to normal…'

Ana: 'We need the money…a lie in, can't wait…'

Ana: '…can't stop shaking…you're the best…the only…'

Rex: 'Your Mom still in the house?'

Ana: 'No, market day…need to go?'

Rex: 'Not yet, your parents get weirder by the day…'

Ana: '…sorry…come back over here…'

The streets are busy. A trailer loaded with a small dinghy stands outside the store. Dave reverses a pickup truck and Storekeeper hitches it to the trailer.

Storekeeper: 'Chainsaw's in the back…want the wood, fair's fair now…'

Dave: 'All yours…don't leave it too long or you'll be chipping it out the ice…when's low tide?'

Storekeeper: 'Soon enough…don't forget to tie it off, big rope behind the seat…'

Dave: '…never hear the end of it…jump in Kid…you can swim…?'

He drives with care on the icy road, stopping where the tarmac ends and gravel track begins.

Dave: 'Snow…not much, risky with the trailer though…help me with the chains…'

Rex: 'Your arm, sorry...how's it...?'

Dave: '...need to get the muscle strong...few weeks...that's it, leave them loose, snow-chains tighten once the wheels move...still need help, least till the river freezes over...'

They arrive at the river.

'... sun never hits this spot, first place to ice up...you jump out, I'll back up...shout when the dinghy hangs over the riverbank...'

Rex: 'Stop!'

Between the icy bank and the swirling water, a low tide mud flat stretches along the river. A hundred yards to their right stands the long wooden footbridge.

Dave: '...release the winch, easy now, I'll guide it down the bank...that's it, on the mud...grab the chainsaw and the rope...

...not being funny, we need to push it to the water...be cold...did say you could swim?'

Rex: 'Mud's deep...jeez, freezing...'

Dave: 'Nearly there...push it off the mud, bit more...'

Rex: '...feet stuck, water rising...Dave...!'

Dave: '...tide's turning, ready...now!'

Dave pulls the starter cord. Rex hauls himself up, out of the mud and flooding tide and flops into the boat. He is shivering.

Dave: '...no other way, need to work fast...tie the rope around that post, there, on the bridge...loop it through...that's it...'

He takes the boat upstream, under the bridge and cuts the throttle. Letting the boat drift back, he pulls hard to start the saw.

Dave: '...cut the support posts...this one first...at the surface, quick...don't fall in, the saw's expensive...'

On his stomach, arms outstretched, Rex leans over the side. He clasps the saw as the dinghy moves with the swirling tide. The cutting is messy, the movements of the boat throwing him off balance. Nearly losing grip as the saw kicks back, the whirring chain slices through the water, just missing the boat.

Dave: 'Now the others...work fast or we'll never get the boat back out…'

Rex: 'It's going to topple over!'

Dave: 'Kill the saw, hold the rope…god's sake don't pull, crash right into us… connect the winch…hurry, can't control it in this tide…

…good job…'

At the top of the riverbank, they secure the rope around a tree before winching the dinghy back onto the trailer.

Rex: 'Covered in freezing mud…can't feel my feet…hands…'

Dave: 'Bag in the truck, got a change of clothes…both of us, boots too…get to it while your fingers still move…throw me some…colder than I thought…'

They sit in the cab of the pickup truck, engine running, heater on, staring at the river.

Dave: 'Tight call…river runs hard around that bend…you did great…feeling warm?'

Rex: 'No longer hypothermic, still cold though…'

Dave: 'Here, drink some more coffee…helps, a bit.'

In the last of the light, the high tide pushes the bridge. They watch it topple over.

Dave: 'The out tide will pull the bridge 'til the rope goes taught…should then get pushed onto the riverbank…stay there, hopefully, stuck and frozen in.

Storekeeper wants to dismantle it, nail by nail, bolt by bolt…sell the wood…good hardwood that, cost some, took an age to build…'

Rex: 'Your land we just cut access to?'

Dave: 'Indian land…suppose so, got a piece of paper if that's what you mean…time to go…chains need taking off before the tarmac road…'

Ana: 'Look at you, have a shower…Mom's making food…Dad's going hunting later tonight…be glad when you're done with this…in the freezing river with a chainsaw, you could have died!'

Rex: 'Your Mom said I'll become just like him…'

Ana: '…you're right about her…weirder by the day, never noticed 'till you turned up…we won't become like them…Rex?'

Rex: '…like him and Ski…'

Ana: 'Oh, don't…'

Later, after supper:

Ana: '…another silent meal, took it as normal once…it's not normal, is it…and Dad's night hunting, always done…with who, where…hunting what? Let's follow him Rex, see where he goes…can use your car, park at the diner, wait for him to pass…'

Rex: 'What for, I'm dog-tired…need to be at the store by eight…'

Ana: '…we can have another lie in…'

Sometime later, huddled in the front seats of the car, they wait.

Rex: 'Can't believe we're stalking your Dad…still cold from the river thing…'

Ana: 'Turn the heater up, this is fun…stay down, mustn't know we're here…'

Rex: 'Not a soul, diner's empty…if he comes this way, sure to see the car…'

Ana: '…course he'll come…not heading for The Boonies…'

Rex: 'That's him! He'll see our lights, not another car in sight…let's not do this Ana…'

Ana: 'Cut the lights, moon's up, new snow on road…follow his taillights…'

Hanging far behind, on a snowy winding road, they follow clear red lights through a pitch-black forest.

Rex: 'It's been half an hour, maybe he's heading for the next town…'

Ana: 'Three hours away, don't think so…Dad's pulling up, there, stop, quick…'

Rex: 'Too close, he'll see us…another car coming, we'll be all lit up, get down…wait…stopping…must be his hunting friend…'

Ana: 'They're getting out…into the back of his, friend's

car…what…?

Rex: 'Ana, another car…in the mirror, pray they don't look out, see us in the headlights…passing now, there…your Dad…oh…'

Ana: '…must be playing tricks…no…Rex, please…say something…drive, now!'

Later, in their bedroom:

Ana: 'Hear that? She's furious, slamming the front door…'

Rex: 'Night walk…'

Ana: 'Don't Rex…she played dumb, said it was imagination, lying cow…'

Rex: 'Maybe saw it wrong, just talking 'bout the hunt…'

Ana: '…saw it both, kissing in the back…my Dad, Rex…'

Rex: '…don't know what to say, need sleep…want a lie in, yes…?'

Ana: 'Going to lie-in everyday from now…won't let you become like him…separate bedrooms, that's how this mess starts…'

Rex: '…we don't know anything…'

Ana: '…parents barely talk, to me, each other…secret…whole town, blank faces, full of secrets….'

Rex: 'Secrets, that's what Dave said…'

Ana: 'Ask him, Rex…if anyone knows this place, it's him.'

Rex: 'Warned me not to ask…'

Ana: 'Please…need to know, something 'bout my Dad!'

Rex: 'Morning Mrs. Petrov…nice jersey…think I'll skip that coffee…'

Dave: 'Smash the ice…good, still thin enough to break…easy now…what's eating you, Kid?'

Rex: '…you don't want to hear…?

Dave: 'Seems I do…tell me at the cabin…

At the cabin:

Dave: …when you stick your nose in, in a place like this, find something soon enough… get a shock…or shot…how she holding up?'

Rex: 'Angry, at them both…asked me to ask, whatever good it does…'

Dave: 'Tell about the jersey?'

Rex: 'She was wearing it this morning…I'm not an idiot…'

Dave: 'North Star still shining in the sky?'

Rex: 'You tell me…?'

Dave: 'Still there, Kid. Want to keep it there?'

Rex: 'Don't want her upset, that's all…couldn't care less about this crazy town.'

Dave: 'Great girl…good parents, done her right, you will too…don't see any problem here.'

Rex: 'Dad hunts shadows in the night…you told me that. She needs to know…something…'

Dave: 'Wasn't legal then, end up in a freezing Gulag, full of murderers, foul disease, food not fit for dogs…certain death for a man, like him.

Worked the boats, jumped ship quick…found the perfect place, this backward town, full of secrets, dirty lies, questions never asked…didn't have to keep it secret, no one would have cared…old habits just die hard…cat's out the bag now…'

Rex: '…Mrs. Petrov? He married her…god's sake…'

Dave: 'Her secrets suited his…some secrets best not known…river's full of secrets, floating out to sea…

…come on, logs to cut and stack…'

Later that evening, back at the house:

Ana: 'Mom says Dad's gone, packed up, back to Russia…says it safe now…think I'll miss him…is it true what Dave said?'

Rex: '…doesn't lie, just shoot you in the head instead…reckon that…yes, true…'

Ana: 'Said he'd write, invite us over…she's not upset at all…one less meal to cook…oh Rex, we'll last, won't we…?'

Rex: 'Forever lie-ins. Found a piece of gold today…look…make a good ring one day, he said.'

Ana: 'Wow, no wonder he took the bridge away…give it here, keep it safe…working tomorrow…?'

Rex: 'Snowstorm coming, river's freezing over, nothing for a week or so…really need a break…'

Ana: '…still up there?'

Rex: 'He came back down with me.'

Ana: 'Mom needs a break too, does that sometimes, goes away…this thing with Dad, too much…had a heart to heart…didn't make new revelations or anything…got the place to ourselves, you and me…don't have to worry 'bout the noise…can't wait!'

Rex: '…been thinking…she looks so young…'

Ana: 'Thirty-four…was young, really young… difficult for her, and Dad…never liked to talk about it…'

Rex: 'He wants me at the store first thing, something about the maps…'

The storm leaves the town white. Although it has passed over, no one ventures out. Streets deserted, crows make the only sound.

Arm in arm, they crunch their way towards the store, their breath steaming in the cold.

Storekeeper: 'Snow's come early, shut the town, winter drinking's started, same thing every year…this your girl?'

Rex: '…know she is…in fact, what don't you know…?'

Storekeeper: 'Left you these…laminated maps, key to cabin, spare one in the outhouse rafter, one you just fixed up…'

Rex: 'Key…?'

Storekeeper: 'How else will you get in? Use her Daddy's skis, when the river's solid, not before…'

Rex: '…walked back with me…where's he…?'

Storekeeper: 'Opera…know it?'

Rex: 'He does…what about the work…?'

Storekeeper: 'Got a list…start tomorrow, take the bridge

apart...frozen to the bank by now...'

    Rex: 'A list, not expecting him back...?'

    Storekeeper: 'Long way Opera...take a winter, least.'

    Ana: 'Rex, your money...'

    Storekeeper: '...said to give you this...worth its weight in gold...'

    Rex: 'Anything else you need to tell me?'

    Storekeeper: '...me and Sheriff only friends you've got...it's the company you keep.

Your Mama's skis should fit you fine, little old...she sure could go...'

Momentarily, the silence of the empty street holds them.

    Ana: 'What's in the box...?'

    Rex: 'Come on, suddenly don't feel safe...'

Ana slams the front door shut and pulls the box from Rex's hands. Sitting on the bottom stair, she opens the lid. A handgun sits on pile of notes. Rex grabs the gun and Ana heads straight upstairs, shouting back down to him.

    Ana: 'Double lock...this has got me spooked....'

    Rex: 'Count it...I'll hide the gun, didn't put it there by accident...'

He joins her on the bed. She's staring at the pile.

    Ana: 'Sixty thousand...can really start a family!'

    Rex: 'If I get out of this alive...'

    Ana: 'Mom, skis...Dave...Storekeeper said it...please Rex, tell me it's not true.'

    Rex: 'They've gone...their secrets too...just you and me now...all I wanted was a cheap degree...'

    Ana: 'Mom always told me he was trouble, said it with a smile, the kind of smile no daughter should ever see her mother smile...Rex...say something...'

    Rex: '...must really like that trouble...anyway, trouble only comes when...'

The Dark Chapel

Published in Scarlet Leaf Review (April 2020)

Six bits of broken sticks
taken from the apple tree
where they tried to hang
the sexton
high.

Six bits of old rough wood
taken where the lightning struck
and cut the tree in two.

It's not quite a ruin but it could be soon, as relentless rain and cold winds try to penetrate and crack the dark, lichen covered granite. Its faded slate roof shows grey and blue in the morning light, just a few loose and crooked tiles, but it's still intact. It sits alone at the back of a steep bracken field, under a broken rocky crag, which rises to the skyline, black with cloud and cut with the occasional burst of light from the hidden sun. From the top of the crag, you can see wild ocean waves crashing on the shore far away and never know that a dark chapel lies a hundred feet below.

Rachel meandered through the fields, thigh deep in browned ferns and wet grass, towards her secret place. It was always wet here, even in midsummer. Three crab apple trees, which may have been part of an orchard once, all gnarled, twisted and laden with fruit, grew behind the chapel sheltered from the harshest storms. Amongst them was an old broken tree, black, cracked and fossilized with time.

She had lifted her dress above her knees to prevent it from getting wet, and Robert looked on from behind as he followed, enjoying the brief view when the sun momentarily broke through clouds making her dress almost transparent.

'I can see right through your dress when the sun shines.'

'God, don't you ever think about anything else?' She said, smiling.

Robert wanted to say no, but didn't, as he gazed up to the gloomy, dank looking building about a hundred yards in front.

'Looks grim.'

'What? No it's not – imagine what a great house it would make.'

But Robert didn't care; he had one thing only on his mind.

'Is it dry in there?'

Rachel smiled to herself, knowing his intentions. She had felt his eyes on her as she lifted the dress to wade through the undergrowth, her bare legs gently brushing against the wet foliage. She liked the feeling of power it gave her, the feeling that she herself had planted the seed of want in him, and like most men, he would now be unsatisfied until he had had her. But for now, he would have to wait.

She stopped in front of the old building and dropped her dress back down, smoothing it around her thighs whilst she waited for Rob to catch her up. Their breath was heavy from the exertion of the climb and they stood together for a moment as their chests settled and their pulses slowed. The heavy dark clouds that had followed them all morning broke open, suddenly letting through shafts of sunlight, which bounced off the wet granite, causing them to both instinctively shield their eyes against the brightness.

Rachel laughed,

'Come on Rob, check it out.'

She unbolted the old rusted wrought iron gate and swung it open whilst looking behind her to see Rob hanging back.

'What's up? Come on...'

'I don't know Rache, I know you've been trying to get me up here for ages, but I just feel a bit uneasy…'

'Fuck's sake! What are you going on about? This place is amazing…I've been coming up here for years and never felt anything weird. Come on, you'll see for yourself once we're in…you're going to love it.'

Rob hesitantly followed her onto the weedy gravel path. Now he just felt annoyed – with her and with himself. He was pissed off he'd let himself get talked into coming all the way up here just because she knew how to push his buttons. He had heard the stories about this place, like everyone else brought up in the area, and had no desire to be there. He also knew there wasn't a chance in hell of getting laid now, which was the only reason he'd agreed to come. He had noticed the shift in her as they had approached the chapel through the field. She had taken on an almost childlike persona, messing about, giggling, teasing him a little, but the way she never shut up about the place, spilling over with her enthusiastic plans, told him sex was the furthest thing from her mind right now.

Rob stopped and watched her, slightly ahead of him, pulling tendrils of brambles away from the old oak door to the side of the building and stamping them down with her feet. He noticed a little window right by him and peered through a small section of the stained glass. The dense cobalt blue in the glass made it difficult to focus his eyes and see beyond his own reflection, but slowly he made out another window positioned on the far wall and beyond that to what looked like an ancient apple tree sitting on the hillside, worn and scarred by the elements. Dark shadows flickered across his vision and the cawing of crows sent a tremor through his cold and tense body.

It felt like fear.

He shook it off, reluctantly following Rachel in through the door. The dank air inside felt thick and his breath got caught in his throat making him stumble. His body suddenly felt very heavy and he was dragged down to the old stone floor. Looking up, he saw the vast and tattered vaulted ceiling and Rachel looking down at him smiling, saying something he could not hear or understand. He felt he was underwater and the sounds were muted somehow. He was confused and began to panic. He desperately tried to get up but nothing happened. Something sat heavy on his chest. He felt a sense of dread but also shame as he realised he was helpless and there she was, watching him, holding out her hand to him. He caught hold of himself then and mustered enough concentration to extend his arm off the floor so she could take his hand and haul him up to his feet. He could hear again and heard her voice, amplified:

'What happened to you?'

'I must have just tripped.'

He was shaking now.

'What's the matter?'

Her easygoing smile was now replaced by a look of concern.

He instinctively wanted to get out of there but felt fixed to the floor and now a terrible fear started to grip him. His mouth was dry and he could feel sweat building on his brow.

Rachel was again saying something which he couldn't hear, and in that moment, between pleading for this strange thing to stop and running for the door, he grabbed her round the waist and kissed her hard – just to feel something normal, just to get back to something he understood. He pushed her up against the wall and tried to get his hand up her dress to pull at her knickers but she quickly fought herself free and roughly pushed him from her. He staggered back ashamed, and looked down to the floor.

'What's wrong with you Rob?'

Now he was angry. He glared at her.

'What's wrong with *you*? Why the hell did you bring me to this damned place if not for sex…'

The words stuck in his throat. Rachel was standing with her back to the open oak door, and he was facing towards it.

'Christ Rob, you look like you've seen a ghost – what the hell is wrong?'

But he didn't say a word, just stared towards the open door making

Rachel urgently turn around and gasp.

And there he stood, watching them; an old bent man with wizened lined features, a rough face that had spent a lifetime outdoors and a grey whisker beard to match. His hair was long, thick and matted under an old black felt hat and he wore something like a dark sacking dress all rough with holes hanging down to frayed ends well below his knees and above his rough and dirty bare feet. But it was the bundle of twigs and sticks he had strapped to his back that really made him out of place and time.

'What the fuck are you looking at?'

The old man was somehow a prop for Rob to return to normality.

'Piss off or I'll deck you.'

'Don't Rob.'

Rachel held his arm but Rob pulled free and headed straight for the old man by the door who didn't move an inch.

Rob lunged hard at him trying to prove his manhood that had just taken such a knock, but he only found some empty air. Rob swung around in panic and saw the man inside the Chapel on the far side and Rachel staring too, her mouth wide open and aghast.

Rob was already half outside the door and the world outside pulled him through; he turned and ran as fast as he could, back towards the town far below.

He stumbled and fell through the field stopping only to retch. He gripped onto the old wooden post by the stile at the far end of the field to steady himself and then wiped his mouth with the back of his hand trying to catch his breath. Still gasping and bent over, he felt clammy and drew his forearm across his forehead wiping away the cold sweat, which had beaded there. As he straightened up, it slowly dawned on him there was no sign of Rachel. Where the hell was she?

He looked again, quickly zoning his vision into all visible points around the chapel. He couldn't see her.

His belly churned and he felt the sickness rising in him again but he ignored it and cast his eyes desperately about. Had she got away? Was she still in there? Where the fuck was the old bloke? He stood on the tips of his toes, straining to see any movement at all but could see nothing.

'Fuck!'

He sighed and took a deep breath. Hands on his hips, he bent slowly forward and then bent back, tipping his head as far as it would go. The tightness in the muscles around his neck stretched and snapped. Then he straightened up and purposefully strode back towards the chapel knowing he had to go back to find her.

'Rob!'

He heard her calling.

'Rachel?' he shouted.

'Where are you?'

He broke into a run now…

'Rachel! ….. Rachel!'

'Rob!'

He saw her, bent over on her knees, her dress pulled up around her waist.

'Oh God!'

He raced towards her.

'Rachel! What's happened? Rachel?'

She turned her face to him, smiling. She held the fabric of her dress out as it hung heavy with the weight of crab apples, which she continued to pick up from the ground.

'Give us a hand Rob, will you? I'm going to drop them as soon as I try to stand up.'

'Are you ok?'

'Yes, fine. Where did you get to?'

'Um…'

Rob suddenly felt rather stupid for running away. He quickly processed what had just happened in the chapel. He realised that he may perhaps have overreacted, that he was sick and wasn't seeing things straight.

'You took off when that old bloke appeared….you should have heard what he had to say…'

'Ur…I came over a bit funny… felt faint and a bit sick. I needed some air. Why? Who is he?'

Rob cast his eye about.

'Has he gone? I didn't mean to have a go – what did he say?'

Rob held his hand out towards her for her to grasp.

She faced him now,

'Six bits of broken sticks….'

'What? But that's just an old wives tale – shit, did he really say that?'

'And then he just vanished, I meant went…oh, I don't know.'

'How did he do that, go from the door to the other side of the chapel in a flash – did you see it?'

They were walking out of the field and onto the stony path that led down through the woods to the back of town. Rachel carrying her treasure carefully in her gathered dress.

'You didn't feel well.'

They were walking in silence, both pondering what had just happened when she mumbled under her breath:

'But yes. Yes, I did.'

They arrived on the outskirts of town, neither having said another word. Rob looked at Rachel, both hands still holding up her heavy dress. He could have kissed her there and then and she wouldn't have been able do a thing about it – no way would she let the apples fall, after having just carried them half way down a mountainside. Then the moment shifted and he realised he had simply lost the urge.

He laughed at this, making Rachel ask:

'What?'

'All that hocus-pocus – bah – let's call it a day.'

'Will you still be coming round tonight?'

She looked down at the apples and lifted her eyes to meet his.

'I'll bake you a pie…'

Rob relented a little,

'I'll be round.'

He grinned and left her standing, looking at him as he headed home.

Crab apples are the oldest apple trees. It is said that if you throw the pips into the fire and they explode then your love is true. Rachel was mulling this over as she took the apple pie out of the oven and then boiled the leftover apples to make into puree to put into her morning yogurt. She picked up a discarded pip and walked into the sitting room where she opened the front of the wood burner and, after placing the pip carefully onto the poker's end, watched it fizz, swell and turn to black.

'Old wives' tales,' she muttered under her breath and slammed the door hard shut.

She was onto her second bowl of yogurt and puree when Rob knocked at the back door – she was bored and couldn't resist sampling her chapel fruit. She had been looking forward to his visit and had felt a little guilty for not delivering the goods high up on the hill. She had kind of made herself in the mood but as soon as the door knocked, felt that switch turn off.

'How are you feeling Rob? Better?' Rachel asked, as she opened the door and stood aside to let him in.

'Better than this morning, I can tell you! Whatever it was, it passed quick enough. I'm feeling on top form now.' He winked and grinned but Rachel looked away and changed the subject.

'Rob, I've been thinking…what do you think that old bloke meant this morning? You know – reciting that poem.'

'Everyone knows that poem, it's in the church records and don't mean a thing – just a stupid old man from fuck knows where, but I'd rather you didn't go up there anymore.'

'Ah Rob, you know how long I've wanted to make that place my home. It's been empty for as long as I can remember. It's crying out for someone to live in it, keeping it dry and warm and from falling down. I'm the only person who goes up there – everyone around here knows that. No one else would be interested, they're all just superstitious and too ready to believe all the bullshit stories about the place…like you do too.'

Rob's face fell. Once again, he lost any urge he might have mustered on the walk over to Rachel's cottage.

'Listen, Rache, I don't know. I have no idea what to believe. But I do know that until you get over your fascination with the chapel, you and I are going nowhere. I hate that place, always have, it's dark and creepy and too isolated up there on the hill. I get a bad feeling up there and just don't understand why you won't leave it alone. I didn't want to say anything but people are beginning to talk. Even tonight in the corner shop I overheard someone saying they'd seen you coming down off the hill with those crab apples – up to no good they said, making more of your potions, they said…'

'For Fuck's sake Rob, I'm not a fucking witch, I'm a homeopath – people around here are just ignorant.'

'Well, regardless, I'm sick of it and do you know what?' He paused for a moment and contemplated what he was about to say.

'After what happened today – you're on your own.'

'What?'

She looked confused,

'Are you saying you don't want to see me anymore?'

Rob didn't even need to think about it.

'Yes,' he said simply before turning around to head for the door where he let himself out. He shut the door behind him, without even the slightest glance back.

Rachel stood still in total disbelief. Just moments before she had been putting pips in the fire to determine if he was her one true love and now he was gone – no discussion, just gone. The pips had spoken true.

It took a moment or two for her to gather herself but the smell of burning caught her attention and she turned back into the little kitchen where she quickly realised her second batch of apple puree was still bubbling away on the stove, almost boiled dry and beginning to burn the bottom of the pan. She snatched it off the heat, set it down by the sink and stirred it with her wooden spoon. It looked ok, but still, she could have cried.

'Sod him,' she figured. 'I won't even worry about it. He was only ever interested in getting me into bed anyway and I need someone who's going to step up and take risks with me and plan adventures and really take care of me.'

Her thoughts wandered back to the chapel and she rested her elbows on the work surface, absent-mindedly scooping up the puree straight from the pan with the wooden spoon, blowing on it gently to cool it enough to take into her mouth.

Moments later, she was scraping the remnants from the sides of the pan. Having eaten the lot, she was beginning to feel a little queasy.

Feeling disgusted with herself, she flung the pan into the sink and hurried into the front room to stoke the fire and throw in another log from the basket.

On standing up, she felt faint and grabbed onto the mantelpiece to steady herself. Her head began to spin and she turned to judge the distance to the couch knowing she would have to make it there in one swift movement or she would come down heavy on the floor or worse, on the old slate hearth. She propelled herself across the room, her legs gave way beneath her and she stumbled forward to collapse face down into the soft cushions where she passed out.

She could see it clear as day but it was night and a fire burned bright, illuminating the scene with eerie shadows darting here and there. The women jeered and cackled, high and intoxicated from the potions of henbane and mandrake they were swilling down from the small flagons that they enthusiastically passed around. Nothing now was going to stop them from what they had come to do.

The chapel stood as it does now, not much different but it looked dark and sinister, and on a huge old crab apple tree, right where she had picked the apples from the ground just that afternoon, a rope was slung with a hangman's noose beckoning for a neck. Sure enough, this hideous crowd of filthy witches had a victim and dragged a bound man to the spot.

'Hang him high – squeeze his neck and spill his blood.'

They squealed and roared excitedly as the noose pulled tight as a dozen of them pulled him from the ground. Laughter spread throughout the crowd. They wanted blood but their joy was short, for a huge crack of thunder rolled across the sky, and without warning, a massive flash suddenly cracked the tree in two. The rope was seared, snapping immediately, and, as the man fell and hit the ground, the witches panicked and began to scatter – running, howling down the mountainside.

She moved closer to the burning tree. The young man's terrified face seemed to recognise her, as Rachel quickly loosened and pulled the noose from around his neck, but before she could fully slacken the ropes around his arms, he had grabbed her wrist with his bony, weathered fingers and seethed between clenched teeth:

'Six bits of broken sticks...'

Then the man grew old before her very eyes.

A cold wind came and blew away the scene, and there the chapel stood, alone as it does now. The tree was still smouldering, and the crows, perched high above the crag, were neatly lined up, staring out across the scene and right into Rachel's eyes.

Rachel woke from the dream feeling disorientated and upset. The room span as she tried to stand and she fell right back down again, vomiting a putrid green across the slate hearth. Again and again she retched, and when she finally stopped, she sobbed until blackness beckoned and she lost consciousness.

The morning was clear and calm. A warm haze hung over the valley and the grass was still damp with dew. Rachel made her way up the hill and through the field, anxious to get up to the chapel as early as possible. Her plan was to kick about up there in the hope of seeing the old man again. Her body felt charged with the expectation of seeing him, which spurred her on. She had so many questions and felt sure he would make himself visible to her if only she laid herself open to it. It was as if her whole life had led her to this moment. She had tried to bring Rob into it with her, but now saw what a mistake that was. This was to be her experience and hers alone. Ever since discovering the abandoned chapel as a little girl, Rachel had been inexplicably drawn to it and was reluctant to share her secret place with anyone. Even at the age of seven or eight, she had gone up there alone and had enjoyed feeling the crunch of the gravel under her shoes and putting her little hands up to the big cold stones to feel the chill of them. Often she had gone in and just sat in the old pews gazing up to the broken alter or tipping back her head to watch the pigeons fly around in the rafters until her head spun. As a teenager, she would make her way up there to sulk after a row with her parents or to lie in the long grass under the crab apple trees looking up through the wizened branches to the forever-shifting sky beyond, her head full of thoughts of one boy or another.

Now, as a young woman with all the usual desires, feeling the need to begin to build a life with a man, she felt she was being thwarted, prevented somehow. Rob was the only person she had ever taken to the chapel. She wasn't stupid, she had seen exactly what had happened the day before and knew she had made a huge error in taking him up there, feeling sure he had been truly warned off. The old man would never have appeared unless it was to get Rob the hell out of there. Rachel knew she had to make amends and placate the chapel's energy, or the old man, or whoever and whatever was upset with her. More than that, she was curious. The visions she had had through her sickness last night had seemed real to her, like omens almost, as if they were trying to tell her something. They had somehow felt urgent.

She quickly came to the edge of the field and crossed over the track and through the old iron gate. As she stepped onto the gravel path, a long, loud, pained scream came violently to her ears through the still air. Rachel stopped, rooted to the spot, terrified. She felt the blood drain from her body and didn't dare to move or make a sound as her eyes darted about searching for where the noise had come from.

Then nothing, only the soft sounds of the subtle breeze against the ferns. Then she saw him, the old man, bent over behind the trees towards the side of the chapel, picking something up. Throwing off any doubt she may have had, she made a beeline straight for him. It seemed to take her an age, even without the chore of having to lift a dress like some proper kind of lady. She smiled at that thought.

He was still bent over as she neared him, both hands close to the ground fiddling with something, snapping something that she couldn't quite make out. What she did see was the very black and burnt tree trunk, kind of split in two, directly behind the old man. She remembered the tree had always been there, but now, after her dream, it took on a different significance and stood out from everything else around. Before it had been just a small, withered trunk, waiting to rot and finally disappear into the ever-encroaching ferns. Now it was in high focus, important and relevant.

She was close to him, and as she looked, she knew – it was definitely the man from her dream, although he was much older now. Having confirmed this to herself, she slowly exhaled her breath, relieved that her suppositions were correct.

He turned to her as she approached and fixed his gaze right on her, seething between his teeth – 'Shhh.'

She could smell him, a musty smell mixed with charcoal that she didn't like. She took a step back. His eyes were deep-set and had that wild look of a wild animal etched within. On his neck, she recognised the scars of the hangman's noose.

He indicated to the chapel with a slight gesture of his head and upper body – 'They'll hear you.'

Rachel could barely understand his soft, thick and strange accent.

'Who?' She said, turning to have a look and seeing only the dark grey of granite blocks.

Then the scream came again, the blood curdling screams of torment…some tortured soul from the other side of midnight's strike.

'Them.'

Her throat felt tight and she made some funny kind of coughing noise that she knew was way too loud. Then she heard some mumbling, the sound getting louder until it became a chant, a frenzied urgency coming from the chapel. Not one, but many voices turning what felt like a magic spell. It was deafening and she clasped her hands to her ears and shut her eyes. But the old man was pulling at her jumper and she dropped her hands only to see and feel him putting something in them. Before she had time to look, he shouted hard over the chanting:

'Run!'

Rachel turned and began to move, but something stopped her. No. This wasn't why she had come here. She needed to know what was going on. She stopped and turned back towards the old man, but he was gone. Yet the lingering scorched smell of him still sat acrid in her throat. She looked down at her hands to see them tightly grasping some twigs. Rachel stared at them for a moment not immediately seeing what they were, all the while aware of the fevered chanting coming from the chapel. She unfurled her grasp to look at them stretched out across her palms. Just a bunch of broken twigs, but then Rachel felt a heat radiating out from them and they twitched and began jumping about in her hands. She instinctively threw them to the floor. Standing back in horror, she watched them come alive in the grass, jumping, fizzing and throwing off sparks. Rachel couldn't believe what she was witnessing. She looked about – was there a fire they had been pulled from? She glanced over to the old, blackened broken tree. It was smouldering as if it had been burning for a very long time. Rachel looked back at the twigs, but they lay still now. She watched to see what would happen next...but there was nothing.

She turned to the chapel and shook her head to gather her thoughts as the noise grew slightly louder and more insistent. There was no doubt Rachel was frightened, but she wasn't afraid of the chapel itself; as strange as it seemed, she knew she was in a good place and whatever was going on was an invasion of it.

It felt as though she was standing in a metaphysical tunnel, out of context with the real world, alongside it but running separately. The sounds she could hear were otherworldly, muted but cacophonous. So much so, that Rachel put her hands up to her ears again, simply to think.

She decided that she had to get close enough to the chapel in order to see what was going on, but was fearful of being discovered.

Remembering the little side window, the stained glass one closest to the entrance gate, handy if she needed to make her escape, she made her way back around the building, keeping one eye on the old oak door as she passed it, afraid it might open and she would be seen. She crept up to the window despite there being no need for quiet – there was no way she would be heard over the frenetic incantations seeping through the very stones of the building.

Hesitantly, Rachel peered through the cobalt blue glass. It took a moment for her to adjust her eyesight, but then into view came the most horrible sight. All at once she saw everything all together, just as she had in her dream, but the terrible chanting wasn't coming from the chapel... no, the scene was being played out through the far window, outside on the rise, beyond the chapel by the ancient apple tree. The tree she had just been standing by with the old man – the tree from which the bits of broken burning sticks had come, which the old man had just forced into her hands. A chill coursed through her bones. In the dream, what had the old man said to her? She frantically searched back through her mind to find the words, all the time watching the witches jeering and heckling over the chanting, which played like a subliminal sound-track in Rachel's ears.

Then it came to her....sticks, six bits of broken sticks! And, as if determined by her sudden realisation, a huge crack of thunder rolled across the sky, and then came the great flash of lightening, striking the ancient tree and cracking it in two. Rachel stood back and gasped. As she watched the assembled crowd disperse, she saw them evaporate as they ran, and all around her strange energies screeched past, ghastly high pitched screams and wails violating her sensibilities, stirring up currents of chilled air, which blew through her very being.

Then, the young man stood up slowly and, as he did so, he aged to an old man, becoming stooped, bent and wizened, and in her ears echoed his words,

'…six bits of broken sticks…'

Just before he seethed those words, the worst bit of all was seeing herself in that other dimension untie the ropes and help him to his feet.

Crows flew up from the crag behind the chapel, squawking, disturbed and menacingly restless against the gloomy sky. Distracted and perturbed by them, Rachel glared up at this mob of mocking birds, and in that moment the spell or whatever she had experienced, was gone, broken.

Only witches like crows, she thought.

It was with some trepidation and a big gulp of air that she cautiously went back to the field behind the building.

All was quiet and still. The tree was there, old and as before, just a stump still showing black from the lightning strike. How could that be? The man, young or old, was simply gone. A low wind blew through the ferns, hissing across the field until it touched her face, and then, like everything else in this strange place – nothing – it just disappeared. She looked down and saw the six bits of broken sticks, now harmless and lying on the ground. Picking them up, she half expected some magic to reignite in the palm of her hand, but no, there was nothing now, only some old, damp and charcoaled black sticks making her hands dirty.

It was very late autumn but she wasn't dressed for it at all. Shuddering and suddenly feeling cold, knowing she still wasn't right from the trials and torments of the night before, she called it a day, a very strange day and headed down, sticks firmly gripped in numbing hands.

It was still morning, much to Rachel's surprise. Feeling famished, cold and at a total loss as to what to do next, she headed to the only café in town.

It wasn't until she had devoured a full breakfast and a huge piece of coffee cake that she warmed up and felt herself again. She didn't think of what had just occurred – thinking about things like that was a fool's game and it would get her nowhere. She just stared blankly around. As she sat there, she saw what she had been missing for the last forty-five minutes: the stares and mumbles of idle gossip directed her way. The room suddenly seemed menacing, vicious almost, and she felt the glare of something she really didn't like. Rob was there with some mates and a pretty girl, but they looked away when she caught their eyes, as if she was to be avoided at all costs.

Then she saw something else – six small dirty black sticks she must have absent-mindedly laid out on the table. The tablecloth was wet and smudged with black. Yes, they must now have cause to think she was well and truly off the wall.

She quickly gathered up the sticks and went to the counter to pay. The waitress couldn't have done her job any faster if she tried.

She thought she would be safe from judgment out on the street, but people stared at her as she hurried away.

She didn't want to go home and face cleaning up the apple puke. What could she do now?

A quiet place, that's all she wanted, someplace else to try to hatch a useful plan. She soon found herself standing in front of the church; a quiet place indeed, and always empty unless it was a Sunday service. But today was Saturday, and she headed on inside.

These timeless places of cold air, whose musty smell refuses to let go of all that's old, suited Rachel very well just then, and she sat down amongst the pews. But she felt restless and fidgety, couldn't think and found herself wandering to the back and through an open door to find the vicar praying by himself in a small and ancient room. He felt her presence without having to look up, and when he did, he knew it was the girl – she had finally come. With a terrible sense of foreboding, he quickly got up and walked right past Rachel to shut the door so they were alone.

He didn't say a thing, just stood high, long and lean waiting for the inevitable. It had been a wait, which had spanned seven hundred years or more. He was ready like all those that went before, but, with a feeling of dread, the realization dawned on him that the task in hand had fallen to him.

He didn't move as Rachel described recent events, showing no emotion at her tale. She did not hold back, even describing the green delights of puree vomit sprayed across the cottage floor.

When she finally stopped pouring out her story, he turned and reached for an old dark book and laid it on the floor.

Rachel looked down at the ancient manuscript and looked back to the vicar.

'What's this?'

'Rachel you must read it. I hope it might bring you the answers you are looking for…'

The vicar's eyes smiled kindly but also held a deep and hidden tension.

She knelt down on the cold stone floor and looked over the old dusty book. Tracing her fingers slowly over the embossed leather bound cover and feeling hesitant, she looked back towards the vicar for some semblance of encouragement.

He smiled knowingly.

'Rachel, I know this may feel far beyond your understanding but please don't think you are alone in this. More people are aware of these circumstances than you might think. It was made known to me that your visit might come in my lifetime. I was just a young curate when I took on this parish and I want you to know I have been waiting and wondering if it would be me you would come to.'

He tried to radiate warmth and confidence but couldn't hide his trepidation.

'I didn't know it would be quite so soon though…'

He laughed nervously.

Rachel allowed herself a smile. His face turned serious now.

'I'm not sure I will be able to actually help you in any way other than give you the information you will need in order to fulfill what I believe to be predestined for you.'

'I don't understand…'

'I wouldn't expect you to, but take a look at the pages I have marked and perhaps you might begin to…'

He didn't finish, for Rachel had turned her eyes back to the old book and carefully lifted the first few heavy pages. She lifted and turned some more until she came to where the vicar had placed a laminated bookmark. which sat there between the old browning pages looking modern and out of place with its beaded tassels and a picture of the Holy land.

She averted her eyes from what appeared to be a rooftop scene of Jerusalem on the bookmark, to see the words jump out at her off the page.

'Six bits of broken sticks…'

It was the poem! She glanced up at the vicar, shocked.

'But I always thought this poem was some local myth…. something made up by kids, like the bogeyman. People used to say that it was written somewhere in the parish records, but to see it actually written down…'

She looked back at the words on the page,

'….this is incredible!'

'Carry on reading,' the vicar said.

Rachel continued. The text was written in an ancient font but it was easy to decipher, as she was so familiar with the poem. She read it aloud as it was written…

'Six bits of broken sticks
taken from the apple tree
where they tried to hang
the sexton
high.

Six bits of old rough wood
taken where the lightning struck

and cut the tree in two…'

Looking back at the vicar, she said gravely,

'I have the six bits of broken sticks. He broke them up and placed them in my hands right up by the smouldering lightening tree….but I still don't understand…'

She thrust her hand into a jean pocket and quickly pulled out the black bits one by one and dropped them on the open pages of the book.

The vicar's face went ashen.

He looked down hard at them and then urgently around the room. He was worried.

But Rachel hadn't noticed, she was already back on the pages reading more but the words made no sense to her at all – were they from another language perhaps or just spelt oddly?

'I can't read it….'

They both froze as a piercing howl suddenly screeched through the vestry. It was deafening. They stared at each other, horrified. The heavy old door aggressively opened and banged shut again, bringing dust and broken pieces of plaster falling down from the whitewashed walls and causing the thick curtains to blow about madly as a terrible haunting high-pitched moan filled the room. Rachel dived over to the vicar, burying her face in his cassock, and he put his arms around her tight to protect her from the demonic onslaught. She clung to him as the noises intensified and echoed around the little room, whipping the pages of the ancient book into a frenzy. The vicar took the crucifix, which hung around his neck between his fingers, put it to his lips and began to pray feverishly,

'Lord Jesus…be with us…protect us….we are your children…blessed are the meek….keep us safe…'

The crazed, fiendish noises reverberated around the room and then, through the terrible din, came a sinister collective of voices chanting slowly and purposefully. The vicar continued to pray, asserting his authority in the house of God, whilst Rachel kept her eyes tight shut, afraid of what she might see if she were to open them. Then, as suddenly as it had begun, the chanting faded out and the air stilled. Feeling encouraged by the vicars incessant prayers, Rachel pried open her eyelids a fraction to find the yellow eyes of a huge black crow staring straight back at her from its perch on the curtain rail, above the old wooden vestry door.

Rachel instinctively broke away from the vicar and again crouched over the book trying hard to grasp and make sense of anything she could. She looked up at the crow, which just stared back and then to the sticks, which were now glowing red and moving, almost jumping off the pages and making the book smoulder before it burst into flames.

An almighty wind rushed through the vestry blowing anything not secured down into a whirlwind, forcing Rachel and the vicar to crouch down low to the floor so as not to be lifted up or flung against a wall.

Then it stopped and a calm silence returned. The crow was gone and the book was just a pile of black cinders – nothing left at all.

'Tell me what it said!'

Rachel was beside herself, screaming at the vicar.

There was some relief on his face, as if it was now over for him, and anymore of this devil-work would not be his concern.

'I don't know what it said, it was in another language, but I'll tell you what was passed on to me ...'

He paused and took a deep breath.

'The chapel has stood for seven hundred years or more. It was built sometime during the 13th century, but before that, something else was there...a meeting place, used by witches. The locals were afraid as it became obvious the coven was getting larger and more powerful and their misdoings were being directed on not only local people but also reaching out far and beyond the vicinity, bringing misfortune onto people many miles away. It was thought by the church that by building a chapel at the witches meeting place God, in his goodness, would overpower their evil and the coven would disband or move away.'

This all made sense to Rachel as it was clear the witches in her visions were angry and vengeful.

'The old man though? Who is he and what's his relevance?'

The vicar continued:

'When the chapel was first built, a sexton was appointed to take care of the building, he was a local woodsman, and newly married. His name was William. He and his wife had a baby and it is said that the baby was taken. Witches were known for bleeding infants and children and he confronted them, convinced they had taken his child. No one can be sure, but it is believed that they cursed him to spend eternity in some God forbidden hell realm and then tried to hang him...he was saved though at the last minute – I think you know the rest.'

'No I don't – what are the six bits of broken sticks?'

He took another deep breath.

'The sexton's wife was a herbalist, perhaps even a sorcerer. It is thought that in her distress at losing her baby and with her husband cursed and about to be sent to the darkness, she desperately tried to expand and use her knowledge to free him from the curse and exorcise the chapel. Whatever happened next is not known, but it is clear that something went wrong as the result of her spell. It only managed to lock the witches and her husband into some kind of eternal bond in a dimension that now exists only in the chapel.'

'But it can't be....the lightning freed him.'

'No, his wife freed him with her magic, and he gave you the sticks before he disappeared into...'

'Where?'

'That place you can see – I've been told that they are all locked in there together, trapped, and imprisoned.'

'But the sticks – I still don't understand...'

Rachel felt confused.

'None of it makes sense.'

'Rachel, do you not see? The six broken sticks are from the spell that William's wife cast to break the curse. She took them from the biggest tree knowing they would hang him there.'

'Oh! The poem – it's a spell. But why me – why did he give them to me?'

Only now could he drop the bombshell, only now did it seem right to tell her.

He paused…hesitant to continue, 'Rachel, look here in this book…'

He opened a very old parish register and turned to a page near the front, handed it to her and watched her closely as she proceeded to take in the words written there.

Rachel instantly recognized it as a marriage record. She read it aloud:

'1223, William Roberts marries…'

Rachel stopped and looked back up to the vicar, alarmed.

'Rachel Ellis?' She exclaimed. 'He marries Rachel Ellis? William? Is he the old man – the sexton?'

The vicar was nodding,

'And Rachel? She has my name…is this the link?'

'Rachel I don't think you quite understand…'

He put his hand out and placed it gently on her shoulder.

'Rachel, this isn't a link….you *are* Rachel Ellis.'

Rachel stared at him in disbelief…

'What? Are you mad? I'm me, I'm here in this time…what are you saying? That I'm over seven hundred years old and that the old man is my husband? You're off your head…how can that be? I was born here, I was a baby and a little girl and I grew up…that makes no sense…'

'Rachel, it's true, you were born and you grew up into the young woman you are today, but within you is Rachel Ellis. Her spirit resides in you, do you understand? She is a part of you and as William's wife it is down to you to rectify the spell and break the witches curse.'

Rachel looked at him open mouthed, not quite able to digest what it was he was telling her. She stumbled a little under the weight of it all, at which point the vicar opened and held the door ajar to indicate the part he had to play in this was over.

'I have told you everything. I can't help you any further.'

Rachel looked at him astounded but knew in her heart the vicar would be true to his word. He had given her the information it had been his duty to impart, and now he would wash his hands of her. As she turned to leave the vestry, she coldly asked:

'And where's your God in all of this?'

Instead of giving an answer, he took a brush and pan and swept up the ashes of the burnt book and sticks from the old stone floor. Rachel waited for a reply, impatiently staring, as he fastidiously made sure he got every grey cinder in the pan. He pondered for a moment, looked around, on seeing what he needed, grabbed a small urn, and carefully filled it with the ash. Only then did he answer, hurriedly, as he briskly walked her to the church entrance down the aisle.

'This is not God's work. You are on your own now and nothing can stop what you have unleashed up on that cursed hill.'

As the low glare of the November sun flooded her eyes making her squint, she protested:

'Me!'

But he wasn't listening anymore as the door closed firmly shut behind her.

'Damn you vicar.'

Looking up the mountainside, she held the warm small urn tightly in her hands.

What had he said? My husband's been locked up for seven hundred years with those witches, waiting for me to turn up again! This is so stupid. What the fuck do I do now? I wish I had never eaten those bloody cursed apples.

Her thoughts were confused as she wandered home, washed out, dragging her heels until she made it to her bedroom and sank down into a deep and empty sleep.

The dream came quickly, short and startlingly clear.

She appeared at the chapel; it was dark and the tree smouldered, cracking loud as bits of trunk exploded, showering orange and red sparks around. The young sexton sat smiling at Rachel. He was sitting at the base of the split trunk amongst the shower of fizzing sparks. Crows were everywhere, hopping and cawing, while looking right at her. One landed on her shoulder and she flinched and brushed it off but others were at her feet pecking. She stepped back as he pointed at her chest, saying:

'The crows will fly
As you lie entwined
In midnight's love sublime'

She woke in a cold sweat.

God damn it, she had had enough of this riddle – better to go back to where she was before and leave all this mumbo jumbo behind; Rob was right, although she was loathe to admit it. It had been just a chapel she had wanted to buy and restore, that was all – not the dark stuff that was now invading and ruining every aspect of her life. No, she would get her life back to normal as soon as possible.

There was a thud on the door. Rachel jumped up and off the bed feeling apprehensive. With some trepidation, she went downstairs and slowly opened the kitchen door.

It was night and she realised that she had slept for some hours. She could see the moon shining full and bright over the hills in the distance, showing between the racing, dark clouds. Before her stood Rob, cocky as always, smiling as if nothing had happened and itching to get in.

'Rob!'

'I've been thinking….'

But Rachel didn't want a long conversation about her sanity and behavior, and blurted out:

'I'm sorry Rob…I was stupid – will you take me back?'

'Sure, forget it ever happened. No weird stuff though, I can't handle it and my mates just laugh 'coz you're such a spooky crank!'

He laughed briefly as he walked through the kitchen towards the lounge carrying a six-pack of beer, but stopped short when he saw the small open urn full of ash on the kitchen counter. Rob looked down and peered in.

'Someone die?'

'Oh…it's…just, um – ash from the stove.'

Rob said nothing, just stared at Rachel who quickly added:

'For the garden, you idiot.'

Relieved, he stepped into the lounge but immediately stopped again, exclaiming and pointing with disgust at the oodles of green puree curdling on the hearth and carpet:

'And what the hell is that? Jesus Rachel!'

'Oh, crab apples – I was such an idiot – let's go to bed.'

Rachel knew it was easy to fob him off like that, especially when he only had one thing on his mind.

She followed his urge.

They drank, laughed, had sex, drank some more, had more sex and now lay entwined half asleep, listening to the gentle wind brushing the trees outside the bedroom window.

Suddenly the wind changed and became a strange noise, humming and reverberating, almost growling at the bedroom window.

'What the fuck is that?'

Rob shot up and looked out of the window.

'Nothing, it's just trees swaying with the wind.'

'No, it wasn't – didn't you hear it?'

'It's just the wind Rob.'

Rachel knew damned well that it wasn't just the wind but something much more sinister. Maybe it would go away if she just ignored it.

'Come here…'

She pulled him down to kiss him softly. He was soon on her, making love and she whispering all those things that seem to make it matter. Rachel tried so very hard, faking her moans and cries in an effort to shut out the sounds, which subtly vibrated through the house.

Soon all they could hear was the sound of a whole flock of birds flapping inside the room – only sounds, not a bird in sight.

Rob jumped out of bed and switched on the light.

'Fuck's sake Rachel, what the hell have you unleashed up there in that God forsaken place?'

'Nothing! It's just birds…um migrating.'

'It's late autumn!'

They were shouting above the din.

Then there was nothing and silence reigned down once again.

'See Rob – just birds.'

'Yeah well, you can't blame me for being jumpy after that thing with the old man – can you?'

They stood naked looking straight at one another and both burst into laughter.

'Jesus – that spooked the hell out of me…'

Rob stopped as the kitchen door banged and shook the house.

They both went white and Rachel tried to calm the moment.

'Maybe I didn't shut it when you came in – I'll have a look.'

She went down, across the lounge and to the kitchen where the door was shut. She hit the light switch and stared at the chipped white paint of the wooden door.

Rob shouted from above:

'What is it?'

'Only the wind I think.'

She opened the door.

The moon was hidden in the clouds and only the dim kitchen light illuminated the old sexton. Rachel gasped and tried to hide her nakedness by crossing her legs and throwing her arms over her breasts.

It was in a brief moment when the moon broke briefly through the clouds that she saw them – a score of crows flying towards the kitchen door and heading straight towards her. Before she had a chance to slam it shut, the sexton pointed at her chest.

Then they were on her, pecking at her, flying in the house and forcing Rachel to retreat to the lounge where she collapsed onto the couch.

She tried to scream but nothing came out, and just when she thought she would go insane with all the crows cawing, screeching and pecking at her, it stopped and everything became still.

Rob had pulled on a pair of jeans and now stood in the middle of the lounge looking down at her, innocently enquiring,

'What was it?'

He hadn't seen or a heard a thing and was looking into the kitchen at the open door.

'You alright – the door's still open?'

He went and shut it, turning the key in the lock.

Rachel shouted after him:

'Yeah, just the wind – thought I'd clean the puke up.'

But something wasn't right at all. Her chest was buzzing and she could feel something almost like a flapping deep inside.

Then it was gone.

Together they cleaned the hearth and carpet, Rob constantly making jokes about witches and curses as Rachel pretended to laugh. Just act normal she kept telling herself.

When they had finished and had flopped on to the couch, Rachel, still naked, thought that this might just be ok now. Whatever had happened had settled down and all was going to be ok.

However, as Rob caressed her, arousing her sexual feelings, she heard a murmur, felt a stirring, not hers but a score of witches who had been locked up for seven hundred years or more. She felt their yearnings, their wants, their anger, and she was on him, overpowering him and without regard, took all that she could get.

The pent up frustrations of a horde of powerful witches and her own desire was all that mattered now. She heard her name called once:

'Rachel – for Fuck's sake.'

But that was all. Later she wondered how her screaming and shaking hadn't shaken the house down as she lay panting on the floor with no regard for Rob who lay motionless on the couch above.

She awoke cold and shivering the next morning and instinctively went to light a fire. As she opened the burner door, she finally noticed Rob lying on the couch, white and ashen, his lifeless eyes staring out in abject horror, reflecting the terror of his last moments.

Those witches, those bitches had fucked the life out of him and she had let them, enjoyed it just like them. Oh God, what the fuck was she going to do now?

Rachel cried for Rob and for herself and for the curse that now lay deep inside.

Looking over at Rob, trousers still around his ankles, lying on his back with his pathetic lifeless head turned towards her, she screamed out as loudly as she could:

'Leave me alone.'

A murmur came back at her, something gentle that she could not understand.

She sobbed some more, desperately trying not to look at him and see the damage she had done.

If only she had listened to him, he would still be alive and things would be just sweet and normal, but no, she had to ruin everything by following some dream that soon became a curse, to its bitter damning end.

She waited until evening. It had been an uneventful day, almost calm in fact. She had had no visitors and the murmurs or things inside her had not revealed themselves. For some inexplicable reason she now felt no remorse for Rob's demise – just some kind of pity that he was no longer around. It all seemed to mean nothing now and it slowly dawned on her what she must do.

Around midnight she tried to lift Rob off the couch. He was too heavy and she dropped him back down the foot or so she had raised him. He was getting stiff now like a proper corpse.

'I need some help here.'

She felt all humanity leave her as she cried out to the things inside, and again tried to pull Rob up. This time however, she easily threw him across her shoulder as if he were a feather.

Rachel laughed aloud:

'That's more like it.'

With some sense of control, she opened the back door and purposefully strode to her car in the gravel drive. The night was dark and the moon well and truly hidden, and with the nearest neighbour some 300 yards away, she felt safe as she offloaded Rob into the boot. He landed with a thud and she slammed the trunk back down.

The quarry lay on the other side of the big hill that sheltered the chapel and the drive went without incident. There was not a car on the road and she confidently pulled into a siding and cut the lights. The quarry was no more than a hundred feet or so in the darkness ahead.

Rachel pulled the body from the boot and once again threw him over her shoulder and edged her way forward until the track ran out and the quarry opened up before her. Below her was a big, dark drop.

Without a second thought, she let Rob fall and heard scraping against rock before the heavy thud as his body stopped at the quarry floor. The moon shone now and she peered over the edge to see him showing pale and eerie against the dark slate far below.

That wouldn't do at all. What had she been thinking? He was now on view to anyone who walked this spot, and there were many from the village that came up here. He needed to be covered up.

'Damn it,' she muttered under her breath.

Murmurs started, just in her head at first, and then all around her. They gained volume and intensity until loose rock started falling, ending with a huge crack and a rumbling below. She peered over the edge again.

Rob was gone, buried under tons of slate.

'Oh Rob, I'm so very sorry.'

But, in the pit of her being, she knew she didn't really care at all.

Rachel was suddenly overcome with tiredness. Her body felt heavy as she dragged herself back to the car, and with a huge effort got herself home.

It then came to her, she felt normal, dog tired but normal as though nothing had happened – no remorse, no fear and no strange noises – just nothing.

She made a fire and warmed herself close to the open door of the burner, soon falling into a deep sleep. No dreams came and the strange sounds stayed away, but she woke suddenly needing the bathroom.

Sitting dozily on the loo looking at her reflection in the mirror on the opposite wall, Rachel spoke:

'Mirror, Mirror on the wall, who is the…'

She paused and let out a laugh as she changed the verse:

'…witchiest of them all?'

Her faced changed before her in the reflection. Rachel gasped with horror. Her mouth went dry as a succession of hideous faces, creatures and monsters started to appear. Some wailed, some made her shake with their pure evil and she wondered if that was fire and smoke coming from her mouth and nostrils.

The stench was awful.

Her stomach churned. She thought she was about to vomit and shot up towards the basin but fell flat on her face as her knickers twisted about her feet.

'Enough…please.'

She sobbed and all went quiet once again.

It was mid afternoon when she finally woke, still lying on the bathroom floor.

Rachel didn't know what to do but one thing was sure – she needed to move, get out of the house, anything just to feel normal.

She dressed quickly and with a lot of nervousness looked into the mirror once again. Nothing – in fact, she looked great – absolutely radiant. Her long dark hair was shining and her hazel eyes burned bright.

Understanding, that if she now stayed calm and didn't ask stupid questions, the witches might stay dormant and not bother her. She headed out. The sun was low in the sky and with the wind still, it was a pleasant walk to the high street.

She didn't know if eating was a good idea but soon found herself in the café having another huge meal. She'd get fat at this rate, she thought, and looked about to see if anyone was looking at her strangely. All seemed ok, but just then Rob's mother walked in and came straight over to her.

Rachel's heart sank.

Oh God, what do I tell her?

'Seen Rob, Rachel? He was meant to come over this morning?'

She hesitated, knowing that hesitation was bad, and quickly blurted out:

'He left early this morning to see a friend about some work.'

Rob's Mum eyed her suspiciously and simply nodded before leaving.

What if they find the body? Now Rachel felt bad, guilty and all confused again. Then the murmurs started.

No, no – stop it!

She had to get out of there.

Fumbling with the cash to pay, feeling embarrassed and self-conscious once again, she knocked her plate on the floor. It landed with a crack and broke in two.

Now people were looking, now they were talking, now she appeared like the old Rachel from the other day again.

Panic.

She quickly fled before something bad might happen.

Trying to quieten the noises inside, trying not to let them get the better of her, she headed round the corner and stood before the church, looking down the path guarded on either side by two enormous yew trees, towards the large oak doors of the main entrance.

The vicar stood in front of them staring hard at her. Rachel wasted no time. She walked right up to him and stood below the step, demanding:

'What the hell has happened to me?'

'You have no business here anymore – you must go.'

The murmurs increased and a chant began.

'Not until you bloody well tell me.'

But the words were not hers and she heard a strange language come from her mouth.

The vicar turned ashen. He started mumbling prayers, turned his back on her and went to open the door, but Rachel was up on the step and violently banged the door shut again whilst consciously aware of the strange sounds she was spouting.

The vicar dropped to his knees.

'You're possessed by those…'

But he couldn't say the word and Rachel felt herself get angry. She let out a scream but nothing came out, and then she realised that the oak door was scorched and smoking. The flames had come straight out of her.

She covered her mouth in horror.

Oh God.

The vicar was praying frantically, attempting to cast the witches out. She knew it wouldn't work and felt furious at him. She had only wanted his advice.

The next thing she knew his cassock had caught alight. He desperately tried to ease the flames, flapping and patting his uniform whilst muttering, 'Oh, Oh my.'

Serves him right, she thought. Then, in an instance, she felt sorry for him and with a big gasp of air from her mouth, she blew the flames out so hard that he banged against the door.

Although the flames were out, he kept on hysterically patting whilst looking up in terror at the monsters he saw hovering and focusing right on him, ready to do their worst, and through the horror of his vision he saw Rachel angrily looking down on him, hands on hip waiting for an answer. He cried out:

'Make them go away.'

'Who?'

'The witches – please…'

'You can see them! What do they look like?' She demanded like an excited child.

'Please…'

He was begging now.

He clasped his hands over his head imploringly.

She didn't really know what to do next, but angrily stamped her feet one after the other, not only at the witches but also at him and the damned predicament she found herself in.

'Thank you.'

He rose shakily.

'What? Have they gone? What did you see – how many?'

Seeing she was impatient, he hastily replied:

'Many terrible beings, tortured souls – evil, but I see you can control them.'

'Can I? How?'

'You just did by stamping your feet.'

'Oh.'

As Rachel changed from feeling defiant to perplexed, he went on:

'They're with you now and I can't do a thing to help you – look after them, that's all they want.'

'Sing them a lullaby – send them to therapy – you're having a laugh aren't you?' She replied, frustrated by his advice.

'Isn't there a prayer or something, I mean it was only last night that I, no we, I mean they, fucked Rob to…'

She stopped mid-sentenced as she realised what she was confessing and clasped her hand over her mouth once again.

'Look,' she demanded, backtracking, 'you're the only one who can help me.'

'Rachel, do you not understand? You surely know that they possess you.'

She knew that alright, and out of sheer frustration, she opened and banged the heavy oak door several times whilst cursing out loud.

Thunder rolled over the town and the sky went dark.

'No Rachel – please don't.'

Then the rain came, hard and heavy. Defeated, she turned and walked away leaving the vicar soaking on the stone steps behind her.

'Six sticks.....remember the sticks...' he called out after her, his voice muffled by the noise of the downpour.

Rachel couldn't think anymore. At a total loss about what to do, where to go, or how to feel, she headed up the lane by the church towards the woods and footpaths that meandered up the hills and through the fields to the old chapel. Where else could she go, she asked herself. It was as if it had all run out for her and she was left with some curse that would never ever leave her alone, and what about those sticks? It all felt too much and she shook her head to clear her thoughts.

She wanted to cry but was far too defiant to let a tear drop. And where had those damned witches gone now – to ground no doubt, silent and hiding in the depths – what ghoulish cowards they must be.

With these thoughts and feelings she entered the wood, purposely striding to the only place she had ever gone to when the world seemed too much to bear. Here she sought solace.

The path was steep and rocky and on reaching the fields, Rachel marveled at her slow and relaxed breathing. Maybe there was something good in all this after all? That thought was short lived as a wailing reverberated through her body. Fear gripped her, not hers but that of others. The witches were scared shitless. 'Good!' She said aloud, and took a step into the field where the old dark chapel came clearly into view. She suddenly felt nauseous and heard the mumblings of discontent and sensed, no knew, that once again trouble was rumbling inside of her.

Nearly a thousand years locked in some hellish time warp linked to the old chapel. No way were they ever going back there.

Rachel took another step and doubled over with the fear and sickness. She knew it wasn't hers but it was in her all the same. She was panicking but calm at the same time because she now understood that the chapel was off limits. Demoralized, she turned and walked with difficulty back down towards the wood.

She felt very alone with nowhere to go and no one to turn to. Rob was gone and the vicar didn't want to know.

Stuck between the inaccessible chapel before her and her defunct life in the town below, Rachel suddenly burst into tears. It just wasn't fair at all, and she threw herself down onto the wet ground and sobbed. This was her spot on the rocky mountainside where she decided to give it up, lie down and just die. She shut her eyes and rolled her body to face the ground, resting her head in her arms.

Then the talking started. She didn't understand the language at first with everyone talking at once, but she got the sense of what they were trying to say – home, go home; home is where the heart is…

Home – what's there, except loneliness and the bad memory of Rob? She protested. Home, she heard again. Damn you, I don't want to go home – there is no home anymore! Over and over, she heard their incessant cries.

Rachel found herself getting up, irritated and pissed off by the incessant pestering. Then silence returned, just that usual nothing that she was getting used to.

She turned towards the dark woods and started walking.

Rachel had been sitting for a long time by the fire, devoid of thought and with very little sense of her place in the world. Just sitting and staring into the fire was all she had the will to do. She had played the mirror game for a while, watching the monsters manifest but that had all got boring, there were too many of them and it all seemed pointless, and besides, they had now become familiar and didn't even scare her anymore.

What had been the point of returning home? None that she could think of, maybe it was the warmth. Do witches feel the cold?

Night had fallen some time before. It was one of those bright, full moon nights where the occasional high white cloud was blown fast across the inky sky. However, down on the ground there was not even a hint of a breeze, the stillness only broken by the crackling of logs burning in the wood stove.

Rachel dozed, lulled by the warmth and sounds of the fire. She saw the orange sparks of the burning tree, and smelt the wood smoke. It soothed her, but then she felt its heat close, very close, and she shot up as a burning ember scorched her forearm. She had left the wood burner door open and shards were being spat out onto the hearth. She slammed the door shut and patted her arm where the dead ember sat.

The kitchen door banged hard – one loud reverberating sound that rattled anything loose in the house. Then nothing, just the sounds of the fire and her thumping heart. Rachel waited, but still nothing, not even a murmuring inside.

So what now? Another flock of crows and the sexton's finger pointing at her chest again – another ride on this spooky merry go round?

She felt weary, fed up and defiantly marched over to the back door and pulled it wide open. The night was chilly and sparkles of frost twinkled on the grass.

There was no one there, but as Rachel went to shut the door to keep the chill out, she caught sight of him standing there.

'Rob! Where the hell did you come from?'

It couldn't be him, could it? He was buried under a ton of black Welsh slate and besides he had already been dead well before then.

But there he stood, naked and with his jeans still around his ankles looking vacant and deathly pale, desperately trying to say something.

'Rob you must be freezing, come in…'

Then, under the clear moonlight, she saw him as he really was; his head was partly crushed, dried blood was everywhere, one arm was totally bent and twisted and his whole body just a proper mess. Was that a bone poking out and, oh God, his eyes…this just couldn't be for real.

'Rob, say something,' she cried in desperation.

However, he just continued to stare, moving his distorted mouth in silence.

'Please Rob, you're frightening me.'

She didn't know if it was fear, the biting chilly night or both, but Rachel was shaking now, almost uncontrollably.

Something propelled her forward and she grabbed Rob's arms and roughly pulled him into the kitchen where she then shoved him into the front room right by the fire. She had felt and heard something pull and snap as she had yanked his arms to get him into the house.

He half collapsed on to the floor next to the hearth as if he had recognized some comfortable resting place. But there was nothing comfortable or resting about him as he sat all twisted and mangled, looking up at Rachel. She could barely look at him and now started feeling sick. Before she could ponder going to the bathroom some sounds finally came from Rob's contorted mouth, half whispered, half breathed but she could just make it out:

'Apples, apples.'

'I ate the apples Rob – you know that.'

A gurgling moan came from deep within him, which she just made out:

'Now I'll die.'

'You're already dead – what happened?'

Rachel immediately wished she hadn't said that – maybe he didn't know he was dead.

The same sound came again:

'The apples.'

As Rob wept and moaned, the shudders made his wounds ooze a dry cake like substance that stank, making Rachel cover her nose and mouth and take a step back.

He was decomposing fast and the fire wasn't helping.

'Speak to me Rob – tell me what to do.'

Rachel was almost beside herself. She didn't know how to help, especially as he was quickly becoming a rotting corpse right in front of her. Her thoughts were confused. What the hell would she do with his body this time? Maybe feed it to the farmer's pigs just across the field from her cottage – they would surely eat the lot – wouldn't they?

What was she thinking? She had to do something.

Then she remembered the apple pie still in the oven.

Rachel raced to the kitchen and pulled the door open. Yes, it was there!

Soon she was back next to Rob trying not to gag on his stench, offering him the bowl of pie and a spoon. His eyes showed some life and with a slight futile upward movement of his arm it was clear to Rachel she would have to spoon-feed him.

But his mouth didn't work and Rachel stepped back and viewed Rob with the spoon sticking out of his broken mouth. No way was he going to be able to get a morsel down.

She knew what she had to do and eased the spoon back out and dropped the bloody mess into the bowl of apple pie.

Working quickly, she loaded the food blender with the whole pie and set it spinning. A rummage through the cupboards found a funnel and in the shed in the back yard she grabbed a small piece of hose and was soon back in the front room ready to try to save her friend from the darkness that fast approached.

Rob had fallen down and his eyes were now glazed and lifeless.

God the place stunk.

She placed the blender and things on the floor and pushed him back up into a sitting position, wedging him up with the back of a chair.

It was a grim moment forcing the hose down into his stomach as she first heard and then felt the ripping and tearing of his rigor mortis flesh.

No response from Rob. Was he dead – well, second dead?

Rachel fixed the funnel to the hose and was about to pour the blended pie into it when she realised it was way too thick – no way would the pie go down.

After another hasty trip to the kitchen, where she added water and turned the blender on again, Rachel poured the thick, green liquid into the funnel, down the hose and into whatever was still alive deep inside of Rob.

The lot went down and Rachel pulled the hose back up and out. What more could she do? That's what he wanted, wasn't it – the apples? As she sat there with his lifeless body, she wasn't so sure.

Rob fell forward and thudded on the floor.

Well, at least I tried, she thought. A brief moment of silence before the wind blew, hissing outside, and the murmurings started, her murmurings it now seemed, increasing until it became a chant filling up the room and house, and then nothing, silence yet again.

A gurgle came from Rob, his body convulsed and a mighty retch shot apple and disgusting red lumps of flesh across the floor. Rob moaned and retched again. The smell was unbearable and Rachel opened a window to let in the hissing wind before going to the bathroom to splash her face with icy water. Slightly relieved she looked into the mirror. Yes, there they were, alive and dancing in the reflection.

So, what now witches? What happens now?

Her body tingled, drawing her back to the front room where she found Rob, still a proper mess, but sitting up and examining his wrecked body.

'Rachel, what happened? Look at me – what will I tell my mum?'

'Rob – is that really you? What happened?'

'I don't know – we were cleaning up your apple puke and the next thing I knew it was pitch black and that old bloke from the chapel was pulling me out of the rocks at the quarry speaking complete gibberish.'

'What then?'

'Nothing much, I remember shuffling across the fields with him, down the mountain by the crags, past the chapel and then the back way through the pig farm to here.'

'Nothing else? What about the old bloke?'

Rob shrugged, looked at himself and then to her imploringly.

'Rachel, what's happened to me? I look like I should be dead.'

This time she refrained from saying that he actually was dead.

'What about the old bloke Rob?' She insisted.

'He just disappeared. Said a bunch of stuff in some weird language and then…I felt a buzzing in my chest and then I was here – I think…'

He paused.

'I can taste apple.'

He looked at the puke on the floor.

'Is that my apple puree? What are those red lumps?'

'You ate some pie Rob. I…um…put beetroot in the pie – you know what I'm like.'

She hated lying, but could hardly speak the truth in his condition.

'I'm tired, can you help me to bed?'

Rachel loathed to touch him – after all a piece of him might just break off. However, she wanted to help – she owed him that much at least.

'I'll get you a blanket – you just rest by the fire tonight.'

Rachel's sleep was deep. She went to a dark place, safe like an impenetrable fortress where she first sensed, then felt and finally saw the witches – transparent, hovering and morphing before her. Not things she would actually be able to describe in waking life, something more subtle, vibrating – a vibrating energy that made her tingle. They were communicating with her now in a way that wasn't familiar. She shuddered with the realization of their meaning and woke up. Immediately they were gone; she heard and felt nothing more. She knew now that the witches were ancient, as old as the rocks that made the chapel and mountains. What about what they had told her?

She didn't know whether to be excited or horrified at what they had said. And Rob, was he dead or still alive somehow downstairs?

With a feeling of urgency and expectation, Rachel pulled the covers aside and jumped out of bed. Scantily dressed she felt the cold and hurriedly went downstairs into the front room where the warmth of the burning embers greeted her. Rob was stoking it with wood.

'Rob!'

'Rachel!'

He stood up to greet her, jeans now around his waist, beaming a huge smile and looking right as rain – not a mark on him.

'What happened to you? You're all, uh, well, um…'

'Apples Rache, magic apples – thank God you saved the pie.'

They stood staring at each other, Rachel dumfounded and shocked and Rob cock sure and full of himself.

'What do you think?' He gestured.

He twirled to show his new mended self.

'Um…'

Rachel was lost, didn't know what to think or say at that moment.

'Imagine what I can do with this!'

Rob looked down at his slim and muscular naked torso and back up at Rachel with an unhinged sense of pride.

'I feel great!'

Rachel thought – he's the same old Rob alright, only a thousand times worse this time.

'Don't you think of anything else?'

'Not really…'

He paused and then added:

'Neither do you. You and those mad old hags killed me, fucked me to death – I remember everything now – it was terrible, like vampires slowly sucking the very life out of me.'

'No I didn't, it was them Rob – not me,' she protested.

'Liar! They couldn't have done it without you. He told me.'

'Who told you?'

Rob's smile vanished.

'Him, I don't know – him – he's here now talking to me – well kind of talking – I don't understand a bleeding' word, but he's talking alright.'

'Who's talking Rob?'

'Him! The old bloke from the chapel, he's here now…'

Rob pointed to his chest with both hands.

'He's a real prude – but I can handle that, it's my body, not his. Wow, I feel great!'

Rob's smile returned as he upped and left, shirtless and shoeless, picking up Rachel's car keys from the kitchen counter on the way out. She heard the car start and the wheels spin as he quickly drove away on the icy gravel track.

Oh my God – the poor sexton, my poor William! What a shock and insult it must be, being locked up in Rob's over-sexed body, with his crude and simple mind. How could she have been 'in love' with him?

Rachel found herself laughing, cackling almost but quickly stopped herself. Damn, it would be so easy to become one of them. She had to get a grip. Despondent, she sat down on the carpet next to the fire, confused and in a place she couldn't understand.

There seemed no way back now.

Even Rob, with all his hatred of anything even hinting at the supernatural, was now involved, possessed by William. How could that have happened? Surely, there must have been some mistake.

There was only one place she could go now, only one voice that might make sense – why hadn't she thought of it before?

With no car, it was quite a hike to her grandmother's cottage on the other side of town some way past the church along the river.

The murmurs and voices had remained silent and Rachel half wondered if they had gone for good until she saw her grandmother dressed in her fur coat and hat waiting impatiently on the lawn outside her closed front door. She hung onto a small shoulder bag with one hand.

This did not bode well.

'You always were a bit slow Rachel, and late…'

Rachel said nothing; she knew her grandmother never said a word more than needed or wasted her breath on anything superfluous.

Without another word, she grabbed Rachel's arm and pulled her up the road with some urgency.

'Why didn't you come sooner?'

'What – what do you mean gran?'

'Stop your pretence, the vicar told me everything.'

'Everything!'

'Yes, everything…'

Rachel hesitated.

'And of poor Rob's demise – how could you do such a terrible thing?'

'Oh, it wasn't me gran…it was, um, them – please believe me.'

How did the hell did the vicar know about that, Rachel wondered.

'Them! You, them, it's all the same now – don't you see?'

She suddenly stopped and took a good look at her granddaughter.

'Oh yes, I can see them clearly now, hovering and morphing – like a soft halo or a subtle rainbow.'

'See them! Can everyone see them?'

'Those who can see them are very rare indeed, and you'd better watch out for those who do.'

'Not more riddles,' she finally protested. 'Spell it out gran!'

'What are they like Rachel?' Her grandmother continued, ignoring her request.

'Really scary at first…but now I quite like them.'

Her grandmother scoffed:

'Yes, you would say that – that's why they waited so long – only you, this Rachel Ellis likes them – to me they are abhorrent.'

'Why me gran – just tell me why!'

Rachel stamped her foot hard.

'Oh Rachel, don't…you have no idea of the power you hold.'

The sky had already darkened and a strong breeze flew through the trees along the riverbank, a stone's throw away.

'Only you, the little girl who took off up to the chapel for no reason whatsoever, whenever she could. All the other Rachel Ellises, including your mother and me, dreaded that place – we never set foot near it. I knew it would be you that would one day unleash something on that hill – the vicar knew it too, although he feigns ignorance and memory loss these days.'

They were walking again but no longer talking. Rachel full of questions and confusion as her grandmother pulled her towards the church. She could see the vicar standing outside the closed oak doors looking ashen and forlorn.

Rachel gasped:

'He looks terrible.'

'And so he should after the dressing down I gave him – he didn't tell you even half the truth when you went to visit him.'

They passed him without a word as Rachel's grandmother practically dragged her to the far side of the churchyard where it edged the riverbank. Here the ground was weedy and overgrown. Right in the corner, where they could go no further, stood an old towering weathered stone statue commanding a fine view across the whole graveyard. Behind this, Rachel's grandmother showed her a small slate gravestone covered in yellow lichen, out of view and well hidden.

Rachel stared dumbfounded at the deeply carved letters.

Rachel Ellis

Born 1205

'Have you never wondered why all the first born girls in our family are called Rachel Ellis, no matter what their fathers' names are?'

Rachel couldn't speak. She knew the witches were there, silent, hiding and waiting deep within her. But waiting for what?

'Every Rachel Ellis and every vicar at this church keeps this stone in good repair to pass onto the next generation. As your mother is no longer with us I ought to pass the care to you...but...'

She seemed lost for words and looked from the stone to Rachel and back again.

Rachel already felt spooked and now started shaking.

'You're scaring me gran – stop it.'

Rachel then felt them move, rise up, a terrifying power, which she herself could throw into the world.

'Tell me!' She pleaded.

The ground shook, a tremor beneath their feet, which quickly ceased the moment the vicar spoke his soft words.

'I'm so sorry Rachel…' he started.

Her grandmother curtly cut in:

'And so you should be – your cowardice has lost us time and may very well have courted disaster.'

'I've had enough of you two! Tell me what's going on,' Rachel demanded, 'Or I'll unleash them without measure.'

The vicar and her grandmother looked at each other gravely, knowingly.

The vicar spoke first:

'In the 13th Century there wasn't much difference between the church and magic. In fact, many sorcerers joined the church to find shelter from persecution. Powerful and ambitious people, who could command the elements with their strange magic.'

He paused to glance up at the dark crags, under which the chapel sat hidden from view.

'What you call The Witches are not ordinary witches, are not part of the world of magic, sorcery or even the Devil – they are something else completely – forgive me, but I know not what.'

He paused again to find the courage to continue.

'They resided up in the old slate quarries and caused havoc with anyone that went near the place – the place where the chapel now stands. People could not take stone to build their houses or gather firewood from the forests that once covered these hills. If some poor foolish soul did venture there, they either disappeared, went mad or worse – they spread fear and illness amongst the village until the church burnt them at the stake. Nothing could placate the place, no prayers, no exorcism, no magic spells – even the cattle and sheep became possessed, attacking farmers and blowing flames. The church and the sorcerers knew that some great power lived up there and they badly wanted it for themselves. If they couldn't have it, they wanted it gone, destroyed and banished for good.

The vicar looked at Mrs. Ellis, who continued:

'The cowardly church and a group of evil sorcerers hatched a deviously clever plan – a trick really. They found William, a simple and pious man and convinced him to build a chapel under the guise of turning the place holy. He had been the only person able to collect firewood up there and for some reason the witches never bothered him. He always maintained he could see them, constantly watching, as if waiting for something. Of course, the church had no interest in the chapel or William whatsoever.'

Rachel was gripped by the story, her mouth agape and eyes wide open.

The vicar found his courage and said:

'The church stole Rachel and William's baby.'

He felt relief – he had finally been able to say it – he had truly dreaded this moment.

'They told William the baby had been taken by the witches for bloodletting and, as a holy man, William needed to confront the witches and threaten them with eternal damnation. At the same time, one of the most powerful sorcerers went as close as he dared to the chapel and warned the witches that William planned to exorcise them and cast them out – and as a holy man with special powers, he would surely succeed. Only hanging him by the neck from the big apple tree would save them…'

The vicar said he had hardly believed the story himself, had wondered if it was all a dream, pure hocus-pocus, but no, he had now seen them for himself, flying in and out of Rachel as she stamped her foot on the church steps. He continued:

'Finally the sorcerers told Rachel Ellis of the witches plan to hang her husband and that the only thing that would possibly save him was a magic spell she had to recite just before the noose pulled tight.

The sorcerers knew that this most powerful spell of theirs could only work if recited by a loved one. Except it was not a spell to save William but a spell to cast the witches out. What happened to William they did not care. They were sure that their plan could not fail and would finally succeed in tricking and banishing the witches...'

The vicar turned to Rachel's grandmother:

'Please Mrs. Ellis, the rest is about your family, it is for you to tell.'

'Rachel, all I know is that Rachel Ellis did as she was asked, reciting the spell as the noose went tight...but, for reasons no one knows, she had collected six pieces of broken sticks from the apple tree and added the six bits of broken sticks poem to the end of the sorcerers' spell. William found the sticks in his hand as Rachel took the noose off. What her spell did we don't really know but the witches did disappear along with William. The sorcerers witnessed everything – it was all recorded in their book, which turned to ash in the church the other day. But no one could ever go to the chapel again, they still can't without feeling sick or terrified, and the sorcerers knew they were still there, locked away somehow, but far from gone.'

Rachel protested:

'What's this got to do with me?'

Her Grandmother continued:

'The church told Rachel that her baby was dead and her husband banished to hell and, in her heartbreak and despair, she threw herself off the top of the crag with her beloved dog and she landed on the burnt apple tree. It's said that the dog survived. They brought her body here...'

Rachel's grandmother pointed to the slate headstone.

'... the sorcerers knew she was somehow still around as her body remained warm and her ghostly eyes could not be shut. With great fear they buried her as quickly as possible without a service and marked the grave with no date of death.'

The vicar finished, as he knew he must:

'It was written in that book that Rachel Ellis would return one day holding six charred bits of broken sticks. The sorcerers left spells to cast her out, but the book has now been burnt, as we both clearly saw and for reasons I can't explain. Anyway, the church no longer delves in magic. You are safe'

Rachel's grandmother shot him a virulent look.

'For Fuck's sake – what's it got to do with me?'

Both the vicar and Rachel's grandmother simultaneously boomed:

'You are Rachel Ellis!'

'And so are you gran – so what?'

'If you hadn't killed Rob we might know what to do now, but no, your lust knew no bounds.'

'Piss off the both of you, and anyway, he's not dead anymore', she screamed.

Again, they boomed together,

'He's alive!'

They looked hard at Rachel, expecting an answer. 'You can go to hell for all I care – if you don't tell me, I won't tell you…' she protested defiantly.

The vicar tried to placate Rachel,

'We don't know – it's like a jigsaw puzzle waiting to be put together, except no one knows the pieces anymore – only you…'

His pause was taken up by Rachel's grandmother:

'…and Rob.'

'I don't bloody know – it's all a riddle – as for Rob – he's off gallivanting – displaying and probably exercising his new found prowess!'

'As if he needs anymore,' Rachel's grandmother snorted.

'Why Rob?' Rachel glanced viciously at the vicar.

'He was available.'

'Available! You can say that again!'

Rachel then told the whole story of Rob's demise and grisly resurrection.

Rachel's grandmother spoke. She reached out and gently touched Rachel's arm, but Rachel flinched and drew back.

'You need to put the pieces together or I feel something terrible will happen. We need to find Rob.'

It didn't take long driving around in the vicar's car. They found Rachel's car nearby parked outside a small cottage. Rachel knew this house and angrily banged on the door.

Rob answered, still shirtless and shoeless beaming a mischievous smile.

Rachel let out a barrage:

'What the hell are you doing here? Where's Sally-Ann? You said you wouldn't see her again. Well?'

'Oh listen to Miss Purity herself – after what you did to me! Jesus vicar, she and those hideous hags fucked me to death – imagine that!'

However, the vicar couldn't, and stayed quiet.

'Stop it you two! Is there anyone else in the house Rob?'

'No.'

Without further ado, Rachel's gran shuttled everyone indoors and pushed the door shut behind her.

'She indicated to the chairs and sofa in the main room. They all quickly sat.

'Jesus Rachel, why did you have to bring them here?'

'My gran and the vicar are the only two people who can help us now, so just shut up Rob and stop being rude.'

'Not them – them!'

Rob pointed, moving his arm around the room.

In the hush that followed, Rachel saw the witches around the edges of the room. She counted at least thirty apparitions – morphing and bobbing.

'Oh', she murmured.

She looked at her grandmother and vicar. They both looked wide-eyed and terrified. The vicar had turned slightly green and was mumbling prayers and her grandmother kept looking from apparition to apparition and then back to Rachel.

Three of the apparitions moved towards Rob and hovered close to him, sometimes going right through him, making Rob shudder.

'Jeez – these three like me…err…the sexton – it's disgusting…'

'Rob, try to focus, tell us what's going on.'

Rob looked at Rachel's grandmother and answered:

'His gibberish is doing my head in – incessant chatting, trying to tell me what to do – even with Sally-Ann'

'Stop it!' Rachel screamed.

Rob sat there transfixed, listening, sometimes mumbling to himself before breaking his concentration, with:

'What the hell.'

He looked at Rachel nervously,

'What the hell have you got me into? I never asked for this.'

Rob looked at Mrs. Ellis' severe face and told William's tale:

'It's not like any of you think – even the church and the sorcerers had it all wrong…I, err, I mean William spent eight hundred years with your witches.'

He focused on Rachel for a moment before continuing:

'Locked up, forced together in what you call the chapel – a space, a vacuum in time. The witches are beings that leaked out of the black slate thousands of years ago during a volcanic eruption. They lived in another dimension, deep inside the earth, but they couldn't get back again and were soon lost, trapped on earth, tormented and afraid. They didn't dare move from that spot in case things changed and they could return…home, I guess.'

'Why couldn't they get back?'

The vicar had perked up, lost his green pallor and was intently following the story.

Rob continued:

'They needed a crack in time – but it never happened, and with the passing of the years they all went slightly, um…what we would call mad. When the sorcerers came along the witches quickly realised that on earth was a magic that could take them back home. It was simple to keep the sorcerers at bay. But no matter how hard the witches searched and no matter how hard they tried to find and make a spell that might work, they just couldn't – the more frustrated they got the madder they became, until one day the church and the sorcerers had had enough and decided to banish them. This is what gave the witches a chance. They knew the sorcerers had great power, could banish them, but they could block it with ease – but they didn't, they just let it play out, except they gave Rachel Ellis…'

Rob looked at Rachel.

'God, it's you, isn't it?'

'Of course it's her, you idiot!' Her grandmother snapped.

Rob continued:

'They gave Rachel Ellis in her dreams a poem to recite. They knew it would end badly for them all, but they had no choice.'

'So what did the extra spell do?'

Rachel urgently needed to know.

'Instead of really banishing them, it locked them and William into a time warp bubble inside the chapel with no chance of escape unless the wheel of time brought around another chance – it was a crazy manoeuvre and they had no idea if it would work– that's how desperate they were.'

'So what happened?'

'You happened, Rachel. The witches needed you to come back and do a spell reversal, but more than that, they needed you to eat the apples and place the burnt sticks on the book with all the sorcerers spells.'

Rob paused and said the next thing very slowly,

'That was their spell – they set the whole thing up – even they can't believe it worked. Can you imagine how grateful they are to you?'

Rob laughed at Rachel,

'They'll never leave you now.'

He turned a little dark as he said the next bit:

'Except for these ghastly three that is.'

Rob shuddered and tried to shake them off in vain.

'William made a pact with them, the kind of pact that you can never go back on or even break. Their fate and your fate are linked, joined for good.'

Everyone was staring hard at Rob, waiting for the bombshell.

'He wanted his life back – you, me – I mean William, and the baby. He would play ball if they would – and for that, a huge compromise was made on both parts. They need William and you, for the next part coming.'

'And what's that Robert?'

He ignored Rachel's grandmother and stared hard at the vicar.

Rachel was so shocked she couldn't get any words out. It was true then what the witches had told her – their fate was linked, come rain, shine or anything else.

'What's the next part – why aren't the witches helping anymore?' She blurted out.

'They can't help because they don't work well in this world – they become monsters in an instant, wreck everything around them. They've gone to ground for now.'

Rob looked at Rachel and then back to the vicar.

'We are running out of time – it will all go wrong soon – won't it vicar?'

After a moment of silence, Rob insisted:

'Damn you – speak!'

The vicar gazed at all the apparitions making them flutter, and then to Rachel and her grandmother.

'I feel so terribly ashamed at what they did – the church.'

Rachel's grandmother tried to ease his tension:

'That was eight hundred years ago, it wasn't your fault.'

'Nevertheless…I'm so sorry Rachel…and you Rob, I…err…mean you William, that the church stole your baby daughter. The burnt book said she was taken to Spain where the church and the sorcerers had a stronghold, a monastic castle, carved into a mountainside…'

The vicar hesitated, trying to find the words,

'The last entry into the burnt book was in 1402. Whoever wrote it had the same handwriting as the first entry in 1089.'

'Are you saying that that someone was more than three hundred years old?'

'No Rachel, I'm saying that they were most probably even older, and my guess is that those demonic sorcerers headed for Spain once the English church no longer tolerated that kind of thing – I'm sure the Inquisition later welcomed them.'

'What are you saying old man – that they're still there, holed up and waiting for bloody judgment day!'

That's Rob speaking – no sign of William there, Rachel thought to herself.

'Not quite, my guess is that they are somewhere, perhaps with what remains of your daughter, hiding behind an obscure catholic sect, deep inside a mountain.'

The vicar lifted his finger.

'And they will be almighty powerful now – your fate lies there, and once they know you're coming – God help you both.'

The vicar crossed himself.

'Why would I go at all – eh?'

The vicar looked straight into Rachel's eyes and said:

'Because William made a pact with the witches – you have no choice but to go there or you will both turn mad and wretched. He wanted his life back – whatever the cost.'

'Is there more?'

Rachel's sternness startled the vicar. He knew she was going to squeeze every last drop of information out of him.

'When this church was finally cleansed of all those evil people and their magic, an oral tradition started about Rachel Ellis. All I know, and all I was told is that the six bits of broken sticks – the ashes in the urn – are somehow the key. I know not more.'

'So where is this place?' Rachel's grandmother pressed.

'I don't know, but it was called Castell del Rei – The King's Castle.'

Again, he lifted his finger:

'Now heed my warning you two – they'll do anything to get that power in you Rachel – the witches power, and they – the witches – are vulnerable now, weakening as every day passes as they are not in the chapel – their crack in time is brief and closing – as is yours.'

Rachel had dropped Rob off at home to pick up his passport and a few clothes for their impending trip to Spain. She had had to plead and coax him until he acquiesced and agreed to come along. God, that guy – he would do anything for sex – more sex she meant – what a pair they made – pious William and slapper Rob. They must both be in some sort of hell, locked together and at odds in the same body.

The back door banged once and Rachel felt the hairs stand up on the back of her neck. No, please make this a nice guest and not another horror show.

She held her breath and pulled the door wide open.

'Rob, you idiot, you'll catch your death out there dressed like that!'

He was still shoeless and shirtless and carrying a small holdall.

'And what the hell is that on your back – Jesus Rob!'

'Oh – I couldn't help myself – he kind of made me – said you needed kindling to start the fire.'

'Tell him we use firelighters these days.'

Rob walked through the kitchen and dropped the large bundle of twigs and sticks he had bundled up and strapped to his back onto the slate hearth.

'Yeah, firelighters are a lot easier – he thinks we are deranged, by the way.'

'Not surprised with what you get up to!'

'Me!'

'Point taken – now just stop it.'

Rachel quickly changed the subject.

'Think I just found the castle – it's not Spanish but Catalan – Castell del Rei – here it is, it's in Mallorca.'

They peered at the computer image of a ruined castle perched on top of a sea cliff, perfectly blended into the craggy landscape to make it look invisible.

'You need a permit to walk anywhere near it and you are not allowed to walk up to it – it's a black vulture breeding site.'

'You sure that's the one?'

'It's the only one, although it doesn't seem to date back that far.'

'What do *they* say?'

'Nothing – and William?'

'He told me to hurry up, then he bloody asks me to collect a whole bunch of sticks for you – Jeez William, get your priorities right!'

'The sticks Rob, oh, I almost forgot.'

Rachel rushed to the kitchen and returned with the urn.

'What are we supposed to do with this?'

Rob just shrugged:

'We could pretend it's your mother's ashes and scatter them in the sea.'

'That's mean – but it has given me an idea.'

It had taken quite some persuading for Rob to put on a shirt and a pair of shoes. He felt warm enough without them. Apparently, William hated his modern clothes. In the end, Rachel got her way using simple facts and threats:

'They won't let you on the bloody plane looking like that – remember what the vicar said – time is running out!'

With Rob quickly suited and booted they drove towards the airport. They didn't speak except for one brief time.

'My three witches don't like that vicar much.'

'And mine nearly killed him on the stone church steps – it was like a deep hatred and disrespect.'

'Well, maybe he was in the Inquisition too!'

'Oooh, now you've got them talking, stirred up – we had better shut up Rob if we want to get there without some huge calamity.'

'Yeah, bloody Church eh!'

They both burst out in hysterical laughter, easing the pent up tensions.

Rob spent most of the flight in the lavatory throwing up. He looked green, pale and very clammy.

During one of his brief stays in his seat, he tried to make light of it all:

'William says it's the Devil's work – pure sorcery – flying in the sky at night. I mean, we don't even have broomsticks.'

'How can he say that after being locked up with them for eight hundred years?'

'Because he's human again…I mean, I'm human.'

'You mean he's you and you're him – right?'

'Jeez, a life of collecting bits of sticks in muddy woods – no thanks Rache.'

And Rob was off again, heading down the aisle hoping he would make it in time.

They awoke to the smell of strong tobacco filtering up from some outside tables below the open window of their hotel room. Was this the smell of Spain, Rachel wondered as she looked down on an early morning smoke and coffee ritual before slamming the window shut.

'Don't do that – it's bleedin' boiling in here.'

'No it's not – you're just used to the driving winds and rain of Wales.'

Rob stretched and threw the sheet off the bed.

'It was almost like old times last night…'

He stopped speaking and looked around.

'Where are we Rache?'

'You fell asleep in the hire car – the old square in Pollenca – come on, move it – we've got a castle to find.'

Picking up the permit from the town hall to access the land around the castle was a simple affair, but they needed more – actual permission to get into the castle. To achieve that, Rachel had an ace up her sleeve.

'I want to scatter my mother's ashes in the sea from the castle – it was one of her favourite spots.'

Rachel produced the urn and quickly removed the lid. She practically shoved the contents into the clerk's face who turned away disgusted, pushing it back to Rachel. Before there could be any reproach, Rachel showed a newspaper cutting of her mother's obituary.

The plan worked and they hastily left the building with permission to do as they pleased.

'That was a cunning move.'

'Actually it was your idea, remember? Anyway, brains can be quite handy sometimes Rob.'

The late autumn breeze rattled the car as they drove through the narrow streets towards the grey crags of the nearby mountains. Once out of town, it was a brief drive along a single-track road to where a green gate marked its end. They parked the car in a layby and followed the track on foot to where a small gorge cut through the sheer rock at the gate.

They pushed the buzzer and a guard appeared to inspect their permits and note their passport numbers. He seemed flummoxed at the extra permission but let them pass without a further word.

They were through, and although Rachel still felt anxious, there was a new underlying feeling of excitement.

Rob felt it too.

'It's beautiful here, so unspoilt and…'

'Timeless Rob – it's timeless.'

They followed the track, which ran besides the small dry river gorge through an old forest of oak and pine. Up they hiked, grateful for the breeze, towards a grassy plateau surrounded by small steep rocky peaks. The woman at the town hall had told them Castell del Rei lay there, almost invisible amongst the crags. They scoured the ridgelines. It wasn't the castle they saw first, it was the vultures, huge and black, perched in a long line along the ridge, their silhouettes ominously black against the brilliance of the sky.

'Give me a crow any day.'

'Why do I now feel it's been all too easy to get here?'

'Is that them, Rache?'

'They're waiting for something.'

'Food probably – us, Jeez, let's go home.'

Rachel had Rob's hand and yanked him towards the stony path that led upwards. Now they saw the castle. It was built into the sheer rock and was much smaller than they had imagined. It was a ruin. On the other side they knew was a sheer drop to the sea.

The path took them through some pines. On exiting the trees near the ridge, the vultures had gone.

'I'm spooked – I can't even feel William or the three witches – this is bad.'

They stopped and peered down at the huge white breakers violently crashing into the sea cliff below, and then to the castle, a stone's throw away from where they stood.

'There's nothing here – it's a total ruin, we must have made a mistake – come on.'

Rob tried to pull her back down along the path but she refused to budge.

'It must be the place – there was no other – we're done for if it's not.'

'And done for if it is.'

'Let's just have a peek.'

Rachel edged along the ridge with Rob following reluctantly behind.

He was right – there was nothing there, just a few parapets cut through with an old window opening here and there and many piles of stones. No one would have lived there for centuries. There was certainly no evidence of it having been a church.

'I'm scared.'

Rachel didn't know what to say to Rob anymore. It was hopeless, there was nothing there except stones and scary vultures which had scarpered at their presence – unlike those pesky crows who had been hell bent on her. But even those crows, the witches, were silent, apparently gone to ground and of no help whatsoever. They were on their own and clueless.

'Do you think it's true what the vicar said?'

Rachel broke from her despondency and answered,

'He said a lot of things, there's something I don't trust about him. It's like we've either been sent on a wild goose chase or into the lion's den – but there is no den.'

Rob was panicking, breathing erratically and playing with his hands.

'You're scaring me Rob – stop it, we need to think.'

'Think! Jesus Rache – duck!'

Rob grabbed Rachel around the waist with both hands and pulled her to the ground.

A huge vulture swept close over them, so close they could see its ghastly eye and beak and smell its pungent odour.

They lay huddled in a small hollow.

'They're all coming – God, no.'

Rob pointed up at the entire flock swooping down from a great height, heading straight for them.

'Come on!'

It was Rob pulling Rachel by the hand this time. He desperately looked around for cover and not seeing any realised they would have to dash like mad for the pines. It was a long shot, but there was no other choice.

'Run!'

As soon as they started, the ground gave way under their feet and they were falling, crashing and tumbling down until they landed with a thud and a joint moan on damp rock.

'Ouch – you ok Rache?'

'I think so.'

They both got to their feet rubbing and nursing their knocks and looked up. The hole was way above them, too far to reach even with Rachel standing on Rob's shoulders.

The dark shadows of vultures momentarily blotted out the light making Rob state the obvious:

'Now we've done it.'

'Don't say that – oh no – look!'

Rachel pointed to the floor. The urn had spilt and the entire contents of ash lay strewn across the floor in a thick, neat line.

'Why did you have to eat those bloody apples?'

Rob was panicking again and Rachel felt an impending dread.

'The ashes have gone, let's just find a way out of here – you were right, I should have listened to you.'

As their eyes adjusted to the light, they could see that they were standing in a chamber carved from solid rock. The walls were rough cut but flat, showing glistening patches of damp here and there. Right by where they stood, was a pile of old broken slabs, and on the wall close by was some old stone masonry cut into the rock suggesting long ago steps had once joined the chamber to the castle above.

'There must be a way out of here.'

Rob started skirting the wall looking for a door or exit, before exclaiming:

'We're trapped, it's all solid rock.'

He came over to Rachel and pulled her close.

'It's over, we've dug our own grave and jumped in.'

She pulled roughly away and pointed to a small light on the chamber wall.

'Just the damp,' Rob said as he sat down on a large slab to hide his head in his hands.

'No it's not – look.'

Rachel was at the wall, picking and gently pulling until a rock came away and the chamber was illuminated by brilliant blue sky.

Rob needed no coaxing and was immediately with her, both of them pushing small slabs of rock outwards until the bricked up window was totally opened.

They yelled with joy, kissed and hugged before peering out down to the huge breakers crashing against the cliff below.

Under the window opening on the sheer limestone cliff was what remained of another stairway. Small stone bricks stuck out of the cliff and stopped about ten feet below beside a black hole, which they reckoned was another window. Above them, the castle parapet was out of reach above a crumbly rocky overhang.

They both moved back into the chamber to ponder their inevitable and dangerous descent down the cliff face.

As they turned away from the sea, they saw something that made them gasp.

Rachel grabbed Rob's arm.

'Jesus, what have we fallen into?'

Under the brilliant light of the sky, the walls showed the faded paint of ages, symbols they both recognized as occult, a strange writing that Rachel remembered seeing in the vicar's old book back home, whose ashes were now strewn across the floor before them.

'I don't want to go down there.'

Rachel pointed towards the window, but Rob was not in the mood for dithering – his panic had subsided and he now felt an urgency to move out of the sinister chamber, whatever the risk.

'Come on, I'll go first.'

Rob was quickly out of the window, lowering himself onto the first brick, before moving carefully to the next. He didn't dare look down at the white foam and boiling water smashing into the cliff hundreds of feet below. The constant crash and boom of waves echoed up the cliff face.

Hands and feet, brick to brick…take care Rob…easy does it, until he stood on the small opening before easing himself through the hole and inside. He was on a narrow winding stone stairway cut out of the rock. Above, it ended at a wall, and below, it disappeared into darkness.

'There's a staircase – come on.'

For Rachel this was her worst nightmare – climbing down a vertical rock face with a constant wind to tip her off balance. It took a long time, with Rob encouraging her, step-by-step, as loose rock broke free, dropping to the sea far below. Finally, she stood on the stairway, trembling and breathing hard.

They didn't talk, just held hands as they descended into what must surely be hell itself.

Does hell have a backdoor out?

The darkness faded as they passed more windows, tiny ones that let through just enough light to mark their descent. The lower they got, the louder the sea became, until they stood where the staircase ended. The floor was soaked from violent waves lashing through another small opening.

Rob daringly moved to the light and peered out.

'Get back!'

He shoved Rachel into the darkness, as a wave pressed through the opening before being sucked back out again. The noise was deafening. They watched the water drain away through cracks in the floor.

'The water is about twenty feet below – it'd be suicide jumping into that – nothing but sharp rocks, reefs and huge pounding waves.'

With no choice, they headed into the mountain, following a dark passageway until their path was blocked by a rusty door with a large rusty ring handle. Rob went to try the handle.

'Oh Rob, no, no.'

But it was too late. He had pulled the door towards them. Musty dry warm air hit them like a sudden wind. There was just enough light to make out another chamber.

They froze at the first growl and at the sound of a chain going tight. There was another growl and again the tensing of a chain.

They could see the dog, massive and black with a huge jaw showing sharp teeth. It didn't look like any dog they could recognize. Its eyes shone green in the dim light, reflecting sea and sky.

Rachel hung onto Rob, as the dog-like creature snapped its jaws closed before growling again. The chain's restraining ring on the wall creaked with strain.

'Oh. It's going to break.'

The dog pulled again, saliva now dripping from its jaw, and the ring moved, twisting in the wall.

Rob tried to shut the door but it had jammed hard against the floor. 'Run Rachel!'

They were soon clambering back up the narrow stairway, both moaning with fear as they heard the ring give way. The dog was free, barking and coming for them.

They had no time to get out onto the cliff face again and continued upwards to where the stairway ended at a blank wall.

The dog was closing, the chain rattling like mad behind it on the stone stairs.

'Do something!'

Rachel was screaming at Rob.

He booted the wall and slammed his hands against it in desperate panic.

'Shit!'

The dog was almost to the last stairway bend below them, but Rob's pounding of the wall was not in vain, as the wall moved and a hidden door revolved, allowing them to scurry though into the chamber into which they had first fallen.

Again, the door wouldn't close, and as soon as Rob saw the dog, he backed off and stood with Rachel under the hole to the sky. She was screaming as the dog leapt through the door and towards them. Frozen with fear, hugging each other with their eyes closed tight, it would be just seconds before they were ripped to pieces and eaten alive.

However, the dog stopped and they opened their eyes. The only noises they could hear were the wind and crashing waves far below and the chattering of their teeth.

The dog looked straight at them. It was huge, its head was as high as Rob's midriff and its body strong – this was no dog, this was a hound from hell itself.

What was it waiting for?

It had lost none of its menace but was now sniffing and licking the ashes before looking straight at them again growling.

'Rob! It's my dog.'

'That's no dog.'

Rachel held out her hand but the dog growled again exposing its terrible teeth before licking the ashes again.

'What have they done to it?'

Her thoughts were quickly overpowered by a sound echoing through the chamber from deep below. Unearthly murmurs and scraping were followed by heavy footsteps on the stairs, slowly coming up towards the chamber.

The dog turned towards the open door and gave a long low growl before licking up some more ash.

'What have we woken up down there? It sounds like the depths of hell...'

Rob was shaking Rachel wanting an answer and she knew exactly what to do.

'The ashes, eat the ashes Rob – look, the dog is showing us.'

She prised herself out of Rob's clutches and went down on her hands and knees, cupping up handfuls of ash and stuffing it in her mouth. She pulled at Rob, who from fear, desperation and want of a better idea joined her. They chewed and munched with great difficulty as their saliva dried up, forcing the dry ash down trying not to retch as another mouthful went in.

The noises from the depths were almost on them but they chose not to focus on that. When the ash was just about gone, the dog howled like a wolf and they both looked up.

The sight was too much to endure and both Rob and Rachel screamed their lungs out. A dark apparition, half man, half dog, dark and evil beyond belief, towered over them.

The world went black and blank.

They awoke simultaneously to find themselves shackled by the wrists and secured to a wall by a chain. The dog sat nearby unrestrained looking as terrifying as it did before.

Lying next to each other on the cold stone floor, they looked around. An eerie greenish glow illuminated the chamber. There were numerous exits and dark passageways cut into the walls. There seemed no source for the greenish light.

'Was that a sorcerer?'

Rob was whispering but it echoed loudly through the tunnels, his voice coming back to him several times.

Rachel nodded.

'And the dog?'

'They must have used it as a guard – it's half sorcerer now I think.'

'Great, a schizoid dog is just what we need – I've got terrible gut ache from those ashes – fat lot of good it did us.'

'Me too.'

Rachel held her guts.

Their whispering echoes had summoned the darkness and the chamber was full of apparitions, abhorrent and morphing like the witches but black and evil.

The pair had gone beyond fear – they were imprisoned and at the mercy of this dark lair.

'What do they want?' Rachel looked at Rob for an answer.

'What's inside us.'

'Let's just give them up and be done with it then.'

'I'm sure that would mean our instant demise – got any more useful comments – anyway, how the hell would we give them up?'

They stayed silent, but the silence only helped to amplify the wail and cry that came next.

Rachel's face dropped, and she sat speechless looking at Rob.

'What?'

She didn't answer him as the cry came again, only this time Rob recognized it as the familiar cry of a baby.

'Oh Rob!'

Rachel burst into tears. Her sobs became uncontrollable, her body shaking as she hung on to Rob with shackled hands. He was perplexed and looked around at the aberrations before him whilst listening to the distinct sounds, which soon became louder and louder, echoing through the room.

Rachel put her hands on her ears and pleaded for them to stop whatever they were doing.

'It's our baby Rob.'

She screamed and implored, was beside herself, now violently shaking, her distraught face screwed tight.

Rob yelled:

'We don't have a fucking baby!'

All went silent and Rachel flopped and lay flat, sobbing and holding her belly. Moments later, she vomited sticky grey ash across the stone floor. Rob followed suit and, as they held their guts moaning, the dog nonchalantly trotted over and instantly devoured the lot.

The cries returned, but this time they were screams of pain, horrific sounds that made Rachel shout:

'I'll do it – just stop please.'

The cries immediately stopped.

'Do what?'

Rachel was still sobbing and did not answer Rob, so he shook her shackled hands, shouting:

'Do what? Fuck's sake Rache – do what?'

She softly spoke,

'Reverse the witches spell – chant their spell.'

Rachel indicated to the apparitions with a slight nod of her head.

'It's a trick – don't do it – they'll kill us, or worse – lock us up forever, please Rache, don't do it…please,' Rob begged.

But the sounds of a spell, a mantra were already being recited, echoing around the chamber over and over again. The sorcerers were agitated, darting about in anticipation as the spell reverberated through the couple until they knew it off by heart.

'I'm sorry Rob but I have to try and save the baby.'

'There is no bloody baby!'

As Rachel muttered the first sounds of the spell, the dog retched and delivered putrid ash on the floor where she now sat.

'Please Rache.'

The dog growled. It was mean and very close. Its disgusting breath made Rachel flinch and reel back. She stopped her recitation. But she soon started again, joining in with the endless echoes filling the chamber.

The dog snapped its huge jaws so close to Rachel's head that it caught her hair and yanked her forward making her fall and crack her head on the stone floor.

The sorcerers moved over the dog making it jump at them, but it only found the air.

The baby howled.

Rob was shaking Rachel who had involuntary started the chant again.

'No Rache, please, we're going to die.'

Then it struck him, and perhaps for the first time in his life he had a good idea.

'The poem Rachel, say the poem – damn you!'

Rob was desperate, but Rachel didn't stop, she just kept copying the chant.

The dog was rabid now, snapping at the apparitions before leaping at Rachel. Its jaws clasped Rachel's head and twisted it to the side, forcing her to scream and stop the chant.

'It wants you to say the poem you stupid cow!'

> *Six bits of broken sticks*
> *taken from the apple tree*
> *where they tried to hang*
> *the sexton*

high.

Six bits of old rough wood
taken where the lightning struck
and cut the tree in two.

She only said it once and the whole world stopped.

Rob found himself floating. That's what it seemed as he looked over at Rachel, who was clutching her bloody head with one hand and hanging onto the thick neck of the now placid dog with the other.

The apparitions were still for a moment and then they seemed to solidify, turning into hideous black creatures with luminous eyes. They looked ready to do battle.

From his detached position, Rob wondered how he could defend himself and Rachel.

His answer came quickly. From somewhere deep within, a place that even he didn't know existed, he heard a rumbling and then they were out. He saw and felt William's three witches leave his body. They also poured out of Rachel.

They looked like molten rock – pure fury itself – red, bubbling and boiling mad. The chamber shook. Dust and debris fell from the roof.

The chamber was a swirl of chaotic energies making noises like trains rushing through a tunnel.

Their shackles snapped and Rob was quickly on his feet, pulling Rachel up, desperately looking for a way out. He noticed the dog madly barking and running in circles by an open passageway and practically dragged Rachel into the darkness following the growling dog whose green eyes were the only source of light.

Rachel had come to and exclaimed:

'My baby – where's my baby?'

'There is no baby – the witches have gone mental and the place is collapsing – come on!'

He was about to pull her along but the dog had stopped by an alcove, and in the very dim light they saw a metal box casket.

'Oh no.'

Rachel opened the lid to find a mummified baby, still clothed and wrapped in silk.

As she silently picked up the corpse, it turned to dust in her arms and a cold wind rushed down the passageway making them shiver.

The dog barked and Rob pushed Rachel behind the dog before she could protest, down a long winding passageway until a crack of daylight told him they were safe.

They exited through a small break in the rock, just big enough to squeeze through, finding themselves in a small and heavily vegetated canyon, way below the castle.

They both looked up and saw a large billowing dust cloud rising above the area where they had fallen through the ground. Then they heard the sound of falling rock. As the noise tailed off, Rob and Rachel stood alone, listening to the hissing wind blowing through the pines.

The dog had gone.

'Did you see how they changed? Looked like red molten rock?'

Rachel didn't answer. She was pale and forlornly gazed down the gorge at a jumble of rock and thorny vegetation to distract herself.

Rob, still eyed the castle:

'They're having a right scrap up there – who do you think's winning?'

He started picking up small sticks scattered around the gorge floor.

Rachel, on hearing Rob's movements, instinctively knew what he was up to and turned towards him.

'William's back.'

Rob threw the sticks to the ground in disgust.

'That was sneaky of him.'

'I think you have your answer.'

Rob turned, as Rachel just had, and looked down the gorge.

'What...oh...'

No longer fire red fury, but luminescence, morphing and bobbing, the witches were spread out along the top of the edge of the gorge.

'Where's my baby – well?'

Rachel turned her grief to anger and stamped her foot hard.

The witches moved, twitched, and moments later were gone.

'Oh no, they're back!'

Rob made a strange undulation with his body – he leant back before raising his spine and pushing his head forward.

A cold wind blew up the gorge making Rob shudder.

'Did you feel that? What the hell happened up there Rache?'

'They want us to go back.'

'But I don't want to go back – I like it here.'

Rachel turned to Rob and vehemently exploded:

'We'll die here or go mad, and anyway – it's not over yet – you must know that...'

'It's like I'm two people – one part wants to go swimming in the Med and get my leg over – the other half wants to pick up fucking stupid sticks and return to that dark sinister chapel of yours, of ours – Jesus. And then there're these three witches...trying to be my friend...'

Rob looked at Rachel imploringly, before adding:

'Fuck's sake – can't you do a reverse apple spell or something and make me normal again?'

Rachel ignored his absurd plea.

'What can your witches do Rob?'

'They're like a boiling cauldron – fuck, how should I know – it's William they like, not me.'

'Be friendly to them.'

'Friendly! I'm just a body, a convenience for them!'

Rachel wondered if that were true – if Rob could be discarded at any moment.

She didn't want that.

'You listen to me, all of you – Rob's my boyfriend – he's for keeps – get used to it...bloody sort it out or we're not going anywhere.'

She felt better and sat down on a rock. Jesus, had she really said that? That was rather rash and committing. She felt herself blush and turned away from Rob who had also sat down, totally perplexed.

'Oh Rache – what have you done?'

She turned back towards him…what had she done? He seemed about to fall forward.

'Rob?'

She shook him to wake him from his daze.

He turned to her.

'Was that a spell? Did you really do that?'

'Do what – what?'

'Make them part of me.'

Now I've gone and done it Rachel thought – there's no going back on this one now.

She feigned ignorance.

'Err…what do you mean?'

'William's thoughts are mine, and those three witches…they're…um…like mine too…oh, I don't know.'

'Is that good?'

'At least I know better than to pick up stupid sticks on a warm Mediterranean island…Jesus, how dumb is that?'

'William's just out of time, that's all…he's safe with you now.'

Poor William, she thought.

'I'm confused Rob…we need to get back ASAP'

'So long as I can get my leg over.'

'Don't you think of anything else?'

They picked the car up from the airport and drove home along dark roads in the wind and rain.

The house was freezing cold so Rob went about making a fire.

'Firelighters William – see? This is how we do it now.'

Rachel smirked at Rob's antics and went to prepare a meal. They were famished.

Eating in silence, hungrily devouring their food, they kept looking at each other smiling. They didn't need words until Rob finally blurted out:

'It's like a last supper or something – tastes great, eh?'

Rachel didn't dare tell him what the witches had told her after Rob had been resurrected with apple puree.

'Err…yeah, great.'

They slept soundly that night, both dreaming of a dark place full of molten fire.

On waking, Rob turned to Rachel and was about to speak, but she cut him off and spoke first.

'Yeah…I dreamt that too…but let's not dwell on these mysteries – time's almost run out – come on.'

She pulled him out of bed and ten minutes later, they were parking outside the church.

'Ooh…this feels spooky.'

'That's because it is.'

They found the vicar in the graveyard standing in front of the statue that hid Rachel Ellis' grave, facing the river.

He turned on hearing footsteps. Standing tall and proud and without emotion, he stated:

'I've done my part – now keep your part as you promised.'

'What's he on about?'

'Shush – listen Rob – I don't know either – the witches kept this part secret from me.'

'Oh great…I hope I'm not gonna get buried under a ton of Welsh slate again.'

The vicar almost smirked as Rachel and Rob stood before him in total ignorance.

'I see they haven't told you. Don't worry – shall I explain, or will you?'

It wasn't Rob or Rachel he addressed, but the things inside them.

Both Rob and Rachel felt disdain and anger, and moments later, a strong wind blew through the graveyard.

Molten red morphed and bobbed around the vicar making him fall to his knees.

'No, you promised me, you made me do it – I did everything you asked, waiting in this miserable church and place for eight hundred years. I've fulfilled my part of the bargain.'

'What's he on about?'

'Shush Rob.'

The vicar looked up at them.

'I don't know what power you hold – it's quite extraordinary and also horrific. We would have done anything to get hold of it, harness it – anything, even steal your baby Rachel.'

He paused, seeming nervous and at the total mercy of the witches power.

'Before our spell was spoken by you, Rachel, all those years ago, they, the witches, paid me a visit.'

'Who the bleeding hell are you?'

'Rob, or should I call you William – and you too Rachel, were such naïve fools listening to our lies…'

Rob felt anger and moved fast to assault the vicar, but his witches were faster, and by the time he had grabbed the vicar hard by the shoulders he was already falling to the ground, lifeless.

What remained standing was a dark and hideous apparition, black like coal, half-human, and half animal with luminous green eyes.

'You're a sorcerer, just like those in the castle.'

It spoke in a whispering murmur.

'You two may have been fooled back then, but your friends here, those within you now, could never be fooled – we learned that too late.'

Rachel stamped her foot and the ground shook.

'No, we had a deal. I kept my part.'

The creature fell to its knees.

'Kill him, Rachel.'

'But we had a deal.'

'You had better start talking fast – none of us seem to care if you live or die right now – you're well past your sell by date it seems.'

The creature continued where the vicar left off:

'The witches knew there was a chance the wheel of time could provide a small window for them to return…'

It paused, then continued after Rachel gave a look of no reprieve.

'…home. They were turning mad and needed to hatch a plan fast. They needed to be suspended in time, locked away until a miracle happened. They used us, yes us – the great sorcerers, the dark that you read about in books and see in films in your modern times. They used our spell to cast them out to their advantage. We thought they had gone until Rachel Ellis was brought down here, still warm, lifeless and staring out with eyes of molten red. We knew they would be back one day and tried to prepare – get ready to steal their power. We took the baby – but – ha, they already had it all worked out. We didn't stand a chance. I suppose I should consider myself lucky not to be locked up forever, under half a mountain in Spain, with no chance or spell to set me free.'

'Like your ugly mates?'

'I betrayed them long ago by staying here in this church – but I had no choice – once the witches came to me, I knew that if they ever returned we would be done for. The only bit I didn't know was that William, yes you…'

He looked at Rob.

'…were to hold the witches to ransom and force their hand – they needed him to give the sticks back to you Rachel – it was in their spell. The rest you know.'

'So how did you know William made a pact?'

Rachel was suspicious.

'As soon as you ate those apples they manifested to me – you could say that they checked up on me. Where would I have gone? The witches would have found me in a flash – they know this earth better than anyone – I just passed from one vicar to the next – what utter tedium.'

'So it was your writing in the book that turned to dust.'

'Of course it was.'

'And what now?'

The creature looked at Rob.

'Now? You promised me my freedom, freedom to walk the earth again.'

'You'll never get a girlfriend looking like that.'

'There may be others like me out there, gone to ground, waiting…'

Rachel had had enough of all the talk.

'What now?'

She stamped the ground.

'Take them home.'

The creature looked up the hill towards the chapel.

'The chapel?'

'No William – the centre of the earth. They are the earth itself, the molten fire that dwells deep within – you have no idea of the power you hold…the chapel is the place they leaked out during a violent eruption millions of years ago – yes, they have been here for that long, waiting and waiting to return through that impenetrable barrier that keeps inside and outside separate.'

The creature paused.

'You have so little time, I suggest you take off now.'

The witches disappeared and once again sat inside the couple. Rob and Rachel gave each other an ominous look and without further ado turned to leave.

Rachel's grandmother stood right before them.

'Gran! What are you doing here?'

But her grandmother was in no mood to chat.

'Have you released him?'

'What?'

'Well Rachel…have you?'

Rachel turned to the creature.

'You mean that thing?'

'Yes, that thing as you call it.'

'What? How?'

'Every Rachel Ellis except you was the same – just like every vicar. The witches made sure that every angle was covered – release him and keep your part of the bargain.'

The witches deep inside murmured and Rachel said:

'You're released.'

Rachel's grandmother was on the ground next to the vicar – another corpse in this ancient graveyard.

'Gran!'

Her shock and grief were short lived, as standing in her grandmother's place was another dark apparition.

'You already had a girlfriend you crafty sod.'

'Rob!'

But there was no time to lament as the witches murmur forced Rob and Rachel to leave the confusing scene and hike towards the hill.

They were being led, forced at a fast pace under a blackening sky. The wind had got up and thunder cracked in the sky above them. The chapel came into view – it was a gloomy sombre sight under the dark sky. A lightning bolt hit its roof, illuminating the entire crag. They saw crows gathering, flying fast with the turbulent winds.

Rachel pulled Rob by the hand towards the gate and then to the door, which she pushed open. The crows flew inside and Rachel slammed the door shut.

All was quiet, not a sound of the storm outside.

'Rachel – it's spooky – I don't like this.'

Rachel didn't answer and Rob lost his fear and confusion as the crows turned red, boiling molten red and started pouring through the cracks in the floor until there was nothing left – just a cold stone floor.

'They've gone Rache.'

But it wasn't true – Rob could still feel them, as could Rachel.

'We're home.'

Yes, we're home, he thought. No firelighters here – better go collect some twigs.

Rob left the chapel. It was a glorious autumn day with a light breeze and racing clouds.

He saw some kids, two boys larking about in the field. He shouted over at them, but they just ignored him. He walked right up to them and started chatting but they just blanked him. Rob felt slightly confused and started to pick up sticks. He came across a tin can and, after picking it up, lobbed it towards the crag above the apple trees. He noticed the burnt tree was no longer burnt, but a huge tree, flowering and in perfect condition. That's not right, he thought, it's November.

The can landed with a crash and the boys froze, nervously speaking while looking around.

'What was that?'

'My dad says it's haunted up here...'

Rob stamped his foot and a thunderclap echoed around the crag as the sky went dark.

The two boys were running through the field towards the wood and town below as if they had just seen a ghost.

Rob headed back to the chapel. Inside he saw Rachel stroking the huge dog. It barked once at Rob.

'It's ok – he likes you.'

'Are we ghosts Rachel? Two kids out there couldn't see me.'

'No Rob, we're not ghosts – you always were a bit slow, William.'

She looked straight at him, her eyes molten red, bubbling and swirling.

'I think I'm pregnant.'

'Can I still get my leg over?'

'Don't you ever think of anything else?'

'Not really.'

OTHER BOOKS BY THE AUTHOR

No Place Like Home – A perilous journey full of love, deception and delusion.

Set in the dramatic and raw landscapes of the Basque Pyrenees, Biafra and the Belgium Congo, the story follows the plight of Jacques Freeman, a lonely brooding bachelor lamenting his days in the south of France after losing his home and family to a violent African revolution. Six powerful characters, three women and three men, interplay in this gritty and exhilarating novel.

The World Peace Journals – A Himalayan journey into madness, mayhem and adventure!

It documents a Nepal not spoken or written about in other travel or adventure stories – not sparing the reader from harsh realities, corruption and madness; a sojourn into the Himalayas that succinctly captures the myths, history, geography and people in a way that shocks but also brilliantly entertains.

Breast Fed by Telephone
A Collection of Modern Poetry

ABOUT THE AUTHOR

Ben Gilbert is an outdoor guide, explorer, life coach and writer. He is a Fellow of the Royal Geographical Society and founder of TheBlueSpace Guides Co-operative – www.bengilbertguide.com.

www.ingramcontent.com/pod-product-compliance
Lightning Source LLC
Chambersburg PA
CBHW071154250626
47159CB00001B/80